Vincenzo

A Debt Owed Enemies to Lovers Dark Mafia Billionaire Romance

Calabresi Mafia
Book 5

L.K. Ryan

Newsletter

Have you signed up for my newsletter?

Join today for all the latest new releases, contests, giveaways, sneak peeks, and more.

www.authorlkryan.com

Table of Contents

*Readers who keep me motivated, love my crazy characters,
and want more.*

Previously in the Calabresi mafia series…

Savio is the eldest brother of five, don of the family, and married to McKayla.

Sante is married to Rena, who is best friends with McKayla. He is the underboss of the family.

Renato, the third brother and enforcer for the family, is married to Sonya.

Elio is engaged to Cora.

The youngest son, Vincenzo, runs the legit family business (or so they thought) and is finally getting his story.

Synopsis

To pay her debt, I'll make my enemy my lover in a marriage of convenience.

Nyla thought she could outsmart me, steal from me, and get away with it.

She was wrong.

Tracking her down wasn't hard. I am a Calabresi, after all, and my family's reach runs far.

I'll make her an offer she can't resist—become my wife in exchange for her uncle's life.

I know she'll resist, but in time, I'll make her mine... willingly.

My brothers have tried to keep me from the family business, but it's time to collect what's mine.

Going against them will be dangerous, but I've never backed down from a challenge.

I'll make Nyla mine and secure my place in the family business.

This Dark Mafia Romance checks all the boxes—forced marriage, forbidden love,

enemies to lovers, and the list goes on. Indulge in the heat and danger in this romance with a guaranteed HEA. Although this book is part of a series, all titles can be read as standalones.

xii

Chapter 1

Vincenzo

I watched her lift the champagne bottle, tilt it toward her mouth, and soak her string bikini with the bubbling remnants.

My friends surrounded me, helping me celebrate closing another property deal while my brothers pursued other activities—except Renato. He'd reserved the entire club, and one or two of the women here were most likely leaving with me.

A blonde rubbed my leg and gyrated next to me, tossing her head back and forth. I let her think she had control while I watched two other girls make out. I was ready to shove my dick down their throats.

Two of my security detail entered as I grabbed another bottle. A leader on my team buzzed updates into my earpiece. Furious at what I heard, I pushed the women aside and stood.

Thirty minutes later, I strode through the casino doors with my guards. Savio had called three times after receiving an alert from our team, but I'd let it go to voice-mail. I needed answers before I spoke to my brother.

My blood ran cold. Who the fuck had the nerve to rob me and my family? Calabresi Casino opened three months ago, and security was tight around the clock. I'd vetted everybody we'd hired—hell, I'd made it my personal responsibility when we announced we were moving forward with our new business venture.

Wealth was important, but continuing the family legacy and proving we could do more than run illegal businesses was paramount.

Leaving the strip club early and cutting my celebrations short had put me in a foul mood.

"Where the fuck are they?" I growled, yanking open the door of the private employee entrance. I glanced at the security guard standing to the side with his head down and slammed my fist into his face.

"Vincenzo! Hold your temper for those who deserve it." Renato patted me on the back, getting between the guard and me.

"I want everybody fired!" I yelled, ignoring my brother.

Renato shoved me into the elevator and pressed the button for the basement. He turned to me with a grin, and I flipped him off.

As the youngest son, my parents didn't want me in the family business. I focused on our legal entities and had no complaints—until I got shot on a mission with my brother, Elio. I hadn't told anyone, but the rush of fighting alongside my brothers and seeing the last breath leave our enemies' bodies was a wake-up call. Savio had no clue, and I'd sworn Renato to secrecy when I joined him for runs after someone had mistaken our kindness for weakness.

Climbing off the elevator, I tugged on my trench coat,

listening to the cries from our private security room where we handled personal matters. I snarled at the guard on duty. He stepped aside, not wanting to be on the receiving end of my wrath, and I stalked into the room. I scanned the faces before me, surprised to discover who had betrayed my trust.

Nyla's long, golden locks were pinned in a high bun atop her head, her silky amber skin flushed. I edged closer, studying her deep brown eyes, which had captivated me since our first meeting.

Her shoulders dropped, and a whimper escaped her throat. "Please don't kill us."

"Us?" I smirked as I pulled out my gun.

"Look, we can pay you back!" The man in the chair beside her trembled, unable to move his bound hands and feet.

I cracked my neck. "Where's my money?"

"I'll tell you if you let us go," he countered, angling his body forward.

I looked at the woman and waved the gun between them. "Who is he to you?"

"My boyfriend," she muttered, pressing her lips thin.

"You love him?" There was no reason for my question, and the confused look Renato sent me confirmed it.

"Y-Yes... Yes," she stuttered.

I turned my attention to the man and pressed the gun to his forehead. "You love her?"

It didn't matter. Getting my money back was the goal here.

He ignored my question. "I can get your money back."

I raised the gun and brought it down on his face, causing him to bellow in pain. "I asked you a question!"

"Please, he can get your money! Just let us go," she pleaded, snot and tears running down her face.

"You thought it was wise to steal from me?"

Blood seeped from his nose and mouth, and he spat on the floor. "Fuck you!"

I backhanded him hard. "Wrong time to piss me off."

"My connections won't let you kill me," he boasted through clenched teeth.

I chuckled. "Connections, huh?" I glanced at Renato. He shook his head, and I sent a bullet through the man's brain.

"No!" Nyla screamed as her boyfriend slumped beside her.

I moved my gaze from his dead body to her. "I'll ask once more. Where is my money?"

Her chest heaved as panic overwhelmed her. I wasn't always an asshole. Being raised by my mother and sisters-in-law saved me from being completely cold-hearted. But I knew I would never find my five million dollars if I gave in to her.

"I can't believe you killed him." She burst into tears.

I knelt in front of her. "Where is my five million dollars, Nyla?"

"I don't know," she whispered miserably.

"You came to me for a job. I helped you, and you stole from me."

She exhaled heavily. "I promise I can get it back."

Her resolve should have come before she'd betrayed me. "How did a beautiful woman like you get mixed up with a guy like him?"

She raised her chin. "His friends are going to look for me."

"Friends who helped you rob my casino? Too bad they left you holding the bag."

Her eyes threw daggers at me. "We weren't supposed to end up dead."

"I'm tired and ready for bed. Where's my money?" If she thought I had any compassion that she'd been left behind, she was sadly mistaken.

She slumped in the chair. "I don't know."

"Then I have to kill you." I stood, ready to kill again and salvage my night.

"Wait! You can't kill me."

I tilted my head. "Why is that?"

"Because my family can pay the debt."

"Your family?"

Tears brimmed in her eyes. "Let me go first."

I leaned forward and grabbed her chin, my lips an inch from hers. Her attempts to negotiate were infuriating.

"Let her talk," Renato interrupted.

I whipped my head around, frowning as he tried to take over the conversation. "Fuck her!" I barked.

Nyla's puppy dog eyes moved between Renato and me, pleading for mercy.

I released her jaw. "Doesn't matter who her family is. She crossed a line."

"It was a setup," Nyla said breathlessly.

I narrowed my eyes at her. "What?"

"He told me he owed someone. I couldn't get that much money from my family, so I had to get a job."

"So, you planned this from the day you walked into my casino, looking for a job."

"Yes," Nyla whispered.

"Say your prayers, Nyla."

The door busted open to a frowning Savio and Sante, and the room filled with our team.

Savio motioned for me to step outside.

"What the fuck is going on?" Yet another interruption, and it irritated me.

"You can't kill her," Sante said.

Noticing Renato's clenched fists, I studied my brothers.

Sante said, "I'm serious. You are not to kill her."

"Why not?" I asked, lounging against the wall.

"Because I said so," Savio replied succinctly.

"Savio, this is my business," I argued.

Savio pushed me hard against the wall, getting in my face. "You need to watch who the fuck you're talking to, Vincenzo."

"Savio's right. Certain things have come to light, and until we get answers, she will remain alive," Sante informed me.

Sante was the next in line to take control when Savio retired. He knew the decision to kill Nyla's boyfriend should have come from him. Savio was like a second father figure to me; disrespecting him would cut him deep.

"She says she knows where the money is hidden."

"For now, she stays alive. Clean up the mess and meet me in the car." Savio offered me a handshake, and I accepted it.

Renato exited the room, wiping blood off his hands.

Savio eyed his blood-splattered clothes. "What were you doing?"

"Having some fun," he said with a shrug.

Renato smirked and headed down the hall to catch up with my brothers. My father was right to have Renato as enforcer. No matter the situation, he had no qualms about taking a life.

Strolling in the room, I stared at the cut-up remains of Nyla's boyfriend. I shook my head at my brother's work and waved at my men. "Take her to the room."

They freed her wrists and helped her to stand.

Nyla fought to get away from their hold. "Let me go!"

"Shut the fuck up, or you'll join your boyfriend in hell."

"Where are you taking me?" she demanded through angry tears.

I grinned. I liked seeing her squirm. "Some place you can't escape."

****

Savio handed me a cell phone with a voice message set to play as I climbed into the limo and shut the door.

My brow furrowed. "What's this?"

"Play it and see."

"I have better things to do than be given the runaround all night."

Savio and Sante locked eyes. Renato chuckled at whatever they were silently communicating. As the two eldest, Savio and Sante thought they had the power to make the decisions, but my father gave us voting power. Nothing could be moved without my father knowing and agreeing.

Casino guests continued sauntering inside with no idea what had happened tonight. Our clean-up crew would wipe the place down, and Sante already had new security arriving.

Savio pointed. "Nyla on the phone. We got recordings of her talking to him."

"Her and her boyfriend."

"Yeah," Sante confirmed.

I played the recording.

"*I can't right now. He has people watching me,*" Nyla said.

"How many recordings do you have?"

"Four or five, and video clips that we should have our people keeping an eye on," Sante emphasized, narrowing his eyes on Renato.

"Too busy trying to get other shit done. I told you that opening a casino would be a bad idea," Renato hissed.

"That's your job!" Sante argued back.

"No. My job is to enforce the rules when someone fucks over the Calabresi name. These petty witch hunts and watching video footage every day is not," Renato countered.

"When I take over—" Sante began.

Savio groaned, familiar with the argument between Sante and Renato every time he brought it up.

"All right, you two. Shut the fuck up. I have bigger problems right now!" I yelled, shocking all three of my brothers.

"What happened to our baby brother?" Renato grinned.

"He fucking grew up, shithead," I said as the limo arrived at Savio's house.

"Go home. We'll discuss business tomorrow." Savio climbed out of the car as his front door opened to McKayla waiting for him.

"She's going to stay pregnant." Renato shook his head.

"Shut the fuck up, Renato." Savio slammed the door and strolled to his wife, pulling her into a hug.

I lifted my index finger. "I need a drink."

"Me too," Renato sighed.

"You have a wife waiting for you. Besides, we have an early meeting tomorrow. I suggest you two get some sleep." Sante motioned for our driver to head to his house.

An hour later, I closed the doors of my penthouse and tossed my jacket and tie on the couch. Grabbing a glass of whiskey to take the edge off, I cracked my neck and rolled my shoulders. I needed a hot shower and some pussy before returning to kill Nyla.

I had no idea what she meant when she mentioned her family, but her debt totaled five million. Adding interest would make the situation even sweeter when I confronted her again.

I took a deep breath and chugged another whiskey. Snatching up the phone Savio had given me in the car, I went to my office to replay the video footage. I kicked off my shoes, reminding myself to find a new housekeeper. I'd been using a service my mother provided through one of her friends, but the woman they'd sent over eye-fucked me rather than working.

Loosening my cuffs, I typed in my password. I logged into the casino security system, rewatching the hour before I arrived. I observed the security guard I'd punched hauling Nyla into the room. He groped her while her boyfriend did nothing and tried to use her as a get-out-of-jail-free card.

"Bitch ass."

Nyla's naivety pissed me off. She'd seemed smart

when she came in for an interview. It upset me that she would choose someone so beneath her.

Now, I tensed as I watched her pleading for herself and her boyfriend. As I watched her boyfriend yell at her, I became upset that I'd killed him so quickly.

Finishing my drink, I left to shower and get ready for bed. For the rest of the night, I contemplated how to get my five million back or kill Nyla's entire family as payment.

****

Loud voices echoed as I entered my parents' home. I hurried to the kitchen to see Rena and Renato going back and forth, bickering as usual. Slapping him on the head, I kissed my mother's cheek, snatched a piece of toast off her plate, and scarfed it down. Pouring a glass of juice, I sat and listened to the banter.

But the banter had ceased, and I suddenly realized I was the focus of attention. "What?"

"You never miss breakfast, Vincenzo," Madre observed.

I grabbed a napkin. "Long night."

"Doing what, exactly?"

Renato rolled his eyes, and Rena elbowed him. Madre glanced between Renato and me, and I wondered if she suspected something.

"Renato, if you involved your brother in family business that I specifically asked your father to keep from him, I'm sure you would tell me, correct?" Madre asked calmly.

Renato scratched his brow nervously.

"Renato!" Madre snapped.

"He's running the casino," he confessed.

I glowered at him, waiting for the interrogation.

"Legal casino business?" Madre stared at me.

I rubbed the back of my neck. "Madre, I'm a grown man."

"You will always be my baby."

"Aww, so sweet," Rena teased.

I flipped her off.

Renato frowned in disapproval. "The only person who can flip Rena off is me, motherfucker."

Our mother pinched his arm. "Watch your mouth, Renato." She slipped off the stool and carried her coffee cup to the sink.

"We have a meeting to get to. You can baby him later," Renato said.

A few hours ago, my life was simple: wake up, run a billion-dollar business, have fun, and get laid. The rule book didn't mention organizing a clean-up crew and searching for stolen money.

I trailed Renato to my father's office, where he sat behind his desk.

"She's still alive," Renato told him as we entered.

My gaze flew to my brother, angry that he'd brought my father in on last night's situation.

Silence filled the room. I could never go wrong with parents like mine. As the youngest, they wanted to keep me from the business, but it felt like they controlled my life. My brothers had also tried to protect me—until I'd proven my worth when Cora was kidnapped.

I balled my fists. "Renato shouldn't have brought you in on the situation."

Father leaned back in the chair, rubbing the full beard my mother loved.

"He's in a bad mood," Renato taunted.

I shoved his shoulder.

Father raised his hand for us to stop. He turned his gaze to me. "I value my boys' opinions, but you were reckless last night, son."

Disappointing my father was the last thing I wanted, but Nyla Jolie was a threat. Her lies had hurt us, and she needed to pay.

Chapter 2

Nyla

*T*hree Months Earlier

"What's the plan, Nyla? You can't keep running," Cassandra chastised on the other end of the phone line.

Cassandra was my best friend. I didn't have many growing up. My parents' deaths had left me with a fear of abandonment, but my trust in people had also died with them. Cassandra had snuck under my defenses. We'd met by chance at the mall and hit it off. My uncle hated how close we were, but Cassandra wasn't intimidated by my family name.

I sighed. "I need a job. Something has to change."

Cassandra grunted. "Well, if you didn't feel so obligated to be with Mark, you could have a life."

Cassandra wasn't shy about speaking the truth. She thought I was stupid for running away from my family and living with Mark. Maybe she was right. I was tired of being locked away, unable to have a life.

My uncle took over my trust fund after my parents died when I was 13 and raised me until I was 18. Pushing his mafia lifestyle on me pissed me off, and we constantly butted heads. The little money he gave me came with rules and regulations. When I turned 20, things took a turn for the worse when Mark and I started dating. I left a year ago to prove a point.

"I didn't call you to complain about my boyfriend."

"Your boyfriend is putting you in danger, Nyla," Cassandra warned.

She and Mark didn't get along. My uncle thought Cassandra was a bad influence, and Cassandra thought Mark was the bad apple. I wanted to deny her words, but Cassandra was right about Mark relying on me, which led to me getting into trouble.

"I hear you, Cassandra. I'll figure it out."

"How? Why not go back to school and get into photography like you always talked about?"

People would describe me as "a whimsical person who needs structure", but my love of traveling and my desire for freedom were a part of me. I hated being tied down. "How will I pay for it with the little money in my account?"

She exhaled a deep breath. "Look, just come by the restaurant, and we can talk."

I had to distract her from starting up again with my boyfriend. She didn't know that Mark needed money, and I'd promised to help pay off his debt. He didn't explain everything, but he'd gotten in deep with some people. Going to my uncle was not an option; he'd kill him before opening the gate.

"I have an interview."

"Where?"

"I'll fill you in later. Promise."

Her sigh reached me down the phone line. "Okay. Call me after."

"I will." I ended the call and dropped my cell in my purse before climbing out of my car. I stared up at the sign for the new Calabresi Casino. Taking a nervous breath, I strolled into the building and headed for the front desk.

"Hello," a customer service rep greeted me with a broad smile.

"Hi. I have an interview with Mr. Calabresi."

"What's your name?"

I gripped my purse to anchor myself. "Nyla Jolie," I replied, giving my mother's maiden name.

I glanced at the beautiful surroundings as the customer service rep typed on her keyboard. The building design inside was reminiscent of old Italy with its marble stone, glass ceilings, wide windows, and original wall art. The Calabresi Family was well known for its wealth, so no expense had been spared on this place.

"Here's your guest pass. Take the elevator on the right to floor three." The rep slid the pass across the counter.

I thanked her and wandered to the employees-only area, scanning my pass to call for the elevator.

A few minutes later, I knocked on the office door of the CEO and owner of Calabresi Casino. I hadn't realized that getting hired would go all the way to the top.

A commanding voice called for me to come in. I tucked a loose curl behind my ear and opened the door.

Mr. Calabresi sat behind a large desk. Leaning back in the leather chair, he ran a hand down the neatly trimmed beard, which only emphasized his chiseled jaw.

His blue eyes narrowed at me, and something told me those eyes could make you reveal your true soul.

"Who are you?" he inquired.

No smile or polite "hello." I contemplated turning around and going home to tell Mark this was a bad idea. "I'm Nyla Jolie. I'm here to interview for the receptionist job."

He stood and stalked around his desk, leaning against the front and crossing his arms. I was five-seven, but he was several inches taller. My eyes lingered too long on his kissable lips, and I shook off my wayward thoughts.

"Receptionist job. How old are you?"

"Twenty-two."

Scoffing, he slid his hands into his pockets. My uncle had tried to keep me in my place since I was a little girl, and I refused to let an asshole who didn't know me do the same.

"I'm old enough to consume alcohol, I've been driving since I was sixteen, and I'm damned sure I could purchase a gun."

That got a reaction from him. He moved suddenly, cutting the distance between us and causing me to stumble back. "Where's your resume?"

I pulled it from my folder and held it out to him.

Taking it, he continued to watch me as he flipped it open. "My team did a background check, and you don't have any warrants."

Mark ensured my background was clear. The goal was to get in here, work for a few weeks, and learn the routine. Once I had it down, I'd give him the information to rob the place.

"The ad stated you were hiring for different positions."

"Sure."

His one-word answer pissed me off.

Looking around the office, I noticed the photos covering the walls. I assumed they were of his family as the men in the pictures resembled him. No doubt his brothers.

He moved to sit behind his desk again, and I sank into the chair opposite.

"I see from your resume that you're not married. Do you have a boyfriend?"

My eyes widened. "I... Yes. But—"

"If your boyfriend is the jealous type, this job is not for you. We never give set hours. Shifts change based on the needs of the business," he barked. "I demand that my employees arrive on time. Don't even think about holidays. Working at the casino is demanding. If you fuck up or bring drama to my business, you will answer to me."

"I understand, Mr. Calabresi."

"Do you? Because tears and crying about him breaking up with you after working late shifts here won't impress me."

Cocking my head to the side. "Why are you so interested in my personal life?"

He chuckled. "Your personal life will no longer matter once you walk through these doors, tesorucci."

"*Little Treasure*," I murmured.

"You speak Italian."

I smiled at his shocked expression. "A little," I lied.

I didn't want to reveal my Black-Italian background. My parents fell in love, and I was created from that love, living for many years in Italy and some in America. My father left his family's lifestyle when he met my mother in Chicago. I was born, and he showed us the world, letting me grow up to be who I wanted to be. Interracial marriage was still frowned upon, but my parents' love allowed me to grow into a confident, intelligent woman.

Mr. Calabresi clicked his pen. "You will be hired on a trial basis."

"Thank you." I smoothed a hand through my hair.

"Don't thank me yet. As I said, you're young in a world where you have no clue how to navigate. I'd hate to see anything happen to you."

His words felt like a gut punch, making me think he knew the real me. "I promise to do my best, Sir."

"Fill out the hiring packet before you leave. Ask my assistant, and she'll show you where to start."

"Thank you, Mr. Calabresi."

Holding my gaze, he took my hand, creating a spark that almost made me shiver.

I had a feeling my life was about to change.

****

I came home from the interview to find Mark bleeding from a cut on his cheek, which was swollen.

"Shit! What did you do?" I demanded, grabbing an ice pack and hurrying to help him.

"Nothing to worry about." Mark rose, snatching the ice pack from my hand.

I frowned as he sidestepped the issue. I could almost hear Cassandra yelling at me for letting him come back home after he cheated on me six months ago. I told him I was done, but we knew our relationship was far from over. It could be toxic sometimes, but Mark was a good guy who made mistakes, like anyone else.

"Of course, I worry. My boyfriend could've been killed! Did you gamble after you promised you'd stop?"

Mark ran his hand through his curly hair. I loved his long hair, especially at night when we were in bed watching TV, and I ran my fingers through it while he snored. "Why do you care?"

Our relationship was nowhere near perfect. He often drank and gambled our money away, so I had to pick up the slack. I remembered the unconditional love he showed, taking care of me when my parents died. I loved him more than anything. It didn't hurt that he was tall, lean, and athletic but not too muscular, and tattoos covered the bronze skin of his hands and neck.

I chewed my bottom lip. "Are you serious right now?"

"Did you get the job, Nyla?" He changed the subject as usual when I called him out on his bullshit.

"I did. What's the next step?" I moved around the couch, interlocked our hands, and rested my head on his shoulder.

He winced as I caressed his cheek.

"Sorry." I lifted onto my toes to capture his lips. "All you bad boys are alike," I teased.

Mark smirked against my mouth. He pulled away as his phone rang, holding a finger to his lips to be quiet as he answered. "Hello."

"You do it yet?" the voice on the other line inquired.

Mark glanced at me. "She got the job. I'll have the money soon."

"Fuck me over, and you're dead." The call ended.

An eerie tingle ran down my back. "Maybe we should rethink the plan, Mark."

He shook his head. "Too late for that. Five million reasons why I can't pull out."

"Are you sure we can pull off a robbery?"

He sat on the couch and tugged me onto his lap. "You worry too much."

"No more gambling, Mark."

He wrapped his arms around me. "I promised you I wouldn't."

"That's what you said last time." I poked my lip out.

He groaned and slid me off his lap, heading to the bedroom.

I stood to follow him. "Where are you going?"

He glanced at me over his shoulder. "To shower and head out for work."

"Mark, we both know going out puts you in danger."

Running the water in the sink, he winced as he wiped the blood off his cheek. "I got everything under control. Besides, your uncle made me promise to take care of his little princess."

****

Mark didn't come home that night. I decided to let him handle his part while I focused on what I could do to get us out of this mess.

I parked in the employee section of the Casino and checked in, going up to the third floor to wait for my trainer.

"Morning."

I lifted my head to see a woman with long blond hair and a kid beside her smiling at me. I waved at him. "Hi."

"Haven't seen you around here before? Are you new?"

Her inquiry caught me off-guard. Maybe she worked

here or knew someone who did. It was unusual to see a child at a casino.

"My first day. Is it obvious?" I joked.

She smiled, lifted the boy onto the reception desk, and held her hand out to me. "I'm Sonya. I'm married to Renato Calabresi."

I shook her hand. "Nice to meet you. I'm Nyla." I directed my attention toward the boy. "Who's the little guy?"

Sonya looked at her son. "RJ, say hi, buddy."

He waved at me shyly, and I gave him a cheerful smile.

"Renato, as in Vincenzo's brother?"

Sonya nodded. "We're meeting him here for lunch."

I started to reply when the elevator dinged, and loud voices could be heard down the hall.

"My business, my decision," Vincenzo snapped, coming into view. The stress lines on his forehead seemed to be more defined as we talked.

"Forget who the big brother is, I guess," the man with him replied. He reminded me of a young Paul Newman with his tall stature and blond hair trimmed at the sides.

"Daddy!" RJ raised his hands.

"Sonya, I told you to wait for me in my office," he barked, grabbing his son from the desk.

I turned to look at Vincenzo. His scowl told me I had already fucked up, and I had no clue how.

Sonya raised an eyebrow. "Renato, we have company."

Everybody stared at me. My cheeks hurt as I forced a smile and waved, wondering if it would be rude to bolt.

"She's new." Sonya's husband pointed at me.

"She won't be here long."

Vincenzo's comment pissed me off. Usually, I would go back at him, but I bit my tongue, reminding myself of Mark's plan.

I offered a handshake to Renato. He ignored it until Sonya punched his arm, and he reluctantly shook my hand. *Friendly guy, like his brother.*

"Have a good first day," Sonya said cheerfully. She grabbed Renato's hand, and they walked away with RJ. Hearing them bickering back and forth was comical.

"Did you come here to work or hang out with my family?" Vincenzo demanded.

I took a deep breath and walked into his office. "Here to work, Sir."

"Go to the employee level and partner with my assistant. She's waiting for you."

I turned to leave. "Thank you."

"And Nyla."

"Yes, sir?"

"If your intentions are not genuine, I will find out."

I let his words seep in. His warning reminded me of my argument with my uncle before I ran away to be with Mark.

Shaking off the memory, I left his office, bypassing his guards. After heading to the employee level, I hopped on the elevator with a few others, staying in the back and listening to their conversation.

I'd noticed that all the women who worked there were young, beautiful, and stacked in all the right places. Vincenzo had a type, and I was *not* it. I wasn't sure why that made me feel sad—not that it mattered, because Mark was the love of my life, and he loved all of me.

Trailing the girls wearing uniforms, I found Vincenzo's assistant talking to Sonya and a red-haired woman.

"Hey, Angelina."

Angelina glanced over her shoulder and plastered on a fake grin. "Sonya, Rena, meet... I'm sorry. What's your name again?" She snapped her fingers at me.

"Nyla. We met yesterday."

"Right, Nyla." She nodded. "You probably won't last a day. Vincenzo hired way more people than he needed to do."

"Weren't you just rehired after getting fired not long ago?" Rena, the redhead, asked.

Angelina pressed her lips, looking like she wanted to claw her eyes out.

"Nice to see you again, Nyla. I apologize for my husband." Sonya smiled.

I waved it off. "You have nothing to apologize for."

Rena extended her hand in greeting. "Hi, Rena Calabresi, married to the second eldest brother, Sante."

"Hi, Rena. I'm Nyla. I was just hired yesterday."

"We're not paying you to sit around and suck up to the family," Angelina spat, stomping off to the elevator.

I forced myself to keep my composure. We'd only had a brief interaction yesterday, but Angelina had been pleasant and professional.

Something had changed since then.

"Ignore her," Rena said, ruffling RJ's hair.

I sighed. "Is she always like that?"

"She was fired and rehired, but she's one of Vincenzo's playthings, and her jealousy shows."

"Jealousy? Why would she be jealous of me?"

"Angelina likes to gossip, and the word around the building is that you were hired without an interview," Sonya explained.

My mouth dropped open in shock.

"Interviews are usually with the hiring manager, but somehow, your file got to Vincenzo's desk, and he requested you come straight to his office," Rena informed me.

I wrinkled my nose. "But—"

"Like I said, ignore her," Sonya continued, grasping RJ's hand. "Not every woman comes here to sleep her way to the top."

"Sonya's right. Angelina is a brat. If she gives you any problems, let Vincenzo know right away."

"Doubt I'll be here that long," I replied as we headed for the elevator.

Rena pressed the button for the third floor. "Why do you doubt yourself?"

I sighed. "Vincenzo didn't seem too excited to hire me."

"He's the youngest in the family. Sweet and charming, but a playboy, nevertheless—and deadly when he wants to be. He probably knew he'd fall for you and tried to push you away." Rena gave me a sideways stare.

"Oh, I have a boyfriend."

Rena held her badge to the elevators to close. "How long have you been together?"

"Almost three years, but we broke up briefly."

Rena propped a hand on her hip. "How old are you?"

"Everybody keeps asking me my age."

Rena smiled. "Because you look innocent, like a college student."

RJ fussed in Sonya's arms as we stepped off the elevator and headed back to the front desk.

"I'm twenty-two. College wasn't for me."

"I'll let you get back to work. Great meeting you, Nyla."

"You too, Rena." I turned to watch Sonya and RJ heading in the opposite direction. "I'll see you two later."

I walked down the hall, looking for Angelina's office. When I found it, the door was open, and Angelina was stacking a pile of files on the desk. My day would be long and exhausting if her attitude didn't change.

"Angelina, I'm not sure what you've heard, but I have no plans to get into a relationship with anyone here. I have a rule not to date coworkers."

Angelina locked a glare on me. "Good. I'm glad we understand each other because I would hate for your job to become difficult."

I gave up and raised my hands. "Understood."

"Great. Take these files and get started at that desk." She motioned for me to sit across from her.

"I thought I would be on the casino level?"

"You will be eventually. For now, Mr. Calabresi wants you here."

Chapter 3

Vincenzo

Hiring Nyla was a bad idea. I was going to pay for it; I just wasn't sure when or how. Her background check came back clean, but my instincts told me she was trouble. So, why had I hired her? My instincts usually screamed at me to avoid trouble.

It was Nyla's second week at the casino. I hadn't spoken to her—beyond saying good morning and goodbye. She learned fast, and Angelina had made it her mission to keep her busy.

Wiping the sweat off my face, I placed the weights back on the stand and gulped my water. I went to the gym at the casino or Calabresi Holdings every day before work. Today, it was the casino. Splitting my focus between both companies left me with little time for my family or socializing. My mother wanted me to settle down now that my brothers had found love, but it wasn't my goal. At twenty-five, I was too young to spend the rest of my life with the same person. Women barely kept my attention for longer than a week. Angelina was the only girl I'd dipped into repeatedly. She could be possessive and jealous, but I'd never promised her exclusivity.

I grabbed my gym bag to answer my ringing phone, preparing to deal with my brother's demands. "What?"

"Working off that sexual tension?" Renato had been fucking with me since he'd seen Nyla at the office.

My mouth twisted in annoyance. "Fuck you. Get off my phone."

"Wait! We need to meet," Renato stalled me.

A surge of air lifted my chest. "Why?"

"Governor wants to throw a party at the casino."

My eyebrows pinched together. "No."

"Not asking for permission."

I sighed in agitation. All my brothers thought they could boss me around, but I made the decisions for the casino. It had been my idea to start something that could bring in legit money and clear our name in the media and around the city. I made the decisions, not Renato.

Sweat trickled down my back. "When?"

"In two weeks."

"We've only been open for three months. Having the governor in our business won't look good."

Renato grunted. "Elio told her it was a one-time situation."

"Elio should have come to me first." I ended the call.

After swiping my badge, I exited the elevator and stalked to my office. Not paying attention, I bumped into a soft body. I dropped my phone and held her arms to stop her from falling.

"Sorry," Nyla murmured.

"Pay attention to where you're walking," I grumbled, bending to pick up my phone.

Nyla shook her head, ignoring my bad mood.

I slammed the office door and dropped my bag on the floor as my phone rang again. I ignored Renato's call, slipping into the bathroom and turning on the shower to wash off the sweat from my workout.

I closed my eyes as water cascaded over my head, bracing myself for Angelina's attitude. Rumors had spread that Nyla and I were sleeping together, which couldn't be further from the truth. It didn't help that I'd personally hired her, a job usually carried out by the employee manager. But when I'd seen Nyla's application photo, she reminded me of someone, so I decided to conduct the interview and dig into her background. She'd come up clean, but I couldn't shake the feeling that something was amiss.

I growled as I heard the bathroom door open.

"You should have invited me to wash your back," Angelina said as I stepped out of the shower and grabbed a towel to dry off.

I slapped her hand away as she ran it up my chest, turned off by her constant flirting. "Get out."

"Why are you acting so cold, Vinny?" Angelina whined. The sudden blast of air had her nipples standing at attention.

"Do you want to get fired again?" I asked, reminding her how things went down the last time she got too possessive.

Angelina pouted and rolled her eyes. "Every day, you show me how little you care."

I shook my head. "I never pretended to care about you."

Her eyes narrowed. "You've found someone else. Is it that new girl?"

I raked my fingers through my wet hair. "Neither of you are sucking my dick, how about that as a solution?"

Snarling, she flipped her hair and marched out.

I sat in the conference room listening to the Governor talk about the party she wanted to have at our casino. Movement caught my attention through the window, and I saw Nyla talking and laughing with Jerry, the security guard. I hated to admit it, but I didn't like seeing her interact with another man.

There was no doubt of her beauty. Her silky, amber-brown skin, plush lips, soft eyes, and sexy curves would have any man begging to taste her. But that way lay danger.

"What do you think?" Elio's question pulled me from my thoughts.

"Huh?"

"The governor asked if you agreed to the plans?" Elio explained. He was the liaison for the transfer of funds and signing of contracts.

I snorted softly. Like I had a fucking choice in the plans. As soon as the governor left, I'd deal with my brothers. "If the contract looks good, we can move forward."

I stood and left the room with Angelina chasing behind me like a frisky puppy.

"Vincenzo, wait!" She clamored to catch up.

"Keep up."

Snatching my arm, she turned me to face her. "What happened back there?"

I pushed her hand away. "Nothing."

"Something did, because you've been snippy all day."

"Cancel my lunch. I have plans," I said, ignoring her question. I pulled out my cell and texted my driver to be ready in five minutes.

"Where are you going? Or should I ask, who are you going to lunch with?" she asked as we reached the elevator.

Angelina was intent on meeting my parents and ensured she was around when my mother came to my office one day for lunch.

I cocked my head. "None of your business."

I rode down in the elevator and hopped in the waiting car. My cell chimed with a group chat text. My brothers wanted to meet at Calabresi Holdings, which wasn't far from the casino. When my driver arrived, I got out of the car and shook hands with the doorman as I went inside, spying Sante and Savio talking.

Sante frowned. "You're late."

"Traffic," I mumbled.

Savio led the way upstairs to his office.

"Elio is sending the contract for the governor's party," I informed him.

We all sat as Renato and Elio joined us, and Sante started the meeting.

****

Two Weeks Later

I fixed my tuxedo as I walked through the lobby. My team had worked around the clock to prepare everything for the governor's party. I groaned at Angelina, plastered against my side, waving at everyone like she was my wife. She hit me up for a ride when I happened to be leaving the Calabresi office, dressed for the party. The casino was closed for this special event;

Governor Constantine Hudson was celebrating her election.

"What is she doing here?" Angelina hissed.

"Who?" I observed the large ballroom decorated with balloons and flowers. Servers hovered with trays holding glasses of champagne.

"Nyla," Angelina spewed.

I saw Nyla in the corner, talking with Sonya and Rena. I dragged my eyes down her body in her red dress, highlighting her plump breasts and wide hips. The long split highlighted her smooth, silky legs. She turned, and her round, plump ass begged to be cupped and squeezed. It aggravated and taunted me.

I shook off my dirty thoughts and released Angelina's arm. "Everyone is invited. Go mingle."

"Are we sitting together?"

I moved away as she pressed her fake breasts against my chest. "Angelina—"

"Vincenzo, please. One night. Let me prove to you I can be a good girlfriend."

I rubbed my temples. "Stop begging. The only connection we have is sex."

An uncomfortable ache stirred in my chest as Sonya, Rena, and Nyla sauntered over. Her presence shouldn't move me either way, but I could only focus on her vibrant red lips.

"The governor sent a bonus to thank you for making the party happen on time," Elio appeared beside me and handed me a check. "Asshole," he grunted as I snatched it from his hand.

I raised my brow at the giggle behind me and turned to glare at Nyla. "Something funny?"

"Vinny, leave her alone," Rena chided, sipping her

drink. She knew I hated that nickname Angelina had started.

"Are you my family or hers?" I gestured between Nyla and me.

Rena waved me off, a small smile curling her lips.

I glared at Nyla, but she didn't shy away. Somehow, she'd become close to the women in my family. I needed to put a stop to their friendship before they became too comfortable.

She's hiding something.

The announcer introduced Governor Hudson's fundraiser for re-election. We hadn't had any problems with her since her husband's death. Elio had a deal in place with her for our casino. The money was helping her more than she could imagine. Most of the bills being passed in Chicago were due to our influence.

I mingled with my family for the rest of the evening, letting Angelina know I wasn't spending the night with her. She threw a tantrum, so I sent her home in a cab, knowing it would cause problems at the office.

****

I entered the casino's main floor with Angelina trailing beside me, taking notes. I observed the crowd coming and going. We'd been open for five months now, and the customers loved the atmosphere, the free drinks, and the VIP area for our top gamblers. Each floor had dedicated areas for slot machines and the high rollers upstairs.

I paused by the main cash station, watching the cashier dish out chips. I noticed a group of men talking to Nyla, their eyes gleaming with interest. It had been weeks since the governor's party, and she and I hadn't run into each other since. So far, there had been no issues with her competence.

Angelina cleared her throat, reminding me why I'd come downstairs before heading to Calabresi Holdings.

"Stare at her any longer, and I'll start to think you like her more than me."

I shook my head, grimacing at her jealousy. She wanted to be on my arm like Rena and Sonya were with my brothers. Elio was pissed when I re-hired her, but I needed someone who knew how to run things, and to her credit, she handled my schedule better than anyone.

"I fired you once. The last time you sucked my dick was a year ago. Let it go."

I watched Nyla with another clerk, barely noticing as Angelina stomped toward her. Taking out my phone, I checked my calendar.

"Do you need a ride tonight, or is your boyfriend picking you up?" she asked Nyla.

"He has to work, so I'll grab a rideshare."

"I can drop you off," the clerk with Nyla offered.

"Thanks, but it's out of your way. I'll be fine." Nyla smiled.

Not sticking around, I headed back upstairs to my office.

Angelina followed, grabbing her purse. "I'll be late coming in tomorrow, so hold all my calls."

"Why?" Angelina quizzed.

My eyebrows lowered in annoyance. "None of your business."

"Fine," Angelina spat, snatching her jacket off the chair and marching to the elevator.

I glanced at my watch—11 PM. I usually tried to

make it home before nine but running two businesses demanded more of my time.

I opened the lobby door to my waiting car and saw Nyla at the pickup area. Tossing my things in the back of the Escalade, I climbed into the back seat and slammed the door, ignoring her standing alone. If her boyfriend cared about her, he'd prioritize picking her up rather than letting her find her own way home.

As my driver pulled away, I looked out the back window to see her still standing alone. I sighed, knowing I was about to do something unusual for me. "Turn around. We need to go back."

"Yes, sir." Carter, my driver, paused at the stop sign on the main road and put the car in reverse. He smirked when I told him to pick up Nyla.

"Wipe the smirk off your face," I grumbled.

The bastard chuckled. He was lucky we'd become close friends since he'd been hired as my driver and guard. Since I'd been shot, Madre had made me promise to increase my security.

Nyla squinted to peer inside as the car drew level with her. She backed up in shock as I rolled the window down.

"Get in."

"No, thank you." She turned away.

"You want to be out here alone when drunks come out looking for a way to find the money they lost?"

Her gaze darted from left to right. "My ride is on its way."

"If it were, then you'd be gone by now. I'm just trying to be nice." I shrugged, rolling the window back up.

"Wait!" Nyla blurted.

Pushing the door open, I slid along the seat to allow her to enter. "Thank you," she said, closing the door.

I angled my head, taking in her features under the streetlights illuminating the car. "Do you wait out there every night?"

She shifted in her seat, drawing my gaze to the voluptuous curves overflowing her dress uniform. "No."

She tucked a lock of hair behind her ear, and the simple gesture sent my tongue darting along my bottom lip. "Where do you live?"

"Not far. Downtown Chicago." She clasped hands in her lap.

"Give Carter your address."

I took in the glow of her amber-brown skin as she did as I asked. She fixed her gaze out the window to avoid mine.

"Keep staring long enough, and I'll think you're interested," Nyla joked.

Chuckling, I leaned back in the seat and pulled out my phone. I scrolled through my messages to see who I could pop in on for a little visit.

"How old are you?" I raised an eyebrow at Nyla's sudden question.

"Why do you want to know?"

She shrugged. "You seem young to be running a casino."

"My age is not your concern," I said coolly.

Nyla's eyes narrowed. "Angelina may let you talk to her like that, but I won't."

Our gazes clashed and held in a stare-off as the car stopped outside Nyla's place.

"Thank you for the ride," she said, reaching the door handle.

Acting instinctively, I leaned across to block her from leaving. Her head whipped around, and she scowled at me.

"My personal life is none of your business."

"Glad you made that clear. Can I go now?" Nyla raised an eyebrow.

I moved back, and she stepped out, slamming the door.

Carter waited for her to walk inside the building before pulling off. "She's different."

"Don't get used to her."

My phone vibrated in my hand.

> **Angelina:** Are you coming over?
>
> **Me:** No.
>
> **Angelina:** Why not?
>
> **Me:** Focus on doing your job, not me.

I sighed. I could be an asshole like Renato when it came to women, but Angelina was a different story. Our clashes were frequent because she wanted to be known as "my girl," the untouchable future wife of Vincenzo Calabresi. I told her it would never happen and that I understood if she couldn't settle for a purely sexual relationship, but years later, she still thought I would change my mind, and I was growing tired of her demands.

> **Angelina:** I apologize for earlier.
>
> **Me:** Thanks.
>
> **Angelina:** Can I make it up to you?
>
> **Me:** Go to sleep.

I needed to figure out why I found Nyla so intriguing.

I let Carter go for the night when we finally arrived at my place. Entering, I turned off the alarm in my three-story home. Having a finger in the real estate market, I'd secured the land to build this place how I wanted—a home that would be mine forever. I had a place closer to the offices but liked coming here at the end of the week to relax and get away.

The Greek marble floors were shipped from overseas. Mom loved helping me decorate because she felt it needed a woman's touch. I'd ensured that my "palace" had enough space for my family to stay if needed. It had indoor and outdoor pools, nine bedrooms, eleven bathrooms, a theater, a man cave, a library, and my office.

I grabbed a bottle of water from the fridge before heading to my bedroom to shower and fall into bed.

Chapter 4

Nyla

While hurrying from the employee lounge, I carried a few empty trays to load up on chips. Getting the hang of working at a casino wasn't too hard—except for the people who lost, got drunk, and yelled at us all night. While rushing from the breakroom, I padded through the halls toward the main floor, watching a few laughing employees come through the door. While keeping my head down, I strolled into the back of the cashier counter, placing my badge back in my pocket.

"Hey, girl." Eunice, one of the longtime cashiers, finished with a customer and focused on me.

"Hey, Eunice. Busy today?"

"Same as usual. People are excited to play and end up losing big later."

Eunice and I got along great from the start, unlike Angelina. Eunice wasn't blinded by the prestige of the casino. All she cared about was working hard and taking care of her family. I admired her and knew we'd be great friends outside the casino had I been staying permanently.

The crowds swelled throughout the day, and a few people were kicked out for disorderly conduct with the servers. Stretching my arms, I yawned, seeing it was almost noon and time for my break.

"Where are you eating today?" Eunice asked.

"The lounge."

"Me too, I brought mine."

"Mind if I join you?"

Eunice grinned. "Sure. Come on, let's go before it gets too busy."

Eunice led the way out, passing the guards and locking the doors behind us. I smiled as I listened to her story about her youngest son not wanting to get up for school in the mornings as we made our way to the elevator.

"Hi, Mr. Calabresi." Eunice waved at our boss.

Since the night Vincenzo had dropped me off, I'd made it a point to stay clear of him. Aside from the sexual tension between us I tried to deny, I felt like he knew I was up to something.

Vincenzo paused as he talked to his assistant. Angelina gave me a death stare. The woman thought everybody wanted him.

He didn't speak but tipped his chin at Eunice and continued to his office.

Eunice puckered her lips. "He is so cute. If I was younger and not married with a kid..."

"Eunice, please." I snickered.

"Girl, you better watch him," she said with a bounce in her step.

"Watch him for what?"

She slid me a knowing glance. "I see the way he looks at you."

"I have a boyfriend," I reminded her.

"Boyfriend, not husband," she said, grabbing her lunch from her locker.

"My boyfriend and I are committed," I replied as we headed for the canteen.

"I wish I could go back to a simple dating lifestyle," she sighed.

I nodded. "Me too."

I paid for my salad and water, and we found a table in the back corner of the canteen.

We ate lunch, and I listened to Eunice talk about her love life.

"Miss Jolie." A security guard appeared beside me.

My heart caught in my throat. "Yes?" Did something happen to Mark? How did they know about his plan to rob the casino?

"Mr. Calabresi needs to see you," the security guard said, his voice giving nothing away.

I looked at Eunice, who shrugged. I set my napkin down on the table. "Do you know what he wants?"

"No, ma'am."

Murmuring that I'd catch up with Eunice later, I followed the guard, who escorted me to Vincenzo's office and left me outside his office.

"What are you doing here?" Angelina demanded with a glare as she exited his office.

"Mr. Calabresi sent for me."

Angelina huffed as she sat behind her desk. Ignoring her tantrum, I edged into Vincenzo's office and waited for him to speak.

"You sent for me?" Even with my slow and even

breathing, my nerves sizzled as his gaze took a lingering sweep of my body.

"I need you to sign these papers."

I approached the desk and glanced at the forms in front of him. Clearing my throat, I asked, "I'm being promoted?"

His steely jawline clenched. "Sign it before I change my mind."

"But... why? I'm still new."

"You've made a good impression on the team and the customers."

I moistened my lips with my tongue, and his eyes dilated as they followed the movement.

He's not interested.

It would be a disaster.

Standing to his full height, he moved around to lean against the front of his desk. "You'll receive a raise and be the lead cashier on the floor."

"What's the catch?"

The corner of his mouth twitched. "I run a tight ship, and when I see someone working hard, I reward them." Vincenzo reached behind him for the papers and held them out to me with a pen.

A jolt of electricity arced up my arm as I took the pen, and our eyes connected. "That's all?"

"Is there something else you'd like?" He tilted his head, and his words sounded like a challenge.

Playing games with my boss would only lead to trouble. Like I'd told Eunice, I loved my boyfriend.

"No. I-I'll sign the papers," I stammered, then did so and passed them back to him.

"Enjoy an extra 20 minutes of your lunch break since I brought you up here."

"Oh, that's not necessary."

"I insist, Nyla."

The sound of my name on his lips raised my pulse. "Thank you, Mr. Calabresi."

I rushed away, leaving his office door open and ignoring Angelina's death stare.

I needed to get control of my emotions and remind myself why I was at the casino.

****

I was tense and irritable. On my way home, I ran out of gas a few blocks from the casino. Not wanting to be stranded again, Mark had agreed to let me use his car. However, he'd forgotten to mention that it was low on gas. I had yet to receive a paycheck, so I couldn't pay for it. My phone was out of battery, so my only choice was to walk home.

I looked up as a familiar SUV approached and pulled up beside me. The window slid down.

"It's a little late to be out here by yourself," Vincenzo said coolly.

"My car ran out of gas."

"We can drop you off."

"Are you sure? I hate to impose."

"Yes, Nyla, I'm sure."

Angelina sat beside him with a snarl targeted at me. "Call her a car service."

"Then you can join her," Vincenzo quipped.

Her mouth snapped shut.

I quickly took out the necessary papers and locked the car. Mark would kill me for leaving his baby on the side of the road. "Will my car be all right here?"

"My people will fill it up and drop it to you later." Vincenzo tapped on his phone.

Angelina's shoulders slumped when he asked her to move across the seat to make room for me. I wondered why she was in his car with him so late.

"Are you coming?" Angelina asked when we reached her house five minutes later. She rubbed her hand along Vincenzo's arm.

He removed her hand. "Goodnight, Angelina."

"Is she going home with you?" Angelina's jealousy was evident as she exited the car.

"Drive, Carter," Vincenzo instructed, slamming the door in her face.

Carter pulled away.

I glanced at Vincenzo. "You could've called for a car service. I hate to be the cause of Angelina's misconceptions."

"Misconceptions?"

I fidgeted with my hands. "That something is going on between us."

Vincenzo laughed loudly as if the idea were ridiculous.

"Asshole," I mumbled as the car arrived outside my building. I shoved the door open.

A hand gripped my wrist, stalling me. "No goodnight?"

I raised my gaze from his hand on my wrist to his smirking face. "Goodnight."

"Goodnight, *asshole*. Isn't that what you really want to say?" Vincenzo taunted, releasing my wrist.

I scrambled from the car and slammed the door, running up the steps into my building. No one had ever made me feel as powerless as Vincenzo.

After tapping the alarm off the next morning, I tossed the covers back and ran a hand through my hair. Mark didn't come home the night before and sleeping alone after having a crazy dream about my boss pissed me off.

After showering and locking up the apartment, I stopped to look at Mark's car out front. Feeling a little hurt by his jab about me minding my business, I shook it off and left to meet up with my friend for the day.

Chapter 5

Nyla

Cassandra and I were shopping and having lunch. She had no idea what I'd planned with Mark, and I wouldn't put her in the middle of my mess, so I pretended everything was fine.

"So, his secretary hates you?" Cassandra asked, flipping through a rack of clothes.

I tugged on a vest. "Yeah, though she has no reason to hate me."

Cassandra gave the vest a thumbs-up. "But?"

"But nothing. She thinks I want her man, which is untrue. I'm happy with Mark."

Cassandra's eyes narrowed. "How are things with Mark?"

"Fine." I held up a pair of silk shirts.

"Good. I know he went MIA for a few weeks." Cassandra draped two dresses over her arm and sauntered to the dressing room.

"He's busy working, but we're much closer than before..." I shrugged, letting my words trail off.

"...before the cheating," Cassandra finished, poking her head from the dressing room.

"I forgave him." I dropped my gaze so she wouldn't see the doubt in my eyes.

She came out of the room, smoothing her hands over the dress and turning in front of the mirror. "You've been working there for two months now, right?"

I shook my head to indicate she should try the other dress. "Almost three."

"I'm proud of you. Any word from your uncle?"

She knew I hated talking about my uncle. He was the reason I had to work since he'd cut me off financially. "No, and before you bring it up, Mark is not keeping me from my family."

My phone rang, and I pulled it from my purse to see Mark's name. A smile touched my lips as I answered. "Hey, baby."

"Hi, Mark!" Cassandra yelled.

"Are you ready for tonight?" Mark asked.

I took the call off speakerphone. "I am. Can I call you back later?"

"Fuck, Cassandra. We have business to sort out," Mark grunted.

My heart skipped a beat as I moved to a private corner. The people Mark owed had told him his time was up, and they were ready to collect. It was going to happen tonight. All I had to do was open a door and let them do the rest.

"Relax, or Cassandra will hear you. I have everything worked out."

"We only get one chance, Nyla."

"I know, baby." Sighing, I leaned against the wall and closed my eyes.

"Once we get the money, we can leave. Get married," Mark promised.

"Really?" I perked up.

"I pay these people off, and we're in the clear. Calabresi won't miss the money," Mark muttered.

"Okay. I need to go. Cassandra's waiting on me." I ended the call and stood, spotting Cassandra at the front counter, paying for her clothes.

"Lunch?" Cassandra asked as I reached her. "I'm starving."

Nodding, I put the blue dress I'd chosen on the counter to pay. "Lunch, and then I have work later."

"Boo, you work too much," Cassandra teased.

We chose a restaurant close to the casino so I could walk to work afterward and clock in for the night. Cassandra sat across from me, scanning the menu, and I asked the server to bring us drinks while we decided.

Cassandra scanned the restaurant. "My first time here."

I tucked my purse into the chair next to me. "I came here with some of my coworkers."

"I'm happy for you, Nyla."

I smiled at my friend. "Aw, thank you."

"You've been through a lot. Losing your parents and having to drop out of school because of your crazy uncle's rules."

I sighed. "I'm glad my parents taught me to always trust my instincts."

"He's low down."

The server arrived with our drinks, and we placed our orders.

"He's sexy," Cassandra murmured, pointing behind me.

I glanced over my shoulder, and my eyes widened as I saw Vincenzo. "Shit," I muttered, shifting in my seat.

"What's wrong?"

"That's my boss."

"So?"

"So, nothing. I'd just rather he didn't see me."

I risked another glance over my shoulder. Vincenzo was with his brother and an older woman.

"Here you go, ladies." Our server placed our meals in front of us.

I smiled. "Thank you. Can I get a to-go box?"

Cassandra frowned. "You're leaving?"

"I forgot I have to cover for someone." I pulled some money from my purse and placed it on the table. Cassandra quickly finished her soda and jumped up to leave.

I waved her off and bent to hug her. "Stay. I'll call you later."

She eyed me skeptically. "Are you sure you're all right, Nyla?"

"Yes, I promise. Enjoy your food."

The server returned with my to-go box, and I quickly left the restaurant. Pulling out my phone, I dialed Mark, but the call went to voicemail. I wasn't looking where I was going as I headed into the casino and dropped my food as I ran into someone.

"What the hell?" Angelina screeched.

"Sorry," I mumbled, bending to grab the to-go box.

"Look where you're going," she hissed.

"I said sorry. Relax."

She jammed her hands on her narrow hips, glaring at me. "I should report you."

"Report me for accidentally bumping into you?" I asked in disbelief.

Angelina pointed her finger in my face. "Vincenzo doesn't see it, but I know you're trouble."

"Bitch," I muttered as she stalked away.

I put my food in my locker in the employee lounge, plastered on a smile, and headed for the cashier counter.

****

Four hours later, I took my break, heading to the back entrance, which led to an alley that no one used.

My phone vibrated, and I answered Mark's call, keeping my voice low. "Hey, babe."

"You ready?"

My fingers clenched around the phone, scanning the area. "Are you sure about not hurting anyone?"

"Only if we have no choice. I have to protect myself, Nyla," Mark rasped.

I bit my lip. "How close are you?"

"Pulling up now."

I pressed my palm to my forehead. "It's almost one a.m. Not much foot traffic, so you have an easy entry."

"Nice job, baby. Go back to work before you're missed," Mark instructed.

"Okay. Love you." I sent a prayer that everything would be over quickly.

"You, too." He hung up.

I repocketed my phone and headed back to my counter. It was just me, the guard, and one other girl working tonight. She took her break once I got back, and I flashed a wide grin at the guard.

"You're working late tonight," he observed.

"You know I work late, Roger."

He rubbed a hand over his beard. "Maybe you and I can get a coffee later."

I winked at him. "Maybe."

His eyes ballooned wide, and his hands flew up in the air as the barrel of a gun pressed to the back of his head.

"Be quiet and do as we say," a raspy voice instructed.

"Do you know who owns these premises?" Roger growled.

The man behind him raised his gun and smashed it against his head.

I jumped back in shock as three more gunmen appeared and covered the cameras. They wore uniforms like mine.

"Where's your badge?" Mark demanded.

I handed it off. "You remember the code?"

"Yeah. Stay close. We have five minutes to get in and out."

The other men pulled Roger's body out of the way and moved to the safe. No sooner had they emptied it than an alarm went off.

"Fuck!" Mark cursed.

Security had somehow been alerted and were heading toward us. Turning, we ran for the back entrance to the alley where a van was waiting.

"How much did you get?" I panted.

"Enough. You did good, baby." Mark captured my lips.

"Hurry that shit up! We have to go!" one of his accomplices shouted.

Mark moved to the front of the van, and I climbed in behind him.

I looked at my boyfriend. "It's over now, right?"

Mark nodded, and in my relief, I missed the glance he exchanged with one of the other men.

Back at our apartment, I showered and changed into shorts and a long-sleeved shirt. I walked down the hall toward the lounge, hearing Mark on the phone.

"She doesn't know anything."

I paused, peeking around the door. Mark was standing by the chair with his back to me.

"You promised me a cut if I kept her around a little longer."

I tensed at his words, but before I could make sense of them, the front door flew off its hinges with a loud splintering.

I screamed as a group of men charged into the apartment. Mark scrambled for his gun, but one of the guys lunged at him and punched him in the face.

Another man grabbed me by my hair. "Where's the money?"

"Please, let me go!" I cried out, trying to jerk myself from his hold.

"Fuck you!" Mark fell to the ground.

"Bring them," another man barked.

"Mark!" I screamed as the man restraining him knocked him unconscious.

****

My entire body ached. Mark and I were restrained in chairs beside each other. I didn't recognize the clinical room with its white walls. We'd been brought here with bags over our heads.

The two other men involved in the robbery had given up our address before our current captors killed them. I'd begged and pleaded with them, promising to return the money in return for our freedom.

Mark grunted as the man landed another punch to his stomach.

"Stop! Please!" I begged.

He lifted my chin. "Bitch, you better pray the Boss doesn't let us have a little fun with you later."

I swallowed the nausea in my throat as the security men laughed.

When the door opened, and I looked up to meet Vincenzo's icy gaze, I knew I would leave this room in a body bag.

****

Present Day

I sat on the floor of a dingy room. I'd been wearing the same clothes for the past two days. I hadn't bathed, eaten, or seen Vincenzo since the guards brought me here.

I wondered if Cassandra had tried to contact me or gone by my apartment. I'd ignored all her warnings about Mark. Sniffing away the tears, I thought about my life and the choices I'd made. My uncle had been right—Mark would be the death of me.

He's dead. Mark is dead.

I backed into the corner as the door opened, and a guard finally came in holding a food tray.

"Eat." He dropped it on the bed.

I looked at the sandwich and bottled water. "Not hungry," I whispered.

He smiled mockingly. "I don't fucking care if you starve to death, but we have plans for you."

My heart pounded. "I don't know where the money is, so you may as well kill me."

His eyes narrowed. "We'll see about that."

He left the room, closing and locking the door behind him. I gazed at the tray and grabbed the water, chugging it like I'd been on a deserted island for a month rather than three days.

Three days since my boyfriend was killed.

Three days since I robbed Vincenzo Calabresi.

Three days since my life changed forever.

Standing, I moved to the door, hearing raised voices. I bit my lip, looking around the room for the hundredth time for something I could use as a weapon.

"Think, Nyla."

They checked on me every so often. *Maybe I could overpower one of them and take his gun.*

My parents had kept me from the mafia world, but I knew how to fight and protect myself.

If I could escape, I could leave the country.

"Whatever you're thinking, it won't work."

I jumped. I'd been so absorbed in my thoughts that I hadn't heard the door open. Vincenzo stood in the doorway.

I backed up, moving closer to the bed as Vincenzo advanced into the room.

"I'm going to ask you a question, and I want an honest answer."

"O-Okay," I stuttered, keeping my eyes on him.

A vein throbbed in his forehead. "Where's my money?"

"Mark kept it," I answered truthfully.

"He's dead. You helped him steal from me."

I was stricken with goosebumps, but not in a good way. "I-I can get your money back."

"How?"

"Mark owed some people. I can tell you where to get it back."

His eyebrows melded together. "Who?"

"Loan sharks over on the west side."

"Why should I trust you?"

I lowered my head in shame. "You have no reason to trust me. But I can return your money."

"Let's go."

"Where?"

Vincenzo lunged at me, gripping me by the jaw. "Question me again and see what happens."

"Sorry. I won't. I promise."

Vincenzo grimaced. "Nyla Sartori, you've made the worst mistake of your life."

Oh no. A cold chill ran up my spine.

He knows my real name.

It would've been better if I'd been killed with Mark. Now that Vincenzo knew my real name, he could easily get rid of me and leave no witnesses who wanted to search for me or ask questions about my whereabouts. He could find and kill everyone who loved me enough to ask questions—and anyone else, he could pay to look the other way.

I fucked up three days ago.

Chapter 6

Vincenzo

Savio watched me as I reached for the glass of bourbon. He'd been quiet since calling the meeting earlier. After picking up Nyla from the warehouse, I had her shower and change because she smelled like shit. She was lucky she was still alive. She had my brothers to thank for staying my hand. Elio had carried out a background search and discovered her real name was Nyla Sartori, the niece of Cono Sartori, a mob boss in Chicago. We had no relationship with him as our businesses never crossed. Did Nyla know her uncle trafficked women?

"She ran away from Cono's protection and has lived independently since she was twenty," Elio explained.

"Her parents died in a car crash?" I investigated, seeing the photos of the crash and newspaper reports.

"You can't kill her," Savio spoke up.

I slammed my hand on the table. "Either she gives me back the five million, or she dies."

"The money will be recovered. We have people researching his loan sharking," Savio explained.

"It's about principles. She set me up," I grunted in reply.

"Vincenzo's right. We let her slide, and we come off weak," Renato backed me up.

Savio stared at him. "How many times have I explained you're not getting involved."

I surged to my feet. "Am I a part of this family or not?"

"Sit down," Savio barked.

Elio raised his hand. "Vincenzo, show some respect. Sit down."

"She played you, and you're pissed. It's understandable, but you're so angry that you're making mistakes," Sante noted.

I flipped him off. "Fuck you, Sante."

Apart from Renato, my family saw me as the little brother, the baby to protect. He knew how hard I'd worked, how my father had taught me to shoot a gun at twelve. I'd been out on jobs with my brothers when someone crossed out our family or messed with our money.

Swallowing my anger, I sat in my chair. If I couldn't get my money back or kill Nyla, I'd become a ruthless asshole likes of which they'd never seen.

Elio finished talking. "Cono Sartori is protected, A Don. Untouchable."

"Word on the street is that Mark had a gambling problem. He lost a lot of money and owed a loan shark," Savio said.

"He was a gambler and a drug addict. We have the information on the loan shark," Renato said, his eyes on his phone.

I nodded. "Let's ride."

Sante stood. "We have family dinner later."

I shook my head. "Not hungry."

"Tell that to your parents and see what happens." Savio slapped me on the back of the head.

I rubbed the sting away, glaring at him.

"Where is Nyla now?" Elio asked as we headed to the cars.

"I put her in the trunk."

My brothers stopped walking and turned to gawp at me.

"You locked her in the trunk?" Savio demanded.

I shrugged. "I needed to ensure she wouldn't run."

Moaning and screaming came from the trunk. Renato stalked over and popped it open. Nyla was handcuffed, gagged, and tied up.

"Get her out of the trunk," Savio snapped.

"Why?"

"We don't treat women like that."

"Weren't you the one almost ready to kill McKayla? And Renato dragged Sonya from a hotel when he found out about his son," I reminded him.

Savio fisted my shirt and said through clenched teeth, "Keep my wife's name out of your mouth."

"Savio, come on. He didn't mean it." Elio tried to calm him down.

I never backed down from anyone, including my brothers. Was I wrong for bringing up their wives? Maybe. But anyone who crossed us had to pay.

I glanced at Nyla, seeing her eyes widen. "Get her out of the trunk."

Savio released me. Going to his car, I opened the passenger door. Nyla climbed into the backseat with a guard on either side of her. I heard her sniffling as I yanked my seatbelt on.

"Your tears can't help you."

She clasped her hands in her lap. "Are you going to kill me?"

"Yes, if I don't get my money back."

We drove toward the city. Elio had given me the address of a bar where the loan shark Mark owed was located.

"I-I know you don't trust me… but my uncle is the only person I know who has that kind of money. He could give you the money, but he won't make it easy. He probably won't pay at all," Nyla said haltingly.

"I'll take my chances. Call him. Put it on speaker." I gestured to my guard to give Nyla his phone.

We arrived at the bar as we waited for the call to go through.

"Who is this?" a gravelly voice demanded.

"Uncle Cono?" Nyla asked hesitantly.

"Nyla?"

She bit her lip. "Uncle Cono, I need your help."

I took the phone from her. "Cono Sartori, you're talking to Vincenzo Calabresi."

Chuckling was heard on the other end. "Vincenzo! What is the point of this call?"

My gaze fell on Nyla, who was staring blankly out the window. "Five million dollars."

"What does that have to do with me?"

Cono's belligerent tone annoyed me. "Your niece owes me five million dollars."

"I haven't talked to my niece in three years. How do you know her?"

"I'd be happy to meet in person to explain."

My words were greeted with a long pause. "Very well. Send me the details."

I ended the call and tossed the phone back to my guard.

Worry darkened Nyla's face. "We can work out a solution."

I frowned. "The only solution is getting back my money."

"He hates me."

"What are you saying?"

"My parents left a trust for me, but my uncle hated my mother. He said she took my father away from the family."

"Your family problems will have to wait until I get my money back."

****

I handcuffed Nyla again before we stepped into the bar. I told her to point out the men who'd dealt with Mark.

"All I know is that his name is Gianney Greco."

My pulse hiked at hearing Greco's name. We'd taken over their areas and business since their Boss had been killed.

"Point him out."

Nyla scanned the room. "I don't see him."

"If you're lying to me—"

"I'm not!" she shouted, trying to squirm away from me.

A few patrons turned at her raised voice.

I grasped her arm and pushed her to the other side of the bar. "Keep your voice down."

"Can I help you?" The bartender's eyes dropped to the handcuffs on Nyla's wrists.

I nodded. "I'm looking for Gianney Greco."

The bartender shook his head. "Never heard of him."

I pushed Nyla toward one of my guards. "Take her outside."

I released her as the guard moved forward, and Nyla made a run for it. I took off after her, exiting the bar and looking left and right. I saw Nyla sprinting up the street, pushing through pedestrians and screaming for help.

"Fuck!" I cursed as she made a beeline for two police officers. Hiding behind a wall, I pulled out my cell phone to call Renato.

He answered on the first ring. "What's up?"

"Nyla got away." Damn. Having the police involved would set us back.

"How?"

"We came to the westside to find the loan shark lover boy owed money to, and guess who it is?"

"Who?"

"Gianney Greco."

Renato was quiet for a moment. "Gianney Greco. Why do I know that name?"

"You know Gianney Greco?"

"Come to the house. We can't talk over the phone. We need to regroup," Renato ended the call.

I watched as the police put Nyla in the back of the police cruiser, debating whether to follow after them or meet with Renato. I opted for the safest option and headed home.

****

Hours later, Savio, Renato, and I sat in Pop's study while Elio tried to find out if Nyla was still in police custody.

Savio frowned. "She said Gianney Greco?"

I nodded. "Yeah. Is that name familiar to anyone?"

"I thought you handled Greco's people." Pops looked at Renato.

Renato puffed his cigar. "We did. Most of his family in Miami and a few here."

"When Victoria pulled that shit with McKayla, I had her taken care of," Savio remarked.

"Must be a long-lost relative. How is he connected to Mark and Nyla?" Pops inquired.

"Her boyfriend robbed the casino," I said, keeping it simple.

"Nyla said he owed money to Greco." Renato backed me up.

"Cono Sartori is her uncle?" Pops ran a hand through his gray hair. At almost 80, he didn't look a year over 65. Madre kept him young, with varied activities and spending time with all the grandkids. They expected all of us to have a lot of grandkids, but since I was the youngest at 25, kids were the last thing on my mind.

"I plan on meeting Cono tomorrow," I confirmed.

Savio shook his head. "It's best if I meet with him."

"It's my casino," I snapped.

"Vincenzo!" Pops barked.

"Go ahead. Take his side, as usual," I scoffed.

Savio frowned. "No sides here. I'm your brother and Don of the family."

"Thought you retired," I grumbled.

"He still has a say in how the family is run. You need

to work together when a problem arises," Pops pointed out.

I blew out a frustrated breath. "I can handle my own business."

Savio pursed his lips. "Yeah, which is how she got away."

Renato elbowed Savio. "Bro, relax. He's our brother."

"Let him say what he wants." I shrugged. "Newsflash, I don't need another father."

I rose from the chair to leave, but Renato stalled me with a hand on my arm.

"Vincenzo, sit down," Pops ordered.

I plopped back down in the chair. "Fine."

"Savio, you're right," Pops stated. His gaze swung to me. "And so is Vincenzo. We've long tried to shield him from the business, but it found him anyway."

Savio's jaw clenched. "So, we're supposed to let him go out on his own to deal with the Greco family?"

"What do you want to do, Vincenzo?"

Pops wanted my opinion. It felt good. "I want to find Nyla and use her to get Cono's money. She told me he controlled her trust. He has offshore accounts and land that could be beneficial for us."

"How much land?" Pops asked.

"Enough for us to expand Calabresi and get our hands in the pockets of a few Senators."

Savio nodded in agreement. "I would do the same thing, little brother."

"So, you'll let me take the lead?"

"Until you fuck up, yeah." Savio extended a hand.

I shook it, then fist-bumped Renato.

"Renato, find Greco immediately. The other Dons will want answers," Pops said.

We filed from the office, hearing the kids playing. I stopped in the kitchen, laughing at my mother, who was learning to do a TikTok video.

"What are you doing?" I took the phone from her.

"Rena is showing me all the latest social media." Madre laughed at my frown.

"Rena needs another hobby."

"Come on, Vinnypoo. Your mom would be a hit on TikTok," Rena taunted.

I cringed at the nickname. "That's not my name."

"Vinnypoo is cute," Madre said.

"His girlfriend made it up." Rena smirked.

"Angelina is not my girlfriend."

Rena quirked a brow. "Really? The last time we talked, she said you were looking at engagement rings."

I glared at her. "Rena, shut up."

Sante strolled into the kitchen. "Hey, don't tell my wife to shut up." He pretended to punch me in the stomach.

"Tell your wife to stay out of my business."

"Where's Nyla? I haven't seen her in a few days," Rena asked.

Sante and I looked at each other.

"Not sure," I responded, picking up a piece of bread from the tray.

"What do you mean?" Rena frowned. "I talked to her at the casino, and we made plans to have lunch."

"How am I supposed to know an employee's social life?"

"Nyla will be out of police custody by the morning, and I have guys waiting at the station," Elio said as he entered the kitchen.

Rena's mouth dropped open as she looked from Elio

to me to Sante. She was three seconds away from hounding us until we confessed.

"Sante, if you ever want to get in my bed again, you better tell me what's going on," Rena stated.

"Not my business." Sante threw his hands up.

"Who is Nyla?" Madre asked, helping my nephew off the stool.

I watched as he ran from the kitchen. "No one."

"A girl he hired three months ago. You'd love her," Rena said.

Mother rinsed her glass in the sink. "Why is she missing or in jail?"

I sighed. "It's nothing for you to worry about."

Rena pointed at me and then Sante. "Talk, or I'll find out for myself."

I shrugged. "Go find out."

"Fine by me. McKayla still has some pull at the police station." Rena stuck her tongue out.

Sante grabbed her before she could get away and lifted her onto the island. "We're here to have a family dinner." Sante dared Rena with his eyes.

Eyeing him, Rena blushed, caressing his cheek. Suddenly, she gripped it hard. "Talk, or no goodies for you."

"She robbed Vincenzo, and he had her kidnapped," Sante blurted.

Elio bowed his head, knowing Cora would be next to ask about Nyla. She'd met all the wives, and they'd hit it off.

Madre turned to me. "You kidnapped someone, Vincenzo?"

"You know I never discuss business, Madre."

She gave me a steely look. "I'm your mother, and I want to know what you're doing."

"Stay out of my business."

She gasped and slapped me across the face. Her hands flew to her mouth, and her eyes widened in shock. "I'm so sorry. I didn't mean—"

"Stop treating me like a kid and trying to control my life! I'm twenty-five and run two successful businesses!" I shouted, stalking from the room.

Rena caught up with me. "Vincenzo, wait."

"What now, Rena? Haven't you done enough?"

She held her hands up. "I come in peace. What happened with Nyla?"

I laced my arms over my chest. "She robbed the casino, and I killed her boyfriend in front of her."

"Oh, my God. She must be terrified."

"Terrified? She knew exactly what she was doing."

Rena saw goodness in everybody. "She's young, Vin. I've been where she is, with the bad boy who gets in your head."

"Not me."

Rena sighed. "Maybe I can help."

"No."

"Listen to me. McKayla, Sonya, and Cora are the only ones who can understand Nyla's current mindset. She's scared and confused, and her being in police custody is bad for our family."

"Her family is connected, Rena."

Rena frowned. "What do you mean? She told me her parents died when she was young."

I barked a laugh at her lies. "Her uncle is Cono Sartori, a mob boss with whom we have no relationship or leverage. This will end badly for Nyla if he doesn't return my money."

Rena's eyes widened. "You can't be serious?"

"I'm very serious."

"Let me talk to her first."

I blew out a frustrated breath. "Do I have a choice?"

A cocky grin spread across Rena's face. "Nope." Before I could reply, she hugged me. "Admit it. I'm your favorite sister-in-law."

"Never." I laughed at her harsh glare but let her drag me back into the kitchen.

Chapter 7

Nyla

I cursed myself for running to the police for help. Now, I was wearing handcuffs, and my hair was all over the place. They interrogated me all night, trying to get answers about who I was running from. I thought about giving up Vincenzo and his family but couldn't be sure he didn't have the police in his back pocket. The cops took my prints and conducted a background check, which revealed my true name.

I went from needing help to being a possible mafia hit. At twenty-two, my life wasn't how I'd hoped.

The little money I could borrow from Cassandra wouldn't get me far enough away from this mess.

Heat flushed my cheeks when I finally stepped out of the police station to find Rena and Vincenzo waiting. My shoulders slumped. I prepared myself to face the music and was surprised when Rena pulled me into a hug.

She dressed in a light pink silk blazer and black pantsuit. "How are you feeling?"

"Exhausted," I said, seeing Vincenzo's disdainful look over Rena's shoulder.

Rena pulled back to look at me. "Vincenzo explained everything."

I tensed. I'd grown fond of Rena and didn't want her to think badly of me. "About the money?"

"Hey, you have nothing to be afraid of," Rena said as Vincenzo climbed into the waiting car.

Tears threatened my eyes. "He hates me."

Rena sighed. "You're not his favorite person right now. What were you thinking?"

"Mark needed help."

"So, you steal from my family?" Rena pressed.

I bit my top lip. "Listen, Rena. I didn't ask you to come down here."

"True, but I thought we were friends. You could've come to me."

"No, I couldn't."

"Mark is dead, Nyla. You need help."

"I'll be fine."

Rena bit back a laugh. "God, you're stubborn like Vincenzo."

I didn't like being compared to him. "He's a jackass."

Rena opened the door. "Get in the car."

"I called a friend," I lied. Cassandra had no clue where I was. I'd been in a holding cell for hours with people who had committed murder. God, my parents would be so disappointed in me.

"That's a lie, and Vincenzo promised not to do anything to you." Rena turned to look at him.

His face was expressionless, showing no sign of the damage I'd caused.

Knots coiled in my belly. "How can you be so sure?"

She frowned. "I trust him, and he's sweet when he wants to be."

"When will that side of him come out exactly?"

Rena threw her head back and laughed.

The car window rolled down, and Vincenzo poked his head out. "What the fuck is taking so long?"

"We're coming. Hold your horses," Rena muttered, climbing into the backseat. She slid over to make room for me.

I eyed the guards on either side of the car. "Where are you taking me?"

"None of your business," Vincenzo bit out.

Rena sucked in a breath. "Vincenzo, you promised to be a little less rough with her."

"Promises are meant to be broken," Vincenzo said sharply.

"Are you taking me back to the warehouse? I'd rather you took me to jail again," I confessed.

Rena gasped in shock and leaned toward Vincenzo in the passenger seat. "You locked her in the warehouse?"

Vincenzo slammed his hand on the dashboard. "Stay out of my business. She's our enemy."

Rena's mouth tightened. "Nyla, you can stay with me."

His eyes burned furiously. "No, she can't."

"She's not going back to the warehouse," Rena insisted.

They argued back and forth for a few minutes before Vincenzo blew out a harsh breath. "She can stay at my condo in the city."

"Is she going to be safe with you?" Rena's eyes narrowed.

"If I wanted her dead, I could do it right now." He snapped his fingers. "Sante has told you plenty of times to stay out of our cartel business."

Rena raised a challenging eyebrow. "You could always let her go. I'm sure she's learned her lesson."

I appreciated Rena fighting on my behalf, but she was right. I'd learned my lesson, and I wasn't about to do it a second time. "Rena, it's fine. I can stay with him."

Rena grasped my hand. "Okay, but you have my number if you need anything."

"We'll settle everything when we meet with her uncle tomorrow," Vincenzo stated.

The mention of my uncle had me shaking beneath the tough façade I was projecting. Mark was dead, but I was pissed at him for leaving me to handle his fuck up and even more pissed at myself for agreeing to his crazy scheme in the first place.

The car approached Vincenzo's massive condo, and we all piled out. I trailed after Vicenzo as he greeted the doorman. He was like a president with all the extra security.

Rena stretched her arm around my waist. "Everything will work out."

I leaned my head on her shoulder. "Thanks for helping, Rena."

"You remind me of myself."

Her words surprised me. "How so?"

"Sweet, full of life, and feisty. But there's a lot of hurt beneath this hard exterior." She tapped my forehead.

We stepped onto the private elevator, and the gold doors whooshed closed. Vincenzo punched the button for the top floor. His cold gaze landed on me, and I dropped my eyes to the floor. I hadn't seen this side of him before: ruthless and deadly.

We exited the elevator, and Vincenzo led us to his high-rise condo.

My eyes widened. The living room alone was bigger than my modest two-bedroom apartment in downtown Chicago.

"When was the last time you stayed here?" Rena asked, looking around.

I wondered that, too, because he didn't seem like a condo type of guy.

"Probably a month. I've been staying at my house." Vincenzo grabbed mail off the stand next to the door.

"Did you hire a housekeeper?" Rena swiped her hand across the fireplace mantel.

Vincenzo put the mail back on the stand. "Yeah, she comes twice a week."

Rena turned to me. "Are you sure you'll be okay here?"

"She won't be alone," Vincenzo said.

"What do you mean?" Rena and I asked.

Vincenzo raked a hand through his hair. "I'm staying here with her."

My stomach dropped.

Rena marched toward him. "Vincenzo, that's not a good idea."

"She's right," I blurted.

Vincenzo ignored our glares. "I'm ensuring my investment doesn't bolt again."

"You don't trust me," I stated.

He moved toward me. "Why would I? Your track record speaks for itself."

"That was a mistake, and I'm here to fix it."

"A mistake is leaving a cup on a table without a coaster. Stealing five million dollars is a fucking choice!"

Our faces were inches apart, our chests heaving.

Rena stepped between us. "Vincenzo, calm down and let me talk to Nyla."

Darting his eyes from me to Rena, Vincenzo walked around her and went to talk to his men at the door.

"Come and sit down." Rena took me by the hand and led me to the couch.

I shook my head. "This is a bad idea."

"Too late now. He's proving a point."

"Which is?"

"You like him."

"What?" I scoffed. "Besides the fact that my boyfriend was killed in front of me, he's the last man I'd ever be interested in."

"I'm married to a Calabresi man, and I can see right through you."

"Rena, nothing is going on between Vincenzo and me. I want to get him his money and move on."

"You had a chance to give him the money."

I stared at her. "You've lost me."

"You could've given up your uncle's information when he snatched you up after the robbery."

I exhaled and stared unseeing at my new home. "My uncle and I don't have the best relationship."

"Are you saying he wouldn't save his niece?"

My mouth twisted bitterly. "Let's just say that I doubt tomorrow's meeting will go in my favor."

Rena studied me for a moment. "I think you and Vincenzo need to have a talk. I noticed the attraction between you the first time I saw you together at the casino."

"Not everyone wants to marry a Calabresi," I said wryly.

"Don't worry, it'll snow in hell first," Vincenzo drawled, catching me off-guard.

"Calm down. It was girl talk," Nyla chided. "I expect you to behave, Vincenzo. Nyla knows to call me if you hurt her."

"Dream on, Nyla," he muttered.

Rena waved goodbye and the door closed behind her.

I twisted my hands, feeling suddenly nervous. "Vincenzo, I—"

"Save it. You can take the guest room."

"The couch is fine."

"You'll stay in the guest room," Vincenzo said calmly. "This place is fitted with cameras, and I'll be sleeping out here to ensure you don't try to escape before our meeting."

"Asshole," I muttered as I trailed behind him to the stairs. He showed me the bathroom, with its large tub and a separate closet for towels. It was stocked with every feminine product I could wish for. "Of course, you have every product a girl needs," I said sarcastically.

"Watch your mouth."

I jumped, not realizing he was right behind me.

The guest bedroom was opposite the bathroom and had a king-size bed, a TV on the wall, and a window nook with a loveseat.

"Do you plan to keep your guards outside all night?" I asked innocently.

His face was impassive. "Not something you need to know."

I pressed a hand to his chest to stop him from leaving. "I need some clothes to change into."

He glanced down at my hand before removing it. "There are shirts and tights in the closet—and before you ask, my sister-in-law keeps stuff here when she visits with my brother."

"Never crossed my mind."

His jaw tightened. "Get some sleep. Tomorrow, we get my money back."

"And if my uncle doesn't give you the money?"

Vincenzo's smile was cold. "Pray for a better outcome."

****

Vincenzo woke me up early to accompany him to the meeting with my uncle. I wished I could ignore his demands. Uncle Cono and I had never gotten along. I moved out because he wanted to control my life and treated me like a chess piece he could move around to suit his needs. If I didn't bow to his way of thinking, he would see it as a betrayal against the family. I prayed for a future outside the world of the cartel. I was constantly looking over my shoulder, wondering if everyone I met would discover my last name and have me killed without even knowing the type of person I was.

Fear tightened my chest. I wouldn't put it past my uncle to force me to come home to live with him.

I adjusted the ring Mark had given me on my thumb, smiling at the pink silver stone. Last night was the first time I hadn't dreamed of him.

"When we get there, I want you to stay quiet," Vincenzo instructed from beside me.

His driver drove through the front gate to a place I hadn't visited in over three years. My stomach fluttered as I recalled our arguments. He never tired of telling me what a disappointment I was to the family. Our last argument had ended with him smacking me in the face.

The guard checked with security inside the house, and we continued up the drive. My uncle prided himself on always being one step ahead of his enemies.

"He won't listen to me anyway," I finally replied.

Carter closed my door after I climbed out of the car. Two more cars I hadn't noticed earlier parked behind us, and more men got out.

"Is this amount of security necessary?" I asked.

Vincenzo's dark gaze raked over me. "Every precaution is necessary when it pertains to my money."

Myles opened the door before we made it up the front steps. He looked older, with gray in his mustache, but his smile was familiar.

"Miss Nyla, wonderful to see you again." Myles reached for my hand, but Vincenzo jerked me away before we could embrace. "Mr. Sartori is expecting you, Mr. Calabresi," Myles said stiffly.

Vincenzo pushed me forward. "We're not here for a family reunion."

I looked around at the same polished art on stands and the paintings he'd fallen in love with over the years on the walls. The brown and black decor was stale trash and reeked of death.

I tensed as Vincenzo placed his hand on my lower back. "I don't plan on running again."

"Good, because I would have to kill you in front of your uncle in his home."

As we walked down the corridor, I saw the man of the hour.

Uncle Cono had aged. His beard was dyed black, and

his thin gray hair was combed over his bald head. A large gut spilled over his pants, wobbling as he approached.

He pulled me into a hug. "My sweet Nyla. *Mi sei mancata.*"

He missed me? What a joke. I plastered on a fake smile and played along. "I missed you more, Uncle Cono."

"We need to talk," Vincenzo said.

"Yes, we have so much to catch up on. How is your father doing?" Uncle Cono gestured for us to follow him into his study.

My gaze was drawn to the pictures on the wall of my father and uncle when they were little and a few of my grandparents. Nothing with my mother.

"Typical," I muttered.

"Did you say something, Nyla?" Uncle Cono asked casually.

I plucked a photo of him and my father from his desk. "Just admiring pictures of you and Daddy."

"Take a seat, please. I was sad to hear the news of Mark's death," Uncle Cono said insincerely.

"Mark and your niece robbed my casino. I've come here to collect," Vincenzo said, getting straight to the point.

Uncle Cono leaned back in his seat. "How much did she steal?"

"Five million."

I kept my head down, avoiding my uncle's eyes. It would be simpler for Vincenzo to kill me and move on with his life. Five million dollars was nothing to him and his family.

"You stole from him, Nyla?" Uncle Cono inquired.

My heart thundered in my chest as I nodded.

I jumped as he slammed his hand on the desk. "Answer me!"

"Yes!"

"Why? Was it Mark's idea? Because you had everything growing up."

It was foolish for me to believe he genuinely cared about me—or the situation Mark put me in. I'd asked him to help with Mark's gambling debts many times and suggested rehab. "Mark needed help."

Uncle Cono turned to Vincenzo. "I apologize for my niece's behavior and the trouble she has caused your family."

Vincenzo shook his head. "Apologizes won't cut it. Mark is dead, which means the debt is yours."

I prayed for death over being returned to my emotionally abusive and manipulative uncle.

"You have a problem, and now I have a problem," Uncle Cono said coolly.

Vincenzo glared at my uncle. "Get to the point, Sartori."

Grim satisfaction flew through me, knowing Uncle Cono and Vincenzo might end up killing each other. Maybe I could get out of this situation after all.

"The money is not accessible. Nyla's trust fund can only be released when she marries."

"*What?*" I leaped to my feet. Why was he lying and telling Vincenzo I had a trust fund?

"Sit down," Vincenzo hissed.

"I promised your father I would protect your money," Uncle Cono stated.

"You lied to me all this time," I accused.

"For your protection."

"I don't care about a trust fund," Vincenzo seethed.

"Whatever issues you have with Nyla can be handled after I get my money."

"Ah, but here's the problem." Uncle Cono leaned forward. "Nyla has something you want, and I can help you get it, but I need something in return."

"You're using me as a bargaining chip," I whispered.

"The first trust fund of one million was used to provide for you after their death. The second trust fund can only be accessed when you are married," Uncle Cono explained.

"Which isn't your decision to make!" I snapped.

"I suggest you show me the respect I deserve, Nyla." Uncle Cono pointed his finger in my face.

I felt nauseous. "I need to get out of here."

"You're not going anywhere," Vincenzo growled, preventing me from leaving.

Tears warmed my cheeks. My life was imploding around me.

Vincenzo slipped his hands into his pockets, his eyes cold. "Mark is dead. Your niece will be next—unless my money is returned to me."

Chapter 8

Vincenzo

"Nyla, wait outside. I want to talk privately with Vincenzo," Cono instructed.

His bloated face was flushed at the idea of pawning his niece. He thought he had the upper hand. He was a fool if he thought he could manipulate me. Cono would live to regret denying me my money.

My fists clenched in my pockets. If there was even a hint that Cono was trying to cross me, I'd put a bullet through his skull.

"Step out for a moment with Romo."

Nyla slowly stood, and the guard escorted her from the office. The other guard remained by the door.

Cono opened his desk drawer, and my hand moved to my gun holster. He removed a file and threw it on the desk. "Something you might want to see."

"I'm not here to play games, Cono."

"Nyla is more valuable than you think."

I picked up the file and scanned the documents inside. My eyes narrowed into slits as I viewed the photographs of Savio at the scene of Viviana Greco's murder. It had been a few years since the incident, but Savio's ex-girlfriend's death still haunted our family.

"Why should I believe these are real?"

"Doesn't matter. The contents of that file could hurt your family."

"Are you blackmailing me?"

Cono ignored my question. "It's a shame our families have never done business. You can change that so we both profit."

"Who knows about these pictures?"

"A few people. I kept it hidden to protect my interests."

"Your interests?"

"You may have the governor's ear, but she can't prevent your family from being indicted for double homicide—not to mention murdering my niece's boyfriend."

Cono was giving me no choice but to kill him before I left—but first, I needed to know how he came upon those pictures. Savio hadn't thought about Viviana in years and was happily married to McKayla.

"Tell me what you want, and I'll decide whether I agree."

"Marry Nyla, and you'll have access to her trust fund to pay off her debt."

"And you get what?"

His lip curled into a smile. "I will get a seat at the table."

I chuckled at his delusion. "I have no say in who sits at the table with the other families."

Cono smiled. "Come now, I'm sure underestimating your influence. Nyla will do what I say. You can annul the marriage after the funds clear. We all win."

"Savio manages the cartel's business."

Cono raised a hand. "I'm certain you can convince him to give me a place. As you know, my business hasn't fared too well lately."

"Not our problem."

He exhaled in frustration. "You know, Vincenzo, your father was selfish when it came to allowing others to make money."

I stepped closer to his desk. "Leave my family out of this discussion."

"Marry Nyla, get the money, and give the Sartori cartel a seat as the sixth family."

"The cartel works with perfectly well five families."

"Perhaps it's time to expand."

"I need all the evidence before I'll consider talking to my brothers."

Cono sat in his chair. "You have twenty-four hours to get back to me. Now, I need to speak to my niece alone."

I turned to leave his office, yanking the door open.

Nyla jumped in fright. "What do you want?"

"What I want is for you not to fuck me over again, or you won't leave here alive."

I pushed her into her uncle's office and closed the door before reaching for my phone.

Me: We have a problem.

Savio: Are you alone?

Renato: Send me your address.

Elio: Call me.

Me: I'm with Cono.

Savio: Did he give you the money?

Me: No, and I'm ready to put a bullet in his head.

Elio: We already have Renato killing people when he's bored. You need to stay calm.
Me: He's saying Nyla and I have to get married.
Savio: Call me.
Renato: Three-way call?
Me: What do we do about the Greco family?

The death of their Don had put a target on our back with the other families. The Greco family had a seat at the table but had done nothing but hinder us and betray my family. Arranged marriages were well known, but Savio had never wanted Vivian Greco as a wife.

Elio: The Greco family are no longer our friends.
Me: I agree. We should reevaluate.

My head snapped up as the door opened. Nyla looked like she'd seen a ghost.

Cono walked out behind her with a satisfied smile and extended a hand. "Call me when you've made your decision."

I left him hanging as I tugged Nyla from the house. She didn't say a word as we climbed into the car.

My phone buzzed, and I answered.

"Where are you?" Savio asked.

"In the car heading back to the office."

My stomach dropped as I thought about Cono revealing what had happened to Viviana Greco and putting our family in danger. Savio and my father had demanded loyalty from Viviana's father and brothers, but their betrayal had put the final nail in the coffin for the Greco family.

"Come here first," Savio instructed.

"Is McKayla there?"

"She is. Why?"

"Something is wrong with Nyla. I thought McKayla could talk to her."

"What do you mean?"

"She hasn't blinked or said a word once since leaving Cono's office."

"Talk to her."

I scoffed at his suggestion. "Talk to her about what?"

"I can hear you," Nyla whispered. Her gaze was fixed out the window as we stopped at a red light.

I narrowed my eyes at her but didn't reply. "We'll be there soon," I told Savio before ending the call.

Nyla tapped her fingers on her thigh nervously. "Uncle Cono told me I had to marry you to pay off the debt. In exchange, the Sartori family will become the sixth family in the alliance."

It was clear from her tone that she wasn't on board with either demand. It seemed we had something in common.

"Did you know?"

She whipped her head to face me. "Did I know what?"

"That he had evidence on my family."

"No. Uncle Cono has never involved me in his affairs."

The car arrived at Savio's home. "I need to meet with my brother. Stay here."

"In the car?"

"Yes. Savio won't welcome the woman who stole from us. He's ten times worse than me when it comes to protecting our family."

****

After hugging McKayla and high-fiving my nephew, I shook hands with my brother and followed him into the living room.

Savio lifted a bottle of St. Jameson's with a raised eyebrow.

I nodded. "Make it a double."

Savio handed me my drink. "It sounds like Cono and his niece are cut from the same cloth. Elio's background check revealed he's in debt."

"Nyla has a five-million trust fund he never told her about. She can only access it when she marries."

"So he proposed you marry his niece to get the money back."

"Yes. He said if I don't marry her, he'll turn in evidence implicating you in the deaths of Viviana and Gennaro Greco."

"Does he not realize that threatening to blackmail the Calabresi family is bad for his health? How long did he give you to decide?"

"Twenty-four hours."

"Elio and Renato need to know. We ensured there would be no leaks after the explosion that killed Viviana."

Their deaths still felt like yesterday. Savio had paid a few higher-ups in law enforcement to cover up the truth.

"I want my money back, but marrying Nyla is out of the question."

"Would it be so bad? She's beautiful."

I bit back my reply. Nyla meant nothing to me beyond money, but I didn't like that my brother had noticed her beauty for some reason.

The door opened, and Renato and Sante entered.

"You didn't answer my text," Renato growled, pouring himself a drink.

I quickly checked my phone. "You want to kill Cono before I get my money?"

Renato shrugged and gulped his drink. "He has a life insurance policy. We take his business and get your money back."

"Cono wants Vincenzo to marry Nyla in exchange for the evidence against me and the five million," Savio told our brothers.

"And he gets what?" Sante demanded.

"The Sartori family is brought into the fold."

Sante's head cocked back in surprise. "As in the round table?"

"It's always been five families, even when our grandfather was the Don," Renato said.

"Six families mean an even split in votes," Savio pointed out.

"So, marry her, then we kill him and get the money. He has limited resources," Renato suggested.

"I'm not the marrying type." My brothers were happy with their wives and kids, but I liked the single life.

"The marriage would only last long enough to get the money and dispose of Cono," Renato said.

I looked up as McKayla entered with Carter and Nyla.

"I told you to stay in the car!" I barked, moving toward her and grabbing her arm.

McKayla looked shocked at my outburst. "She needs to use the restroom."

"McKayla, stay out of his business," Savio said softly.

Nyla jerked herself from my grip. I went to grab her again, but McKayla blocked me.

"Move, McKayla!" I growled.

"Watch yourself when you talk to my wife!" Savio shoved me aside.

I sighed. "I apologize, McKayla."

"Would someone like to explain why Nyla is so distressed?" McKayla's glare dared us to ignore her question.

"It's my fault. I robbed the casino," Nyla whispered.

McKayla turned to face her. "I see."

Nyla looked from McKayla to me, her eyes pleading. "I need to use the bathroom."

"I'll take you," McKayla said.

"No!" we all said in unison.

"Nyla won't harm me. She made a bad choice, but no one in this family is perfect," McKayla stated before sweeping Nyla from the room.

Savio turned to Sante. "Get me Sartori's financial records. And check if he has any offshore accounts."

Sante pulled out his phone. "I get Elio on it, but it'll take time."

"We have twenty-four hours."

A few minutes later, Nyla and McKayla returned to the room.

"Nyla, it was nice meeting you—even though my brother-in-law is not his usual charming self," McKayla teased.

"Let's go, Nyla." I gestured to the door.

Nyla's head stayed down as she walked from the house back to the car. She'd made choices that hurt my business—and my family—because of her connection to Cono Sartori.

. . .

***

"I don't want to get married," Nyla said as we entered the condo.

The tears streaking her cheeks softened my scowl. Seeing a woman cry always sparked my protective instincts, but I clamped down on them. "What you want isn't important. Lives are at stake," I said through gritted teeth.

She leaned wearily against the wall. "My uncle is not a good man. I think he's lying about the money."

"Seems you have a lot in common."

"What if you find out where the trust is held, and I sign a document transferring the funds to you?" Nyla asked, her voice trembling.

"Trust funds don't work like that. They're set up in a specific name."

"I'm too young to get married. We barely know each other."

"Agreed. I have until tomorrow to decide."

"He'll betray you."

"Another thing you have in common," I sneer.

She gasps and raises her hand to strike me, but I block her.

"The men in your life have made you delusional, gullible, and dependent on them. Blame yourself for your situation."

Her eyes narrowed in anger. "Like I care what you think of me! Opinions hold no weight with me. You, Cono, and Mark all have one thing in common—you want control. But you have none, and you're pissed."

I ignore her taunts. "Carter and Romo will watch you until I get back."

"He won't go away easily," Nyla said.

Her words made me suspicious. "Did Cono say something you're not telling me?"

She moved away from me. "No."

"Get some rest."

I left, telling my team to keep an eye on her.

Chapter 9

Nyla

"**Y**ou've always been a fuckup, but maybe Mark put you in a position to help your family for once," Uncle Cono argued.

"What are you saying?"

"Marry Vincenzo and you're free."

"Free?"

"He gets the money you stole, and I leave you alone for good. The second trust fund holds thirty million dollars."

I frowned. "Pay him five, and I keep the rest with no strings?"

"Yes."

"No. I'm not marrying to satisfy your egos," I said stubbornly.

Uncle Cono stalked around his desk, wrapped his hand around my neck, and squeezed, cutting off my air. "Bitch. I never liked you. I never understood what my brother saw in your mother," he snarled before loosening his grip.

Coughing, I rubbed my throat to soothe the ache. "What are you saying?"

"I'm saying you mean nothing to me. I'm glad Mark

took you away. He saved me the trouble of looking out for your spoiled ass."

Tears spilled down my cheeks. "How can you say these things to me?"

He reached behind him to remove a cigar and lit it up. "I paid him to date you."

"You're lying."

"I had no interest in parenting a child my brother was foolish in bringing into the world."

"My father loved me!"

"He's not your father," Uncle Cono sneered.

My chest tightened with shock. "W-What?" I stammered, slowly rising from the chair.

Uncle Cono sighed. "Little girl, your mother should've told you the truth—but everything was left to me. What I've told you stays in this room. If I could've removed you altogether, I would have done it years ago."

I went rigid in my seat. "He's not my father?"

"My brother adopted you." He shook his head in frustration.

The air felt thick around me. "That's a lie."

"Believe me or don't, but it's true."

"You hate me so much that you'd pawn me off?"

"You brought this on yourself with your little robbery attempt. I plan to use it to my advantage."

"I refuse to marry Vincenzo."

Uncle Cono shrugged. "Then he kills you, or I do."

He moved back behind his desk, removing what looked like a recording device from the drawer.

"What's that?"

"Shut up and listen."

He pressed play, and I immediately recognized the man's voice.

"She's not here right now," Mark said.

"What I'm about to say stays between us," Cono insisted.

"I hear you."

"Nyla is not a Sartori. She was adopted by my brother."

"Why are you telling me this?"

"Because I need you to keep her until I figure out how to get her to sign over the money to me. The bitch refused to listen to me, and I'm not raising a child who is not mine." Cono grunted.

"She wants to move in with me. I wasn't expecting to have a full-on relationship," Mark groaned.

"Think of it as a favor, and we both come out clean."

"I want my money upfront."

"You'll get half now and the rest after she gives me her share."

"She's not stupid."

"She's like her stupid mother. My brother was a fool to adopt her and sign over a fortune. The money should have remained in the family."

"All right. I think I hear her coming." The recording ended as Mark hung up.

I stood and backed up to the wall, knocking the picture of my dad when he was younger. I'd skipped the typical teen years, living in fear of the unknown. Discovering that the man I thought was my biological father had adopted me pushed me to want to know the truth—no matter how hard it would be to hear.

"Who's my father?"

"You don't need to know. Yet," Cono stated.

I straightened the picture almost absently before turning my gaze on my uncle. "You're disgusting."

A grim smile spread across Cono's lips. "Now, now, Nyla. It's simply business."

****

Tossing and turning in bed, I pushed the covers off me and sat up, restless from the nightmares replaying in my head. Cono Sartori wasn't my uncle. My entire life was a lie.

"How can this be true?" I mumbled to myself.

I glanced at the bedside clock—2 AM. I rummaged through the closet, grabbed a robe, and left the bedroom in search of a phone. I tiptoed down the hall to the living room to find it empty. "He must have a phone around here."

I remembered the landline phone attached to the kitchen wall. Snatching it up, I dialed the number. "Cassandra, please be home," I whispered, looking over my shoulder to check I was still alone. It rang and rang, but no one picked up. "Shit, she must be out partying."

I redialed the number, and this time, it was finally picked up. "Hello."

"Cassandra?"

"Nyla!" Cassandra gasped.

"Cassandra, I need your help."

"Where are you? I've been calling you for days. I even stopped at your place, and your neighbors said there was some kind of trouble."

"Cassandra, I—" The call ended abruptly.

"Did you think I wouldn't have you monitored?" a familiar voice asked.

Fear gripped me as I turned to look at Vincenzo.

Dropping the phone, I eased back, scanning the counter for something to use as protection.

Vincenzo stepped closer. He looked handsome, dressed casually in a plain T-shirt, jeans, and sneakers. His thick muscles sent a shock wave to my throbbing core. Damn, this wasn't the time to be attracted to the man who held my life in his hands.

"It's not what you think."

"Tell me what I think, Nyla." His smirk indicated he knew a lie was coming.

"I called Cassandra."

"Cassandra?"

"She's my best friend. We talk every day, sometimes talking twice a day."

Vincenzo popped his knuckles as he walked around the island. "The phone is tapped. I have cameras everywhere to keep an eye on my property."

"What are you planning to do?"

He moved closer, trapping me in the back corner near the fridge.

"I checked my cameras and saw you moving around. I had to leave what I was doing to see what escape you were planning."

I caught a waft of perfume from his clothing, and it suddenly dawned on me what—or rather *who*—he was "doing." "Please don't keep your girlfriend waiting on my account."

The tension in his jaw and the hate in his eyes told me I was on borrowed time. "My personal life will remain unaffected by our marriage."

"Is your girlfriend okay with you marrying a stranger?"

"*If* I had a girlfriend, it would be none of her

concern."

I thought of another way to get him to back down. Honesty. "Cono is lying to you."

"Like uncle, like niece." Vincenzo shrugged and reached behind me, opening the fridge and taking out a beer.

"He has a backup plan to take the money if I marry you."

"How?"

"I heard a recording of him with Mark."

Vincenzo placed the beer bottle on the counter. "Say that again."

"He played it in his office. He and Mark were working together."

Vincenzo sighed and rubbed a hand down his face. "Either way, you stole from me, and your uncle has sensitive information on my family."

"He's blackmailing you?" My throat tightened. Did my uncle and Mark have a backup plan in case the robbery failed?

"Details don't matter, but you're the key to finding out where he's keeping the evidence."

"Me? We hate each other," I reminded him.

Vincenzo ignored my statement. "Can you think of anything my brother could use to ascertain a clause in the trust?"

I shook my head as I trailed Vincenzo out of the kitchen. "Uncle Cono is always two steps ahead and will have thought of everything."

"He thinks he's smart, but I'm smarter."

"Can I ask a favor?"

He paused and turned to face me.

I sighed. "I know I have no right asking for a favor, but

please let me visit my friend one last time before..." I bit my lip.

"Before what?"

"Before I die by your hand or my uncle's."

Taking my chin, he stared at me intently. "What are you talking about?"

It was a surprise to be touched so intimately, and I licked my lips nervously. He also sensed it and dropped his hand.

"He threatened to kill me if I didn't marry you," I whispered.

Vincenzo took a step back.

"Loyalty doesn't run in my family like yours."

"We never put money above our family. Our parents taught us to stick together."

"Can I see Cassandra? Please?" Vincenzo hated me, but for a split second, I glimpsed compassion in his eyes at the despair in my voice.

Vincenzo walked away. "Get to bed, Nyla. The car will be waiting for you in the morning."

****

Sitting in the coffee shop, I was excited but nervous to see my best friend. It seemed Vincenzo did have a heart buried somewhere by allowing me to see Cassandra. Although it was probably because he expected me to fall in line by marrying him. The coffee shop was closed to the public, so we could meet while Vincenzo's guards hovered nearby. He'd allowed me this brief meeting to let Cassandra know I was okay but wouldn't be able to contact her in the near future.

The door swung open, and Cassandra entered, her

braids swinging left to right. I stood and lifted my hand in a wave.

Cassandra hurried over to hug me. "Nyla! I missed you so much." After a moment, she pulled back, looked me over, and hugged me tightly again.

Cassandra sat opposite me, and I grabbed the menu to see if she wanted to order.

Removing her jacket, she reached for my hand and gave it a squeeze. "Tell me from the beginning. Where have you been? And why are all of these men gawking at you?"

"Um, Cassandra, I have to tell you something."

"Shoot."

"What I am about to say isn't easy. I need you to let me get it all out first."

Her eyes darkened with concern. "You're scaring me, Nyla."

I blew out a breath. "You and me both."

"Tell me. Whatever you need, I'm here for you."

"Thank you. Mark and I did something stupid."

My hands fell from her grasp. "What did you do?"

"I helped Mark rob the casino where I worked." I spoke low.

"What?" she shouted.

"Keep your voice down," I muttered, aware that the guards were watching our every move.

Cassandra shook her head and whispered, "Did I hear you right? You robbed a casino?"

"Mark needed to pay off a debt, and I foolishly helped him."

"Nyla, of all the things in the world I expected, that wasn't it."

"There's more."

"Oh, God. Please don't tell me he's dead."

"He's dead."

Her eyes widened in shock.

"Vincenzo sent his men to our apartment and kidnapped us."

"How much did you take?"

I lowered my eyes at her look of disappointment. "Five million."

"*Five* million?" she hissed.

"Vincenzo killed Mark right in front of me, Cassandra."

"Nyla, what were you thinking?"

"I wasn't, that's the problem. Helping Mark was all I thought about."

"He always got you involved in his shit," she spat.

"I know that now, and thinking back, I should've seen the signs the first time he cheated."

"Did you give the money back? Can you go home now?"

"No, that's why I asked to meet with you."

I wouldn't blame my best friend if she hated me after confessing my sins. Falling for Mark had only brought me pain and hurt the people I loved. Cassandra was the only true friend I had left in the world.

Her palm tightened around my wrist. "Vincenzo threatened to kill you if you don't give the money back?"

"Yes."

"Then give it to him."

"It's not that simple."

"What do you mean?"

"I never saw any of the money; Mark and his accomplices had it. I know it was stupid, but I just wanted him to pay off his debt so we could move on."

"How much was his debt?"

I sipped my water to ease my dry mouth. "One million as far as I know."

"But he stole *five* million." She pointed out the obvious.

"Please, Cassandra. Judge me later and let me explain the rest."

"There's more? Shit, Nyla."

I nodded, grasping the glass of water. "Uncle Cono is forcing me to marry Vincenzo."

Cassandra exhaled in surprise. "*Why?*"

"To get my trust, which is allegedly thirty million. I'll give Vincenzo his half, and I can leave with the rest."

"So marry him," she said in a hushed but firm tone.

"We can't be in the same room without cursing each other out. Besides, I think my uncle is lying."

"About the money?"

"Yes, and other things. He told me I was adopted. He's not my biological uncle, but he's forcing me to go ahead with the marriage to get the money."

Cassandra fanned herself. "My God, your life is like a scary soap opera."

Now the truth was out, I was even angrier at my parents for not being honest with me. Not knowing my birth father and my real family hurt.

Movement caught my eye as a woman entered the cafe. She made a beeline for one of the guards.

"Carter, what are you doing here?" she asked, hugging him.

Carter was my guard and driver. We'd talked a little during the past few days, and he seemed like a decent guy. Compared to Vincenzo's rough, aggressive attitude, Carter was older and kinder, making me feel safe.

"Hey, Miss Cora. We're here on business," Carter replied, glancing at me. "Are you here alone?"

Cora pointed at the black SUV parked outside. "No. I'm grabbing a coffee before I head into the clinic. I thought this place was closed for a second, and then I saw you inside."

He nodded and headed to the counter.

"Hi, I'm Cora." She waved at me.

I returned her gesture hesitantly. "Hi, I'm Nyla, and this is my best friend, Cassandra."

"Nice to meet you. I think Rena told me about you. Elio is my fiancé."

Hearing Rena's name eased my nervousness. "Elio is the lawyer, right?'

Cora nodded. "That's him. Short dark hair and a mustache."

"It's hard keeping up with who's who. I think the blond brother, Renato, hates me," I declared.

Cora laughed. "Renato hates everybody."

"Are you a doctor?" I inquired, recalling her comment about returning to the clinic.

"Veterinarian," Cora answered.

Carter reappeared with a muffin and coffee for Cora.

"You remembered what I like," she beamed at the guard before returning her attention to us. "It's nice to meet you, Nyla and Cassandra. You should come to family dinner sometime so we can have a proper chat."

I grimaced. "Thanks, but I doubt Vincenzo will keep me around much longer."

Cora frowned. "What do you mean?"

I shrugged. "I'm sure you must know what happened."

Cora scanned my face. "I really don't."

"It's a long story, but I made a bad choice, and Vincenzo hates me."

"The men in my family are no angels," Cora stated. "If I know Vincenzo, he'll forgive you." She patted my shoulder and left the cafe with a cheery "goodbye."

"She seemed cool," Cassandra observed, sipping the iced latte the server placed in front of her.

I nodded. "All the women in the family are cool."

"I can't tell you what to do, Nyla, but you need to make a decision fast."

"You think marriage is the answer? He'll probably kill me as soon as he gets his money."

"Then we go to the police," Cassandra whispered.

I shook my head. Bringing the police into cartel business could be deadly. "I know my fate. I die betraying my uncle, or I die betraying Vincenzo."

"Negotiate," Cassandra urged. "Maybe your uncle will reconsider if you hand over the money."

"No. He hates me. I never asked to be in his life." It would be best for everyone if I took off.

"What other option do you have?"

I bit my lip, looking at Carter, then back at Cassandra. I took her hand and stood. "Carter, I need to use the restroom. It's, uh, that time of the month."

"I'll walk you back there," he said immediately.

I gestured at the other men surrounding us. "I can't escape, Carter. Vincenzo has security everywhere. I promise to come back." I smiled, and Cassandra looked at me like I was nuts, but it did the trick as Carter nodded.

Stepping into the bathroom, I locked the door and checked each stall to ensure we were alone. Moving to the sinks, I turned on the faucets to drown out our voices.

"My other option is to leave," I whispered to Cassandra.

Her eyes widened as if to say, *Bitch are you crazy?*

I smiled. "Before you say it, I'm not crazy."

"How are you planning to leave? You're my best friend, and I love you, Nyla, but you continue to make stupid choices."

"What would you suggest I do?"

"Marry him. Pretend for a few months, then leave. You may even end up happy," Cassandra said, like it was all so simple.

"Happy? With Vincenzo? Never. He keeps me under surveillance in his condo, but I know an opportunity will come at some point."

"And where will you go?"

"I could leave the country."

"Nyla, the Calabresi family has connections everywhere. Why put yourself in a bigger bind?"

Groaning, I buried my head in my hands. "Cassandra, please. I need your help. I won't ask for anything again."

Cassandra stared at me for a long time before finally nodding. "All right. How do you want to do this? And please don't tell me you have no idea."

I smiled, already feeling better. "Well, I think when I get back to the condo, you can follow me."

A knock on the door had us both jumping in panic.

"Nyla, are you all right?" Carter asked.

I stepped up to the door. "Fine, Carter. Give me five minutes."

"That was close," Cassandra muttered.

I needed Cassandra to trust me. If I could get to the safe in my closet, I had a little money stashed there—if Vincenzo and his people hadn't already found it.

Chapter 10

Vincenzo

arter checked in and told me Nyla and Cassandra were leaving the cafe, mentioning that Cora had stopped in and introduced herself. I wanted to get back to the condo to ensure nothing fishy had happened. Cora was sweet and saw the goodness in everyone. It would be best if she kept her distance from Nyla. My desire to kill her had decreased with each passing day.

Running the money through the counter machine, Renato packed it up in the bag, and I marked off everyone we had to collect from for the month.

"Do you plan to attend the car line-up?" Renato asked, pulling me from my thoughts.

Sitting in the basement of Calabresi Holdings, I'd finished a few minutes earlier when he came in and needed to check the drop-offs.

"Yeah, I'm interested in a few."

I bought and sold limited edition classic cars as well as managing the casino. Growing up, I had a passion for working and fixing up cars. While the other kids were hanging out and drinking, I was learning the family business and studying the luxury cars my father brought home.

"How many are you expecting to buy?" Renato asked, lifting the next bag.

"Two classic Lamborghinis."

The door opened, and Elio stepped inside. He slapped my back and shook Renato's hand. "How's it going?" he investigated, placing his things on the table.

"We have four bags; two checked out at two million," I replied, watching our counter lift another stack onto the scale.

Elio nodded and looked at me. "I've been thinking about your situation."

"Talking me out of killing Cono won't help."

"She's not worth marrying. Let me put her out of her misery, along with her uncle," Renato said with a scowl. "We can make back the money she stole in twenty-four hours."

"Sonya must have pissed you off today," I taunted him.

"Why is Nyla still alive? A mistake is putting the wrong gas in a car. Stealing money from my family is a death sentence," Renato stated.

Renato hated that Nyla had gotten close to his wife after stealing from our family. He wanted nothing to do with her. It reminded him of how Sonya had stolen from him before he found out about his son.

Elio shrugged. "Don't use your past with Sonya against Vincenzo."

My phone rang, and I grabbed it from the table. "Carter, tell me she hasn't run off."

He sighed. "Sir, she tried, but I stopped her."

"I'm going to kill her."

I heard yelling in the background.

"Sir, I think you should listen to her before doing anything rash." Carter pleaded.

"Put her on the line."

Elio and Renato listened to the call on the speaker.

"Nyla, it's Mr. Calabresi," Carter said.

"Let me go!" Nyla screamed in the background.

"Nyla," I growled. "Do you want to be buried next to your uncle and parents?"

Her gasp of shock could be heard over the line. "Kill me, and you'll never get your money. Cora was right about you."

"That bitch threatened your fiancé!" Renato fixed his gaze on Elio.

Nyla was making enemies of everyone today.

"What did she say?" Elio snatched my phone from my hand.

"Watch your mouth," I gritted.

My brothers' eyebrows hiked in surprise at my rebuke.

"Cora came into the café and told me Vincenzo was calmer than his brother, but it was a lie," Nyla snapped.

Hearing her compare me to my brothers was like a hit to the gut.

I took the phone from Elio. "I'm heading back to the condo now."

I ended the call and left the basement with Renato and Elio trailing behind me.

Nyla had pushed my buttons from the moment she entered my casino. She had no idea who she was playing with.

"Try to be calm, little brother," Elio suggested.

We jogged to the car and climbed in, pulling up the camera feed on my phone, watching as Nyla jerked from Carter's grasp and paced in frustration. She rubbed her arms as tears flowed down her cheeks. A strange sensation squeezed my chest. Her tears shouldn't bother me.

"Take me to the condo," I directed my driver.

Another call came through on my phone.

"Vincenzo, I heard you left for the day. What happened?" Angelina asked.

"You don't get to question me, Angelina."

"You have meetings lined up, and as your assistant, I should be informed if I need to reschedule."

She had a point.

"Reschedule my meetings for the day after tomorrow. I have a family thing."

"Is something wrong? Maybe I can help," Angelina responded.

I hung up without responding.

Elio shook his head in disappointment. "She should have stayed fired."

I rubbed my forehead as a headache threatened. I still had to get the location of the cars to check them out.

"See what happens when you leave problems unresolved?" Renato demanded. "How about I handle Nyla for you?"

I flipped him off. "Killing her before I get my money back doesn't work for me."

Renato quirked an eyebrow. "You like her."

I rolled my eyes. "Fuck off."

Elio stared at me for a long time. "Either you like her, or you feel sorry for her."

"Neither. I want my money."

The driver dodged traffic and returned us to my

condo in minutes. Renato and Elio got out and talked to the extra detail downstairs.

"Don't go in there ready for war," Elio advised.

I ignored him.

****

Nyla and Cassandra were sitting on the couch, holding hands.

"You. Out," I said, pointing at Nyla's best friend.

"Why does she have to leave?" Nyla demanded, jumping in front of Cassandra.

I ignored her. "Carter, ensure Cassandra gets home safely."

Cassandra's eyes widened as I said her name.

"Nyla, call me if you can," Cassandra said, hugging Nyla.

Nyla whispered something in her ear, and Cassandra nodded.

Carter hovered by the door. "It's fine, Carter."

"Wait! I need him here," Nyla said.

Jealousy hit me. "Why?" Did she think Carter would offer her protection from me? I had no reason to be jealous. *Nyla meant nothing to me. Right?*

"Nyla, you're safe with Mr. Calabresi," Carter reassured her.

She rubbed her arm, and I noticed a dark bruise. "What happened to your arm? How did you get this bruise?"

"Like you care!" Nyla moved away from me.

"Who. Hurt. You?" I enunciated each word.

"Nobody," Nyla mumbled.

"Either you tell me, or Carter will."

"One of your men," Nyla huffed. "Wait! What are you doing?" She rushed to stop me as I moved toward the door.

"Who did it?" I opened the door and motioned between four guards.

Nyla lowered her eyes and crossed her arms to hide the bruise. "Why does it matter? You plan to kill me anyway."

"Carter, do you know who did this?" I demanded.

He nodded. "One of the new guys downstairs. I didn't see it happen."

"Take him to the cabin." I turned back to Nyla. "As for you, get inside."

I held the door open, and Nyla walked inside with me. I took out the first aid kit and sat her down. She also had a bruise on her shoulder and a small cut on her forehead.

"Why are you doing this, Vincenzo?" Nyla whispered.

The defeat in her voice sent a chill down my spine. My throat tightened, and I avoided her question. "The twenty-four hours are up. I can't think of another plan unless we can get our hands on the trust fund documents. Do you know where he keeps his important papers?"

"Sometimes, he stored papers in a safe," Nyla answered.

My fingers trailed down her cheek. "Can you access the safe?"

She shrugged. "Not sure."

I tipped her head back to get a good look at the bruise. "You're so young."

Nyla frowned. "What does that mean? You're only three years older than me."

"And you haven't matured, Nyla."

"Oh, please. Don't patronize me. You're no better than me." She snatched the bandage from my hands.

I looked up as Renato and Elio entered, wearing grim expressions.

I left Nyla to it and went to the kitchen, grabbed a glass of water, and gulped it down.

"We have dinner plans tonight, and you're required to bring your guests," Elio informed me as he entered the kitchen.

"Huh?"

"Madre wants to meet Nyla."

"No."

"It's not up to you. She found out from the girls."

"What?" I was furious.

Angelina had never met my folks, and she worked for me. Now they wanted to meet the woman I was being forced to marry? The same woman who'd stolen from me?

"Cora and Rena were talking," Elio confessed.

I concluded that Rena was interfering again. "Keep your fiancé out of my business."

"Too late, little brother," Elio chuckled, leaving the kitchen.

I returned to the lounge, where Nyla sat on the end of the couch with the remote. Renato glared at her coldly.

"Keep glaring. It won't change anything," Nyla snapped.

Renato reached into his holster, removed his gun, and pointed it at her from across the room. "I should have killed you that night."

"Yes, you should have."

We were all shocked by Nyla's response.

"Go shower and get dressed," I told her. "We're going

to dinner." Dinner with my parents would be better than remaining here.

"Where?" Nyla asked.

"With my family."

Her eyes widened. "Seriously?"

"Time is running out, Nyla. My patience with you is wearing thin. Now, go shower and get dressed," I repeated.

"Is Cassandra okay? You won't hurt her, will you?" Nyla challenged.

"*Should* I hurt her? I mean, you lied to me and tried to escape." I took a bold step closer, trying to get in her face.

Nyla backed up. "Cassandra only did what I asked," she pleaded.

"Then I suggest you behave, or Cassandra will end up like Mark," I said softly before stalking to my room to shower and change.

****

Renato and Elio left before us to handle the guard who'd disrespected my home by putting their hands on Nyla. I'd threatened Nyla plenty of times, but I was the only one who enforced my threats and no one else.

My thoughts ran rampant as I sat in the back of the town car. Nyla and I hadn't spoken since getting in the car. As usual, roadworks set our travel time back by ten minutes, and Madre blew up my phone twice for being late. Nyla sat as far away from me as possible, biting her nails.

"Nervousness is not a good look on you," I taunted, laughing when she rolled her eyes. I knew being a jerk would bring out the fighter in her.

"If I help you get the papers from my uncle, will you let me go?"

"It's not that easy."

"I don't see why. I sign off, and you take the money and leave me alone."

"What if the clause says I have to wait thirty days before I get my money? Then what?"

Nyla opened her mouth to reply but was distracted as we passed through the gates to my parents' place. "You live here?" Her astonishment was palpable.

I nodded to let Carter know I would help Nyla out of the car. "It's the family home."

"Why am I here?"

"Seems your little game worked. My mother wants to meet you."

"What game?"

"Nyla, stop acting innocent. Rena and Cora are your biggest supporters."

She smirked as I guided her up the steps to the front door. "Cora and Rena are nice. Their husbands, not so much."

Laughing at her, I removed her jacket as Sante and Rena came into view.

"About time. Nyla, I heard about today," Rena said, glaring at me.

"Hi, Rena," Nyla greeted.

"Glad you came to dinner." Rena grabbed Nyla by the hand.

I jumped in front of them. "She's not here on a friendly visit."

"Vinny, move," Rena sassed.

"Bro, let her go. We need to talk." Sante grabbed and shoved me toward the dining room.

"Rena's overstepping."

Sante bumped my shoulder. "Relax. I need to tell you something."

"What?"

Sante handed me his phone.

I took it from him and watched a video of Cono and another man talking outside my brother's club. "Who is he talking with?"

"We're still trying to identify him through a database at the police station." Sante took the phone back.

"Cono is fucking with my money," I muttered.

"I agree. Savio is on his way. We think marrying her and keeping Cono close would be wise."

Angry and frustrated, I threw my hands up in the air. "Come on, Sante."

"Cono has too many secrets, and his niece is the key to discovering what he's up to."

"They don't even get along."

"Make her."

"And my money?"

"Still a priority. Nyla can help us get the evidence he's holding, plus the money."

"Nobody will believe I'm getting married."

"Make it believable. You wanted to get into the cartel business, so here's your chance to prove you can manage it," Sante said, leaving me alone.

Marrying Nyla was the only option to get what we needed at the cost of my personal life crashing down around my ears. I shouldn't have to take on the responsibility of a wife.

"Fuck!" I shouted, kicking the back of the chair.

I passed the kitchen as I went to use the bathroom

and heard Nyla and my mother talking. I paused outside the door.

Madre handed Nyla a glass of juice. "You're very beautiful, Nyla."

"Thank you, Mrs. Calabresi."

"My sons have kept you a secret from me. My daughter-in-law said you deserved a second chance."

"Honestly, I'm shocked to still be here," Nyla responded.

"So, you robbed my son's casino?" Madre challenged.

"Yes," Nyla whispered.

"For your boyfriend, I understand," Madre continued.

Nyla nodded. "Stupid, I know."

"Men make you feel like the only way to be special in their lives is to go off a cliff for them to prove your loyalty. But you know something, Nyla?" Madre paused at Nyla's questioning look. "Loyalty should be to yourself before anyone else. Your boyfriend didn't love or respect you because a real man would never put you in that situation." Madre echoed the same thoughts I had about Nyla's situation.

After finishing in the bathroom, I returned to the dining room to find everybody seated at the table.

"You were late, Vincenzo. Where were you?" Madre asked.

Her question annoyed me. She still couldn't understand that I was an adult and no longer the family's baby. "Work." I pulled my chair out to sit and high-fived RJ.

"How are your brothers here on time, yet they work at the same office?" Madre rambled on.

"Probably because they left the mess for me to clean up," I murmured, taking the wine bottle from Cora.

"Watch yourself." Savio smacked me on the back of the head.

I flipped him off.

"Savio, stop hitting your brother," Madre snapped, spooning peas onto SJ's plate.

I chuckled at him getting into trouble. Savio had kids and was still intimidated when our mom yelled at him.

"Vincenzo, did you sign off on the building inspection?" Pop asked, and I nodded.

"When are you boys going to give me more grandkids?" Madre pointed at Elio and me.

"Never," I replied, catching Nyla's eye.

Elio rubbed the back of his neck. It was a nervous habit that meant he was keeping secrets.

"What's for dinner?" I changed the subject.

"You're trying to avoid my questions." Madre frowned.

"Pop, please deal with your wife."

Pop chuckled, and everybody burst into laughter. It was rare that we were all together for a family dinner. Now that Savio, Sante, and Renato had families, it was hard to get them here at the family home all at once.

"She grilled us the same way." Sante grinned.

"Anyway, Vincenzo, we wanted to know if you've thought about bringing on a second assistant," Rena prodded.

"No, the assistant I have now is fine."

"Your current one got fired," Pop said.

"Angelina's good at her job."

Madre pointed her fork at me. "Is she not in love with you because you can't keep it in your pants?"

I felt cheeks turning red at them knowing about

Angelina and me. I'd had a few one-night stands with previous assistants, but I had them all sign NDAs.

"Either you find love and marry, or I'll do it for you," Madre stated.

"Welcome to the club, brother." Renato held a fist out for me to bump, and I ignored Madre's glare.

Madre turned to Nyla. "Nyla, are you not hungry?"

"I already ate," she answered.

"Even though my son has kept you locked up in his condo, has he treated you respectfully?"

"Yes, Mrs. Calabresi," Nyla replied.

"Good."

"We're getting married," I blurted.

My father paused with his fork halfway to his mouth, Rena choked on her food, and Renato glared at me.

Chapter 11

Nyla

The entire room fell silent after Vincenzo declared that we were getting married.

My mind went into overdrive, thinking about how I could be *anyone's* wife, let alone a mobster's. What did he expect of me? Would I have to live with him for longer than he needed? Where would I fit into his world? And sex had its own issues that I hadn't even brought up.

A week later, I was still blind to the answers. Vincenzo went to work, and when he came home, he checked in with Carter on what I was doing. The plan was to get me back into Uncle Cono's house to find the safe and grab the trust fund papers. I tried calling Cono to meet, and he blew me off every time, making me worry that it was all a game to him.

Sighing, I slipped my feet into my slippers and strolled to the kitchen, putting a plate on the counter to cut into the pot roast that his mother made last night and sent home with Vincenzo.

After hearing the locks on the door open, I hurried

from the kitchen, but my excitement died when I saw Angelina with a nasty snarl.

"He's not here." I turned to walk back to the kitchen.

"This was our place," Angelina enlightened me.

I was pissed for a split second before regaining control of my emotions. "Why are you telling me?"

"Vincenzo told me you were staying here."

Her confession made me angry. Having her in my business was the last thing I needed. Bitches like her thrived off attention. *Do I really care?*

"That happens when you get married." I raised my hand, wiggling my fingers and showing her the five-carat diamond ring.

After the announcement at his parents' house, Vincenzo and I returned to his condo and talked. We agreed that neither of us expected it to last more than a month, that we both needed to play our parts, and he would let me walk away once I got my hands on the trust fund.

"You're lying!" Angelina rushed at me, grasping my hand and checking out the ring.

I yanked away, and she pushed my shoulder. "Push me again and find out what I'm capable of, bitch!" I snarled, pointing my finger in her face.

"You tricked him. Vincenzo is mine," Angelina spat.

"Not anymore. Maybe if you talk to me nicely, I'll hook you up with one of his cousins," I sassed, remembering him talking about his extended family in New York. Surprisingly, our conversations had been cordial for the last two days.

"Whatever you did to him, I'll find out. I'm warning you now: getting comfortable will be your downfall." She flipped her hair in my face as she whirled around.

She gasped as she saw Vincenzo scowling at the front door.

Vincenzo stalked forward, slamming the door behind him. "What are you doing here, Angelina?" he growled.

Angelina backed up. "I-I was dropping off some paperwork."

"You've never been to my condo before. How did you know where to come?" Vincenzo asked.

"I followed you," Angelina murmured the admission.

"You're fired," Vincenzo stated.

Her mouth dropped open. "What?"

Firing her seemed a bit drastic. "Vincenzo—"

He held up his hand for me to pause. "Get out," he told Angelina.

"Vincenzo, you can't fire me." Angelina tried to grab his shirt.

Vincenzo stepped out of her hold. "You've shown me time after time that you can't be trusted."

"But she's lying to you! Why would you marry her? I love you," Angelina wailed, falling to the floor in tears.

"Have some dignity," Carter said, entering the room and seeing her on the floor.

Vincenzo held out a hand to help her to stand, but Angelina shoved it away.

"Fuck you, Vinny. She's using you. You'll come crawling back to me," she hissed before flouncing from the condo.

Vincenzo closed the door behind her and turned to me. "Are you hungry?" he asked as if nothing had happened.

I gaped at him. He hadn't once asked me about food or any other comforts. "I was going to have the leftover food your mom cooked."

"We need to talk and I'm starving. Get dressed, and we'll go out to eat."

"You mean a date?"

"Think of it as a business meeting."

"Business. Right." I ignored the pang of disappointment.

I went to my room to freshen up, putting my hair into a high bun and applying lip gloss. Slipping my feet in the sandals, I looked at myself in the mirror, reminding myself that this wasn't a date.

"Ready." I swished out of the guest bedroom.

Vincenzo froze, dragging his eyes from my feet to my face.

I frowned. "What?"

"Nothing." Vincenzo opened the door and placed his hand on my lower back to lead me out.

****

I couldn't remember the last time I'd dined out with a man. Mark and I had been together for so long that I was used to hanging out at home or with his friends. Vincenzo took us to a nice restaurant near downtown.

"Do you come here often?"

Vincenzo sat back, staring at me. "For business, mostly."

"Oh."

"Have you made contact with your uncle?"

I placed my drink on the table. "Not yet."

"Why not?"

"Thinking to wait until the ink dries on the paperwork before hounding him."

His brow creased. "You think getting my money is hounding him."

"No. But Cono is conniving. He won't even tell me who my parents banked with, so I wanted to wait for you."

"We'll go tomorrow after my party."

"Party?"

"I have a business event to attend and need you on my arm."

I raised an eyebrow. "Another date?"

"Call it what you want." He shrugged.

"Vincenzo, how long do you plan on hating me?"

"Playing the victim again?" he taunted.

"Better than playing the asshole," I spat. I grabbed my purse and stood.

Vincenzo grabbed my arm. "Sit down."

"I need to use the restroom."

"I'm not falling for another of your escape plans."

I parked a hand on my hip. "You don't believe me."

"The past few months have proved you a liar."

"Come with me."

Surprised swept across his face. "What?"

"Come to the restroom and stand outside."

He sighed. "Go ahead."

I didn't miss the flash of lust in his eyes as he checked me out in my little black backless dress. I hadn't had sex in months, and that look was causing a throbbing between my legs.

The server appeared and placed our food on the table. I smiled, thanked her, and headed to the back to refresh my makeup.

Exiting the bathroom a few minutes later, I paused in the hallway when I saw a familiar face. Gianney, a friend of Mark's. My eyes darted to our table in the corner. Vincenzo's back was to the door. The guards stood a short distance away outside. I needed to move quickly.

Another waitress came from the kitchen, holding a tray.

I slowly stopped and blocked her from moving. "Excuse me, do you know how to get in touch with the owner of the restaurant?"

"Is something wrong with your meal?" she asked as I'd hoped she might.

"No, I wanted to ask if you all catered. The food is delicious."

"Yes, we cater. I can get your information after I drop these plates off."

"You know, that would be wonderful. Let me walk with you." I snapped my fingers as suddenly remembering something. "I just remembered you have business cards up front. I'll grab one from there."

She walked up to the front with me, and I slipped to the right toward the table where I'd seen Mark's friend being escorted.

He raised his eyes as I stopped at his table. "Nyla?"

"Yeah. Can we talk?" I glanced at his girlfriend, knowing I only had a few minutes before Vincenzo noticed I was missing.

"About what?"

"Mark."

"Nyla."

I jumped at Vincenzo's voice.

Gianney's face fell.

"How do you know him?" Vincenzo asked me.

"Gianney is a friend of Mark's."

Vincenzo held out his hand toward me. "Let's go."

"Wait. He can help me with my uncle."

Vincenzo tugged my hand, pulling me away from Gianney's table. Carter and the rest of the guards stood near the front door as he led me from the restaurant. Embarrassed, I tried to jerk from his grip.

Vincenzo pushed me against the car, pressing his body to mine and blocking my line of sight. "Gianney Greco is a friend of Mark's, and you never told me you knew him?" he seethed.

"Gianney might be able to help. Can you move?" I pushed against his chest.

He grabbed my hands and nudged my legs apart. My throat tightened and my chest heaved. My arousal was heightened by our intimacy. I didn't want to be attracted to the man who'd killed my boyfriend, but here I was, marrying him out of necessity.

"You want me to move?"

Averted his deep gaze.

Pinching my eyes closed, I counted to five to calm my best friend down. She hadn't been awake in a while.

"Nyla." My eyes popped open at my name being called.

"Please, let me handle him," I begged.

Vincenzo released his hold. I started to walk toward Gianney, but Vincenzo wrapped a hand around my waist, pulling me to his side.

"Are you with him now?" Gianney investigated.

"Gianney, we have to talk about Mark."

"He killed Mark and you're running around town dating the man that pulled the trigger," Gianney argued.

"She's married." Vincenzo raised my hand up like I was a puppet, and I jerked away.

"Stop it!" I hissed.

"Nyla can't save you; I know you were in on the robbery," Vincenzo claimed.

That surprised me, because Gianney and I hadn't talked in a few months.

"He wasn't there," I blurted out.

"He's collaborating with your uncle," Vincenzo informed me.

I knew Cono and Mark set me up, but I hadn't discovered that more people were involved. I was still lying to Vincenzo about the board, and Cono wanting stock options.

"I heard he had inside help for the casino robbery; Nyla would know about that, right?" Gianney egged him on.

"All right, you two. Gianney, tell me what you know."

Gianney walked backwards to his car. "Mark left the details out. He owed a lot of people money."

"Gianney, wait!" I called out.

Vincenzo held me back from running after him. I shoved his hand away, yanking the door open. Vincenzo hovered over me, leaning against my ear. "Our marriage isn't for love, but you won't disrespect me in public."

A few seconds later, he glanced into my eyes, his lips just a few feet away. I wanted to kiss him or push him away, but my mind and heart couldn't decide.

After pulling back without a kiss, I regarded him in a daze, as he stalked to the other side of the car, daring me not to get in with him. One part of me wanted to continue fighting, and another felt aroused by how he handled me.

In a way, Mark had been controlling and possessive, making me feel afraid because of his need for money, and he always said that if I cared about him, then I would give him anything to help him. Vincenzo felt different. It was a strange connection I couldn't explain. Despite our hatred for each other in the beginning, I felt like he wanted to protect me on some level.

Slamming the door behind me, my reaction to pout and throw a tantrum came naturally. Exhaling a long breath, he ignored me and continued texting on his phone.

"Stay away from Gianney Greco."

"You don't get to tell me who my friends are."

"I just did."

I swiftly turned, leaned over the seat, and got in his face. "And I said no." I watched his eyes bounce up from my lips again. Tension in the car, my stubbornness, his possessiveness, and not having him around the condo pissed me off.

He turned his head and checked back down at his phone. "Sit back and put on your seatbelt."

Something came over me, and I snatched his phone from his hand and tossed it in between my breasts, then sat back in my seat, ignoring him.

He growled. "Give me my phone Nyla and stop acting childish."

"Gianney Greco is my friend. What are you keeping from me?"

"All you need to worry about is getting along with your uncle." Vincenzo held out his hand for the phone.

I taunted him. "What do you want?"

"My phone."

I slapped his hand high-five. "Tonight, you promised me a date. No phones."

"You realize we are not a real couple." A smirk formed.

"You realize I never asked to marry you," I countered.

He chuckled at my response and for the first time I could see the boyish look in his demeanor. "Dinner only."

"Same thing."

"Woman, you are batshit crazy," Vincenzo grumbled, and I cackled at his pout.

Removing the phone from my blouse, I said, "Here, you crybaby."

"Serious about Greco."

"Be real with me, Vinny."

His brows creased together in a frown. "Don't call me that."

"Angelina calls you Vinny."

"She doesn't mean anything to me."

"Oh."

"My brother found out that Greco and your uncle met up once."

"So."

"Think he's in on the robbery."

"Gianney's always been kind to me."

"Probably the same way you said Mark got into your head, Cono has played you since you moved in with him."

Taking in his words, I tried to think back on our conversations and Gianney felt like a big brother, especially when Mark cheated on me a few times and I kicked him out.

"Shit."

"What?"

"Rena talked my mom into throwing a party for us."

"Party."

"Since we got married at the courthouse, she wanted a reception at the house."

"Wow, your mom is really taking the marriage seriously."

"I told her it's not real and will be divorced soon, it goes in one ear and out the other."

"What's the harm in a small gathering?"

"She's inviting 200 guests." Vincenzo grimaced, texting away on his phone. I reached out to stop him, taking the phone from his hand and seeing what the thread message said.

Madre: Vincenzo, this might be the only time you get married.

Vincenzo: Leave it alone.

Rena: Why? A party would be fun.

Vincenzo: Stay out of my business, Rena.

Sante: Rena he's right.

Rena: Shut up Sante or else.

I giggled at Rena's response. She and Sante made me giggle all the time.

Vincenzo: This is Nyla. I would love to have a party, Mrs. Calabresi. We'll be there.

"What are you doing?" Vincenzo tried to grab the phone from my hand.

I whipped around with my back to him. "One second."

I felt his arm drape around my waist. He pulled me against his chest. "Nyla, I swear to God if you—"

Rena: Yes! I knew you would agree.

Madre: Glad you came around to the idea, see you soon.
Vincenzo: Still pretty new at the marriage thing, you've
          been kind and remind me of my mother

.I handed his phone back to him, letting him read my response.

"Having a party means spending money to fake it to our friends."

"I'm good at faking things." I winked at him, on the sly remark.

"Meaning."

"You know."

"No, I don't."

"A woman faking it with you."

"Never happened."

Smacked my lips. "Vincenzo let the ego relax for a second, you've never had a woman fake it with you during sex?"

"Hell, no!"

"Hard to believe." I pursed my lips together.

"I can more than satisfy a woman, see Angelina is still calling."

"She's a stalker, so it doesn't count." I chuckled at my joke, and he laughed for the first time seeing his smile felt warm.

He wiped his hand down his face.

The car arrived at a different location, which caused me to perk up. The guard at the gate nodded at Carter, then opened the gate for the limo to pull inside. My breath halted for a split-second. A huge mansion sat on large acres of land. Cars sat out front.

"Where are we?"

"My house."

"Why?"

"I need to change and go to a party."

"What about me?"

"You're staying here."

"No, I'm not."

"Yes, you are." Vincenzo hopped out of the car.

I chased him.

"You are locking me up again." I accused him of continuing to punish me for my mistakes.

"For your safety."

I pouted, stomped my foot. "Not fair, Vinny."

He abruptly halted his steps, turning and causing me to bump into chest. "How many times do I need to say not to call me Vinny?" Stretching his arms around my waist.

"Once you give me the real reason."

"Vincenzo is my name."

"I like calling you Vinny," I teased, trying to get under his skin. He sensed I pissed him off on purpose, but he made it easy.

"Vinny is a nickname that Angelina thinks I like. She's one of many women who I let suck my dick. Now, unless you want to be one of those women..." He cocked a brow up, taunting me.

I squeezed my thighs tight. I could keep the games up, but him leaving me alone while he went out to have fun was out of line.

"Seriously, Vincenzo, I want to come with you—or you can drop me off at Cassandra's place."

He sighed. "If I take you with me, then you have to keep your mouth shut. Understand?"

"Great, where are we going?"

He turned to head into the house, and I jogged up the

steps to keep up. I could tell that the walls he had put up were slowly coming down.

He turned off the alarm. I stopped and scanned the foyer, I was amazed at the warmth and feeling of the home. It was completely different from his condo. I looked at the cream-colored foyer, oval-shaped bay windows, family pictures, and antiques hanging on the walls.

"Your home is beautiful," I said, staring at the painting of him as a young boy with his siblings.

"Don't touch anything."

"Promise not to rob you," I joked.

"You can change in the guest bedroom upstairs on the right."

His home had to be sitting on a few acres, so I peeked at another house in the back. "Shocked you let me see your place."

"We have fifteen minutes before I leave you." He ignored my statement.

Chapter 12

Vincenzo

Tonight, I was already going to be 10 minutes late. A few cars were coming in, and I'd set aside the time to have dinner and try to get Nyla and I on the same page. A private eye whom my brother hired hadn't found anything since the video of him with Gianney, so when I took Nyla out, and we bumped into him, it made me suspicious that she knew. Based on the look in her eyes, I could tell she had no clue about our relationship with Cono and Mark. Having her schedule a meeting with a lawyer and finding the paperwork were on my agenda for this week. Soon after, we'd end the marriage, and I could go back to my normal life.

While coming from the bedroom, I heard singing to my left. I pushed the door slightly open to see Nyla, letting her hair fall from her ponytail and flow down her back. She had changed into a black leather dress, with thin, strappy red heels, and I told her it was a business event. The way she was dressing and displaying her plump breasts and round ass ignited something in me. I hated her for causing me so many problems. I was jealous of the men who would flirt with her, and it baffled me. I never noticed how women I slept with dressed before. Meeting my eyes, she whirled around, waiting for me to say something.

Clearing my throat. "Car is waiting."

"Where are we going again?" She picked up her coat and clutch.

I'd had clothes purchased for her and left here in case I had a business function. Our wedding day at the courthouse was basic, simple, and fast. She'd asked me if Cassandra could be her witness, and at first, I started to protest, but after thinking it over, having her best friend there made sense in case we needed to confirm anything with the lawyer. Carter drove us all downtown, and I had arrangements made for us to have dinner afterwards alone with a chef at the condo. Nyla and I sat and talked most of the night about her parents, and how she wanted to have a better life.

****

"I know I have said it a hundred times, but I am sorry for what I did," Nyla said, *sitting across the dinner table.*

Guzzling my wine, I said, "Taking the steps to fix it means a lot to me and my family."

Smiling, she cut into her lamb, moaning from the flavors. "Your chef is amazing." Nyla took another bite.

"Pay him enough, thanks."

"If we get the money, are you going to let me go?" she wondered.

****

That was a problem I had debated for a while, and at first, my family's code was to get rid of all our enemies, but my brothers forgave their spouses and saw a change. I always thought that anyone who stole from needed to die, but Nyla made me see a different side of things.

"Hey, you're making me feel like I'm a bad date." Nyla tittered, bringing me from my daze.

"Thinking."

I helped her to slide her coat on, walking out of the house, held her hand taking the stairs, and Romo unlocked the front passenger seat.

"Driving in your Bentley?" Nyla looked at me.

Security would trail me and give me a heads-up as to how tonight would go. We didn't need too much protection.

"I can drive."

"Shocking."

"How so?" I shut the door, came around to the other side, then slid in and closed the door.

"You come across uptight, figure you never lifted a hand for anything."

Staring at her with my back to the door. "I give off that impression?"

"No offense."

"None taken. My parents never handed us anything. Yeah we lived a privileged life, private school, nice clothes, but we had to work and learn the family business. My brother Savio had it worst, trying to live in my father's shadow."

"He's the one married to McKayla. At the house we stopped at that day."

"Yeah."

"Renato is married to Sonya, right?"

"Yeah. Renato and I are the closest."

"I can tell."

I shifted the car forward, then stopped at a red light. I lived a few miles from my parents, in an exclusive area. Privacy was extremely important to me, which was the reason I never brought a woman home or to meet my parents—unless I felt she was the one. Nyla being this close to me made the hair on my neck stand up. My dick jumped, and we hadn't even kissed. It confused me.

"Everyone you've dated ... are they like Angelina?" Nyla interrogated me unexpectedly.

"Like Angelina how?" My gaze aimed at her, driving off to the destination in Edison Park at Calabresi Cars. Parking around back, turning off the ignition, and slipping the seatbelt off, waited for her answer.

"Blond, self-entitled, can't-take-no-for-an-answer."

"Angelina's smart in business, anything outside of that has caused problems. Come on, I have something to check out." Seeing the team unloading the cars, Nyla started to open the door, and I frowned.

"Sorry, forgot you have a thing about doors."

"Women shouldn't open doors if a man is around."

She held her hand up to salute, then giggled at my frown. "You do have manners."

"Let's go." I took her hand out of habit, and we both peered down at our interlocked palms. She smiled. "Have to make it look good," I explained.

The smile fell from her face, and I wondered what if it had something to do with my words.

Shaking hands with my delivery driver, he explained the papers were in the office, and I could take the keys and car for a ride now.

"How much are you planning on selling it for?" Nyla

released my hand, running her palm over the hood of the car.

"Between eight-hundred and a million."

The Reventón was a rare and exclusive car; only a select few in the world had one. The vintage '66 red Ford Mustang sitting next to it brought a smile to my face.

Nyla whistled, catching sight of the vehicle. "Has to be worth a good $100,000—especially if the engine is good. Not too many miles," Nyla commented.

I settled my stare on her. "You know about cars?"

"My Dad and I used to work on his cars. I'm not just a pretty face," Nyla said, waving her hand at the car.

Feeling my phone vibrate in my pocket, seeing my friends asking if I was coming to the race.

"Time to go."

"I thought you had business to do."

"This is part of the business."

After approaching Grant Park minutes later, the race had already started, and few of the people whose drivers I sponsored were gearing up to go. I shook hands with two of my friends from the cartel family, Custant and Pirtinaci. All of us grew up in strict households with a family-first mentality. The cartel was in our blood.

"Are you racing today?" I interrogated, Custant the hot head out of the three of us. Reminded me of my brother Renato, he works under him as an enforcer.

"Not tonight, who's the girl?" Custant quipped.

"Nyla, my wife." All eyes were aimed at us, and I knew she felt out of place. To reassure her, I wrapped my hand around her waist, hugging her close.

"Vincenzo must really like you," Pirtinaci taunted, eyeing her seductively.

"Watch your eyes." I pointed at him, making him back up and hold his hand to his chest, like he was hurt.

Nyla laughed at our play fighting.

"Why do you say that?"

"He never brings a girl around," Custant assured.

"I keep hearing that from his family. What about Angelina?"

Shaking my head, she had no idea. "Angelina was business only, and now that I hired someone new to run my schedule, I was happy to let her go."

The race began, and I held Nyla close. I stared behind me. Carter and Romo stood back, giving us space. After taking in the large crowd, my jaw clenched upon seeing Gianney Greco across from us, staring right at me.

"Calabresi Motors," Nyla whispered.

"I sponsor them."

Then she lifted her head in awe and stared at me. "You're a jack of all trades."

"I try to be."

Announcers blew through the horn, engines revved up as the flag came down, and everybody cheered, clapping their hands watching to see who'd come out on top. The more I got involved, the more it could come to fruition to invest in a major team in NASCAR as a silent partner in a big money business. Having the Calabresi name on the national level in legal business was my goal.

"Wait, is that Gianney?" Nyla stated, trying to walk over until I pulled her back.

"What are you doing?"

"Gianney, I need to see him."

"He's going to be dealt with, Nyla. You can't go warning him."

I couldn't hold onto her, as she jerked away. "He's my friend."

Finally pulling back up, my guy won, and most of the crowd huddled together. I pulled Nyla to the side, gently pushing her up against the wall.

"Let me make myself clear. You are my wife, and Gianney is my enemy."

Her eyes darkened in my direction. "So, an enemy of yours is an enemy of mine. No conversation."

"Yes, that's how the cartel works. Being a Sartori, you should know the rules."

"I don't follow rules."

"As my wife you will."

"If I don't?" she challenged me.

Gunfire struck out, and the crowds disbursed, running in all directions. I grabbed Nyla and ran through the crowd, searching for shelter. My men boxed us in from the front and back.

"Keep her safe!" I removed my gun, directing Carter and Romo to get her back to the car, I went looking for my friends. Shoving through, I saw Gianney tapping his men on the arm to cover him.

"Vin!" Custant called my name, I rushed toward him, covering him as he reloaded.

"Who the fuck is shooting?" I hissed.

"Has to be a rival cartel out here, they know we have the block covered."

"Cartel or someone." I eyed the smirk on Gianney's face.

"Fuck! Too many innocent bodies out here."

"I need to call my brothers."

"Renato's going to be pissed."

"He's not the only one," I shot back, hitting someone on the shoulder.

Sirens blared in the distance. I tapped him on the back, motioning that we needed to get out of there. While jogging back to our cars, people were crying and consoling each other. After tucking my gun away, I ambled back to my Bentley. I saw Nyla standing outside, pacing back and forth.

"Vincenzo!" Nyla rushed me, wrapping her arms around my neck, sobbing in tears.

Rubbing her back gently, I shot daggers at Carter and Romo. They shrugged, not having a clue. The tears flowed down her cheeks as I lifted her arms away from me, gently wiping them away. Unthinkingly, I placed my lips on top of hers, wanting to reassure her that I was fine and to calm her down.

"I'm fine."

Her tongue slipped over my lips. She tightened her grip on my neck and moaned, closing the gap between us.

Hearing a throat clear, I took a step back, remembering we weren't alone.

"Sorry," I said.

"Are you hurt?"

"No, we need to get out of here." I opened the door, motioning for Custant and Pirtinaci to call me.

"What happened back there?" Nyla hopped in, unlocking my side of the car. Carter and Romo waited for me to take off before moving.

"Your friend thought it would be a good idea to shoot at me."

"Gianney?"

"Yeah, do you have any other friends I should worry about?" I didn't mean to bark at her, but it was time for her to realize people she knew had no interest in her safety.

"I can't believe it."

A few blocks away, we turned off the road. As I shifted into park, I turned my attention to her. She stared at me with her chin raised.

"Nyla, you're not as innocent as you like to think you are, but the people you're surrounded with would leave you to the worst enemies of the world."

"I got it, Vincenzo," she growled, hating to be chastised.

"Stop acting like a little girl and realize Gianney, Mark, and Cono will do anything to use you for power and money."

"I know," she mumbled, putting her head down.

"Look at me."

"I said you're right."

"Is there anything I need to know about before we get home?"

"Home?"

"Huh?"

"You said once we get home. Are you taking me to your house or the condo?" she pressed, raking her eyes over me.

"Answer my question first."

"What question?"

"Anything else I need to know you're keeping from me?"

"Are we both being honest?"

"Nyla." I glowered, removing my jacket and unbuckling my seatbelt.

She squinted at me confused when I undid her seatbelt, but then I pulled her into my lap.

"Vincenzo!" she shrieked.

Smacking her on the butt gently, she cried out, and I rubbed the sting away. Thanks to the tinted windows in my car, nobody could see her or hear her. Nyla licked her lips as she rubbed my shaft, forcing me to close my eyes and count to five before we fucked in the car. We didn't consummate the night of the wedding because I wasn't sure if I wanted to proceed with faking a marriage. Slowly, Nyla leaned forward staring at my lips.

I firmly held both sides of her face, stopping her movement. "Are you sure?"

Nodding her head.

"No, I need to hear the words, baby."

The moment I called her *baby*, she stiffened. As she raked her fingernails along my thigh, her tongue brushed across my bottom lip.

Do I want to fall victim to her trap? Here I am, with the woman that stole money from me, on my lap, with a ring on her finger that I bought.

Then again, all of my brothers fell in love unconventionally.

Nyla cooed, "Yes, I'm sure."

I had to admit that our kissing was no longer just comfort; it became passionate and intense. There was a need to explore her and make her mine.

"Shit!"

After jumping apart at the knock on the driver's side window, I helped her scramble back into her seat. She pulled her dress down. I put the gun away after rolling the window down and seeing it was Carter.

"Sir, I want to make sure everything is fine," Carter wondered, looking from Nyla to me.

"We are headed to my house. Have the cars delivered to me. I'm staying in for the rest of the night."

I checked the time on the radio. It was going on 2 AM. I knew she was pretty tired, and we wanted her to come with us to meet with her uncle and the lawyers in the morning.

"Yes, Sir."

I slipped the keys from my pants pocket and passed them to Carter. Besides my brothers and my friends, he was the only person whom I trusted to drive my personal vehicles.

I locked the front door, shut it behind us, and set the alarm. Nyla stood off to the side, watching my next movements. The last thing I wanted was for her to feel like she was being treated like Angelina, or like a one-night stand.

"Same as the condo, you can have the guest room upstairs where you got dressed."

"We're sleeping in separate beds?"

"Did you want to sleep in the same bed?"

Her attention was focused on her purse instead of looking up. My hand sank into my pocket as I groaned, exhausted from the day and unprepared to hear my brother's words. The only thing I could do to clear my head of confusion was sleep.

Nyla muttered. "Is that what you want?"

"Nyla."

"Forget it, Vincenzo."

The moment Nyla began to walk away, I grabbed her by the hand and pulled her close to me.

"Tonight was a mistake."

Her eyes held sadness, and confusion. "Right. It was a mistake. Can you have someone take me to the condo?"

"No. I—"

She held a hand up halting my words. "We both know it's only temporary, I have a big day tomorrow, so do you."

Releasing my hand from around her arms, I stepped back to give her space. "You can sleep upstairs, and before you start, it's two in the morning, the last thing you need to be is out alone."

"Fine." Nyla, in a fit, stomped off to the stairs, and I wanted to pick her up and throw her over my shoulder for pissing me off. For reminding me of how young she really is mentally compared to me.

In the shower, running water beat down on my skin. The thought of Nyla trusting Gianney that much seemed sketchy, and it frustrated me to no end. Tomorrow, we needed to sit down and discuss how to approach finding him and bringing him to the cabin to get the real truth from his mouth.

As soon as I dried off, brushed my teeth, and got into bed, the weight of the day fell off. My mind drifted to Nyla's silky, warm skin, curvy hips, and tight ass in my lap.

Squeezing my erection in my hand under the covers, I tried to relieve some of the pressure.

"Relax," I told myself.

I should not be having a sex dream about my wife.

Following morning I came downstairs, hearing laughter or a TV playing. My new assistant knew I wasn't coming in until later to check in on a few things, but mostly was working from my phone. Checking the screenshot Carter sent me of my car parked out front, I smiled, ready to sell it for double the price.

"Here's Mr. Batman."

Looking up, I grimaced in annoyance to see Rena, Cora, and Sonya sitting at the table with Nyla.

"What are you three doing here?"

The chef moved around the kitchen, setting plates out for each girl, and then handing me mine.

"We asked if we could come for breakfast with Nyla," Cora said.

I joked. "Aren't you all married to husbands that need you in the morning?"

Rena rolled her eyes. "Sante knows where I am at all times."

"Because you two track each other like spies," I teased.

"Makes for great makeup sex," Rena responded.

Nyla spit out her juice, and the girls jumped up to help her. I pushed my plate back not hungry anymore.

Darting her eyes around the room, Nyla picked up the paper towel to clean up.

"Vincenzo, we want to hang out with Nyla and get to know her better," Cora suggested.

"Yeah, I thought since you had to work, and the guards already follow your sisters-in-law, I could go shopping and do lunch," Nyla probed.

"Not today, we have that thing."

"What thing?" Rena peered at me.

"Business."

"Business can wait, she's newly married," Rena pressed.

Pointing my fork at Nyla, I said, "Unlike you and Sante, Nyla has responsibilities she can't get out of."

"What is that supposed to mean?" Rena hissed.

"Vincenzo, that's not fair," Cora pitied.

"Maybe you should go suck his dick a little longer Nyla and he will relax more," Rena jested.

"Oh, God." Nyla tossed her head back.

"Did you tell her something?"

"What no!" Nyla fussed.

"You two are having sex, right?" Rena checked.

I argued, "None of your business, Rena."

Cora begged, "Rena, stay out of it, please."

"Angelina wasn't a good fit for him, and finally a girl we like comes along, and he's blowing it up," Rena hinted.

"Sex is not the issue."

"Then what is it?"

My eyes grew large at Nyla's confrontation, in front of everyone. "Nothing, I will talk about it later."

"He doesn't want to sleep with me because of my past," Nyla blurted out.

"That's bullshit!" I shouted.

Nyla jumped out of her seat, pointed in my face. "Then tell me the truth. You kissed me last night and walked away."

Running a hand down my face and exhaled seeing the hurt in her eyes. "Nyla, I was—"

"No, keep your excuses, just like Mark." Nyla walked out of the kitchen while throwing her napkin on the table.

"What just happened?" Rena checked.

Her piqued interest got me thinking, as well. We had a decent night out together before the shooting. We came home, and I tried to respect her desires and not cross the line. Even though I should have hated her, over time, it became clearer that she needed protection, and the bitterness I kept holding onto was putting her in a defensive mood whenever we were together.

"Let me go talk to her." Cora rose from her chair.

I confessed, "We kissed last night."

Rena's hand ran down my face. "I can see you fighting your feelings."

"Rena, it's business."

"Convince yourself. It might be business, but you're in deep, little brother."

"How does Sante put up with you?"

Picking up the cup of juice, she grinned while taking a sip. "Marrying your soulmate makes it worth the battle," Rena replied.

Chapter 13

Nyla

Marriage is not what the fairytales make it out to be. Feeling rejected in front of the girls by Vincenzo fucked me up inside. Probably dumb for even wanting him to like me for real, but the simple fact of the matter is that I put myself in the situation, and I needed to get out as soon as possible.

"Hey."

After peering up, Cora walked over and sat beside me in the game room. Early in the morning, before everybody got there, and while Vincenzo was still asleep, I explored more of the house and saw he had a man cave and a game room; I figured they were for his nieces and nephews when they came over. The chef told me about a theater and bowling alley near the basement, plus the pool outside. It was like a big playhouse that anyone could get lost in if they wanted to.

"Hey."

"No real advice to give," Cora said.

"Thanks." I chuckled.

She smiled. "He's a really sweet guy, give him a chance."

"Business only, Cora."

Cora shrieked. "None of us believe you two are only doing it for business."

"After today's confirmation, I do."

Cora melted in the chair. "You really like him?"

"I don't know."

"Guilt."

I looked at her, feeling like an open book. "My ex really fucked me up."

"My ex and now current husband fucked me up." Cora laughed.

"You married your ex?"

Cora's cheeks bunched into a smile. "I did. Long story."

"How did that happen? Like did he cheat on you?"

"Elio and I have a history like a roller-coaster ride. Would I trade him for someone new? Never, because what we've built is the truth. Love is never easy. If it were, then many people would experience it."

"I thought I had true love with Mark."

"Mark cared about you in his own way, probably, but in love? I doubt."

"Why would you say something like that?"

"No guy would willingly put someone they love in a situation to get hurt." Cora was saying the same things that Vincenzo had said to me that day.

Cora seemed genuine, and she's closer to my age than the other girls. Her coming over with Rena and Sonya made me feel good and not excluded from the group of wives.

"If Vincenzo and I were to really give the relationship a chance, would that make me look selfish?"

Raising her hand to my lap, she patted me on the back. "Judging yourself or caring what other people think or say is not any way to live."

"You are right. My uncle is a bastard, and all he's ever done is basically tell me I'm the cause of everything that's bad in my life."

"Tell your uncle he can suck a dick," Cora joked, covering her mouth.

"Rena has rubbed off on you," I cackled.

"Seriously, if Vincenzo has forgiven you, wants to try a real relationship, and you want to see where it goes, that's what matters."

"Cora." We turned to see Rena, stepping into the living room with the phone in her hand.

"Elio said he's been trying to call you." Rena held up the phone for her to take.

"Oh. Give me a second, Nyla." Cora answered the call, leaving to have some privacy.

"Feel better yet?" Rena squatted down next to me.

"Yeah, are you and Vincenzo always so combative?"

"He's really like a little brother to me," Rena answered.

"Is he still in the kitchen?"

"No, in his office."

"Give me a moment. Are you three still going shopping?"

"Probably, unless Elio wants Cora to come home," Rena explained.

I huffed. "Marriage."

After sauntering down the hall, I gently knocked on his office door and heard him shout that it was open. I slowly pushed forward, poking my head inside. He held the phone to his ear and gestured for me to wait a minute. After closing the door behind me, I stood near the wall, folding my arms and looking at everything—except him.

"Send the papers to my email, and I can sign them," Vincenzo demanded, hanging up the call.

"I think we should talk."

"I agree."

"Last night, you said it was a mistake."

"No, I didn't."

"Vincenzo, if you're not going to be honest, we can end the entire plan." I aimed for the door, but he leapt up and yanked me into his grasp.

"Stop assuming shit," he growled in my ear, nuzzling his nose between my neck and shoulder.

I felt limp as a noodle in his arms. "Vincenzo," I moaned.

"You jumped to what you thought I was going to say, by mistake."

"Then explain it to me now."

"Last night, putting you in that position to be shot at was a mistake on my part. Having you vulnerable in a situation even though I was next to you, that could have ended terribly."

While he held me tight, he reached out and touched my cheek with his hand.

"Thank you."

"For what?"

It was unexpected to see a different side of him. "Actually caring about me."

"Surprised?"

My lips parted. "Yeah."

"Me too."

"Can I kiss you?" I struggled for a breath.

"You don't have to ask to kiss your husband."

Grinning, I ran a hand up his chest, leaned up to capture his lips, nibbling on his bottom lip, and sucking it into my mouth. Feeling his strong arms wrap around me, lifting me up, I automatically wrapped my legs around his waist. Placing me on top of his desk, I reached down to unbuckle his pants.

"We can't." He grasped my hands, together.

Out of breath, I asked, "Why?" I whined, wanting to taste it in my mouth.

"Your uncle, remember? You're supposed to go and find the papers."

"Right. That way we can get the fake marriage over with faster." I snatched myself from his hold, trying to push him away and jump down.

His eyes darkened, and he lifted his hand around my throat, making me weak at the knees and feeling aroused at his dominance.

"Did I say you could get down?" He pecked me on the chin, then my forehead.

Closing my eyes, I whispered, "No." I shuddered at the aggressiveness in his commanding voice.

"When we get the papers and look everything over, we can talk about us."

His touch.

His voice.

His intelligence all turns me on.

"For real."

Vincenzo fingers ran up my thigh, split in between my legs, pushing up my skirt, only my panties between us, hovering his thumb over my panty line.

"You want me to touch her?" He studied.

"Yes." The way my legs automatically spread wider shocked me.

He grinned, kissed me on the mouth, and removed his hands. "Later. Right now, we need to handle business."

"Uhm, what are you doing?" I jumped off the desk, practically following him out of the office in a huff.

"Go get dressed and meet me in the car. We have work to do." He smacked me on the ass.

"Vincenzo!" I shouted.

He laughed with his back to me. Rena and Cora came from the living room, glanced at me, and burst into laughter.

"He's an asshole like his brothers," Rena quipped, and I couldn't do anything except turn and go upstairs to get dressed to leave for my uncle's house.

****

An hour later, we pulled up to Uncle Cono's house. Vincenzo hadn't taken his hand off my thigh. Every time I knocked it down, he put it right back, and I sucked my teeth, irritated by him teasing me earlier.

"I do like you, Nyla. I can admit I was out for revenge at first, wanting to make you pay."

My heart rate sped up at his confession. Hearing how he really feels about me felt different from the relationship between me and Mark.

"Okay."

He chuckled at my response, squeezing my thigh. "If the papers show we have to be married for a year before I get the money, then are you willing to stay in the marriage?" he asked.

A gulp of air filled my lungs. "Is that what you want?"

"Only way we work is communication. Mark might have led you into rocky waters, but baby, I'm a real man that needs you to speak up and tell him how you really feel even if it pisses me off."

"I like you and want to see where we can go."

"All right, here's the plan: Cono is expecting you, but not me. I'm going to distract him while you search for the papers."

"What if I can't get in the safe or he comes back before I figure out the lock system?"

Vincenzo lifted his shirt, showing his gun. "Cono will be distracted."

"Tell me you're not going to hurt him. Are you?"

"Depends on if he disrespects you."

"Nobody's ever stood up for me—besides my mom and dad."

"Mark?"

"Thinking back, it was more about him in the relationship than us building something together. At one point, I left him after he cheated. I still loved him, so I forgave him, and then the gambling got worse, and I told him to stop."

"He's a boy, not a man."

"Do you think I'm crazy for liking you, knowing you killed him?"

His eye twitched, and I could tell that the conversation was going in a direction that he'd shut down any minute.

"Focus on the future. Mark is your past, and if you decide tomorrow that you can't handle my world—"

"You'll let me go."

He gritted his teeth. "Nyla, you're mine even if we get

divorced today and live in separate rooms. The second I put my lips on you, it was over."

Lifting my eyes, I saw Cono, standing in the doorway. "He's waiting." I pointed at my uncle.

Vincenzo turned to look at him. "Give him a show."

He leaned toward me, and I grabbed his shirt, pulling him into me closer and sucking on his top lip.

"PG-13 only," I teased, releasing him, and wiping red lipstick off his lips.

After climbing from the car, Vincenzo took my hand and escorted me up the steps.

I reached out to hug my uncle, and he patted me on the arm, then shook Vincenzo's hand.

"Glad you two made it today. I heard from the lawyer, and he wants to wrap up the paperwork."

"You heard from the lawyer?" I asked, shocked at him.

"Of course, dear. Come have a seat—and Vincenzo, you sit here." Cono had coffee and muffins on the coffee table.

"I need to use the restroom, do you mind?"

Cono glared at me for a brief second, then smiled. "You remember your way around, Nyla," he joked, and I played along, jumping up and strolling from the living room.

I bumped into one of his guards.

"Excuse me," I said, walking around him.

Rubbing the back of my neck, I took another glance behind me and quickly opened the bathroom door pretending to go inside. The guard looked back forward and I slowly shut the door, walking around the pillar of the stairs into his office. I ran quietly to the back of the bookshelf, remembering a fake Abraham Lincoln biography that opened his shelf. Waiting for a brief moment, nothing happened, and thinking quickly, I pushed more books forward, getting the same results. Staring up at a picture on the wall, I took a chance and felt around the sides of the frame, feeling a clasp opening to a safe.

"Bingo."

Typing in his birthday, nothing happened. I tried the year next, then my year with the same results.

"Fuck. What is the code?"

After trying my dad's birthday, I checked the handle. It didn't move. An idea popped into my head, and I used the date of his death. Then it finally opened.

"Real asshole for using my father's date of death."

After seeing piles of money and a few documents, I snatched the documents from the safe, folded them up, and placed them in my bag. I shut the door to the safe and closed the painting. I slowly peeked out of the door, making sure that the guard was still looking forward, and then I snuck out, shutting the door and hearing loud voices from the living room. I tiptoed back to the bathroom, sighed, and smiled right as the guard turned back around. I walked back to the living room.

"Give me the evidence or you'll regret it, Cono."

"I told you: Once my niece gives you the money, it will be squared away." Cono rose from his chair.

To block Vincenzo from choking my uncle, I jumped in front of him, pushing him backwards. "Are you two crazy?"

"He thinks because he's a Calabresi I am supposed to be scared," Uncle Cono argued.

Vincenzo winked at me, and I caught on that he was just pretending to get him worked up. "Well, Uncle Cono, we are related now, so we need to try and have peace."

"If he gives me a seat at the table."

"Fuck you," Vincenzo cursed.

Cono smirked, lit his cigar, and sat back down. "I can have the evidence shown all over the internet in a split-second. Nothing will be traced back to me," Cono taunted.

"If it hurts me, then what?" I wanted to know.

"He doesn't care anymore than Mark." Vincenzo cuffed my hand.

"I saw Gianney."

His face fell in surprise. "Gianney Greco?"

"Gianney Greco and Mark were friends," I answered.

"Never knew that," Cono replied.

"You're lying," I hissed, getting in his face.

Vincenzo pulled me back.

"Nyla, I suggest you sit, be a dutiful wife, and be quiet," Uncle Cono chastised.

"It's more than clear you've hated me all my life. Now tell me who my real father is, Cono."

"What?" Vincenzo dropped his hands from my arms, turned me to him.

"I'll explain later."

"All you should be worried about is living the life as the wife of Vincenzo here."

"Mark was right about you." I stormed from the house.

Vincenzo called my name and stopped me from getting in the car. "What the hell was that back there?"

My voice trembled. "Can we just go?"

Picking up my chin, Vincenzo wiped the tears away. "Look at me."

I shook my head no.

"Nyla."

Opening my eyes, his upper lip curled into a smile. "You have a family now."

"Are you sure they want me?"

He unlocked the car door and opened it for me. "More than sure. Tell me you got the papers."

Removing what I had in my purse, I passed them to Vincenzo as the car pulled away. He studied the documents with a deep frown. "Did you read these?"

"No, I just took everything and left."

"He's lying."

"Lying about what?" I snatched the papers from his hands.

"There is no trust fund. Fuck!" Vincenzo cursed.

"Huh?"

"It's all a plan to get a seat in the cartel—and now, if we refuse, then he'll put the evidence out about my brothers killing Greco."

"Wait, Greco as in Gianney Greco's people?"

"There's more to the story."

"Oh, shit." Revelation creeped into my head, and I slouched in my seat.

"What?"

"He played us both."

"Played us?" Vincenzo repeated.

"Remember I told you Mark and Cono were on a recording together?"

"Yeah, something about them working together."

"All this time, it was a setup for you and me to get married, so he could be in the cartel. He never loved me; he just went along like he cared when I started dating Mark."

"Help me understand."

"Cono told me I was adopted; I wasn't really a Sartori by blood."

"Hold up, Nyla, you have to be confused."

"I wish, but no. I'm sorry I didn't tell you earlier. He forced me to go along with his plan."

"For what?"

I sighed. I didn't know how to tell him about the stocks, and the seat on the board. He'll probably think I went behind his back and planned it with my uncle.

"Can you promise to not kill him?"

"Nyla, I can't make that promise."

"He hasn't told me who my birth father is, and I'd like to meet him, and that side of my family."

"I understand you need closure, but my family are on the line, and they come first."

"Right, your family."

****

I sat on the fence about whether I should spill the entire story or try to get the truth from my uncle on my own. I listened to Cassandra on the phone, talking about her latest date. It made me miss being single and meeting new people.

"I'm so glad he let you have a phone again, so we can FaceTime each other like old times." Cassandra held up a blue dress, wanting my opinion on her first date.

I pushed the spoon in the ice cream tub, sulking in the house after we got back home from my uncle's. Vincenzo told me to wait for him to get off the phone with his family, and I had no plans on spending any more time with him after today.

"Something happened."

I dropped the tub on the table. "No, why do you ask?"

"You have that sour puss face," Cassandra teased.

Reaching for the napkin, I wiped my hands. "Ugh, I hate you."

Cassandra thrust a makeup bag at me. "All love over here."

"Where is he taking you?"

"To a jazz club."

"That sounds nice."

Cassandra puffed her hair up. "Our official first date since he had to cancel last time."

"Why did he cancel?"

"Work."

"Lucky you."

"What did hubby do now?" Cassandra joked.

"I can't talk about it right now."

"Must have pissed you off. You are almost halfway finished with the tub of ice cream."

Peering down at the strawberry, chocolate, and vanilla mixture, I started to feel sick from letting him get to me to the point I binged on ice cream.

"What time is he picking you up?"

"In an hour. Why?"

"I need a favor."

"What?"

"Can I crash? I promise to give you your space. But I need to get out of this house, or I'll go crazy."

"I don't know, Nyla; your man is crazy, and the last thing I want is him blowing up the club with me in it—or messing up my dick appointment."

"He doesn't have to know."

"See now you're starting off the marriage wrong."

"One, not a real marriage, and two, I might find some-body new tonight."

Cassandra wiggled her finger in my face. "Ohhh... Playing with fire, baby."

"Who says I'm playing? Vincenzo doesn't own me."

"True, but he probably respects the ring on your finger, and you wouldn't want him going out on dates with other women."

While thinking over her statement, Angelina popped into my mind, along with the last time she came to the condo. How did she have a key to his place if they weren't an official couple? After shaking off those thoughts, I hopped out of bed, holding the phone and moving toward the closet.

"One drink and maybe a dance or two."

"Fine child, remember I warned you. Be ready in forty minutes, and I'll pick you up."

"Actually, I can meet you there."

"Is he going to let you out?"

"I can get out on my own."

"How?"

"My new sisters-in-law." I winked at her and ended the call, going to the group chat message.

Me: Hey ladies I need a favor.

Rena: Hey babes.

Sonya: I'm here.

Me: Cassandra's going on a date, and she's worried the guy might be a dud. I was thinking of going and staying in the background, but you know Vincenzo won't let me out of the house.

Biting my bottom lip, I waited to see if the buttons would pop up and they'd be on my side.

Rena: What time is the date?
Me: I have to meet her in an hour.
Sonya: Renato has RJ at his parents' house. I can go.

"Yes." I excitedly fist pumped the air.

Rena: I can pick you up, Sonya, then run by to grab Nyla.
Me: Thank you, ladies.
Rena: Tell Vincenzo we'll see him soon.
Me: He's out at a business meeting.

I hurriedly messaged them, not wanting them to catch onto my lies. The faster I could get dressed and sneak outside, the better.

Logging out of the group chat, I ran in the backroom for a quick hoe bath, fixed my hair, and touched up my makeup. I eyed a black leopard jumpsuit in the closet and figured tonight I would let loose and find my inner self.

Thirty minutes later, I got a text from Rena. She was outside. I ran from the bedroom, checking to make sure Vincenzo was still locked in his office. I smiled at my plan and slowly disabled the alarm, then reset it. Upon seeing Carter in the car talking to the girls, I walked downstairs and opened the door.

"Mrs. Calabresi, Vincenzo let you out of the house without a fight?" he joked.

"He did, and I promised to be home early, so we better get going."

"Have a good night, ladies." Carter waved at us.

I tossed my things to the side, then hugged Sonya and waved at Rena. Their driver left the wraparound driveway, and I stayed low to avoid seeing any more of the guards at the gate

Chapter 14

Vincenzo

Renato snarled. "Are you crazy?"

As soon as we got back from Cono's house, I went into my office to get my brothers on a call. Renato, Sante, and Elio had each beat it into my head that I should have had Cono come to the office on neutral ground. Giving him the luxury of being in his own home had given him an ego boost.

"Renato's right, Cono should never have the upper hand to make demands," Sante explained.

"Savio needs to be aware of what happened," Elio tossed out.

"He's going to be pissed."

"Not if I go and kill Cono right now," Renato growled.

"How's Nyla handling your threats?" Sante inquired.

"She hates her uncle, but wants him alive, especially since she found out she's adopted and not a real Sartori."

"I can understand her seeking information for herself," Elio commented.

"She's a fucking Calabresi now by marriage. Fuck the

Sartori's," Renato barked, in frustration.

"Renato, watch what you say about her," I fussed.

"Are you taking up for her now?" Renato remarked, and I didn't know at the moment that I was backing her up.

"All I'm saying is that she's been through a lot."

"She fucking robbed us!" Renato shouted.

"Renato's right, but Nyla's been around us, and she's not into anything shady," Sante insisted.

"Are we sure?" Renato pried, and I felt it in my gut I needed to fill them in on the stock seat.

"Well, there's something else I need to tell you."

"What is it now?" Elio asked.

"Cono not only wants Sartori in the alliance of families, but he's trying to go after a board seat at Calabresi Holdings."

As he chuckled through the phone, I could tell Renato was ready for a bloodbath. "Listen, fuck your wife and her family," he grunted.

"Renato, you're my brother, but keep my wife's name out of your mouth."

"How will you handle this, little brother?" Renato taunted.

"Both of you need to calm down. We're brothers. The last time we fought was back in our teen years. Act like grown men," Sante shouted.

"Sante's right; crumbling is what Cono wants, and I refuse to give into his demands," Elio preached.

"I'm giving you twenty-four hours to bring her to me," Renato demanded.

I screwed up my face at the phone. "What are you saying?"

"We hold her to get Cono to come to us, and I kill

them both. Our lawyers can get rid of the evidence," Renato directed.

"I have a great record, but some things I can't make disappear, Renato," Elio muttered.

"Not bringing her to you to kill."

"Better yet, I'll come to you. I love making house calls," Renato taunted.

"Fuck you, Renato!" I slammed the phone down, pissed at everyone.

After sliding from the chair, I yanked the door open and marched down the hall. I stepped into the kitchen, seeing that our chef had prepared dinner.

"Has Nyla come down?" Picking up the bottle of wine from the counter.

"She left."

Looking at him in confusion, I glared at him. "What do you mean she left?"

"Uhm..." he stammered.

I dropped the bottle on the counter, ran upstairs, and pushed the bedroom door open. My eyes scanned the empty room, and I saw a heap of clothes laying on the bed.

"Fuck!"

Slamming the door back, I rushed downstairs, picking up my keys and phone from the office, and sprinted down the front stairs.

"She fucking left!" I shouted.

Carter and Romo squinted at me in confusion. "Mrs. Calabresi left with Rena and the girls."

"When?" I ran to my Bentley, hopping in the driver's seat.

"About fifteen minutes ago. She said you were asleep and knew they were going to hang out," Carter emphasized and I shook my head.

"She lied and skipped out."

Carter jumped in the passenger seat of my Bentley. Romo trailed in the other car. I sped from the driveway, not stopping.

"Call Renato," I commanded.

"I don't have time for your bullshit, Vincenzo," Renato remarked.

"Call Sante and Elio. She skipped out with the girls."

"Who skipped out?" Renato pried.

"Nyla."

Laughing at my expense, I wanted to wring his neck. "Renato, now is not the time to piss me off."

"All of our wives are caught up in your girl's bullshit, and if something happens to Sonya, I'm personally holding your wife accountable." Renato ended the call before I could respond.

"Did she say where they're going?"

Carter sent a message to the team. "No, I assumed you knew."

"Call Rena on my phone."

After picking up my cell, he dialed her from my contact list, and I listened while it rang. It went straight to voicemail, and I told him to dial again.

"She's not picking up," Carter informed me, taking the phone from his hand and making another call.

I pressed my foot on the gas, blowing through the light and getting on Highway 41.

"Renato called me already," Sante answered without saying hello.

"Are you tracking Rena's phone?"

"She's at the Jazz Showcase club," Sante responded.

After swerving in traffic, I stepped on the brake. "I'm ten minutes away."

"Savio wants to be updated as soon as you have her," Sante said.

After hitting the end-call button, I shoved the phone in my pocket and slowed down. After pulling up, I slammed the car into park and jumped out with my team behind me. I saw Renato stomp down the block next to Elio. Sante arrived in the parking lot, shaking his head at me. I placed my hand on Renato's chest, blocking him from moving forward.

"Let me handle it."

Pushing my hand down, he said, "You have five minutes before I burn the place down." Renato walked alongside me, scanning the room.

Searching for Nyla, my eyes shot to a group of women in the back corner and a man laughing at something Nyla said. "She's out of her mind." I stalked through the room, and Elio rushed and jumped in front of me. Sonya saw us and tried to grab Nyla's hand.

Elio said, "We're in public, keep your cool."

"Move."

Stepping out of my way, Elio threw his hands in the air.

Leaning down, I whispered in her ear. "Get up."

Nyla froze in place. "What are you doing here?"

"Either you get up now or find out what I will do."

"Who are they?" the man next to Nyla pried.

"That's her husband," her friend Cassandra mumbled.

He stuck his hand out at me, and I glared at it.

Nyla slowly stood up, pressing her hand on my chest. "Vincenzo, please try to be calm."

"Nyla, are you alright? Do you need me to go with you?" Cassandra reached for her hand.

"Renato, leave me alone. We just wanted to have a girls' night out," Sonya argued, propping her hand on her hip.

While snarling at her, he wrapped a hand around her neck, pulling her in close. "Who are you talking to like that?" Renato asked before he pecked her on the lips.

Rolling her eyes, Rena jumped up, blocking me and Nyla. "She's with us, Vinny."

"Rena, stay out of it."

Sante cuffed her hand, pulling her away. "He's right Rena, let's go."

"Grab your things," I said.

"No," Nyla spat.

Over her tantrums, I bent down and lifted her over my shoulder.

"Put her down, Vincenzo," Cassandra shouted, rising from her chair. "Help her, Ralph."

The man sitting next to her looked from Cassandra to me to my brothers. "Cassandra, stay out of that man's business," Ralph said.

Cassandra glared at him and sat back down.

While wiggling her legs, Nyla hit me on the back and screamed, "Vincenzo! Oh, my God, put me down!"

"Take her things and put them in the car," I told Sonya.

Sonya nodded, then helped calm Nyla down.

The crowd around us stood back, whispering at the scene.

Once we were out of the club, I placed her on her feet, gently shoved her against the car door, blocking her eyeline of the girls.

"Seriously, you are a fucking asshole."

"What are your issues?"

"Why do you even care? You plan on getting rid of me, anyway. I might as well have a night of fun." Ignoring my stare, she lifted her chin.

Quietly, I told her why I cared. "Cono is going to die. He's crossed the line, and now you're out here making yourself a target."

"Target? He's not going to hurt me."

"Gianney and Cono have something going on, and you're the focal point."

Kicking the rock next to feet, dipping her head low. "Why do you even care?"

"Nyla."

"Keep it real, Vincenzo. Are you interested in me for me, or just to get the evidence back and your money?"

"Get in the car."

After shaking her head, she turned and climbed into the car. After talking with my brothers, we planned to meet in the next few days to come up with a plan to handle Cono and Gianney.

****

While standing in the middle of the bar in my man cave with my sleeves rolled up, I guzzled another shot of bourbon. Once we got back to the house, Nyla went in and locked herself in the bedroom, ignoring me.

During the car ride, her soft tears had stabbed me in the chest, and the moment I tried to reach out to comfort her, she moved closer to the window.

Sante and Renato texted to say that Savio heard about the way I acted, but I didn't care, since all three of them had done way worse than me.

"Come in." I looked up at the chef standing in the middle of the doorway.

"Sir, I'm leaving for the night," he informed me.

"Thanks, I left a check for you on the counter."

"Thank you, and I have her favorite meals in the fridge."

"Has she eaten?" I probed.

"I tried, but she wasn't hungry," he stated.

"She needs to eat."

"I agree." He turned to leave.

After slamming the glass on the end of the bar, I stomped from the room and then upstairs. I was frustrated at how my day had ended in another fight with Nyla after she jumped to conclusions. I shoved the door open without knocking. Her bed was half-made, her clothes were tossed around. The bathroom door was open a smidge, and steam was coming from the running shower. I moved in further, shutting and locking the door behind me. After peeking in, I saw the steam fill the room. I peered around at the lit candles on the counter and opened the shower door.

"Oh shit!" Nyla jumped back, covering herself.

"You didn't eat."

Her hair was wrapped to protect it from the water. "What?"

"I paid the chef to prepare dinner, and you told him you're not hungry."

She turned to step under the faucet. "I'm not."

"Nyla, we need to talk."

"Can you leave so I can have some privacy?"

I licked my lips as her small hands tried to cover her plump breasts, and the curve of her hips and thick thighs glistened under the water.

"Vincenzo!" she called my name and softly gasped.

Reaching in and turning off the water, bending down and lifting her in my arms, she wrapped her arms around my neck.

Fumbling to hold on, she asked, "What are you doing?" Her words turned into moans as my hands squeezed her ass. Rubbing against her, I told myself not to go there with her. This was a business arrangement.

A cry eased through her lips as I smashed my mouth on top of hers, plunging between her lips, groaning at the feel of her grinding against my dick.

"Baby," she cooed, sliding her hands to the back of my head.

Hearing her calling me baby, my dick grew harder. I trailed kisses across her shoulders, down to her arm and her palm.

"Nyla, I'm telling you now. I'm not playing any more games with you."

Nodding her head. "I want you," Nyla whimpered in a longing plea.

I caressed a hand against her skin, flicking my tongue to her nipple.

"Ohhh... yes."

I tried to control the intense rage of how beautiful she'd looked tonight, of having other men see what belonged to me.

She belongs to me.

Cupping her breasts together, I spread her legs wider, and her juices coated my left hand. Nyla's lust-filled eyes lingered on me.

"Stop playing with me," I demanded, and she nodded at my request. The prolonged anticipation was unbearable.

"Please fuck me, now," Nyla asked and stared longingly at me.

"First I need to eat my pussy." Popping her titty out, I dove into her warm, succulent pussy, devouring her sweet nectar. I was carried away by her own response.

"Yes, right there." She humped my face, gripping it tight.

Her intoxicating smell filled the air, drowning me. Drowning in her was the only way I would be willing to leave her on this Earth.

I ran my tongue across her swollen lips. "Fuck, you're so delectable, baby."

Her cheeks were flushed, and her body shuddered beneath me. The bed was covered not only in the water from the shower, but in her juices trickling down her thighs. After pinching her nipple, I moved back, took off my shirt, then yanked off my pants and shoes. While standing back in a daze, I gazed at her smooth skin, and she ran her leg along my chest. I took hold of it and kissed the arch of her foot. She'd become my prized possession, and nothing would come between us—not even herself.

"You know you've fucked me over multiple times, baby."

"Punish me."

My heart jolted at her submission. "You like being a bad girl?"

"Only for you, I can be a naughty little bitch."

Positioning her to the end of the bed. "My bitch, you're mine. Show me how dirty you can get."

Smirking, she lifted on her knees, roping her hand around my dick. My head fell back at the warmth of her full lips when she wrapped them around it. Holding the back of her head, she showed the control I struggled to let go of when she licked the tip. As the soft lighting illuminated her amber brown complexion, Nyla took me further down her throat.

"Shit, Nyla, hold up."

While grinning at me, she shook her head, then ran her long nails up my chest. She pulled back, popped my dick out, squeezed it, and kissed up my chest.

Pushing her hair back, I held her around the waist. "Scared?"

"No, are you?" she challenged me.

My feelings for her intensified. "My type of girl."

Laying her down, I ran the head of my dick down to her entrance. She was tight, and I pulled back.

"Hold on," I said, placing her legs on top of my shoulder, getting as deep as possible. Slowly pushing forward, her tightness had my dick in a chokehold.

"Vi-Vincenzo," she stuttered, closing her eyes.

Staring down at our combined bodies, the sight of being inside of her drove me crazy, and I pondered why Mark would fuck up on the masterpiece in front of me.

"Yes, yes, fuck me."

"Rob me of this sweet pussy again, Nyla, and I'll fuck you up," I growled.

"I promise!"

While pounding her repeatedly, I slammed my mouth on top of hers and sucked on her top lip. She pulled me flat on top of her, causing the bed to shift.

"Fuck!" We both groaned at the impact. Her shit was sloppy wet, and my head nuzzled in between her neck, hearing her heavy breathing.

"Are you ready for more?"

Her reaction was so powerful to my touch. "Yes! Oh, aghhh."

"Stop running off, thinking I'm not for you."

"Okay. Please, Vincenzo," she sobbed.

Prolonging her torture, I said, "Let me know how bad you're ready to go?"

She bit her bottom lip. "Oh, God!"

"He's not in this room, understand me?"

Throwing her head back, cupping her chin, I snaked my tongue in her mouth and tweaked her nipple, rising up and picking up my strokes.

"Come, now!" I commanded, watching her body tremble at my voice. Giving her orgasms became my new favorite task at that moment as she squirted. It was the first of many to come, and happened right as I had my own release while holding her in my arms.

"I didn't expect that." She buried her face in her hands.

I grinned. "Expect what?"

"You to be that good." She grinned, making me smirk, pulling out of her and lying flat on my back.

"Fucking crazy girl," I sighed.

"And you're fucking huge, at least nine inches. My pussy is going to be sore tomorrow," Nyla said.

Feeling in between her thighs, I said, "I'll be gentle next go round." I pressed against her cheek.

"Next go round." She smiled.

"Pretty lady, I might like you in my bed at all times." I pinched her cheek.

"What happened to me being your bad bitch?"

"Based on those moves, in the bedroom you are my bad bitch. In public though, you're my wife."

"I like that." She pecked me on the lips.

"Kinky ass." Brushing a hand against her butt, slapping it, I rubbed off the sting.

Watching her yawn, I wanted to have another taste before we got fully deep into sleep. Lifting her up, she popped her eyes open.

"What are you—? Wait, Vincenzo!" she panted, gliding down my pole, planting her hands on my chest. Slowly, I helped her to ride me back and forth.

"Go at your own pace, pretty lady."

"Too much. I can't, Vincenzo." Her trembling limbs clung to me.

After thrusting up, she cried out. I wrapped my hand around her throat, pushing into her again.

"Show me what you can do. You are my wife right?" My brow hiked, suspended until she gently slapped me across the face.

Softly, her breath fanned my face as she bent down, kissing me with a hunger that belied her outward calm. My hands folded over her perfect, mouthwatering globes. Flesh against flesh, imprisoned in a web of arousal. I bucked deeper into her and growled, then jerked her head back and branded her neck with a reminder of who she was fucking right at that moment and would be for the rest of her future.

She cried out for release. "Fucking play with me, Vincenzo."

"Where's the grown woman that knows how to take my dick?"

"She's right here." Nyla rolled her hips, reached behind herself and massaging my balls.

Her arousal dripped down my pole, giving me the gift I'd been waiting for since we joined in marriage.

All night, we made love. I finally emptied my balls, and we showered together, then fell into bed in our room.

I told her she'd be moving her things over tomorrow.

Chapter 15

Nyla

A month passed, and my uncle had ignored all my calls—even to the point of changing his number. After speaking with a lawyer, he explained the papers were fabrications, and that the trust fund was used years ago. Sitting in his office and hearing how my uncle spent my money without consulting me aggravated my soul. To him, I was just a bank; he could draw money and leave a negative balance without paying it back. The second I ran away with Mark, he never tried to find me to rectify the situation.

After throwing the phone on the table, I listened to the girls laugh and talk about the boys, nagging at them about the night that Vincenzo came and yanked me away.

I invited Cassandra for lunch. I wanted to apologize because Ralph hadn't spoken to her since. "Cass, will you ignore me all day?"

"I should, since I haven't had sex in over a month," Cassandra spat.

Rena had been cackling at our back-and-forth arguing from the moment Cassandra came into her house. During an early morning group chat, I added Cassandra, so she could see the havoc that went on with the Calabresi men's wives.

"Cassandra, you like to hold a grudge, same as me. I like you." Rena clinked her glass with Cassandra.

"Rena, please."

"Thank you, my new bestie," Cassandra teased me.

"How about I invite you on a trip with me and the girls?"

"So, you and your husband get along now?" Cora challenged.

Avoiding all of the stares, I gulped the rest of the mimosa and refilled my glass.

"She got laid," Cassandra blurted out.

"No, I didn't."

All of them gave me a face of "you're lying".

"If I did?"

"Nothing to be ashamed about, we're all married," Rena reminded me.

"I could have been if your husband had some got damn sense," Cassandra blasted.

"He's a work in progress." I shrugged.

"Oh, she's definitely getting laid." In response, Rena held up her hand for a high-five.

My attention focused on my cell, vibrating on the table from back-to-back messages. After lifting it, I saw it was Vincenzo, checking to see how my day was going.

Vincenzo: Whatever Rena says is a lie.

Me: Leave her alone.

Vincenzo: She's a menace.

Me: You love your sister-in-law.

Vincenzo: Sometimes. I'm in a business meeting, and I'll be home late.

Me: Okay, I tried Cono again, no answer.

Vincenzo: Leave him to me.

Me: But he's trying to take advantage of the deal.

Vincenzo: I will handle him and Gianney.

"See. She's sitting there ignoring us for her man," Cassandra tittered, throwing a grape in her mouth.

"Vincenzo is just checking up on me," I answered.

"You two probably stay making googly eyes all day," Sonya teased me.

"What about kids?" Rena pried, and I hadn't even thought about having kids with him.

"We haven't talked about kids."

Sonya reminded me, "You should; you're married—and more than likely, having unprotected sex."

"Are you scared to have kids with him?" Rena asked.

"Honestly, I never thought about kids—or being with him after getting the money back."

"So, you two are going to stay married?" Cassandra asked, confused.

"Uhm, we haven't talked about long-term."

"How about we stop hounding the girl and have some fun today. McKayla's on deadline so she can't be here," Cora insisted.

"What do you have in mind?" Rena poured another round of drinks.

"A trip would be great, maybe Las Vegas or Hawaii," Cora remarked.

"Just the women?"

"I want my husband with me," Rena said.

"For someone that always complains about their husband, you sure stay under him every chance on the hour," Sonya jokes.

"Like Renato doesn't stalk you." Rena reached out and pushed her on the shoulder.

Waving her comment off, I said, "I agree, a trip with our husbands would be fun, and Cassandra you can invite Ralph, all expenses paid."

"He blocked me." Cassandra pouted.

The entire room burst into laughter. Sonya extended an arm around Cassandra's neck, pulling her into a hug. "Sorry, friend. He's missing out."

"Glad you found love."

"Love."

"Yeah, you love Vincenzo, or is it just lust because of the dick?" Cassandra picked up the plate of croissants.

"He's my husband."

"A husband that you've grown close with over the past few weeks," Cassandra emphasized.

"Can we change the subject?"

"She's right, we're here because Rena wanted all of us to come together and connect." Sonya pointed around the room.

"Sorry."

"Never apologize for how you feel," Cassandra said.

Rena probed. "What are your plans for work?"

"I used to be in college, then I dropped out, but I have a love for photography."

"That sounds wonderful, and you can do your own thing without having to do a regular job," Cora said.

"I know you have your own clinic."

Cora replied. "My passion is helping animals. You should look into the new school year."

"Maybe. First, I need to handle things with my uncle."

"He's still not answering your calls."

"No, and Vincenzo refuses to allow me to go see him," I sighed.

"I heard from Sante that Cono is trying to get you to sign over your board shares to him." Rena stared at me.

"I won't."

"Cono's playing a dangerous game." Rena scratched the back of her ear.

I answered, "He's manipulative, and after lying about the trust fund, I refuse to give in to him."

Rena swung her head to me. "Have you seen the evidence?"

"What evidence?" Cassandra probed.

Since Cassandra only knew bits and pieces, letting her into all the drama might put her at risk since my uncle knew we were close, and he might try to use her against me as leverage.

"Uncle Cono planned for me to marry Vincenzo so that he could get a higher position in Calabresi Holdings —Vincenzo's family's company—as well as his other illegal businesses."

"And he's still alive?" Cassandra quipped.

"He has evidence on our husbands, and until they can find all the copies, they have to keep him alive," Rena answered.

"Nyla, as a best friend, I'm going to always worry about you. So, are you sure you are safe?" Cassandra checked.

Reaching across the table, I covered her palm. "Vincenzo has my back."

"It was McKayla and Adelina. They want to come on the trip." Sonya placed her phone on the table.

Rena ducked her chin. "Might as well make it a family vacation," she said, drinking her mimosa.

"Kids and all."

"Renato might kill me for setting it up before talking with him." Sonya laughed.

"At what point will he like me?"

"Take a while for him to grow on you," Rena said.

"She's right, just ignore him," Sonya suggested, knowing how her husband could quickly change into a monster.

Sonya leaned over Rena's shoulder scanning the vacation packages for Hawaii, while I answered my ringing phone, seeing an unknown number. "Hello?"

"Nyla?"

"Who is this?"

Loud yelling in the background crackled through the phone. "Gianney. I need to talk to you."

After standing, I moved from the dining room swiftly.

"Gianney, how did you get my number?" Standing near the corner of the entryway, I peered up at the girls smiling, lifting a finger to give me one moment.

"Nyla, it's not hard to find you," Gianney remarked.

"Why are you calling me?"

Gianney managed a slow disarming tone. "Something you should be aware of about your uncle."

"My uncle."

"He's lying to you."

"I can't talk right now."

"Is he there?" he prodded.

I was pissed off at his nosiness. "Who?"

"Who else? The man of the hour, the one you let kill

my best friend," Gianney snapped.

"Mark got himself killed," I grumbled.

"Does that help you sleep at night?"

"Gianney, you've been a great friend to Mark and me."

Gianney chortled. "He's already brainwashed you."

"Mark put me in harm's way," I preached.

Frustrated with the conversation, I leaned up against the wall, head lifted in the air.

Gianney's accusations would have sent me down a spiral of revenge on anyone who hurt someone I loved, but after the time Vincenzo and I had spent together, I had realized our entire relationship was going down the wrong path.

"Meet me and I can explain more," he says.

"Have you contacted Cono?"

"Rather not say over the phone." Gianney's line dropped, I exhaled walking back into the room, placing the phone on the table.

"Everything okay?" Cassandra asked, looking at me.

I put on a brave face, letting the thoughts of my uncle and Gianney disappear. "Fine. Did you get anywhere with the plans?"

"First, we had an idea if you're on board," Rena suggested.

"What's the idea?"

"Well, Adelina is throwing you and Vincenzo a party, correct?" Cora inquired.

"Yeah, no exact date though."

"Maybe we can combine the trip with the party," Cora suggested.

"So have the party in another country or state?"

"You said that when you were growing up, your

parents traveled and showed you the world. So, what's the one place you all constantly visited that means the most to you?" Cora passed the computer to me.

"Wow, I hadn't even thought to do something like that." I searched for the locations on the map. I could only remember the one place my mom took us to every year like clockwork.

"Greece."

"Greece sounds nice," Cassandra said.

"Where did you stay?"

"Mykonos."

Rena raised her hands in the air, clapping in excitement. "Greece is our trip."

"Adelina will love planning and forcing the boys to put business aside." Cora giggled.

"Thanks, ladies. I have to get home and change; my man is taking me out for dinner." After standing, I grabbed my phone and purse.

Cassandra rose from her seat.

"Let me know if you need any help with the work hunt," Cora yelled out.

"I will, thank you." Walking around the table, I hugged each one and waved goodbye.

Sitting back in the car, Cassandra tittered at something on her phone, pushing it in front of my face.

"He sent an apology." She waved the photo of flowers on her front porch.

"Ralph seemed cool; you should give him another chance."

"Probably, but I need someone not easily intimidated," Cassandra mentioned.

"Carter, can you run to the salon? I have an appointment in five minutes."

Figured I would get my hair refreshed before the big date with Vincenzo.

"Yes, ma'am."

"Lana squeezed you in?" Cassandra inquired.

"Yep, I promised her an extra bonus—plus I would throw in some advertisements through Vincenzo's casino."

"You actually liked working at the casino?"

"It was cool."

"Why not do something officially there?"

"Like what?"

"Advertising, setting up events, you know, being a real socialite."

I laughed and waved off her comment. "Vincenzo would never let me go back to work for him.

"Have you talked to him?"

"No, and I would rather keep our thing personal without mixing business."

She opened and closed her mouth.

"I know it's a contradiction after what happened, but it's better for us."

"As long as you're happy."

Carter arrived at Lana's salon and boutique on Michigan Drive. After closing the door, he escorted us inside, checked around, then stood off to the side. Vincenzo forced me to have extra-tight security while my uncle was trying to blackmail us.

Lana pushed her arms out for me, and I squeezed her close.

"Baby girl, you look so good. How long has it been?" Lana had done my hair for the longest time; only recently, after the entire Vincenzo debacle, I had stopped getting it done professionally and started managing it on my own.

"About four or five months."

Lana sifted a hand through my hair. "Well, it looks like you kept it fresh."

"I tried. You remember Cassandra."

"Hey, Cassandra, how are you?" Lana quizzed.

"Lana, you've upgraded the salon since we last saw you." Cassandra commented on the kids' playpen in the back corner and large TV hanging on the wall.

"Trying to extend my clientele." Lana motioned for me to follow to the chair.

"Still busy."

Lana swung out a comb. "Love the noise, helps pass the time."

"So, what are you getting?" Lana wrapped the cap around my neck, as I plopped down in the chair.

"Just a little refresh on some of my locks, have a dinner to attend."

"I heard you got married. You finally got Mark to calm down?" She giggled.

Cassandra eye's connected with mine.

"Actually, Mark and I broke up; I'm married to someone else."

"Wait, you broke up when?" In shock, Lana's eyes opened wide.

"He passed away."

She hugged my shoulders. "Oh, God, Nyla, I had no idea."

"Thanks, it's something I still have a hard time talking about."

"So, you married another guy?"

Clearing my throat. "Vincenzo Calabresi."

That same look of confusion was evident. "Vincenzo Calabresi, the billionaire?" she quizzed.

"Yes, but that's not why I married him."

"Shit, he's fine." She cursed, and I cackled at her flushed cheeks. Vincenzo's extremely attractive, and I wouldn't be a girl's girl if I can't acknowledge how his presence alone makes my panties wet.

"Thanks."

"So, you and Vincenzo knew each other for a long time or something? He's always seen on social media with other women—usually, some blond." Lana pulled my hair out of my bun.

"Angelina's his assistant."

"Oooh, so you know about her." Lana tapped me on the shoulder.

"She's nothing to him."

"Claiming your man," Lana joked.

"Believe me I would have never married him if he had someone seriously."

Lana washed the sink next to her station. "Men love to play games."

For the rest of the visit, she and I tittered, joking about her latest boytoy. An hour passed, and we hopped back into the car.

I made it home to meet Vincenzo in the bedroom, fresh out of the shower.

"Hi," I said.

He dropped his towel on the floor, then reached out to pull me to his chest. He pecked me on the lips. "You smell delicious." Vincenzo cradled the back of my head.

"We have dinner reservations," I told him, pressing a kiss on his cheek.

Vincenzo smacked and groped my ass, sitting me on top of the dresser. Pushing my legs apart, his palm clasped my thigh. I could practically taste the desire from his lips.

He grinned, pushing his tongue into my mouth. "Have my full meal right here."

I pressed my breasts against his chest. One corner of my mouth pulled into a slight smile, and I dreamed of being crushed within his embrace.

Ran my hand down his chest. "I'm hungry, can we go eat please, and later I promise we can do whatever you like."

Groaning, he stood back and kissed me again, helping me down. "Give me a second to get dressed."

"Wear that brown sweater. I think you're sexy in it, like you're a professor and I'm the student. Maybe we can play dress up." Happiness filled me as I talked, and for the first time ever, it seemed real.

He threw his head back in a laugh.

I skipped into the bathroom to freshen up and change clothes.

Forty minutes later, we arrived, holding hands. He pulled out my chair and kissed me again.

"You have a little red lipstick, babe." Picking up the napkin, I wiped it off the side of his lip.

Gazing up, I smiled at our waitress as she laid the menus down on the table. "What are your specials?" I quizzed.

She explained. "For today we have the sea bass and steamed vegetables."

"Bring me the special of the day please and a side of fries." I was starving, after lunch earlier I didn't eat much. As Vincenzo started to give his order, I saw my phone glow with an unknown number showing. Opening I saw a message from stating to meet tomorrow.

"What has your attention?" Vincenzo investigated.

"Cassandra texting about Ralph," I lied, ignoring the

text thread. Reaching for his hand, I interlocked our fingers.

"You look beautiful."

"Thank you, Vinny," I cooed, cupping my chin, mesmerized by his dazzling blue eyes.

After lifting the bottle of champagne, he filled our glasses.

"Vincenzo, are you okay with me?"

"Okay, how?"

"Building a real marriage. The money from the trust fund isn't real, and I can't pay back the money. Cono won't let it slide if I don't sign over anything to him. Maybe we should look into an annulment."

"He's not getting a dime from me and my family."

"I know, and that's why I think we might need to just end it before anything more happens."

"Cono thinks you're just a young girl he can manipulate. You are my wife and a Calabresi."

"But your money."

"I'll get it back. I already have a plan in motion."

"What plan?"

"Once I catch up with Gianney and learn what he knows, we can get Cono at the same time."

"Not sure it's that easy."

"Cono Sartori will get handled, trust me."

Pulling my hand to his lips, I said, "There's something else I want to talk to you about."

"Go ahead."

Now would be the perfect opportunity to ask about me meeting with Gianney. Maybe the girls are right to leave it alone between the men and let them handle the cartel.

"So, if I wanted to look for a job, you wouldn't mind?"

"What type of job?"

Cutting into my food, I took a piece of fish. "Haven't figured out if I want to go back to studying nursing or something else."

"You're young, and you have my support."

"Growing up, did your mom work?"

"She was a stay-at-home mom. What about yours?"

I stroked his hand. "She was a stay-at-home mom. My dad, as you know, renounced the family business."

"They raised a beautiful woman."

"Even the evil bitch that robbed you?" I tested.

Vincenzo laid his fork on the table. "Nothing about you is evil or a bitch. Let's take this food to go and get to the dessert."

Cupping my chin, I grinned. "Ready to spend the rest of the evening in bed?"

"I had a long day of meetings, and Angelina left my schedule in chaos."

Angelina would have been worse if he'd actually had a relationship with her. "Thank God you got rid of her. Does she know any of your side businesses? Like, are you worried she'll expose your family's cartel information?"

I leaned forward, and he grasped my hand, kissing the back of my palm. I was mesmerized by how attentive Vincenzo was when it came to me.

The waitress approached with the bill, and Vincenzo signed and left a tip in cash. "Do you need any money?"

He glared at me. "Never will you have to pay when out with me." Vincenzo cupped me close with his hand on my back. I tapped him on the nose, pressing a kiss on his lips.

Chapter 16

Vincenzo

With the new week rolling around, I decided to keep some of the details of what we were preparing for Cono to myself—especially after having dinner with Nyla and hearing her concerns about Angelina, and how she'd been keeping it under wraps that Cono had started to make a name for himself by reaching out to other board members and threatening them into supporting his seat.

Right now, I stood in front of our people at Calabresi Holdings, listening to the latest updates. Cono's whereabouts had come in, and he was staying away from his property. If I were in his shoes, then I'd do the same. Renato was already conducting searches for him at the locations we'd learned he liked to frequent.

"Vincenzo, tell us how we should go about keeping Cono from getting a vote on the board?" one of our oldest members asked.

"Cono Sartori set up his niece. My brothers and I are working on locating him as we speak."

"Well, the rumor running around is that he's not her uncle. Is that true?" another member interrogated me.

"Personal family matters won't get discussed today."

"Maybe we should discuss, I mean he's threatening all of us!" he blasted, and Savio connected eye contact with me.

"Clear the room," I demanded, hovering over my seat.

Each one filed from the room, leaving my brothers and father alone.

Savio demanded, "How the fuck did he find out this information?"

"You knew about the adoption?" my father challenged me.

"I just confirmed it before I came here to the office. Renato was supposed to keep the information to himself." I grimaced.

"She's become more of an issue than we need," Renato seethed.

"No more than Sonya." I cocked my head to the side, meeting his stare.

Renato jumped over the table, trying to reach for me, and Savio blocked him and pulled him back into his seat.

"Renato, sit down!" my father shouted.

Shoving him back, Savio shook his head at the both of us. "Cono wants us to fight so we're distracted. Renato we might not like the way Nyla came into our lives, but she's here now."

Renato, nibbled on bottom lip. "Keep Sonya out of your mouth."

"Same goes for Nyla."

"She fucking robbed you, and now you're playing fucking house. Fuck off!" Renato argued.

I balled up my fist, ready to go to war with my own

family. I raised my fist and punched him in the nose. Savio wasn't fast enough to stop me, and Renato stuck his tongue out, licking the excess blood.

"Is that all you got little brother?" Renato hounded.

Yanking off my jacket, throwing it on the chair. "What do you think?" I taunted, ready to bust him again. Sante stood to the side, rubbing his forehead.

"All right, you two need to cool off," my father said.

"He needs to grow up and learn it's the big boy's league now." Renato shoved his hands in his pocket.

"Fuck you, Renato. Right on time with the bully shit about my age. I've run Calabresi Holdings since I was 20; nothing about me is young and dumb."

Scoffing, he took the handkerchief from Savio's hand.

"Vincenzo is right, *and* Renato is right," Savio emphasized.

"Here we go, placing the blame all around," Renato mumbled to Savio.

"Take your attitude up with the wrong one, Renato, and see what happens. Vincenzo has run the family business fine. Yes, I step in when I should, but nothing has gone too off-the-rails," Savio said.

"He's gotten ahead of himself after getting shot during Cora's kidnapping," Renato brought up.

"What's that supposed to mean?" I sniped.

"Savio has no clue. You've put yourself into more of the cartel business than you should. Your role is corporate life. Let me do the real work." Renato pushed his chair out of the way, stalking from the room.

"Give him a little time, he's frustrated," Sante expressed.

"No reason to take it out on the family," my father growled, slamming his hand down on the table.

After turning off the video, I was left with Savio and Sante. "All right, leave him alone, so he can cool off. We need to get Cono," Savio insisted.

"I say we check out the strip club he owns and check Gianney out."

Sante kept his eyes on the printed photos of Gianney and Cono together. "Gianney's going to be a problem if we can't catch up with him."

"Cono knows we have our next meeting tomorrow. He's going to try to make a statement," Savio said.

"I agree, we can't let him get away with forcing our hand."

Savio passed my coat and chuckled. "Call Renato and tell him to meet us at the location."

"He's an asshole."

"He is—but truthfully, I noticed you coming around more at the meetings. I told you our father didn't want you involved in the cartel," Savio said.

"You and your brother need to understand, I'm grown and a part of the family. I have a right to be involved."

He stopped me before we got on the elevator. "If I felt you would not be protected, then you would not be permitted to attend family meetings. Understand that I might be looking into retiring, but I still have power, little brother." Savio clapped me on the back, then stepped onto the elevator.

I listened to Savio and Sante giving me the same fatherly advice to give Renato some space. I ignored it all as we made it to the Sartori's Lively Ladies Strip Club. After climbing out of the car, I shut the door, shifted my gun, and walked up to the guard.

He held up his hand to block us. "No guns," he said.

"Were going in with our guns. Cono wouldn't like for his family to be held back."

"Let me check with management."

Reaching for his hand, I pulled it behind his back and shoved him up against the wall.

"Get the fuck off me!" he yelled.

"Shut up and understand I can pop your shit out of the socket, or you can ignore us having a gun and keep your life," I threatened, pulling it up further, he hissed.

"All right, man!" he cried out.

"Glad you understand."

After removing my hand, he rubbed the soreness and stood off to the side, waving for us to go ahead. After stalking through the entrance, women walking around in only thongs smiled at me and my brothers.

Smoke filled the air, and women flirted with us from the DJ booth to the stage, making it known with their penetrating stares that if we wanted their company, then they'd be willing.

"You see him?"

Turning my head left to right through the crowd, I narrowed in on a crowd of men sitting in the back corner smacking on a girl's ass. A few glanced our way.

"We got company." Sante pointed at a few standing up coming in our direction.

"Cono must have alerted them."

"You're on the wrong side of town." The man was tall, the leader of the pack with tattoos around his neck of Sartori family.

"We're in the right place."

"Calabresi has a habit of going to places they don't need to be," he grunted, narrowing his eyes.

"Where's Cono?"

"Not here," he answered.

"If he's here and we leave, it won't be good for him."

"Sartori runs the entire block. Find you something to play with, maybe that sweet little pussy you call a wife," his friend said.

After quickly unholstering my weapon, I shot him between the eyes. He fell into the hands of his friends.

"Oh, my God!" a woman screamed.

"Shit, Vincenzo," Sante grumbled, pulling out his gun.

"You shot him!" their leader shouted, taking out his gun.

"We can end this now or figure out a way to coexist."

"Fuck coexisting. Cono told us about you trying to stiff him out of a seat with the alliance," their leader pushed.

"Savio!" A loud voice came from the back, and we saw Cono march into the room as other people scrambled to leave.

"Let's go."

"I'm not working off your emotions. Business is business, I have a right to get in the alliance," Cono suggested.

"We have more to talk about, unless you'd like to see more of your people dead." I shoved the gun into his chest.

"If you do anything to me, my niece will never forgive you," Cono taunted.

His comment made me think twice about putting the trigger. Nyla had tried daily to build a relationship with him—and even though he lied to her, it wouldn't be fair to end him without her knowing the full story.

"Take him with us." Snagging him around the shirt, I pushed him toward my guards, walking back to our car.

"Where are you taking me?" Cono investigated.

"We need information on Gianney."

"Gianney who?" Cono replied.

"Stop acting dumb." Pushing him up against the wall, I pressed the gun underneath his chin.

"We have evidence of you with Gianney. What are you two hiding?" Renato appeared next to me.

Cono scanned the sight of Calabresi surrounding him.

"I don't know Gianney," Cono spat, and Renato raised his fist and punched him in the stomach.

Dropping down low, Renato whispered in his ear, and Cono's eyes showed he was shocked.

"Bring him on," Renato said.

"Hold up," I said, lifting my ringing phone to answer.

My assistant spoke. "Mr. Calabresi."

"Yeah?"

"I have Angelina here wanting to talk to you," my assistant informed me.

"Tell her to leave."

"Sir, I tried, but she refused to leave," my assistant complained.

"Get security."

My assistant growled. "Yes, Sir."

"What happened?" Sante asked as I tucked my phone in my pocket.

"Angelina's acting stupid."

"Seems like she's becoming a problem." Sante walked to the left passenger door, I hopped in the back.

"She's not my problem."

Turning my phone on silent, I slide it back in my pocket and watch my men put Cono in the car and pull into traffic.

"Renato riding with them?" I pressed for confirmation from Sante.

"He's going to make sure that we get him to talk," Sante explained. While reading over emails, I listened to Sante and Savio discuss the kids having a playdate soon.

"Watch it!" Romo shouted, swerving to the right.

I dropped my phone on my lap. Looking up, I saw two cars box in Renato's van at the light, yank the door open, and stick a gun to his head. They removed Cono from the back. Six masked men rushed to get him in the back of their car, then drove off quickly.

"Turn around!" I shoved the door open, about to jump out, when I felt a hand on the back of my jacket, pulling me back inside.

Romo was driving backwards, stopping traffic so we could get to Renato, right as one of the men lifted the gun in the air.

"Get down!" I ran to the back and helped Sante cover Savio, as he helped Renato out of the van.

****

Renato paced back and forth in anger, holding an ice pack to the back of his head, annoyed at being caught so easily. All of us had come to my parents' home to regroup and figure out who they'd sent to take Cono away.

"I promise as soon as we catch them, they're all dead," Renato shouted.

"Calm down before you scare the women." I glanced in the backyard at the women talking and laughing.

"How many men were there?" Pops probed.

"Six, I counted six," I responded, standing next to Pops in the hallway.

"We need to talk to Nyla."

"No."

"Not up for debate. She's closer to him," my father said.

I pinned my arms over my chest. "She's still holding love for him."

My father stood firmly. "That can work in our favor."

Renato dragged on the cigar. "She's going to be pissed when she finds her real family."

"I want Nyla far away from Cono."

"Can't help it until we get him."

Nyla came into the house with Sonya drinking and laughing together.

"Hey baby." She roped her arm around my neck, pushing her lips on my chin.

"We need to talk," Renato said.

Nyla scanned the harsh faces of all my family.

"What's wrong?" Nyla waited, and Sonya stood next to her.

"Sonya, this is private," Renato remarked.

Sonya sassed, "Nyla wants me here."

"No, it's fine," Nyla replied.

Extending a hand to pull her into my lap, I pressed a kiss on her shoulder. "She'll be fine."

"Cono was kidnapped," Savio said, and Nyla stiffened in my arms.

Nyla's legs buckled. "Kidnapped for what?"

"We went to see him to talk," I said.

Nyla looked down at me. "Talk."

"Nyla, let us not play the innocent and naive route, you know what your uncle is trying to do." Renato blew smoke from his lungs.

"Renato," I demanded.

Nyla squinted her eyes. "I know he's out to try and get your family's company, but I wouldn't allow it to happen."

Renato guzzled down his glass of Gnarly Head 1924. "How can we trust you?"

I defended, "I trust her."

"Vincenzo knows I would do anything to get Cono to back off," Nyla pleaded.

"He's no longer going to have to worry about backing off; we're killing him," Renato announced, walking out of the room.

Nyla dropped her glass, jumped out of my lap, and ran from the house.

"Nyla!" I yelled, following to catch up, but Sonya stepped in front of me. "Let me try," she said.

"I will give you a minute, then I'm coming after her."

Sonya nodded, leaving me alone with my thoughts.

She won't leave me.

The ride home was quiet. Nyla ignored everything I said. Even when I tried to touch her hand, she pushed me away. After walking into the house, she went straight upstairs, not letting me explain the real reason behind Cono's situation. After jogging upstairs, I entered the bedroom before she could shut the door, then I slammed it behind us.

"Are we ignoring each other for the entire night, or are you willing to hear me out?"

"Nothing to explain."

I watched her remove her shoes and earrings.

I pinched the end of my nose. "Chef made dinner."

"Not hungry."

"Nyla, listen to me."

"I understand my mistakes, Vincenzo, no worries."

"Cono has you brainwashed."

She went rigid, turned to face me. "Brainwashed?"

"Yes," I said, undoing my cufflinks.

"He's the only thing I have left!" Nyla screamed.

I pointed at myself. "And me?" We've gotten close over the past few weeks and to know her motives weren't pure would confuse me.

"Vincenzo."

She tried to reach for my hand, and I took a step back. "My family has been patient with you, when most times we never do."

"I know what he's doing is wrong, but I need time to move on."

"Time has run out, Nyla."

"You can convince your brothers to give me more time."

Chuckling at her comment. "Come on now, Nyla. You grew up around him, and now Cono will use anyone to get ahead."

"Then I can talk with Gianney."

I gulped down a steady breath. "Why is Gianney so important to you?"

"He's my friend."

"You don't have friends; you have me—and that's enough."

She pitched her hands in the air. "Vincenzo, be serious."

I went into the bathroom, turning on the shower, pulled the shirt over my head, and threw it to the floor. Nyla stood at the counter watching me undress.

"My plan would be safe," Nyla announced.

"Safety is my priority."

"So let me do this one time."

"Nyla, drop it."

After stomping from the bathroom, I slammed the door. I was not up for her pretending to ignore me for the rest of the night.

****

An hour into my sleep, I turned over and felt the bed empty. After flinging the covers back, I turned the light on and searched the room. Not seeing Nyla, I reached into the nightstand, removed my gun, and marched into the bathroom, then checked the closet. I checked the guest bedroom next to me, pushing the door slightly open, and my chest relaxed after seeing her in bed, curled up. After placing the gun on top of the dresser, I bent down, shoved the covers back, and lifted Nyla into my arms.

"Mmmm, Vincenzo."

"Shush, go back to sleep."

"What are you doing?"

"Taking you back to bed."

She opened one eye, staring at me. "I was sleeping fine."

"I wasn't."

Nyla turned her back to me. "Not my problem."

"It is when you're not in my bed."

I laid her flat down on the bed, kissing her on the forehead. "Go to sleep."

She tried to get out of bed, and I pushed her back down. The tiny shorts she wore pushed up her toned thighs and had me licking my lips.

Nyla grumbled. "You can't force me to sleep in here with you."

"As my wife, you will sleep where I am and vice versa."

"Meaning?" she asked, crossing her arms, pushing her perky, plump breasts together.

"Either we sleep together here or in the guest bed, but I'd rather be here because the bed is firmer."

Nyla tried to step around me, and I cupped both sides of her hip.

"Move, Vincenzo." She moaned when I kissed her on the forehead and pulled her tight in my arms, caressing her cheek.

"I promise to keep you updated on Cono."

"You won't kill him?"

I pressed a kiss between her breasts. "Nyla, I can't promise you that he will live."

"He's wrong for lying, but Vincenzo, I still need answers."

"If he hasn't given you anything now, then he won't. It's emotional blackmail at this point, and I'd rather see him dead than torturing you even further."

Nyla nodded, dropping her arms, and fell into bed, letting me snuggle up next to her.

"Will your brothers always hate me?"

After pushing her hair from her face, I ran a hand up and down her arm. "Renato's just agitated. It's taking longer to get Cono."

Nyla released a strangled breath. "Renato scares me."

"Why?"

"I know he's married to Sonya, but if you had to, would you go behind my back and do what your brother suggests?"

"We can talk tomorrow."

Nyla's nostrils flared. "I need to know, Vincenzo."

"At the end of the day, my loyalty is to you and my family."

Turning in the bed, she faced the ceiling. "Maybe I can help you."

"Help how?" I clasped our hands together, kissing the back of her knuckles.

"Gianney reached out to me."

"Nyla, I told you if any contact happens to block him."

"He has something to tell me."

"Gianney and Cono are using you."

"Fine, Vincenzo. Face it. You have no faith in me." Whirling around to face the wall, Nyla shoved the covers over her body.

Rather than fight with her, I fell into a comfortable sleep, listening to her breathing slowly, as her soft snores poured throughout the room.

Chapter 17

Nyla

Sleep never really came. My head constantly went over our conversation. So, meeting with Gianney was the only solution to end all Vincenzo's problems. Cassandra hated to be disturbed from her sleep, but I had to put something in motion.

After tossing my napkin in the trash, I pushed my hair behind my ear, peering around, happy it wasn't cold or raining today.

"I need your help."

"What type of favor?"

"I need to meet with Gianney."

"Nyla, leave it alone."

"Cass, I'm begging you as my best friend."

Cassandra was able to meet me at the park after I called early in the morning. On Fridays, she usually had a lighter workload. I scooped more ice cream in my mouth, watching the runners go through the park.

"Shouldn't you leave it alone? It could be dangerous, Ny."

"Gianney messaged me the other day, when we were at lunch."

"What does he want?"

Shrugging my shoulders. "Not sure, he just wanted to meet to tell me something important."

"Where are you meeting him?"

"I told him about a café near my apartment."

"You mean your *old* apartment." Cassandra laughed.

I bumped her in the shoulder. "Come on! I won't take long; we can go to your place." I grabbed my purse and keys.

She rose from the bench. My guards trailed us a few feet back. Cassandra's face creased into a frown. "If anything crazy happens, then I'm calling the police."

I got in the car and shut the door. Cassandra dumped her cone in the trash then plopped in next to me.

"Carter, I need to go to Cassandra's apartment to pick something up."

The look on Carter's face said he didn't believe me.

"Promise nothing funny is going on," I said, holding up two fingers to show I wasn't hiding anything.

Carter explained, "We have orders to take you straight form the park to grocery store, ma'am."

"I know. I want to cook for my husband, but can you just run me quickly to Cassandra's."

Cassandra slid up further in the seat. "Mr. Carter, are you married?" she asked, flirting to try and distract him.

"What about Ralph?" I asked, nudging her in the arm.

Carter laughed at her, and she winked at him. "He didn't say no," Cassandra flirted.

As we left the park, I dug in my purse, reaching for my phone and sending a message.

Me: I can meet you at Cassandra's place.

Gianney: Is this a setup?

Me: Gianney, you know me better than anyone.

Gianney: All right, give me 30 minutes.

Me: Thanks.

Gianney: Cono is with me.

Me: Good he has some things to explain.

Gianney: A lot is going to be explained.

"Ma'am, I just got word your husband wants to meet for lunch," Carter announced.

"What restaurant?" I pouted, frustrated with my plans getting changed.

"His assistant said the lobby near Calabresi Holdings," Carter replied.

I sighed. "All right, I have a few minutes."

Me: Change of plans I can't meet now. How about in an hour or two?

Gianney: Vincenzo must have you on lockdown.

Me: Leave my husband out of it Gianney.

We arrived minutes later, and I hopped out of the car. Cassandra followed me into the lobby restaurant. The doors opened, and the hostess greeted me at the front.

Pushing my purse up on my shoulder, I said, "Hi, I'm meeting my husband for lunch."

"Name?"

"Calabresi."

She glanced at the reservation booklet, back up to me. "Is something wrong?"

"No, I have your table waiting," she expressed, walking me and Cassandra over.

I was taken aback by her weird behavior, but I shook it off, sauntering through the back, near the restricted area. She opened the door. My smile dropped the moment I noticed Angelina sitting at the table.

"Who is she?" Cassandra cocked her head to Angelina's table.

"Vincenzo's old assistant."

"His girlfriend," Angelina teased.

"Can I get you something to drink?" the hostess asked.

"No, I won't be staying."

"Come on, Nyla." Cassandra turned, grabbing my hand to escort me out.

"Vincenzo is only babying you until he can get rid of your uncle," Angelina spat.

Panic set in at her knowing our business. "What?"

Angelina sloped her head to the side. "I heard him."

"Heard what?"

"Vincenzo and his brothers, talking about your uncle's plans."

"Angelina, you have no idea what you're talking about."

"The more you push him away, the more he tells me things." Angelina's lips turned into a taunting grin.

"Vincenzo assured me that you no longer work with him, and his dick belongs to me." I got in her face.

"For *now*—but he knows when the baby comes, I'm going to be wearing that ring," Angelina taunted.

I struck up my hand to smack her across the face, but Cassandra pulled me back before I made contact.

"Please hit a pregnant woman and see what happens to you," Angelina pushed.

"What evidence do you have of Vincenzo being the father? Even you being pregnant is farfetched."

Sticking her hand in her purse, she pulled out a pregnancy test and laid it on the table.

"Ewe, that's nasty," Cassandra shivered.

"Keep your lies and the fake pregnancy test to yourself; we're good." As I walked away, I felt my heart drop at him having a baby with her.

"You don't believe her, do you?" Cassandra stopped me at the door.

"I mean it's weird she's still around after he said she was gone."

"Nyla, don't let her get under your skin." Cassandra reached out to pull me in for a hug.

"Thanks. Let's get to your place before I forget."

"Well, hopefully, Gianney will be a little saner." Cassandra slapped hands with me, and we locked our arms together.

****

Talking with Cassandra reminded me to give Vincenzo a heads-up. Carter stopped outside her building, and I went to unbuckle my seatbelt.

"Put your hands in the air!" a masked man suddenly demanded.

"Oh, my God!"

"Cassandra, relax."

"What you're doing won't end well," Carter announced, and I looked out of the window searching for anyone I could signal, when my eyes squinted at the end of the street, seeing Gianney standing there, smoking a cigarette.

"Wait! Carter, it's fine."

"Nyla, what are you saying?" Cassandra hissed at me, tears rolling down her cheek.

"I will be right back."

"Nyla, no!" Carter tried to reach for me, and the gunman hit him over the head.

"Stop! Leave him alone. I can handle it, Carter. Just stop hitting him," I pleaded with the gunman.

Carter safe, Gianney had his men pulling a gun out on my guards, which would cause more attention than we needed.

I shoved the door open, leaving my phone and purse, walking slowly down the street to meet Gianney. Dropping the cigarette, he held both arms open, I leaned forward returning his hug.

"Nyla, it has been a while," Gianney said.

"I would say I missed you, Gianney, but you have a weird way of showing your feelings."

"Sorry, I had to make sure we weren't coming into a trap."

"My friend is in that car, tell your men to fall back."

"Can't do that."

"Gianney, explain to me what you want."

Gianney flickered a crimpling glower at me like I was behind all of his problems. "Cono was kidnapped, did you know?"

"Yes."

What I would never do was let Gianney cause me to doubt my husband or show weakness that he could use against our marriage.

"By your husband."

"I know and he promised not to hurt him."

"Well before he made that promise, a few of my men grabbed him."

Bile pooled at my throat. "Cono is hiding with you?"

Gianney hit me with a bladed stare. "Yes, he wants to see you."

"I've tried to see him. But he keeps dodging me." Holding all of my family secrets to blackmail me and Vincenzo shows Cono only cares about himself.

Gianney pushed his hand out to touch my arm, and I jerked back.

"You have no real protection out here besides me, Nyla."

"Why do you say that?"

"Cono tell you about your family?"

"Yes, I'm adopted."

"Did he tell you who your real father is?"

"No, did he tell you?"

"Look, Mark and Cono kept a lot of shit from you."

"Just tell me the truth."

Gianney stepped close to me. "Greco. Does that name mean anything to you?"

"Gianney, I know your last name. Get to the point." I waved my hand in the air.

"Greco is one of the founding families in the alliance. Your birth father is Gennaro, and your sister is Viviana, an ex-girlfriend of Savio's."

My stomach twisted in knots. I stumbled back, not believing any of his words.

"Gianney, I think you are confused."

"No, I'm your brother, my father and I didn't get along. He basically disowned me, and the public had no clue about me. I learned about their deaths, and Cono has helped me track down the real killers."

"I have to go." I started to jog away.

He grasped me by my hand. "Nyla! Wait."

I snatched away. "No! Leave me alone."

"He's trying to kill you and wipe our family out; you need to work with us!" Gianney yelled.

I hopped back in the car, and his gunman backed up, letting us drive away.

My body convulsed, tears streaming down my cheek.

"Nyla, breathe, please," Cassandra begged.

"I need to get home."

"Carter, are you good to drive?" Cassandra evaluated.

"I will be fine. Keep her relaxed, we're going to the hospital."

"No!" I screamed.

"Nyla, you're shaking. You need to see a doctor," Cassandra pleaded.

I wanted to ignore them both. "Take me home, I will be fine."

"We can have the family doctor come and check her out," Carter said, ending his phone call.

"Who were you talking to just now?" If Vincenzo found out Gianney and I met up, hell on earth would start.

"Mr. Calabresi said to bring you straight home."

"Where is he?"

"At the office."

"Probably with his bimbo," I mumbled under my breath.

"Nyla, you can't believe her after everything."

"Cassandra, not now."

Sighing, she released my hand. "Having an attitude with me won't help your situation," Cassandra remarked.

The hurt in her voice made me think twice before I pushed her away. "Cass, I'm sorry."

She stared at me, then nodded.

Arriving back home, I tossed my head on the pillow, looking at old pictures in my photo album I got from my old apartment. Cassandra decided to go back home, and Carter sent her with another escort so he could wait for Vincenzo to get there and talk about the details of my meeting.

The loud beeping of the alarm distracted me, and I dropped the pictures in the box, then walked out of the game room. After climbing the stairs, I heard low voices, and I paused at the top of the stairs, against the wall.

"Angelina did what?" Vincenzo questioned.

"She ambushed Nyla at the restaurant. She thought it was you, and somehow, we got word from your assistant that she thought you wanted to meet her," Carter went on.

I peeked my head out to watch.

"Find Angelina and bring her to the cabin."

"She said she's pregnant," Carter responded.

"Does Nyla know?"

"She does."

"How pissed is she?"

"There's more."

He pinched his brows. "Fuck."

"Gianney had his men at her friend's place."

To avoid being seen by either of them, I hid behind the wall.

"How the fuck did he get close to her again? I'm paying top of the line for security, Carter."

"I agree, and I will rectify the issue," Carter emphasized.

"What did he tell her?"

"She hasn't said a word since we got back."

"All right. Get my brothers on the line and find out what Cassandra knows and Angelina."

As I stepped into the room, they stopped and stared. I threw a hand between them. "Don't let me get in your way."

"Nyla." Vincenzo stalked toward me.

"Vincenzo, did you know Angelina is claiming to be pregnant by you?"

He sighed. "Carter just told me."

"Congrats."

He frowned. "She's not pregnant—at least, not by me." He walked up to me.

"Stay there."

"I can't touch you now?"

"Distance is better, I can't think straight with you this close."

He smirked and lifted my chin. "I'm distracting you."

"Vincenzo, right now the smirk is not helping you."

"Gianney and Angelina are two people not in this room right now."

"Are we even now?" I asked.

Chapter 18

Vincenzo

I kicked off my shoes and tossed my jacket onto the chair, then I shook my head. As if seeing her for the first time, I could not believe how beautiful she was —whether she was dressed up or wearing a simple shirt and shorts around the house. The clothes she wore now didn't do her body justice. Her white panties covered her sweet pussy, and I could not resist freezing the picture in my mind forever.

"Vincenzo, you can't go around killing people."

In a hurry, I climbed onto the bed, spread her legs wide, and grabbed both of her hands above her head.

"Since when do you make demands?"

It was apparent that she was starting to cry. I needed her not to fear me and understand that my feelings are real, although it was a mistake in the beginning of getting together. I had to bring her around my family and see how she reacted and if she could handle my world.

"Just let me go," she cried out as I slowly slid a finger deep inside her.

"No."

Her eyes began to shine even more when I wrapped my hands around her neck gently.

It was clear from the first day she walked into my casino that she was different, that this would be different. I gave one long luscious lick to her that caused her to shudder.

"What do you want from me?"

"Everything." I dipped my head low, pressing my lips against hers, took my left hand, and pulled her panties down slowly as her essence dripped onto the sheets.

I smirked. "She's ready for me."

Her nipples strained against her blouse for me to taste them. I heard her breathless moans escape her lips. Nyla could act out if she wanted, and play like she didn't want or need me, but I knew the truth. With my hands lifting her legs up, she crossed her ankles, and I selfishly stared at her smooth, bald pussy, retracting in heat. I nuzzled my nose in her slickness, and her arousal pushed my dick straight up, ready to make love.

I never made love.

Nyla placed her hand around my hardness. "Aghhh, please, fuck me."

"Is that what you want?"

I watched her eyes delve into a lustful haze, and all my logic melted at her touch.

Nodding her head wouldn't suffice for me, she had to say the words for me to know it was a done deal.

"No more doubts."

Wildly she stroked my dick. "None."

I moved down as her hand dropped from my dick, peppered her sensitive skin with my finger then tongue.

I could tell her past lovers never made it about her pleasure, so tonight she'd be showered as the Queen I knew that she was and should be treated like. Nibbling on the back of her thighs, I reached, caressing with my right hand up to her feet. I wanted to see how many orgasms I could get out of her from both my tongue and penetrating her pussy. Trembling beneath me, Nyla held onto the sheets, and I moved to her right leg giving her the same light nibbles. Easing my tongue in slowly, automatically she tried to grab the back of my head ,and I gently smacked it away.

"Enjoy the ride."

Her legs started to fall down. "I can't take it...." she panted.

I spat on her pussy, diving back as if it were my last meal, touching her pearl as she arched her back in pleasurable cries.

I felt pre-cum already forming, and I needed to be inside of her now. I stood, removed my pants, twisted her body to the side, got on the bed, and pushed my dick in slow, with my head tossed back, and my eyes closed. Her thighs glistened after the first few thrusts.

I might have to deny how much her body is making me feel things, and it was starting to piss me off how Mark had the opportunity to even look at her pussy. My thoughts got the better of me, but hearing Nyla's moans pulled me back at the scene in front of me where my dick was soaked in her nectar.

"God damn, Nyla."

"Kiss me."

I flicked my tongue around her nipples, hovering over her body, as her legs were draped over my shoulders, giving me extra room to dive into her warmth.

"Keep your eyes open."

The hazed look in her eyes spoke volumes that something was transpiring between us. If we could call it a mix between lust and love, but much deeper connection I never had with any other woman. *She had a hold on me.*

Pounding my hips, pumping harder, her lips parted and her hand clawed at my arm, nails hooking. I abruptly pulled out, feeling her pussy grip my dick. I wasn't ready for her to come.

"You... oh...Vincenzo," she gasped, biting her lower lip.

I smirked at her response. "Nobody can fuck you like this, Tesoro."

"No one," she agreed.

I circled my hips, turned her over, helped her to her knees, closed her legs together, and stroked her faster. I caressed her back, kneaded her ass, and groped her breasts. I thrusted in and out, seeing the ripple of her ass, and her stretch marks moving in sync. My dick swelled and betrayed me once again, and I moved faster against her, teasing her to ecstasy, as she arched her back. I kissed a blazing trail down her throat. I heard the mixture of my groans and her moans, and our bodies were ready to explode. I already knew we'd go another two or three rounds before I let her sleep tonight. While paying extra attention to her sensitive nipples, I curled my tongue and enjoyed her reaction. Her hands moved from my head down to my back, and her face curved in deep passion. The way she defied me and her smart mouth turned me on and pissed me off at the same time, I had the biggest nut orgasm arising, as my spine tingled and my toes curled.

"Fuck, Nyla!"

"Please let me come," she whimpered.

Wrapping my arms tight around her waist, I brought my right leg up higher for a deeper angle. My head fell back, feeling her waterfall turn into squirting all over my stomach and the bed.

"Ohhh... I'm coming," Nyla shuddered.

I pulled out of her, stroking my dick, as my orgasm spurted ropes of come onto the bed and across her ass.

Flopping back on the bed, I held her close, while our breathing subsided. I kissed her on the forehead.

"You fucked the feeling out of my leg," Nyla said with a frown, and I threw my head back in laughter.

"I can carry you to the shower."

"Too tired to shower."

"No sleep until you at least have three more orgasms tonight."

Her eyes popped open dramatically. "Three more."

"That's your punishment."

"I could get used to that."

"Mouth needs to handle something else for right now, get up so we can take a shower."

After stretching her arm around my neck, I carried her into the bathroom, then turned the shower on. I made the water the temperature we both liked and let her enter. While she started to shower, I changed the sheets, and then jumped back into the shower to fuck her again before we headed to bed.

Chapter 19

Vincenzo

lasses clinked around the room, and voices complimented the good food that our chef made every night. Her feelings were hurt from being confronted by Angelina's fake pregnancy, and I had my people on the lookout to find her. Angelina never took being fired easily, and my brothers told me that a woman scorned would do anything to get my attention. The ultimate disrespect was talking to my wife and making her think I had a meaningful relationship besides the one we'd built together.

Her tantalizing smell still lingered on my nose as I'd had her bent on the very table where we ate dinner in our home.

"Vincenzo, did you hear anything I said?" Madre broke me from my daze.

Taking a gulp of water, I cleared my throat. "Sorry, tell me again."

My mother's brows drew together in confusion. "The trip to Greece."

"I have to see if I can get time off."

"You own the company," Rena blurted out.

I frowned. "Rena, your comments aren't helpful."

"She's right," Sonya joined in on bashing me.

"Rena, Sonya. Leave it alone please," Nyla defended me, and my eyebrow went up, watching the stare between Rena and Sonya toward me.

"How is business going for you? You're newly married; I think spending time with your wife is more important," Madre complained, giving me more of a headache than the girls.

"Our marriage is fine."

"Nyla, do you agree?" Madre's face twisted in surprise.

"Adelina, leave it alone. All the boys know the most important thing about a marriage is keeping it between the two people involved," my father said, backing me up.

"I promise we'll be fine." Nyla smiled, her facial expression back to normal.

"What about the rest of your family on your mom's side?" Sonya inquired.

She played with her food. "Sadly, I haven't kept up with my mom's side; all my life was spent with the Sartori side."

Soon as dinner was finished, the guys came down to my man cave for a late-night drink. Unlocking the cabinet, I poured my finest bourbon, and Pops lit his cigar, taking a seat in the lounge chair.

"Your mother is nosy; you have to forgive her," my father said.

I lifted a glass, passing one to Savio, then Sante. Ignoring his statement, I went into business mode. "Renato, find out if Gianney's place is guarded with double security."

Savio's pinched glare matched my father's. Learning to keep our disagreements to ourselves is the best way we can move forward, unlike my brothers' wives. Any problems they had, the girls would involve me in some way and put us at odds. I refuse to make our marriage a topic of discussion at dinner, or alone with the guys.

Sante rose up to refill his glass. I took a seat at the bar next to Renato. "How many guys are you talking?" Sante marched back to the couch.

"At least a dozen. Cono was seen a few times entering and leaving," Renato explained, displaying the photos on his phone.

"Are you prepared to kill him?"

"Yes, why wouldn't I be?"

"He's her uncle; no matter what, it's going to be hard for her," Savio recalled. A worried expression flashed over his face.

"She will get over it once we can live peacefully."

"Not if you're destroying the little family she has left," Savio mentioned.

I flinched at the thought of her having to deal with the betrayal of her parents.

They made valid points, but it was time to move on from the lies and the corruption of the Sartori family, along with Greco.

"Tomorrow, we meet with Greco's higher-ups and see if they've had contact with Gianney. Afterwards, we take him down." I chugged my drink. Each one raised a glass in the air, concluding our night and leaving.

I stood at the window, staring out at the silent night in the backyard. When I first built this home, I never wanted a family, and now, seeing the gazebo and the garden of fresh flowers I gladly had installed for Nyla, it spoke to what she'd brought into my life.

After sprinting upstairs, I checked to make sure that the alarm was set. I wanted to get a good rest before tomorrow's events. It could either be a point of no return for our relationship, or the beginning of better memories after all the pain people had brought into her life.

****

The next night, we sat in the back of the club, watching the Greco cartel sit around, laughing and drinking together. Our money came in on time every month, so Savio had no reason to confront us about any issues. If I were them, then I'd hate us, since we killed their boss and all their top-made men, then put our own leadership into place over their territory.

Duran appeared, extending his hand for me to take. "You asked to meet."

My eyes scanned his right-hand man, Macario, who cocked his chin up, standing, while Duran pulled his chair out in front of us.

"New team is running business smoothly," Savio said.

"No problems so far," Duran answered, tracking each man with his eyes.

"We have a problem, and I hope you and your men aren't involved." Catching the eye of his next in command, his top lip twitched, showing he knew what I was about to bring up.

I reached into my pocket, lifted the two photos of Gianney, and pushed them into Duran's face.

"Where is he?"

"We have no contact with Gianney."

"Duran, you and our men eat off our product. The time for games is over."

He looked away from me. I sensed the lies were about to roll off his tongue.

"Look, Gianney came to me because he wanted to find some sister of his."

"Sister?" I repeated, icy glare pinned onto them.

"Some girl, Natalie, Nikki, what was the name?" Duran snapped his fingers in thought.

"Nyla," Macario said, making a rush of fear fill my body.

Jerking the photo from his hand, I lunged at him, pushing the bottles and ice on the ground.

"What the fuck are you talking about sister?"

Duran held hands in the air. "He came around one night talking about she's his sister and they were supposed to reconnect."

Releasing him, I slipped my cell out to dial Nyla's number, hearing it go straight to voicemail.

"What else did Gianney say?"

"We're not a part of whatever beef Gianney has going on." Duran tried to wiggle out of having to answer for any lies.

Gianney texted Nyla a few days ago and probably put into her head that we were the enemy and that she should stay away from us. His random appearance after all of these years only showed that he was trying to take us down.

Duran trailed behind us out of the club. "Whatever you have going on with Gianney, is that going to be a problem for us?"

"Nyla, pick up," I growled into the phone. I paused in front of the club, frustrated that she was not answering.

"Bring Gianney to me, and we'll discuss it later."

"Greco territory has nothing to do with Gianney," Macario grimaced.

After waving a dismissing hand, Renato put them in order, and we drove back to the house. I sat in the back with Savio and Sante sitting across from me as the car left the parking structure.

"I told you something was up with her and Greco," Renato huffed.

"You think they're really related?"

"What other reason would he have to want her on his side?"

"We found the truth about Cono and Gianney working together. Maybe Gianney would lie to save himself," I answered, searching my phone for the private investigator we'd used in the past.

"Who are you calling?" Renato challenged.

"Private investigator. There's more to this story."

"Story is that Gianney has Nyla in his web, and if she plays you again, I promise she's dead," Renato argued.

"Carter gets us to the house," I say, placing the phone on speaker.

"Vincenzo, glad you called," Manual said.

"Tell me something good, Manual."

"I have some news you might not like, and before you chew my head off, the information is factual."

"Savio and Renato are listening."

"All right. I looked into Gianney Greco's relationship to Cono, and it goes back to when he was a child."

"In what way?"

Manual stated, "He's a god-uncle to him, and their families have done business for many years."

"Shit."

"I'm thinking that when he was a teenager, he found out his father was a big mobster, and he learned of his sister's lineage."

"Get to how Nyla fits in the Greco world."

"Her mother had a brief relationship with Gennaro Greco; as usual, he wanted nothing to do with the baby, and her mother found love with Cono's brother and got married."

"Did Nyla spend any time with the Greco family?"

Manual described, "From what I have gathered her mother was still pregnant when she left him, so none of the family even saw the baby."

"Damn."

"No type of contact, and now he's using it as advantage to go against us."

"As revenge."

"Nyla's going to be devastated."

"Cono knows about everything?"

"He's been in correspondence for years with Greco, making sure he knows what to do once Nyla is told the truth. Cono had a letter drawn up making it look like her mother and stepfather.

"Motherfucker needs to die now," I fussed, grinding my teeth.

"For now, calm down; working yourself up when you're about to see her for the night won't help."

"Are you saying I should keep it to myself?"

"No, we're saying wait until you have a moment to gather all the information," Savio stated.

Renato unlocked the car door, climbing out. "Savio's

got a point. Throwing out accusations will make her shut down."

"All right, Manual. Send me everything tonight."

"I will, Vincenzo."

Gianney: She's going to know the truth.

Whether it's tonight, tomorrow, or next week. Gianney decided to play with the wrong one, and his feelings must be hurt from not being the golden boy in his father's eye. Reading his text message fuels my ideas on how much he's going to suffer at my hands.

Me: She might be your sister, but she's my wife.
Gianney: Funny because she's still in love with Mark.
Me: If I was insecure like you, that would have me questioning my woman, but I have real boss moves to make.
Gianney: Have your fun now, but Nyla won't be around you much longer.
Me: Real boss would meet in person.
Gianney: Soon.

Maybe it was wrong to taunt him further, but fucking with me was no longer an option.

Savio hung around the bar in the living room. I flung my jacket on the couch, then ran out to find Nyla. I didn't see her in the kitchen, or my office.

"Nyla!" Calling her name, I pushed the bedroom door wide, seeing the bed made and her things still in the closet.

"Where did she go?" Renato startled me, as he walked into my bedroom.

"Probably with your wife."

"Hey, babe."

I swiveled around to Nyla holding bags in her hands. "Where were you?" I grabbed the bags from her hands, placing them on top of the bed.

Kicking off her heels, Nyla took her purse and put it on top of the dresser. "Out shopping with Cassandra for my birthday."

"Your birthday."

"Yeah, I turned 23," Nyla answered, peering between Renato and me.

"Why didn't you tell me?"

Renato stepped out of our bedroom.

"Honestly, I didn't think you would care."

"You are my wife, Nyla."

"I get that, but we're still learning each other, and putting stress on you to do something for my birthday felt wrong."

Catching her hands, I pressed them to my lips. "Celebrating you is important to me."

Grinning, she said, "Thank you."

"So, what do you want to do?"

Nyla picked at my suit jacket. "Um, Cassandra and I planned dinner."

"Cancel it."

"Vincenzo, you do a lot for me already."

"That's what a husband is supposed to do for the woman he loves." I rubbed my hands up her arms, down her back.

Blinking her eyes. "You love me."

"Yes, which means a big celebration is needed."

"As long as I have you there."

I kidded and pulled her close to me gently slapping me on the chest. "Listen before we get too far ahead, I want to talk with you," I said.

"Okay."

Hesitating, I sat her on my lap and ran a hand up her thigh, then pushed her hair from her face and admired the dimples in her cheeks.

"I—" My phone blew up, interrupting me.

"Could be about business. Go ahead. I'm going to take a shower and get dinner started."

"You're cooking?"

Nyla stood, sauntering to the bathroom. "The food at your parents was fine, but I'm still not completely full."

"Let me get rid of whoever is calling." Checking the unknown number, I stood up and walked out of the bedroom.

"Vincenzo?" There was a whisper of fear in the voice.

"Who's asking?"

"Angelina."

"Angelina, why are you calling me?"

She confessed, "I miss you."

"We've never been more than a fuck buddies. Get it out of your head." I shut my office door behind me.

Angelina taunted, "Does she know you're going to be a father?"

"She told me about you trying to ambush her." I adjusted my tie.

"That girl is blind to what we have, and you know she's not worth the time. You need someone who understands your world."

"Angelina, get it out of your head, we are done when I find you."

Angelina's chilling voice stabbed me in the chest. "You're threatening me, Vincenzo? Is that what happened to Viviana Greco?"

I froze at her statement. "Angelina."

"No, you listen—and clearly—to me."

There was a knock at my door, and when I pushed it open, Renato stood waiting to enter.

"Nyla will be fine once you divorce her and marry me."

My jaw slackened. "How would that happen?"

"Draw up the papers and have her sign, then I can promise to get the evidence you and your brothers have been looking for to destroy."

Hovering at my desk. "Cono contacted you?"

Irritation at her taunting voice crept up my spine. "Crazy to believe I have to go about threatening you to get you to see the real me."

"Angelina, know we will be seeing each other soon." Hanging up the phone, I cast it on the desk.

"Angelina is still lurking around?"

"Everyone has to die."

"It's time you learned that giving people the chance to change doesn't end well for a Calabresi." Renato watched me pace back and forth.

"Nyla's birthday is next week I need to get the girls to help me plan something on short notice."

"Call them and keep her distracted so you can focus on finding our enemies."

"We can start pulling all of his old locations where he's done business." Slouching down in my chair, I jumped on my computer and started searching where Greco's distribution of products used to come from before we took over.

"Savio is going to make some calls," Renato remarked.

"Can you check out phone records and find Angelina? Living at her old place is out of the question since she knows about the blackmail."

"I will be in touch." Renato swiveled around and left my office.

Informing Nyla about Gianney—on top of planning her birthday with Angelina still sniffing around—would put us back in a place we'd moved away from. Having to protect her at all costs meant handling any problems without her getting hurt.

Chapter 20

Nyla

"Nyla, what are we doing here?"

"I need to get some information from Gianney."

Cassandra poked her lip out, staying behind me as we walked to the location where Gianney wanted me to meet him without Vincenzo. I gripped her hand, then looked down at the address on the paper, and then back up at the empty building.

"This is the place."

"Do you see anyone?"

"No, let me knock."

She yanked me back. "Nyla, are you sure about meeting him alone? What if Vincenzo finds out?"

"Cassandra, stop worrying. Vincenzo will understand."

I raised my hand up to knock and it opened automatically. "Who are you?" a tall figure with long arms asked, with a gun in his hand pointed at our faces.

"Oh, my God!" Cassandra shrieked, gripping tight to my hand.

I pushed her behind me, with my chest poking out.

"Is Gianney here?"

"Marciao chill out." I heard Gianney's voice come up to the door.

Marciao probed, "Who is she?"

"No one for you to worry about." Gianney gestured for us to come inside, shutting the door behind me.

Keeping my eyes on the guy with the shotgun, I was rethinking coming here to talk when Vincenzo told me to stay away from him, even though I knew Gianney had always been a friend during the early days of meeting him and Mark.

"Does he know you're here?" Gianney sat on top of his desk, and I stood next to Cassandra.

"Who?"

"Vincenzo, your husband." Gianney reached down, picking up a cigarette and a lighter, then puffing out smoke.

"I'm not here to talk about my husband."

Smirking and nodding, he scanned Cassandra with his eyes. "Your friend looks scared."

I turned to Cassandra. Her eyes stayed glued to the guards in the room.

"Gianney, you texted and left me wondering about my family."

"Did you find out any more information?"

"Not yet, so tell me the truth."

"The Greco cartel is well-known. I learned about my family's name when I was younger."

"How am I connected?"

"Vivianna is our sister. The Calabresis killed our family."

I stepped closer. Cassandra pulled me back by my

arm, but I nudged her hand loose. "How do I know that's true?"

"Vincenzo told you his brother made the call?" Gianney answered.

Relaxing my shoulders, Gianney wasn't giving me anything concrete. "Tell me the truth or I'm walking out of here and never coming back."

"Cono is right, you need to get him a seat at Calabresi Holdings and alliance."

"I have nothing to do with Vincenzo's businesses."

"As a wife, you have a perfect setup to get him onboard. We can get the Greco and Sartori families at the head of the alliance."

"Vincenzo never talks to me about business. I doubt he would even believe me if I canvassed to put Cono in as a voting power."

"Either he backs you up, or his brothers will have to contend with the other families coming together to take them out." Gianney lifted a piece of paper off the desk, then extended it to me.

"Is this my mother?"

"With the Greco family when she was pregnant by my father."

"What else do you have?"

"More pictures and a letter of my father giving you up."

"Let me see it?"

"Only when I get what I want."

"If were related then you should want to help me find the truth."

"Cono is expecting you to hold up your end of the bargain."

"Vincenzo trusts me now, and I am no longer using

him for someone else's gain." After whipping around, Cassandra and I marched out, leaving him calling my name. After coming to the door, I yanked it open to a pile of men and Vincenzo standing there, with a scowl on his face.

"Should I be worried?"

"Very." Vincenzo extended his hand, and I slipped my palm into his, scanning all the deep frowns on their faces. After opening the door and climbing in next to Renato and Savio, I felt like I was a kid in trouble.

"Cassandra is coming with me."

"She's seen too much. After we have a talk, you can contact her." Vincenzo slammed the door on me.

Cassandra had a worried look in her eyes.

I slammed my hand against the window. "Vincenzo, I am not a child."

Renato motioned to Gianney's business. "Are you working for him?"

"I refuse to talk to you unless you tell me what I want to know."

"Nyla, my brother and I feel Gianney and Cono are using you," Savio explained.

"Funny. He said the same thing about you and your brothers."

"In what sense?" Savio squared his shoulders.

"Tell me the truth about Vivanna Greco and how she died."

"We have plans for your birthday." Vincenzo placed a hand on top of my thigh and squeezed.

"Keep playing these games, Vincenzo. Gianney's starting to sound right."

****

231

"Here, since you want to know what my family is trying to keep hidden and protected." Vincenzo dumped a pile of papers in front of me.

"Where did you get these?"

"A private investigator found out Gianney is using our beef to come back into the alliance." Vincenzo stood over the bed.

Picking up the files, I see Cono's name on a few letters between my mother and father.

While covering my mouth, I sat back, disgusted at how Cono played my parents and me for years, lying about the adoption and plotting with the Greco cartel to take down the Calabresis.

"He worked with Greco to take me from my parents when I was a baby."

"Cono's dangerous, Nyla."

I rubbed my temples and lied back on the bed, tears pooling in my eyes. Every picture-perfect moment was a setup to use me as a pawn.

"Gianney will do anything to bring you back into his lies. He doesn't mean you any good."

"I hear you."

"What do you want to do for your birthday?"

"I'm still going out with the girls." Turning to rise out of bed, I sit at the vanity mirror, checking my foundation and blush.

"The Casino has a room ready for you."

"Thank you. We will more than likely walk the floor a little and do some gambling."

"All right, just stick with Carter for the rest of the night."

Coming up behind me, Vincenzo ran a hand up the back of my neck, pressing a kiss on the top of my head.

"Will you drop by and hang out?"

"Soon as I make sure things are good for you and your friends, I will join you."

"Great. It's time we start enjoying ourselves and leaving my family's drama out."

"Here's my present." Slipping his hands down my back, he takes ahold of both ass cheeks, grinning.

"Down boy."

Biting his top lip, he groaned, and I captured his lips one more time then released him, grabbing my purse and shawl.

Turning 23 was not a big deal, but I was grateful to have a husband who wanted me to be happy and protected me and his family.

We piled in our respective cars. The girls each had a car with their husbands, leaving the kids at home with the grandparents to come out and celebrate my birthday. Renato and Savio had reservations about me, but I honestly ignored our last conversation to focus on my relationship with Vincenzo. One thing I did learn was how to put what was important first, above everyone else.

While interlocking our hands on the drive, I listened to Vincenzo give out orders to the staff that we'd be arriving soon. He did all the planning with the girls and set up a private area in the restaurant at the casino for about twenty of us. Cassandra decided to bring Ralph after talking with him these past few weeks.

Glistening lights filled the front entrance, along with a red carpet and photographers, like we were real celebrities.

"Vincenzo, you went all out."

"Anything for you."

"Thank you, but don't you need to keep a low profile."

"We're businessmen above all else, baby." Vincenzo winked, pushed the door open, helped me out, and shut it behind me. He wrapped his arm around my waist and grinned for the cameras.

"Mr and Mrs. Calabresi, over here." A photographer called our name as more cars pulled up, guests waving and stepping to the side waiting to get in the picture.

Cassandra barged through the crowd, grinning wide. "Nyla, you look amazing."

"Thank you, so do you. I see Ralph is here." Sticking my finger out, I poke in her arm.

"Taking it one day at a time."

I leaned forward, whispering in her ear, "He must have eaten that pussy."

"Ate it all up." Cassandra giggled and had me dying laughing. Vincenzo shook Ralph's hand. I guess he'd learned not every guy is trying to fuck his wife.

Vincenzo directed everyone to follow inside through the front entrance. I lifted the train of my black Gucci gown. Vincenzo's money had come with a new wardrobe upgrade, and I had to tell myself not to turn it down every time I came across what I liked. The wives reminded me that spending their billionaires' money was what they wanted us to do.

The restaurant had a large sign on the front entrance with a picture of me posing from a photo that Vincenzo must have taken when I wasn't looking. My locks were high on top of my head, my long diamond earrings were dangling, and I was showing my curves in a pink lacy dress.

Cupping my chin, I tried to will the tears away from falling. Missing my parents was the worst, but having a new family to enjoy these moments made me feel better.

"Here's your private area, Mr. Calabresi." The hostess motioned to the back room, a long table decorated in pink and black, my favorite colors.

"Baby, you've done too much." I walked around the room. The table had name cards; Cassandra was next to me, and Vincenzo sat at the other end of the table.

"There's more coming, and I have the club ready whenever you want to go." Vincenzo grasped my chin, sticking his tongue in my mouth.

"Save the love for when you're home please," Rena huffed.

Vincenzo stepped back, wiping the lipstick off his lips. I took a seat as the waitstaff poured our champagne.

"Toast before I go check on the food. To my beautiful wife, you and I came in like bulls, clashing in the beginning, but I have no regrets and I love you more and more every day," Vincenzo said.

"I love you." Raising my glass in the air, I danced in my seat in excitement. Vincenzo left the room as I listened to Cassandra and Ralph read the menu.

"A preset menu?" Cassandra emphasized.

"All of my favorites."

"After, we have the club, right?" Cassandra investigated.

"Yes, and we have a VIP section," I acknowledge.

Our appetizers appeared, but Vincenzo hadn't returned. I finished off one glass and poured another.

"Can I get something a little stronger? It's my birthday!" I laughed, slapping hands with Cassandra.

A two-hour meal with friends and family—plus presents—became the highlight of my night next to dancing in the DJ booth. I dropped my purse and shawl with some of the girls in the VIP section while Cassandra and Rena came with me to dance on the main floor. The guys told us to not get too out-of-hand. For the most part, we stayed together and respected their request. As soon as the song changed, I jumped up to stand next to the DJ to see the crowd really get turnt up for Rihanna.

Popping my fingers, and bending over dancing with Cassandra, we showed out. Ralph came up behind her, holding her close, and I thought he'd started to loosen up with the group as a whole.

"I need to get something to drink. I will be right back," I said, fanning myself.

"I'm coming with you," Cassandra replied.

"No, you're fine. Keep dancing. Won't take but a second." After climbing downstairs, I moved through the crowd, then headed to the bar. I felt the sweat dripping down my face. I grabbed a napkin to clean up a little and gestured to the bartender to give me another drink.

"Here's to the birthday girl." The bartender passed me my drink. I gave him a thumbs-up and stepped off the stool, rocking my hips left to right. I gulped the rest of my drink, placed it back on the counter, and almost tripped when I felt arms around my waist, catching me.

"You need to be careful."

Smiling, I turned and dropped the smile from my face and back up from the cocky smile on Gianney's little friend Macario."

"How did you get in here?"

"Just exploring the club, baby."

"Yeah right." I pushed by him, darting from the DJ booth to the VIP area, not seeing Vincenzo or his friends. Stomping down the hall, I approached the bathroom, and figured he might be in his office. Turning around, I headed to the employees only hallway. I slipped a hand up to knock on Vincenzo's door when I noticed it was partially open. I pressed up against it, listening to multiple voices.

"He dies now."

"She's going to want to know."

"She's your wife, you explain it to her. When it comes down to it, she's a Calabresi now and loyalty belongs to the family."

"I get it, Renato; but killing Cono and Gianney isn't easy when we still don't have the evidence."

"They're bluffing."

"Giving any type of leeway will show our weakness to the alliance."

"Vincenzo is right. If Gianney has the evidence hidden, we need to have Nyla find it and destroy it," Savio argued.

"What if she decides to use the evidence on you or blackmail the entire family? Are you willing to get rid of her for the family?" Renato challenged.

"Do you hear yourself?"

"Sonya knows the discussions we've made when it pertains to the business. The Calabresi name is to be upheld," Renato said.

"Calm down. Renato isn't so quick to agree with killing his wife," Savio assured us.

"Because you made the choice years ago to protect McKayla after what she witnessed," Renato examined.

"I will do it for the family," Vincenzo responded, agreeing to kill me.

I stumbled back. My stomach felt sick; everything I ate at dinner was starting to come back. I needed to figure out a way to get the evidence before they did.

After running out, I bumped into a few women, and

they congratulated me on my birthday. I put on a fake smile, then left to find Cassandra. While glancing around the club, I noticed her back in the VIP room with the other wives. Rena and I made eye contact, and I felt she knew something was up.

I sighed to keep my composure, then I went back to the VIP room to take a bottled water from the ice bucket.

"Where did you go?" Cassandra tapped me on the lap.

"Um, to the restroom. Actually, I'm not feeling well. Do you ladies mind if I leave early?"

"Do you need aspirin or food?" Rena checked.

"Probably sleep, been a long day."

"Will walk with you out." Sonya rose from the booth, and I waved her off.

"Promise to call you all when I get settled. Tell Vincenzo I will see him later."

"You don't want him to leave with you?" Rena asked.

"Uhm, he's enjoying himself."

"Nyla, what is going on?" Sonya and Rena folded their arms, huddled around me.

"I can't talk here."

"All right, we can leave," Rena said.

I raised my hand up in the sky. "No, it would look too crazy if everybody leaves."

"Did Vincenzo do something to you?" Cassandra chimed in. Her fists balled up.

"Cassandra, I promise to call you later." I left a kiss on her cheek, hugged Sonya and Rena goodbye, and rushed out of the club.

After seeing Carter standing next to the car, I hid behind a group of strangers, hailed a cab, and hopped inside.

"Take me to this address please." Lifting my phone, I

showed him the address from the loose paper Gianney gave me.

"Yes, ma'am." The cab driver hit the gas, driving out of the parking structure.

I turned off my phone to avoid any distractions. Coming over late in the evening would make Vincenzo upset with me, but Gianney gave me no choice. While leaning my head back on the car seat, I thought about Vincenzo, constantly being in the position to choose either me or his family, and I felt it might be better to leave the marriage and start over fresh in another country. His life was a nonstop roller coaster of me inserting myself and my family that had lied to me and cheated me. My mom loved a man who didn't love her and pushed off his child to be raised by another man over a business arrangement. She and my stepdad wanted me for me; they never looked at me as a means to money.

"We're here, ma'am." The cab driver stopped.

I slipped $50 from my purse, handed it to him, and shut the door. I looked around the streets at a few people standing around, then I came to the door and knocked. One good thing about living with Mark was knowing how to break into a place. After walking around the side, I noticed a window, and the lights off inside. I climbed onto the garbage bin, tested the window, and saw that it was locked. After taking a rock, I tapped it gently to break the glass, then slipped my hand through, praying I wouldn't cut myself too much, then I unlocked it. After climbing in, I pushed it back down. The room was empty, and it looked to be abandoned, like the entire building. After strolling to the door, I peeked into the empty hallway. After remembering the office that he had down the hall, I sauntered toward the room, tried the doorknob, and shoved the door open.

"Look for the evidence," I whispered to myself. Running to the desk, I pulled each drawer open, only seeing a few sheets of dates and times for visits.

"Where is he keeping the evidence?" I put my hands on my hips. There was no computer in the room, only a couch, chair, and a desk.

Before I could check, I heard loud talking coming from the front door.

"He's out with Nyla. It's the perfect opportunity to take her now," Gianney's voice growled.

Unable to hide, I grabbed my purse, slipped behind the door, and waited for him to leave.

"I have it on the flash drive. The copies will get destroyed once I know we have the alliance on our side. Fuck Calabresi Holdings. You keep trying to be one of them, and you will find yourself dead." Gianney chuckled evilly.

I heard the footsteps stop.

"Wait, I think someone's here," Gianney whispered.

I covered my mouth to hold in the cries of help.

"There's glass on the floor, and the window is broken. Fuck! Meet me here."

Ending the call, Gianney took slow steps, and my heart pounded as I waited for him to catch me. Coming here without any support was foolish and naive.

A loud smash startled me, followed by more loud voices, then gunshots.

"Where the fuck is my wife?" Vincenzo shouted.

Chapter 21

Vincenzo

"**B**oss, are you alright?"

I turned to my guard who had just gotten out of his car which was parked behind mine. "I'm fine." I kept my composure—before cursing everybody out for letting her slip out of the club and take on Gianney herself.

After having the doctor check her vitals, I stood outside the bedroom, waiting to go in and see if she was awake.

As soon as Cassandra came to me looking for Nyla, I had the entire casino shut down to keep anyone from doing something underhanded—especially if they worked at my place of business and helped them take her. I had too much on my plate from Angelina to Gianney and Cono, thinking we'd back down and let it slide. It was shocking that they came together against a common enemy, but it was also understandable. All three were jealous of who we were, and what we'd accomplished as a cartel family and business.

Unable to hold out any longer, I turned the knob,

gently shoving the door open, and I spotted Nyla, with her eyes wide.

Doctor, a long-time physician for the family, followed her gaze to me.

"Mr. Calabresi, she's going to be fine."

"Thank you. Can I have a moment with her?"

"Sure. Remember, she needs rest," the doctor answered.

I cupped her hand and stroked her cheek, but she avoided eye contact. "Tell me what you're thinking," I said.

"You hate me."

"If you dented my car, I could hate you, but putting yourself in danger is never an option," I said, joking to break the mood.

Trying to sit up, she flinched at the pain. "Gianney's my brother."

"I know."

"He's using me to get under your skin."

"I heard."

"I overheard you were planning on killing him."

"How do you feel about him?"

Shrugging her shoulders, she said, "Be real with me, Vincenzo."

"Always, Nyla."

"Where would we be if I never robbed your casino?"

I ignored her question. "Aren't you the one who told me we should leave the past there?" I was focused on her getting better and enjoying a real birthday.

"Gianney said the evidence is on a flash drive."

"Why would you go alone, Nyla?"

"Because I felt everything having to do with Cono and Gianney was my fault."

"Baby, they've been after us for years. You were just their pawn to use and dangle in my face."

"Can you forgive me?"

"Never was mad, but going off and doing things on your own is not an option."

"I want to help."

"No."

"Vincenzo, I'm a big girl, I can handle Gianney, let me talk to him."

"You already tried talking to Cono, and nothing came out of it."

"It will be different this time."

"How?"

"By having you there. By going as a team."

"He's held up at the cabin."

"You caught him?"

"Before you passed out, we wounded him and got him locked up. He's not talking, but we were able to search his place of business and his clubs. Nothing was found."

"I might be able to help." Shoving the covers back, Nyla reached for her purse and tensed up at the pain.

"What are looking for?"

"I need my purse."

I picked it up from the nightstand and handed it to her.

Searching her bag, she removed her cell phone, scrolling through messages. "At first when I saw him, he gave me directions to his place of business."

"Okay. We searched and didn't find anything."

"What if the numbers were to a safe?"

"Maybe, our tech team will need to descramble the numbers." I groaned and started to stand to leave.

"Wait! I'm coming."

"Nyla, you need sleep."

"No, we need to get to the bottom of the bullshit together." Grabbing ahold of her robe, she tightened it around her waist.

"One hour you can stay up with me, while I make some calls."

After clasping our hands together, I stepped out of the room and strolled to my office. Most of the guys lingered around, on the phone, coming and going, while the guards stood on alert. My parents called all night, checking up on Nyla, wanting to be there, but I felt it would be too much —plus, her friend and my sisters-in-law hovering only kept her from resting.

"Sit here on the couch." I pointed, watching her roll her eyes and slowly sit back with her legs kicked up under the pillow.

"While you make calls, I should have the guys search Gianney's bank records."

"Already being handled."

She cocked her head against her arm. "So, you thought of everything."

"Soon as you left the casino, you had me worried, so I had to put as much force behind finding you."

"There's something else we need to talk about."

"What?"

"Angelina."

"I know."

"Are you doubting I believe her?"

"No, she and I were never an item or serious."

"I get it, Vincenzo; but she's convinced you're the father of her child."

"A lie, and she's going to get dealt with because she's working with Cono and Gianney."

"You are lying!"

"Sit down and relax, before you pass out again." I rushed around from the desk, helping her to sit.

"Sorry, I moved too quickly."

I stood and headed back to my desk, then lifted the phone and dialed my private eye. I put them on a three-way call with my tech team.

"Manual, we need additional information."

"I got word on Cono," Manual answered.

Nyla and I gazed locked in at his comment. "Where?"

"A home he's using near Chesterton."

"Hiding in plain sight."

"I can send the location and get a few police on payroll to keep a lookout."

"No, that will spook him. Send the address." Ending the call, I glanced up at Sante, standing in the doorway.

"Gianney's on ice if you're ready."

"I want all three of them."

"I'm coming with you." Nyla rose from the couch.

"No. Rest is the only thing I want you to do to save your strength." I peppered kisses along her cheek and shoulder.

"You promised to not leave me out."

"Promise. I'm going to grab him and bring him back."

"Okay, and Angelina needs to be handled."

I stared back at her. She had a pout on her face. "Get dressed and stay quiet," I demanded.

"I can come?"

"Yeah, stay in the car until I can make sure everything is safe." I slid the coat on my shoulders.

Grasping the back of my head, Nyla kissed me on the forehead. "Thank you."

"Anything for my wife."

****

We were sitting outside the restaurant Angelina was spotted in. Traffic wasn't too heavy in the late afternoon, and I'd made the trip with Nyla, so she'd know my loyalty belonged to her only and no one else. I was tired of playing games with people who thought they ran our lives. Nyla gripped my hand tight, and I held the door open. Angelina sat at a small table with another woman.

After peering at Nyla's perplexed gaze, I stopped her from moving forward. "You look like you've seen a ghost."

"She's here."

"Who?"

"Nancy." A hard glare crossed her face.

"Nancy?"

"Mark's mother."

Taking in the older woman sitting with Angelina again sent sickness to my stomach. Angelina stepped to the lowest form to get back at Nyla and expected me to fall back in her arms.

"Wait!" I tried to hold Nyla back, but she stalked to the table in a huff—even though she was still in recovery after passing out.

"Nancy, what are you doing here?" Nyla challenged.

Nancy glared at Nyla. Scanning Angelina's snarky smirk made me wish I'd brought Rena with us to smack that look off her face.

"Nyla, good to see you for once," Nancy snapped.

"Excuse me? What are you talking about?"

"Vincenzo, you married a woman who abandoned the family of the man she claimed to love," Angelina snarled at Nyla.

"Nancy, whatever you think you've heard is a lie," Nyla announced.

"My son is dead, and you're with the man who killed him!" Nancy shouted.

A few guests turned to look at us.

Nyla's mouth dropped agape in shock.

A small smirk was on Angelina's face. A better way to get under a snake like her would be to remove all her options.

"Your son deserved to die." I gritted my teeth, and Nancy gasped in shock.

"Vincenzo, let me handle it," Nyla begged, blocking my eyeline of Mark's mother.

"How dare you? My son would never rob a person like you! I'm calling the police." Nancy slid her hand into her pocket.

Nyla turned swiftly, plucking it from her hand.

"See I told you, Nancy. She's just as corrupt and probably had Mark killed to marry him in the first place."

The entire restaurant went quiet when the backhand slap went across Angelina's face.

"Fuck you, Angelina. Nancy, if you think I will take the fall for your son's crimes, you are sadly mistaken."

"What I know is that you've disappeared and never returned my calls." Nancy jumped out of the chair.

"My life has not been easy, and after Mark's death I had to figure out how to pay off his debts."

"She found a way," Angelina hinted, pointing at Nyla's ring finger.

Nancy's eyes zeroed in on Nyla's hand, then she reached out and snatched it. Nyla yanked it from her grip.

"He told me you would be the death of him one day. I begged him to leave you alone."

"Same thing I said about him."

"His entire life revolved around making you happy. I think it was your idea to rob him and set my son up," Nancy claimed.

"You can believe whatever you want, but if you try my hand, I will get the police involved," Nyla muttered, stepping in her face.

"Or what?" Nancy replied.

"Fuck around and find out, Nancy. My husband doesn't play about me."

After lifting her bag from the chair, Nancy stormed out of the restaurant. Not wanting her to get too far away, I nodded at my security and directed them to follow her.

"All of your threats won't work on me," Angelina taunted, picking up the wine glass and taking a sip.

"If you want to walk out of here without a fight, I suggest you stand up," Nyla voiced low.

"So, you can kill me?!" Angelina shouted.

I'd had enough of her childish antics. After taking out my gun, I placed it on the table and took a seat, pulling Nyla onto my lap. I stroked her cheek, gently brushed my lips on top of hers, then slowly crushed our lips together, guiding my tongue into her mouth.

"Vincenzo! Get the fuck away from her." Angelina stretched her hand out to shove Nyla away.

On reflex, I raised the gun and shot her in the chest.

Nyla jumped in my lap. I laid the gun down and held her close. After standing, I grasped her wrist. I stared into Angelina's eyes, watching the rise and fall of her chest.

"Nyla is right where she belongs. I warned you."

"Vincenzo, people are looking," Nyla whispered, gripping my arm and peering around the restaurant, half full. Shoving my gun away, guards picked up

Angelina, dragging her out to the van we had on standby.

"Get their information and make sure that we have no issues," I explained to the manager and hostess of the restaurant.

After helping Nyla into the back of the car, Renato appeared with Elio near the van. After kissing Nyla on top of her head, I stepped away to talk about clearing the restaurant out.

Elio glowered at the drama I created for him to clean up. "How many people saw what happened?"

"Enough to know we'll either have to pay some off or handle them accordingly."

"Cameras are probably installed," Renato commented.

"All right. Anything else I have to fix?"

"Nancy was here with Angelina."

Elio hiked a brow. "Nancy."

"Mark's mother."

"You let her get away?"

"No security is trailing; she's making threats about knowing we killed Mark."

"Handle Angelina first and send the men to keep an eye on Nancy's house," Elio commanded.

"You want her to disappear?" Renato slipped black gloves on his hands.

"Like she never existed."

"Sante said you're heading to pick up Cono in Chesterton," Elio reminded me.

After shaking hands with my brothers, I hopped in the car. Renato went into the restaurant with Elio after talking to the manager and hostess outside. Carter rushed from the area. I dialed Savio to give him an update.

"Renato informed me you took it upon yourself to make a move in public," Savio grimaced.

"Had to be done, she wouldn't stop."

"Cleaning up behind you is pissing me off, Vincenzo," Savio voiced.

I take a glimpse at Nyla's worried stare. "Then don't."

"Where are you heading to now?"

"Handle Cono."

"Then you've made your decision, and I can't stop you."

"No, you can't."

Hanging up on Savio would have us in a fistfight, but I had already decided to put an end to everyone who was trying to play with our relationship.

Traffic had us arriving an hour later.

"Stay here while I check out the scene."

"No, I'm going with you."

"Nyla, you need to stay here. The less you're involved, the better."

"There's blood on your shirt." Nyla ran a hand down my sleeve.

"Once I take care of him, we can go home."

"Not this time, Vincenzo. You took care of Angelina. Let me prove my loyalty."

Cuffing her cheeks, I said, "Your loyalty was proven when you married me."

"It would be better if I go. He's not expecting me, and his guard will be down."

Facing the small gray-stoned home, we saw a car in the driveway.

"I'm going with you."

"Give me your gun."

"No."

"I know how to shoot, and I promise to be careful."

"Never wanted you this deep in cartel business."

"Nothing will happen to me. Cono is finished, and he can't manipulate me anymore."

I took in her words and felt she would be safer if she were next to me when I killed him, so I agreed to let her go in—only to see me make sure that he took his last breath.

"Keep the car running," I told Carter.

Nyla grasped my hand. Most of the neighborhood was inside or gone; the street was pretty quiet. After looking around, I raised my foot, kicked the door, and knocked it off its hinges.

I saw Cono jump in fear and try to run off. After lunging toward him, I shoved him back in his chair.

"Cono," Nyla called his name.

"Get your fucking hands off me," Cono growled.

"Cono, where's the flash drive," Nyla hissed.

"Fucking slut!" Cono snapped, and I balled my fist and punched him in the face.

"Where is it?!" Nyla screamed, snatched my gun from my holster, and pointed it at his head.

Both of us were caught off-guard by her boldness. "Nyla, give me the gun." I released Cono, reaching for her hand.

"No, back up, Vincenzo. Cono doesn't scare me anymore."

"You think because he married and gave you the Calabresi name that means something?" Cono growled.

"What I know and believe is that we're leaving either way with you dead," Nyla responded.

Nyla's stark response sent arousal to my dick. It might have been wrong to want to fuck her after she killed her uncle, but the way she wasn't scared and was ready to end him after torturing her for years was making me proud.

Squinting his eyes, Cono glanced back at me. "How did you know I had it?"

"Gianney. What made you pull Angelina into your little trick?" Nyla voiced.

"I thought that if you were distracted by Angelina, then I could use her to take him down."

"Why? I'm your niece."

Cono held Nyla hostage with guilt. "Nyla, you were never my niece, just a way for me to get ahead."

"Did you have something to do with my parents' death?"

"Answer her!" I barked.

"He got in the way," Cono explained.

"Speak up," Nyla chided.

"Your mother and my brother learned of what I was doing, and I put a hit out on them. I made it look like an accident."

"For money, all of it over money," Nyla muttered.

"Think of what you can do if our family is in the alliance. Forget Chicago; we could go to the highest and make moves with our names in rooms," Cono examined.

Tears fell down her cheek.

"Sorry," Nyla murmured to him.

"Nyla, as your uncle you have to understand my choices were to keep the Sartori family from crumbling. Debts had to be paid."

"And Mark... I was so stupid."

"Mark couldn't do anything right, and I wish I was the one that killed him," Cono griped.

"One thing we agree on, Uncle Cono."

Nyla took off the safety.

Cono raised his hands in the air. "Nyla, think about what you're doing!"

"I have."

"Talk to her! Killing me would start a war."

"A war you started long ago Cono," I said.

"Nyla, give me the gun. We can talk and come up with an alternative," Cono pleaded, trying to look around for an escape.

"I would ask you to tell my parents I love them, but we both know you're going to hell." Nyla's finger pressed the trigger, blasting him repeatedly with bullets.

I slowly walked over to her, gently slipped my hand around the gun, and took it from her hands, whispering in her ear, "I'm here. I'm here." I kissed her on the forehead.

"I shot him," Nyla whispered in shock.

"Nyla, listen to me."

"Vincenzo, I killed him."

"Baby, you had no choice. He was never going to stop."

Wiping her tears, Nyla nodded, rubbing her hands down her pants. "What about the neighbors?"

"Elio will have someone make it look like a robbery. Let's go."

After putting the gun away and slipping from the area, we climbed in the car with Carter. I stared at Nyla between texting with my brothers about our next moves.

Chapter 22

Nyla

I was in the bathroom, showering after having tossed my clothes in the trash. Vincenzo stood at the bathroom door, watching me rinse off the suds.

Carter had run through as many lights as he could to get us back home and away from the scene.

Killing Cono gave me a weird feeling. I kept switching from not caring to becoming a little upset that he pushed me to make that decision. Cono had to have the last word and make my husband out to be the bad guy, when all along, he and Gianney were trying to destroy us. Turning off the water, he held a large bath towel in his hands for me to grab. Removing my shower cap, I walked to the sink and brushed my teeth, and moisturized my skin. My stomach growled, reminding me I hadn't eaten since earlier in the morning.

Feeling strong hands around my waist, a longing set of eyes captured my gaze.

"Tell me the truth."

"I have."

Running a hand up my shoulder, around my neck. "You're still shaking, Nyla."

"My first time using a gun." Turning in his hold, I faced him.

"It was a decision you didn't have to make."

"You took care of Angelina; it was only right I handled my uncle."

"A husband handles any threat coming at you."

I closed my eyes, inhaled his scent. "What about Gianney?"

He leaned back and smiled. "He's next on my list."

"Can I come?"

"No."

His stubbornness seeped through, and I slowly backed up on the counter and slipped on top, opening my legs wide for him to enter. Unbuttoning his shirt, I stared into his eyes.

"Mmmm..." I moaned, peppering kisses along each finger, then sucking them into my mouth.

"Nyla, tesoro, you're playing a dangerous game."

My fingers entwined with his. "Right, then punish me."

He removed the fingers I had in my mouth and slipped them into my pussy, gripping the back of my neck and sucking on my throat.

"Vincenzo!"

"Fuck, you're sexy to me right now." He grinded against my pelvis.

I bent back a little, giving him more room, pulling my towel away. Watching his intense stare, he twisted my nipples, and I threw my head back as he latched on, sucking like a baby.

I reached out to touch his beard. "Aghhh, yes!"

"Baby, you're fucking intoxicating."

"Vincenzo, fuck me now!"

After lifting me off the counter, he moved us into the bedroom, and I snatched his shirt and pants off. We climbed into bed, and he flipped me over onto my stomach. After locking his mouth onto mine, he breathed life into me.

"Aghhh!"

After smacking me on my ass, he moved down to kiss the sting away. I held the back of his head, looking over my shoulder at him as he ate my pussy.

"Right there!"

Shaking his head, he wrinkled his nose. "You fucking killed for me."

I brushed a thumb over his soft plump bottom lip. "I would do it again in a heartbeat."

Vincenzo's lips curled, and he released my right breast and moved to the left one.

"My wife is a fucking lady." He pinched my nipple.

"I'm your lady and your bitch."

"My pretty bitch. Can you handle this dick, baby?"

Vincenzo teased me, running the head along my entrance before pulling back.

"Stop playing!" I hissed, backing into him.

He chuckled and pushed me flat on the bed, taking both of my hands, binding them together, and trailing kisses along my back, sticking his tongue in my ass.

"Fuck! Sweet and tight for me."

"Too much for you, Vinny," I taunted, feeling another sting to my ass, and then the feel of his dick pushing forward.

"Oh, God!" I cried. His dick filled me up.

"Take the dick like you're supposed to, Nyla. Show me what you can do."

His words were a challenge, and I knew if I gave him a reason to think he outfucked me, then we'd have a debate forever.

Releasing my hands, he fell flat on top of me, pumping faster, whispering in my ear all the things he wants to do me for the rest of our lives.

"Vincenzo, I love you."

Slipping my leg out a little more gave me more access to go deeper, and we both groaned in pleasure. The obsession Vincenzo has me in I can admit started when we first met, and I wondered how he'd be in bed, and each time has lived up to those expectations.

"I need to come!"

"Only come when I tell you to, pretty lady." Easing out, he slipped his fingers inside like a dick stroking me fast. My eyesight became blurry and skin tingly, seeing stars.

"Vincenzo! Please, oh, God."

"Listen to me, Nyla, and listen good."

"Yes! Anything I promise." His tongue became my favorite toy, taking his groan into my mouth, savoring my taste. Driving his long thick dick to my entrance, his hands journeyed from my hips to my waist, resting just shy of my breasts. Circling his hips, he pulled me close to his chest, anchoring his leg on the bed. Breathing heavily, his fingers playing with my clit gave me double pleasure.

"You are mine, and when I tell you something for your own safety, you listen."

"Okay," I whimpered.

He drove hard, lifting my head with a hand around my throat, the other on my stomach, squeezing not too tight, but enough to make me feel his presence. Right when I thought he could do nothing else, he smacked my pussy, over and over. Grunting in my ear how I will take his dick every time like a good little wife.

"Oh yes, shit... keep going." I shuddered and almost fell when he held onto me tightly as I came, then he released his own orgasm right behind.

I turned to face him. He hovered over me. We fought with our lips to be the top alpha, and I relaxed in his arms, wrapped my legs around him, took hold of his dick again, and slid him into my pussy. He roared in my ear after slamming into me. Sensations tightened in my chest; it felt like we were floating in the air. The entire room seemed to spin as I felt his bare, slick skin against me, and we came together again, then caught our breath.

"How do you feel about me going to talk to Nancy?"

Opening his eyes. "Talk to her for what?"

"Maybe I can convince her we had nothing to do with Mark's death." Flipping on my stomach, I ran a hand through his hair, watching the frown on his face turn into a scowl.

"Nyla, you want me to be honest with you?"

"Yes."

"She's already dead."

After catching his gaze, I didn't flinch. "I guess it was a matter of time. She spoke too much in public."

"We thrive on loyalty, and the moment someone challenges our name, it becomes a problem we need to eliminate."

"I understand."

"How do you feel about killing Cono?"

"Are you asking if I'm sad?"

"Any type of feeling is something."

After straddling his lap, I lied flat on his chest, kissing each nipple, then along his throat, before gently biting and sucking on his ear.

"Your dick is still hard."

Our moment of pleasure came to a halt as we heard loud banging at the front door.

Vincenzo picked me up, moved me to the side, yanked the drawer open, took out a gun, and then took his phone off the charger.

"What's going on?"

"Carter's at the door." Vincenzo slipped on his boxers and pants, then rushed downstairs.

"Wait, Vincenzo."

Whipping around to face me, he shouted, "Stay in the room."

"No."

"Nyla, I need you safe."

"I'm safer with you."

He shook his head, grumbling under his breath. "Put some clothes on."

After rushing into the bedroom, I snatched my robe, tights, and a t-shirt. "Oh, my God." I quickly jolted from the window after seeing a few cars outside the property. I sprinted downstairs to find Vincenzo at the door with Carter.

"Greco's people sent a message. If you don't release Gianney, they'll make a move."

Vincenzo watched his men shoot at the vehicles outside our house.

I turned and ran back to his office. After picking up the phone, I dialed the first number I could remember.

"This better be good," Renato grumbled, through the phone.

"Renato, it's Nyla."

"Nyla, why the fuck are you calling me from this line?" Renato blurted out.

I shook my hand, afraid to think the worst. "Um, Vincenzo is shooting at someone."

"Nyla, calm down and talk slowly. What happened to my brother?"

Calming my breathing down. "Carter came to the door and said Greco sent a message."

"Stay inside. Vincenzo will be fine, and I'm on my way," Renato declared, ending the call.

Running back to the front foyer, Vincenzo wasn't there.

"Vincenzo! Vincenzo!" I screamed, running outside, watching him stand in the middle of the font yard with a gun in each hand, shooting back.

The bullets sparked off the railings, the gate, and the cars.

"Vincenzo!" I shouted his name, he turned to look back.

"Get in the house!" he shouted, and my heart dropped when he fell to his knees.

"No!!!" I panicked, running to him.

All eyes stared back at me. When I saw my husband pass out, blood seeping from his body, adrenaline kicked in and I wanted revenge, even more than what happened to Mark. When I saw his body start to fall, I was grateful for how quickly Renato came when I called. At first, I was worried that he thought I had something to do with Vincenzo getting shot, but we had security cameras installed, and Carter explained how two cars rode by suspiciously twice and started blasting warning shots. Savio, Sante, and Elio checked in on me almost every 30 minutes while Renato was out front, going over the cleanup. The luxury of living away from prying eyes made it easier, because with no neighbors close by, no cops were called to investigate.

It took two of his men to carry him into the bedroom. Carter called the doctor and gathered more men to cover for the rest of the night—in case they came back.

"Vin, are you hurt?" Renato and Savio helped him to sit down in the chair, Elio played the video from the surveillance.

Watching him try to hold back on the pain, he said, "I'm fine," and rubbed a hand down his face.

I stayed, hovering around the doctor in our bedroom while he checked the bullet wound. "I'm not leaving him."

"Please, help me out," he begged the doctor to be on his side.

"Vincenzo, you were shot."

"A graze wound, pretty lady." He sat up from the bed, and Doctor packed up his supplies, to leave.

"I know you won't listen but get some rest. You still have soreness from the first time you got shot," the doctor said.

"Don't worry, Doctor, I will make sure he stays in bed."

Vincenzo's upper lip rose into a smirk.

"Sleep, not fucking," Renato said, sauntering into the room.

"Renato, watch your mouth," Savio huffed.

Shrugging, he moved in closer to check over his little brother, and they slapped hands in greeting. Vincenzo got up and moved to the chair in the corner. He picked up his robe and put on the grey sweatpants that he usually wore around the house.

"Where are you going?"

"To talk with my brothers." Vincenzo wrapped his arm around my shoulder, kissed me on top of my head.

"The Doctor said you needed to rest."

"I will, once we check the camera."

"Renato already checked the cameras."

"Nyla, we're not about to argue."

Throwing a tantrum would send us back to square one, so doing the next best thing, I smiled in agreement. "Let's check the cameras."

"You're not coming."

"Why not?"

"It's business."

"She sounds like Rena," Sante mentioned.

My eyes darted over to him, and they all snickered.

"Either way, you're not leaving my sight."

Vincenzo sighed, stretched his hand out for me to take, and locked his around my palm.

I leaned on my toes and kissed him on the lips.

"Glad you're safe."

"Takes more than one drive-by to kill me, baby." He ran his hand down to my ass.

I nudged it away, embarrassed at his brothers seeing him flirting. I hinted at what was next. "Gianney's people made a move, so now we have to retaliate?"

"She's right—even though I hate to admit it right after a shooting," Sante remarked.

I tried to wiggle off Vincenzo's lap, but he had a tight hold on my waist.

"Are you sure I'm not too heavy?"

"No," he answered.

I cupped his chin, and he grinned. I rolled my eyes at his playfulness."Not funny."

"Duran, Marciao, all of them need to be taken out—even if they weren't in on the shooting," Vincenzo announced.

Savio, Elio, and Sante all nodded.

"Can I handle Gianney?" I asked.

"You already have one death under you; maybe you should lay low," Renato suggested.

"They touched what belongs to me."

Vincenzo's left hand grazed up my back. "What's that?"

"My husband."

I made myself a target the minute I told him I loved him and that I never helped Cono with his plan. There was no turning back now.

Savio took his ringing cell phone and left the room. Elio and Sante watched the video back-to-back, whispering together.

"Are you hungry?"

"Huh?"

"I asked are you hungry?"

"Vincenzo, why are you asking me about food right now? You were shot."

"A normal routine in our line of work."

"Is this why your brothers never wanted you in the cartel side of business?"

"Bingo." Renato scrambled something on a piece of paper, slipping it in his pocket.

"Go out with your friends and do some shopping."

"You're just trying to distract me."

"Yes," Vincenzo answered, nuzzling his head in my neck.

"All right, but I won't be gone for long."

"Take Carter and Romo," Vincenzo said.

"Soon as you move on Gianney, I want to be there."

"Promise."

"Renato, make sure he keeps his word," I pushed.

****

Two Hours Later

"Carter, you let her talk you into doing some crazy shit," Cassandra huffed from the back seat.

"We're going shopping, I promise. Then we can have dinner at my place."

"Does your husband know you're going to your ex-deceased, best friend's house?" Cassandra smacked her lips.

"Ohhh...why so angry?"

"All right, wannabe housewife, this ain't a reality show."

"I won't be long. Vincenzo said he's expecting to confront Gianney and his men about the attack." I shoved the door open, knowing that Nancy, Cono, and Angelina were already dead. A feeling in my gut told me that Gianney could have the missing flash drive stashed in his place after the shooting at the office building. The blackmail that Mark and my so-called "uncle" tried to do was finally over, and I was no longer afraid to live my life fully. I crept up to the door, taking in the quiet scenery at his gated, one-story home, covered with "No Trespassing" signs.

"We are going with you," Carter imposed, getting out of the car.

It was around lunchtime, and there weren't too many cars around. I was glad that it was a Thursday, and not the weekend, since he lived on a street with a lot of kids.

Carter scanned the area. "You know how to break into a house?"

"Yeah."

Carter's eyes grew wide.

"My ex-boyfriend unfortunately taught me a lot of things that I will take to my grave." After picking the lock, I remembered that he didn't have an alarm, so luckily, it opened without a problem.

"What are you doing?" I asked Cassandra as she stalked up behind me.

"Praying that you change your mind. I'm not stupid enough to stay in a car if something goes down," Cassandra responded.

"Gianney had a small safe that Mark told me about where he had his most important papers. If he worked with Gianney, then Angelina got ahold of a copy."

The living room was painted in modest browns and tans, with a small fireplace, and a TV hanging on the wall.

"When's the last time you were here?" Cassandra remarked.

"Probably a year or so ago." While checking out the pictures on the wall, my head did a double take after seeing Mark and Gianney when they were younger. Both had to be no more than 17 or 18, and they looked ready to cause trouble.

"Here." I strolled into the bedroom, pushing the closet

door open, shoving the rack of clothes to the side, and on the floor a small steel safe sat.

"Let me grab it," Carter mentioned, and I stood back.

"Do you think something is inside?" Cassandra challenged.

"Probably. Take it with us."

Carter untucked his gun, holding the safe in the other walking in front of us for protection.

"What if we were Gianney's people?" Vincenzo's wide smirk on his face told me I was in trouble.

"How did you know I would be here?"

"My wife wants to protect me and all I want to do is protect her, so I figured coming here would be the spot." Vincenzo approached, holding out his hand for me to take.

"Your arm."

"Pretty lady, I'm fine."

"Can we save the making up for after we leave here? This place creeps me out," Cassandra whined.

"Cassandra, are you riding with me back to our place?"

"No, I would rather not sit around a married couple making googly eyes." Cassandra waved a hand at me.

"Best friend, I'm sorry I messed up our planned shopping trip."

"Oh, I'm still shopping on your dime; I'll just be alone," Cassandra informed me.

I opened and closed my mouth, then snarled at Carter and Vincenzo for laughing at the scene.

"Get in the car." Vincenzo helped me inside.

"Do you have a way to open the safe?"

"Were taking it to the source."

"Right now?"

"No better time than the present." He ran his hand up and down my thigh, then pecked me on the lips.

An older woman and a younger kid walked past our vehicle as we pulled out. He waved at the car, and she jerked him away to keep moving forward. I couldn't fault her reaction at seeing four black Escalades in an upscale suburb during the day.

Chapter 23

Vincenzo

"We can do things the easy way, Gianney, or the hard way. Either way, you know you are dying today."

I turned to look at Nyla off to the side, studying her reaction. After killing Cono, I thought she might close herself off and keep me away, but it only drew us closer.

Now, my chest was tight. We'd had Savio bring in all the leaders of the alliance to witness what was about to go down with Gianney. Renato already took care of the rest of the team. Duran pleaded for his life; Marciao only gloated. I appreciated his confidence, and how he hadn't let his enemies see him on his knees.

"Fuck you and the rest of you motherfuckers that turned your back on me," Gianney cursed, blood dripping down his eye, nose. Our men beat him up the first day after taking him from his office, starving him and Renato had fun torturing the rest. I straight kill them with a bullet and leave it alone.

I picked up a piece of the safe after it was blow-torched open. The flash drive was placed in the laptop. It displayed not only my family's pictures, but Nyla growing up. Cono had made it his mission to have her followed. Even though he'd played like he didn't care about her running off with Mark; all along, she was monitored.

"You let him kill your own brother. You're just like him," Gianney spat.

Nyla started to walk over, and Savio's arm went up to stop her.

"Never speak to my wife. You talk to me, motherfucker." I placed my hand around his neck and squeezed.

"Vincenzo!" Nyla shouted, and I froze, turning to look at her.

"My brothers thought that getting rid of Vivianna and your father would be the end of the Grecos in our business. Unfortunately, we learned it wasn't enough. You'd better believe the entire Greco lineage will be wiped out by my orders."

Gianney tried to wiggle out of the restraints.

"Duran, and the rest of your boys are dead, and I heard your grandmother in Boca is still alive in a nursing home."

His eyes broadened in surprise.

"Yeah, I had everything about you traced, down to your blood type, bitch."

Again, he tried to move, and the ties on his wrists and legs kept him in place.

I lifted the gun and checked the chamber. I turned around to face him again.

"Nyla, come here."

Savio stepped to the side, and she appeared next to me. Taking her hand, I helped to grip the gun, pulling her to stand in front of me with her legs cocked open in a firm stance.

Her breathing picked up.

"I'm here. All you have to do is squeeze, Tesoro, and it's all over."

"Gianney!" she called his name.

He looked up at her. Darkness showed on his face. "Mark said you'd be the death of me if I told the truth. He was right." Nyla pulled the trigger twice, hitting him in the chest and the eye.

I took the gun from her hand and tucked it away. She whipped around, stretching her arms wide around my back.

"You alright?"

"I'm fine. Actually, better than great," Nyla answered.

"Let's go home."

"What about the evidence?" Nyla pointed at the computer.

Elio picked up the laptop, took out the flash drive, and placed in his pocket.

"No longer anything to worry about. We'll get it wiped clean, and eliminate all traces," Elio explained, shaking hands with me, and hugging Nyla.

"Renato."

"Cleanup is right outside," Renato answered, waving me off.

"Vincenzo we are deeply grateful for the steps you took in securing all of our positions." Tommaso expressed, being one of the older bosses in the alliance."

"Savio and I talked and understood that keeping it with five families is the only way for our futures to stay viable."

After shaking hands with a few men from the Brambilla cartel family, I led Nyla from the cabin to head home.

"The next meeting, if you're looking to sit at the table, then we'd like to have you as a deciding member," Tommaso explained.

I left it alone, clasping hands with Nyla and kissing the back of her palm. After starting the car, Carter drove from the backwoods around the small cabin we kept to discard bodies close to the lake. I was ready to get back to being with my wife and having her all to myself, without any more outside interference.

****

We were sitting in the shallow water of the warm pool under the waterfall. I reached over, grabbed her arm, pulled her mouth to mine, inhaled the warmth of her sweet tongue, and felt her legs wrap around my waist. I cupped her ass. I slowly untied her bikini top, flung it to the side, came up for air, and caressed her cheek.

"I want to show you something."

"I will after we finish here."

"Tell me."

"It's a surprise for your birthday that we really didn't get to celebrate."

Grinning, Nyla wiped a hand across my forehead. "My dinner was enough for me."

"That's what makes me want to do more for you."

Wedged between her thighs, I engulfed her lips again, flicking a thumb over her nipples.

She threw her head back in excitement, slowly grinding against my lap. I shoved her thong off, flipped us around, and pushed her body up a little to sit on the steps. I stuck my tongue into her perfectly shaped lips, soaking in her juices, ready for her to feed me.

"Agghhh…" she groaned.

"How does it feel?"

"Amazing…" Nyla started to hump my face. She clawed her nails in my arm and back. In and out, I paced my movements and saw the lovely arousal on her face. "Ohhh, baby." Nyla struggled when I put my tongue into her asshole, wanting to see how she reacted further. I slipped my thumb in between, sucking on her pussy at the same time.

"Vincenzo, wait!" she shouted.

Pumping in and out like it was dick, hearing her cries and grunts, caused my dick to strain in my shorts.

"Fuck, you're beautiful to me, Nyla."

"Come here." Nyla tightened her legs around my waist.

I slipped my thumb out, craned my neck, kissed her, and pushed my shorts down at the same time, then plunged inside, not moving.

I shake my head like always, forgetting how much she had a grip on my rod. Lifting off the side of the pool steps, I drop my hands around her waist, staring at my dick moving in and out of her pussy.

"Yesss, keep going."

"Fuck." I panted, not ready to come, feeling my arm on fire. Covering my pain, I flicked my tongue over her plump breasts, sucking and nibbling. Her screams grew louder.

Would she mind being tied up for the rest of her life?

"Ahhh!" Nyla screamed, as I pumped faster, pushing her left leg in the crook of my arm.

"Stop running, tesoro."

I looked up, seeing tears fall down her cheek. I didn't know whether I hurt her or not. "Baby, what's wrong?"

She hid her face, wiping her tears. "Nothing. You just feel so good; us being here is good."

"That's why you're crying?"

Nodding, moving her hand up my chest, she pulled me down on top of her.

"Mmmm," she moaned.

I lifted her up from the pool and walked us over to the cabana bed. I guided her wet hair out of her face, moving in and out slowly and kissing the tip of her nose. Seeing Nyla vulnerable made me fall more in love with her spirit, and it gave me a purpose: I wanted to protect her always.

"Come for me, tesoro."

Arching her back, I sped up my strokes, our skin slapping louder and louder, seeing her essence drip down her thighs, making me miss feeling her juices on my tongue.

"Shit, you ready for me, baby?"

"Mmmm... give it all to me."

Her words made my arm go stiff, my spine locked as my orgasm creeped up and she came with me.

She collapsed on top of my chest.

I gathered my thoughts. There was ringing in my ear. I kept her close in my arms, thumbing her clit and feeling her arm stroke up and down my back.

"I like you."

I burst into laughter at her comment. "Where did that come from?"

Sighing, she puckered her lips and kissed the nape of my neck. "I don't know if I ever told you that I liked you."

"Good, I'm glad you like me, pretty lady. Come on, I have a surprise."

After rising from the lounge chair, I reached out to help her stand, and we both walked naked back into the house and upstairs to our bedroom.

"Is the surprise in the bedroom?"

"No, you're getting dressed first."

"Why? You don't trust yourself." She poked me in the stomach.

Tapping her butt, I said, "I don't. Chef is coming to cook dinner for us, and I'd rather not have my wife naked. That's only for my eyes.

"In a few days, we leave for our trip. Are you excited?" Nyla slid her arms into the silky pink robe.

"A vacation alone with you in a private suite." I winked, taking my robe off the back of the bathroom door.

"All right, so where's the surprise?" Nyla held out her hand.

"Downstairs and you have to close your eyes."

"Vincenzo... really."

"Tell me, what's the one thing you loved to do with your parents when you were younger?" I walked her out of the bedroom, downstairs, and down the hall to the other side of the house, next to the game room.

"Travel and take pictures."

"Open the door."

"What's behind the door?"

"Open it and see."

She looked perplexed, turning the knob, pushing it open, watching the expression of shock across her face.

"Oh, my God, you didn't." Nyla clasped her hand against her mouth, tears falling. She wandered around the room, staring at large, blown-up pictures of herself when she was younger. I'd had my team clean up a spare room and turn it into a photography darkroom for her to do what she loved and missed most.

"How did you even have time to do this?"

I drank in the comfort of her nearness. "Pays to be a billionaire."

"I'm speechless." She admired the room, and I felt her caress my arm.

"You like it?"

"*Like it?* Vincenzo, you amaze me."

The idea of her eagerness excited me. "Are you about to cry again?"

"A happy cry, because you looked beyond what mistakes I made and saw the real me."

"Your past is the past."

"Thank you." The very air around her seemed electrified.

"You're welcome."

"Does this mean I can take photos of you?"

"No."

She whined, stomping her feet. "Why not?" she asked, gliding her hand on my back.

"Baby, we don't leave photos around for evidence."

Her mouth dropped, and she shook her head.

"What if I take photos of me, on my knees, sucking your dick?" Nyla slid down to her knees in front of me.

I brought this untried naughty part of her senses to life. "What are you doing?"

"I want thank you properly."

"First, we need to eat. I need to rest. Your pussy has my chest and arm aching."

Nyla cackled at my reply. "Poor baby, I put that good pussy on you."

"Keep talking." I closed the door, and we walked hand-in-hand into the kitchen.

The chef had prepared some of Nyla's favorites as a follow-up to her birthday.

"So much food, we won't be able to eat all of it tonight."

"Save some for tomorrow."

"Let me fix your plate and then we'll sit in the theater and watch movies for the rest of the night."

I picked up a bottle of red wine, took two glasses with me, and listened to her plan her first photoshoots with the kids.

Chapter 24

Nyla

One Week Later

One I stepped through the thick field of grass. I hadn't been here in over five years, and I felt guilty. I bent to wipe the dirt from the double stone with both their names and a picture of us all together. While laying the flowers down, tears were already pooling in my eyes before I could get a word out. The sun was shining. It was a Saturday, right before we were going to fly out of the country.

"I miss you every day."

Closing my eyes, I felt Vincenzo's arms on my lower back, controlling my composure.

"Your little girl got married. Mom, Dad, this is Vincenzo." He came up next to me, keeping his arm securely around my neck.

"Sorry I never came sooner, so much has happened, and I hate not being able to talk to you. I know the truth, and I still love you both. Vincenzo has helped me and even got me a therapist to talk with if I want."

I ran a hand through my hair. "At 23, I have a family

again, people who care about me. The Calabresis stepped in when I could barely hold myself up."

I dropped to my knees, feeling a loud sob pierce my stomach.

Vincenzo came up behind me and rubbed my back.

"I wish you both were here."

"They're always with you, Nyla," Vincenzo whispered in my war.

I nodded. "You're right. My mom would tell me to stop crying and look up in the sky whenever I needed to talk to her."

"She's right."

"When I get back from out of town, I promise to make it up to you and come visit more. I love you." Kissing my first two fingers, I place them on the headstone. I stood up, holding his hand and walking back to the car.

"Do you need more time?"

"No, I needed to come here and let it out."

"Once we get on the island, you can relax and enjoy yourself." Vincenzo helped me in the SUV.

"Did your mom tell you what time they'll be at the airport?"

"In thirty minutes."

"Perfect. Thanks for coming with me." I leaned my head on his shoulder.

Grief was something I always pushed to the back of my mind, never really dealing with the knowledge that I was alone in the world. After meeting through special circumstances, Vincenzo had found ways to remind me how much he cared for me and wanted me—no matter how I came to him.

Romo drove, Carter in the passenger seat on guard. Even with the Grecos gone, Vincenzo stated that being in the cartel would always make people want a piece of us. The heavy-duty caravans driving in front of us and behind us would always be a testament to my new life.

After arriving at the airport, our cars lined up. Renato and Sonya helped their kids upstairs, with Adelina and her husband behind them.

"You have two planes here?"

"I wanted us to have privacy."

"Vincenzo, you didn't." I was caught up in his enthusiasm.

"My parents understood."

"I'm so embarrassed," I said, shaking my head.

"Why?"

My emotions caught up with me and his vibrant nearness. "Because they will know what we're doing."

"Have you realized my parents have five boys?"

"I really don't want to think about your parents having sex," I tittered.

"The only sex on your mind will be ours."

"Still. Two private jets?"

Stopping the car beside the plane and unhooking our seatbelts, we climbed out and came around to the door of the plane, greeting the staff. He hooked a finger under my chin, sucking my bottom lip, snaking his tongue inside. Pulling back, he had food, drinks, music laid out for the long flight.

"What do you want to do first when we get to Greece?"

The wheels started turning, and the pilot came on the intercom, giving directions.

"Mr. Calabresi, we are preparing for takeoff."

Watching the airport fade away as we take off, I

thought of how beautiful it will be to see some of the places I saw as a child with my new family.

****

Once we landed in Santorini and rested in our suites, we had an early breakfast on the table from the private chef, and then we went sightseeing and hung out with the kids and his parents.

Afterward, Adelina planned a dinner for the family. Nothing would ever compare to seeing all their faces and the love we all had for each other. Wine was poured, and food was brought to our table. When the Calabresis made their presence known, everything stopped, and the staff rolled out the red carpet. We were sitting at the table, and the two of them were going back and forth about how she wanted the next few days to go for everyone, and how he wanted to just relax with his wife, without any real plans. I laughed at Renato and Adelina, arguing back and forth. I couldn't help but wonder how a stone-cold killer could always back down when his mother put him in his place.

"Nyla, we planned everything around you and Vincenzo. You have the final say."

Putting my fork down, I linked hands with Vincenzo on the table. "Honestly, I would like to make it like a trip where everyone can do their own thing."

She exhaled. Renato winked at me, and his mother smacked the back of his head.

"Eat your food," Adelina spat.

"The party's tomorrow, right?"

"Yes, we have the party tomorrow night, afterwards you two can do whatever you'd like."

"Okay."

"Nyla, how is the photography coming along?" Sonya investigated.

"So far, it's great. I bought my camera with me and plan on taking pictures, so be prepared to be sick of me.

"I was born a star, so I'm ready," Rena joked.

"You're not eating; what's wrong?" Vincenzo tapped me on the shoulder.

"I'm fine, just listening to your family."

"Come here." Vincenzo scooted back in his chair, helping me to stand.

"Where are we going?"

"You'll see."

"Another surprise?"

"Nope." Vincenzo guided me away from the table, and a few people backed away, as our security directed us through the crowd. We came up to a restricted area, and our security stood on guard with their backs turned to us. Vincenzo turned me to face the moon shining down on the water.

"Keep looking." He caressed his hands under my dress, pulled my thong down, and slipped it into his pocket.

"Out here?"

"Tesoro." He pressed a kiss on my forehead.

"Yes."

He buried his face in my neck. I heard the rattle of his belt loosening, and then came his massive pole. Inch by inch, he drew in and out. Goosebumps rose on my arms and back.

"Our party...Fuck.... is a celebration."

"Yesss...Vincenzo."

"Tell me you're ready to do forever with me."

I'm unable to verbalize my answer, from the pounding and tight hold on my waist, taking my breath away.

"Tell me!" he shouted.

"Forever! I promise. Forever."

Right as I came, he released and kissed behind my ear, pulling my face around to kiss me.

"Come on, our parents us waiting on us."

"Our parents."

"You are a Calabresi, baby."

"Thank you for the trip."

****

The next night, Adelina quickly rushed us all to be on time for the reception, with a special request to wear red in celebration of love. While clasping the diamond earrings and bracelet she gifted me, I stepped out of the bathroom and sauntered to the living room, stopping when I saw the red roses on the floor.

"Vincenzo, you are making me feel terrible."

A violinist played, and he reached for my hand, walking me into his embrace for a slow dance.

"Spoiled yet?"

My heart danced with joy from his thoughtfulness. "Beyond."

Pressing a kiss to my forehead, he said, "Then I'm doing my job well."

"How many more surprises are there?"

"None." He grinned.

"Liar." We burst into laughter, strolling out to the deck, and saw that most of the guests had arrived.

"It's beautiful."

Adelina had tables and chairs lined up with us facing each other over candlelight. There was also a large sign on the back of the wall with our names and congratulations. Colors red and white covered the table and chairs, and napkins with place cards and inscription of different quotes on the plates.

"I should get a picture while everyone is standing."

"We have a photographer; you relax and enjoy yourself."

"Is that a demand?"

"Yes."

"Have I told you how much I like you?"

He blushed, turned his head, and I tittered at making the big bad mobster blush.

"I have to give a toast for the happy couple." Adelina raised her glass.

Taking a champagne from the waiter, I held it up in the sky.

"Nyla, each of my daughters-in-law have come to me in a special way, and you are no exception," Adelina said, and Vincenzo rolled his eyes.

"Thank you, Adelina."

"I know my son, and he's probably embarrassed for being put on the spot, but he chose well, and he's in good hands." Adelina took a sip of her drink, and I gulped mine down.

Rena appeared with McKayla and Savio. "Ladies, are you enjoying yourselves?"

"We are, and you look amazing, Nyla." Rena extended arm out for a hug.

"Adelina picked it out."

"She has taste because the villa is gorgeous." McKayla

smiled, holding Savio's hand. Vincenzo and Savio went over to their brothers, talking in a huddle.

"Did you love the surprise at the house?"

I motioned between them. "You two knew?"

Rena clapped her hands together. "He called us to help."

"Honestly, Vincenzo has blown my mind, unlike any guy I've ever dated."

"You love him. I can tell." McKayla pulled my cards.

Everything within me knew it was right to be with him. "I do."

"Happy for you and him, after the situation with your uncle."

"I hadn't even thought about him."

"Then clearly Vincenzo is doing a great job keeping you busy."

"More than you know."

"Ladies, do you mind if I dance with my lovely wife?" Vincenzo took my champagne from my hand and placed it on the table.

He was so handsome in his black slacks; my breath caught in my throat when his dick twitched under my grip. "You're ready to dance again?"

"No, I want to be alone with you."

I giggled at him, lying to his family to sneak off. "Vincenzo, that's terrible."

"Sorry, I'll apologize later."

Chapter 25

Vincenzo

ne Month Later

OMy phone was still buzzing with notifications of magazines wanting to do interviews with me about the casino, which was the hottest place in Chicago. Everyone was calling it "the place to be if you want to be seen." All the celebrities were showing up—even wanting to take pictures with me and my brothers, but we declined.

After shutting my phone off and sliding it into my pocket, I joined the conversation. I listened as the gentleman proposed an offer to go into business with me for hotels in four different states.

"How much of a cut are you talking about?"

"Twenty percent. Plus, if the four hotels do amazing —and I know they will—then we can revisit doing international property," Oliver explained.

Flicking my pen on the desk, I ran the numbers in my head and what they've brought to the table.

"Thank you for coming."

"You're declining."

"Honestly what you've shown me really isn't profitable, and I could make triple by myself."

"What about your brothers?"

"The casino is run by me, and decisions start and stop here." I pointed at myself.

Oliver gulped and nodded. "Thank you for your time."

"Maybe in a year or two when I see what you've made in profit we can revisit."

"Thank you, Mr. Calabresi." He stretched his hand toward me, gathered his things, and left.

"He sounded like he knew good business." Elio stood beside me at the window in my office.

"Based on the reviews of his hotel, they need more than what we can offer."

Elio flung his hands in his pockets. "How is married life treating you?"

"Good. In fact, I need to head home early. We have plans."

"Glad to see you happy."

"Same to you."

My assistant poked her head in the door. "Mr. Calabresi, you have a call on line three." Since being back, our lives have gotten into a routine and I've made it a priority to be home for us to spend time together at least three times out of the week.

"Thanks."

Elio treaded along to the door. "Let me get out of here, I need to meet Cora at her clinic."

"Tell her I said hi."

Elio chucked his chin up goodbye.

"This is Vincenzo."

Nyla purred into the phone, "Hello, Mr. Calabresi." Her sultry voice reminded me of our late-night swim.

"Mrs. Calabresi, what can I do for you?"

"I was checking to see if you're leaving work early today."

I answered, "I am."

"Great, I have a surprise for you."

"I hate surprises."

Nyla grunted. "Vincenzo, don't start."

"All I need is you."

"I'm happy about that, but you will get a surprise," she divulged.

"Sounds like you've been talking to Rena."

Snickering at my response, Nyla told me she loved me and hung up.

I stood up, I walked out of my office and checked the main casino floor to see how business was doing.

A few of my staff greeted with me waves. "Hello, Mr. Calabresi."

"How are things looking down here?"

"Great sir. Traffic has picked up," the man at the counter service answered.

"Any problems?"

"No sir, the new system is running smoothly," she proclaimed.

We had installed back-up alarms and placed codes on the doors inside that changed every thirty seconds. Plus, we had a failsafe that I was notified of at all times on my phone.

"Keep me updated if anything changes." I looked around, seeing the guests, laughing and enjoying the slot machines.

After strolling out of the building to see Carter waiting, I jumped in and shut the door.

"Where to next, Mr. Calabresi?"

"Warehouse."

Forty minutes later, the guards pulled the door open for me to enter. I saw each member sitting and waiting, as Savio stood in the front.

"About time you arrived," Renato grumbled and I flipped him off.

"Gentlemen, sorry I'm late."

"Ready?" Savio asked.

"Go ahead."

"The alliance is going through a change; we all saw it happen when we were younger, and now it's time to grow even further. Over the past few months, I've explained how I eventually want to step down and be with my family more," Savio continued.

"So, are you for sure going through with leaving?" Alvize asked.

"Yes, and Sante is taking over as Don."

"Who's the underboss?"

"Me," I answered.

Silence filled the room. The original plan was to have Elio move in the role, but after talking with Cora, things changed and I understood him wanting to be around more since they were separated for so long.

"Are you ready for that position?" Renato inquired.

"Vincenzo knows how I feel about him taking on a cartel position—especially one so high up—but he's a man whom I respect and will support, as long as he's happy," Savio remarked.

"The decision wasn't taken likely," I explained. "I know I'm young, and I'm looked at as a kid, but Calabresi blood runs through my veins, and any enemy of my family will be destroyed."

"Any objections?" Savio probed, scanning all eyes.

"Then it's settled. Welcome to the alliance, Vincenzo Calabresi." Sante stood, taking my hand and pulling me into a hug.

Renato's eyes contacted with mine and he smirked.

"I look forward to working closely with you, Vincenzo," Alvize said.

"You're a fast learner. I don't doubt you will be ready for what's to come," Savio said.

"I agree, and the first order of business is checking our transactions in New York. I wanted to wait to discuss, but some things with our cousins have me alarmed."

"No time like the present to figure out how we can help." Savio moved to the third chair.

Sante sat at the head of the table, and me beside him. We called up our cousins for a conference call in the middle of the day to get some background on what they needed.

****

Carrying the newspaper inside, I dumped it on the counter in the kitchen. Opening the fridge to grab a bottle of water, I craned my neck to work out the kinks. Nyla rushed in, talking on the phone with who I could only assume was her best friend as she tossed her head back in laughter.

"He's still dressed in business attire." Nyla rolled her eyes.

Chucking the bottle on the counter, I stared at her with my arms folded.

"Yeah, let me call you back; I have his attention now." Nyla smirked.

"Do you, now?"

Nyla sauntered toward me, closing the space between us. "Hi." Latching her arms around my neck, she stood on her toes, capturing my lips.

"Hi."

Nyla pulled back, burying her face in my chest. "Tired?"

"Not for you."

She grinned. "Ready for your surprise?"

Groaning, I patted her on the butt. "I hate surprises." I brushed my lips across hers.

"Come on, silly man." She pulled back, took my hand, and walked me from the kitchen to the living room, which had no furniture.

"Where's the furniture?"

"I moved it to storage."

"Why?"

"Just for today. I'll bring it back in once were done."

"Done with what?"

Nyla picked up a strawberry and tossed it into her mouth. "You will see. Sit down."

"What are you up to, Nyla?"

"I want to have a picnic and take pictures of us together."

"Huh?"

"I'm not able to give you the extravagant things. You're already rich, so I thought it would be cute to do a little picnic and photo shoot," she said with a shrug.

"Baby, you're rich."

She waved me off. "No, I'm not."

"You have bank accounts with millions of dollars in your name."

Nyla pulled the camera up to her eye and snapped. "That money is yours."

"What's mine is yours, never forget that."

She sighed and reached for another strawberry. "I hear you, but for now, do you like the picnic?" Focusing the camera on me again, she snapped.

"It's nice."

"Really? You're not just saying that to gas me up?"

Chuckling, I kicked off my shoes, losing my shirt and plopping down on the floor, popping the bottle of white wine open.

"There's something I need to talk to you about."

Nyla snapped pictures of me and sat down next to me. "Go ahead."

"I had a meeting today."

"You always have meetings." She fed me a grape.

"True, but it was a little different."

"In what way?" Nyla scooped pasta salad onto a fork and lifted it to my mouth.

"You cooked that?"

"Yep, I gave the chef today off."

"I'm the underboss of the cartel," I blurted out.

Nyla choked on her food, and I raised my hand to pat her back.

Placing her camera on the floor to eat, she repeated, "Underboss?"

"Remember when everything went down, and I was grilled about whether I wanted to go in fully?"

"A little." She rubbed her temples.

"Today, I took the offer."

"How dangerous is it going to be now?"

"Honest?"

"Honest."

"Ten times as dangerous. I sit at the side of the Don. Sante took over for Savio."

"So, you're going to be gone a lot more?"

"Yes, and making decisions you won't understand, but I have to do what keeps you safe."

"Wow." She stood up swiftly.

"Tell me what you're thinking." I jumped up, walked up to her back, and wrapped my arms around her waist as she stood in front of the mirror.

"I'm scared for you."

"I know what I'm doing."

"Seems like we just started to know each other as a couple, and now you'll be gone more."

"My goal is to always have you in mind whenever I need to do anything, and I promise to put you first."

"I trust you."

"Good, come take more pictures and finish this picnic."

"You're ready to just fuck." Nyla cackled.

Grinning at her comment, I reached up and tweaked her nipple. "When it comes to you always."

After picking up her camera, she took a picture of us together, then a few separate ones of me. We laughed and joked about how we met.

"That was fun," Nyla expressed sitting with her back to my chest in the bathtub.

"Thank you for the picnic."

"How do you feel about being underboss really?"

"I'm ready to see what it brings. My goal is to protect my brothers at all times."

"Do your parents know?"

"Not yet."

"I think you mother is going to have a problem with you moving in that direction."

"She will at first—but understand that it would have happened in some other capacity; it's our bloodline."

"Well, I have to say going for the job interview did work out for me after all."

Running a hand up to her neck, I glide it across her shoulder. "Glad I didn't fire you when I had the chance."

Nyla giggled and turned her head to peck me on the lips, moaning in my mouth.

"Mark did one thing right."

"What's that?" she asked.

"He brought you to me," I answered.

Epilogue

Nyla

*S*ix *Months Later*

After falling for Vincenzo, discovering the real him and how his family dynamics worked made me love him even more. Unlike his older brothers, he wasn't good or bad; the decisions he made were based on protecting himself and the people he loved.

After slipping off the house shoes that I kept under my desk, I double-checked my makeup in the mirror and gazed at the diamond ring on my hand. Thinking back to our wedding reception in Greece brought back wonderful memories that I planned on reliving every year that we were married.

Vincenzo's trust in me gave me more purpose to work my ass off and show him that I could be the rock he needed beside him. I no longer worried about his decisions because the best gift he could have given me was renewing our vows.

Scanning the pictures on the wall from our picnic made me happy. I got him to put up a few without a hassle.

He was off to New York and New Jersey for a scheduled meeting with his cousin Bosco to see about opening a casino in Atlantic City and look into the security structure that he would need.

"I thought I'd find you here." Cassandra stood in the doorway.

"Come in, girl."

"How long have you been working today?" Cassandra scrunched down in the seat.

"Since eight. What are you doing here?"

"Came to surprise you for lunch."

"I have too much work," I said, waving my hand around the desk.

"Vincenzo's assistant said you haven't eaten since breakfast this morning, when you rushed out to handle a photo shoot," Cassandra fussed.

I scratched the back of my neck. Vincenzo and I both led busy lives, and I was slacking on spending time with Cassandra or any of the girls. I knew my best friend missed me. My photography business was going so well; I even had local mom-and-pop stores hiring me.

"Who told you I was here anyway?"

"The girls."

All of the wives loved Cassandra, and she'd become one of the crew. Now we hang out as a group along with Cora's friends.

"Y'all always in my business."

Smirking, I said, "But that's why you love me."

"Love, way those options," I joked.

"Hush, Vincenzo has you spoiled."

I scooted back, stood up and walked to the filing cabinet, and put away the last stack of reports Vincenzo had left.

The first thing out of his mouth when I told him to let me handle the office at Calabresi Holdings was that I only had to do it for a few hours, and then go home. He wasn't against me working in general, but I liked being around the people at the casino and doing my own thing with my photos.

"Where are you planning lunch?"

"Probably the Lobby."

"My favorite."

"I know, so grab your purse and let's go."

"All right, I still need to get some work done when I come back."

"Nope, your secretary explained that you're supposed to work only until lunch and go home afterwards," Cassandra said, bossing me around.

"Ralph lucked out," I muttered.

She scoffed. "Ralph's not going anywhere."

"You two back together?"

"Yes, I told you he can't stay away."

"Glad you're happy, boo."

"Thanks bestie, now come on. Vincenzo is probably ready for you to get home and do some phone sex."

"Is that what you and Ralph do?"

"Act like you two don't."

Cassandra and Ralph made it official with a relationship at my reception dinner six months ago. Her going on dates with other guys made him see how much Cassandra meant to him. I sucked my teeth, propping up my bag and coat, and stepped in my heels.

"Did you make a reservation already?" Leaving the office, I locked the door. Cassandra waved to the assistant.

"Yep, under the Calabresi name."

"Okay, Carter should have the car ready."

"Already texted him. You're driving with me."

"And he didn't put up a fight?"

"Girl, he's going to follow us." Cassandra cackled and stepped onto the elevator.

****

I snickered at Cassandra doing a little wiggle getting out of the car, happy to get a few drinks in her system. Driving as usual through downtown Chicago could bring a headache, and Carter approached, holding the door for us.

"Thank you, Carter."

"Anytime, Mrs. Calabresi."

The debt I owed Vincenzo came back to me in so many ways; I could never repay him. Looking around at all the balloons and signs, with pictures of me and my family growing up tugged at my heart. Seeing myself age through every stage of my life up until our marriage had me choking back tears.

"Cassandra what did you do?" Pressing a hand to my chest, for several seconds I took in the group of friends and extended family standing clapping coming toward me.

"Vincenzo wanted you to feel special for the anniversary of the day you met."

"But."

She threw her hand in the air. "To making new memories, Nyla, and letting go of the past."

Vincenzo moved through the group of friends, and it made me even more ready to fall into a crying fit.

"I thought you were out of town." Wiping the snot

from my nose with a napkin, Vincenzo kissed me longingly on the lips, hugging me close.

"I flew on a private jet to get back to celebrate my favorite girl."

"Favorite and only girl."

"How are you doing?" Vincenzo glanced at my worry lines.

"Happy you are here."

Those damn deep, pleading blue eyes speared my heart. *God, I love this man.*

Removing the little space between us, he hooked an arm around my waist, caressing my ass.

"People are going to think you want to have sex with me right here." I moaned, blinking back the tears.

"I missed you," Vincenzo kidded, turning to face our family and friends.

Patting him on the chest, clasping our hands together, Vincenzo led me around the room of the restaurant to hug everyone.

"What happened with the casino and your meeting with Bosco?"

"Fine, I will have some more conversations—but right now, I want to celebrate us."

"Happy anniversary you two, I knew it was meant to be when you forced her to live with you," Rena joked.

"Thank you, Rena," I smiled.

"My son has you glowing, Nyla," Adelina broke up our teasing moment.

"Thank you, Adelina." I sighed, embarrassed at the amount of sex we had that kept me nonstop ready to commit a crime when I went too long without his dick.

"The longer I stay away, the more she jumps on my

bones," Vincenzo countered, pressing me close, pulling me on top of his lap.

I feel like I'm whole again, having a family, a man, friends, and owning a business. My age would make a lot of people think I'm too young, but it made me determined to hold onto my happiness and celebrate every moment Vincenzo and I created together.

"Can I tell you something?"

"Anything." Vincenzo snaked his arm around my waist.

"Thank you for seeing me and supporting me through my fears; your love healed the broken heart that Mark and so many others left behind."

Vincenzo stared into my eyes. "You were never broken; you are perfect the way you are." He crushed his lips to mine.

I held the back of his head and slipped him my tongue. After remembering we were not alone, I pulled back, smiling at all the wide, grinning faces watching us in awe.

"Maybe next time we can do a surprise that only includes us," I whispered in his ear, and he groped my thigh, nuzzling his nose in my neck.

* * *

I hope you enjoyed Vincenzo and Nyla's story. Check out the sneak peek of Giouse's story coming soon.

Check out where it all began with a Dark Mafia Arranged Marriage **Savio: Dark Mafia Billionaire Romance**: Book 1 https://books2read.com/u/mlEAW7

Follow it up with a Dark Mafia Enemies to Lovers

Arranged Marriage **Sante: Dark Mafia Billionaire Romance:** Book 2 https://books2read.com/u/mdd1oW

Also, if you love Hate to Love, Marriage of Convenience **Renato: Dark Mafia Billionaire Romance:** Book 3 https://books2read.com/u/4AjAQd

Plus, a Second chance, Dark Mafia Romance **Elio: Dark Mafia Billionaire Romance**: Book 4 https://books2read.com/u/4j5yjD

Fans of Debt romance will continue to love. **Vincenzo: A Debt Owed, Enemies to Lovers Dark Mafia Billionaire Romance**: Book 5 https://books2read.com/u/4EEYYo

Giouse's: A Dark Mafia Stalker Billionaire Romance Book 6

Lawyer by day, escort by night – the perfect prey for billionaire mafia boss.

Penelope has always dreamed of becoming a lawyer, but law school is more expensive than she had anticipated. She has found a way to keep up with her education bills, whilst earning some life experience of her own. Becoming an escort was the most profitable and most dangerous thing, Penelope has ever done.

Giouse Calabresi operates by a personal code. Blood, honor and vengeance, are three words he lives by as a mafia boss. And of course, claiming any women he desires. For months he has been stalking Penelope, curious about this versatile seductress.

When he finally makes himself known, all bets are off. Will he claim the seductress or will she seduce him instead?

Upcoming Releases

Vincenzo
Giosuè
Armani
Bosco

About the Author

L.K. Ryan is an author of Romantic Suspense, Dark Romance, and Contemporary Novels. Join my newsletter and sign up for the latest news and updates on my books and releases:

Calabresi Mafia Series

Savio: Book 1
https://books2read.com/u/mlEAW7
Sante: Book 2
https://books2read.com/u/mdd1oW
Renato: Book 3
https://books2read.com/u/4AjAQd
Elio Jr: Book 4
https://books2read.com/u/4j5yjD
Vincenzo: Book 5
https://books2read.com/u/4EEYYo

Thank you so much for reading. If you enjoyed the crazy ride and decide to leave a review, we'd appreciate the support.

www.ingramcontent.com/pod-product-compliance
Lightning Source LLC
Chambersburg PA
CBHW071210210726
48293CB00002B/369

Chapter One

Dead bodies interrupted my dessert course.

It's not that I don't enjoy discussing what lies on a slab in the city morgue, but the majestic puff pastry conceived by the master chef of the most luxurious hotel in Alenbonné deserves its due.

Besides, there is no need to rush when discussing the dead. They don't go anywhere. Normally.

From the far end of the banquet room, I saw the hotel manager, Henri Colbert, about to move protectively towards me, but I shook my head. Sergeant Dupont was a rude bore and wouldn't harm me. Besides, even an elite establishment like the Crown must obey the law, unless enough royal coins crossed palms.

To Sergeant Dupont I commanded, "Sit, and be silent. I will not have a guardia ruin a work of art made by the incomparable Crown chef, Gerhard Perdersen."

Dupont collapsed into a chair with as much refinement as a sack filled with a week's worth of laundry. The man lacked presence. His round face had the impassive slackness of a bored cow, and his wrinkled guardia uniform of navy blue with red trim had a grease stain on the lapel.

My demand for order rose in me and I scolded him, "You're in a hotel where your annual salary wouldn't pay for a night's rest. Remove your hat and show some respect."

He grabbed the flat hard cap off his head with pudgy hands.

Taking another bite, I tried to recapture the bliss in my mouth: the caramelized sugar-coated flaky pastry layers, sandwiched with the softness of cream, juxtaposed with the very slight hardness of chopped pistachios— No, my delight was over. Thoughts of murder were too distracting. I opened my eyes and sighed, dabbing my cloth napkin at the corners of my mouth, before saying. "Now, begin again."

"A body from the river. Dead perhaps three days. The inspector wants you to make it talk, Madame Chalamet."

"Oh, he does, does he?" I waved over a server, a clean-shaved young man wearing the traditional service colors of black trousers and a vest with a starched white shirt. He had too much oil in his hair, but his nails were clean and manicured, and his shoes polished to a mirror shine. Dupont could take some tips.

"You may take my plate away. Bring two coffees, one for myself and another for my guest."

"No time, madame." The cow bent forward, gaining a little animation to his features. "We cannot keep mysir de duke waiting."

My breath quickened at his words. Why would a noble be interested in the death of a nameless body? "A duke? Alenbonné has only three in residence."

"Mysir de Archambeau."

I stood. "Come, sergeant, if Mysir de Archambeau wishes the dead to speak, we must not delay him. You gain us a quick-cab while I retrieve my bag from my rooms."

~

As I entered my hotel suite, I called for my assistant, Anne-Marie. Wiping her hands with a dishtowel, she entered the main room from the door leading to our kitchenette. She was a thin girl, in her teens, quick-footed, and smart as a whip.

"We have a case. Tell me what you know of Mysir de Archambeau."

Her hazel eyes gleamed like bright stars in her brown face, for the girl loved gossip and was thus an invaluable resource, besides being a hard worker. She followed me to the dressing room next to my bedroom. One armoire held my clothes, the other the tools of my Ghost Talking trade.

The walnut cabinet once stored my father's jewelry-making tools and supplies. I stroked the dark brown wood, and opening the two doors released the fragrance of the stored herbs. Taking a moment, I breathed in deeply, relishing in the scents that spelled magic for me. Shelves now held rows of amber glass bottles filled with my custom tinctures. Depending on the need, there were solutions to encourage or discourage the dead. Powders, resins, leaf, and root.

My fingers ran over their corked tops and paper packets, deciding which I might need tonight. Definitely Eyesbright to enhance my sight. Something for protection; the dead always attracted corruption. And another to persuade the conscious to give way.

While I packed my leather satchel, Anne-Marie told me what she knew.

"Mysir de duke is in his mid-thirties and has a townhouse with a decent address. It's near the government offices, but not what I would call the fashionable side of town. While an aristo, he has not claimed his family seat in parliament. Instead, the consensus is that he acts as a general dogsbody for King Guénard."

"Any recent deaths of relatives or those he might care about?"

"He's a widower, but she died some years ago. A natural death, but I'd have to look in the newspaper archives to be sure."

"Find out the details for me."

In the drawer, I pulled out my man-stopper, a small pistol that could easily fit inside a woman's muff or purse. It could fire two shots. It was a pretty little piece with a mother-of-pearl handle and was a gift from Anne-Marie's sailor father. I tucked it into a deep pocket of my skirt, designed to hold it. It was always best to have it close at hand when dealing with the dead.

"I'm heading to the city morgue and don't know when I'll return. Don't wait up."

"Happy Haunting," she said as I headed out the door.

I handed my bag up to the Sergeant and then gathered my skirts up to mount the step into the quick-cab. The vehicle was a small rig, designed to maneuver easily through city traffic, but the interior was designed for two people to sit side by side. However, the sergeant's bulk put me close to him and the scent of boiled cabbage was penetrating.

With a crack of the whip, we surged forward and the dessert at the Crown hotel faded from memory to be replaced with another thrill. With Mysir de Archambeau involved, it meant this case would be important and unusual. A lout from the streets being rolled for coin and dumped into one of the city's many canals would not interest an aristo. No, this was something far more important.

No, the victim would be someone significant, or possibly have relatives of some stature. Or perhaps he was a master criminal, stealing state secrets? Something would have captured the duke's attention.

"Tell me about this body," I said to Dupont.

"Male, late thirties. Maybe early forties. Dead."

"Do you know why Mysir de Archambeau is interested?"

My question received only a blank stare from the dull-witted sergeant. It made me wonder why his superior, Inspector Barbier, a man fastidious in dress and manner, kept the crude Dupont as his man. But once when I had seen Dupont wade into a riot without thought, pitching men to the left and right like he was mowing hay with a scythe, it became clear. The inspector was small for a man, and with one leg shorter than the other, he was slow to give chase. Dupont was his nightstick, his club.

The whip cracked over our heads and the quick-cab exited the drive of the Crown hotel and flew into the traffic of the avenue with such force that I grabbed the shoulder strap to prevent myself from falling into Dupont's lap. We narrowly missed colliding into a farmer's cart filled with hay. Truly, a city driver with the heart of a lion!

Fortunately, our pace slowed when our driver found himself behind a legal clerk in his black robes, riding an unflappable horse. The cab driver shouted at him to give the road over, but horse and rider kept steady with their bone-rattling pace, and the traffic to the side did not permit a safe pass.

The crescent-shaped street ran parallel to the curving of the canal. Leaving the hotel district, we passed the houses of the well-to-do merchants and tradesmen, all neat, tidy, and proud with their well-swept doorsteps and painted shutters.

We turned to cross the humpback bridge and onto Rue Brasseries. Finally escaping our clerk and his horse, our cab surged forward along this boulevard, where gossip was traded over hot or cold drinks, and platters filled with crackers, olives, and slices of that salty and expensive delicacy of thinly sliced Dibiko ham were consumed with relish.

Most of the trees had lost their autumn leaves and the evening chill was settling in as the gas streetlights were lit. The crowds were gone and only the staff remained to remove the outdoor tables and chairs, storing them away until tomorrow.

The city of Alenbonné was changing, putting on her evening clothes, readying herself for a night of dining and theater in the entertainment district. Pockets would be picked, and drunk fools seduced, while in the working areas of the city a family would sit down around the fireplace after a long day's work.

A few more blocks and our path took us to the student district, Rue Beausoleil. Named for its founder, only those mocking the area called it a 'beautiful sun' anymore. When King Guénard took the throne, his interest in funding education was minimal and, as royal patronage ceased, the aristocracy followed suit. The area had fallen accordingly. There were no decorative trees, no wide pavements for strolling, no street lamps or genteel cafés. Ironwork here was serviceable, not decorative. Boards covered doors and windows, and grime darkened the exterior brick.

Vagrants huddled in doorways, their hands tucked into their armpits, hats pulled down low, like sleeping birds. But they were city birds, dull in plumage and faded into their corners.

There was an element of defiance about the place I always admired; like an unrepentant youth that sings a taunting tune when hauled off by the gendarmes for stealing a pear from a street vendor's cart. So I gave a smirk when the cabdriver opened the roof flap to tell us, "Streets blocked ahead. Another protest about the king's treaty, I expect. Do you want me to take an alley? Try to get around?"

"No!" I said, alarmed at his recklessness of trying to push through a crowd. People could get hurt or frightened. "Let's wait a moment. I'll compensate you for your time."

The door flap shut. I heard shouting and saw hand-painted signs being waved. It seemed they were angry that King Guénard was once again planning to raise taxes on imports when we renewed our treaty with Perino.

Students were still optimistic enough to attempt changing a world that dismissed them as next to worthless. It either made you want to laugh or cry.

The crowd moved, streaming around us. One rapped the door

of the closed carriage ahead of us and when an angry face emerged, they gave him a raspberry before laughing and moving onward.

A cheeky lad tipped his hat to me, and I had to suppress a desire to give him a smile back. The dozen or so students behind shoved him forward, and then they were all gone. Their ditty about a cockerel only suited for the cooking pot faded away; the ribald lyrics were amusing, but not a great compliment to our good king.

With the street clear, we reached our destination, the university's medical school, which also served as the city morgue. Here, scholars amused themselves by slicing open the less fortunate while I researched their departed spirits.

The carriage passed through the security gates. When the coach stopped, I popped open the door and jumped down the step. Dupont handed me out my leather valise, and after paying the cabbie, we walked to the solid anonymous door that was the portal to the medical wing. As the sergeant opened it, I smelled death.

Down the hall were angry voices, and entering the surgery, I gave Inspector Barbier standing at the doorway a nod of acknowledgment.

"Thanks for coming, Elinor. Welcome to the circus."

Unlike his sergeant, he wore every-day clothes for the working man: a brown tweed coat, with matching trousers and a waistcoat with black buttons. Barbier's long dour face was that of a mournful hound disappointed with his life: large brown eyes, flat hollow cheeks, and a long black mustache that brushed the corners of his mouth. With his chin tucked to his chest, he was slowly stroking the ends, a sign of deep concentration.

It was the surgeon, Doctor LaRue, who was arguing. She was at least twenty years older than my almost-thirty, rail thin, like a vine bean, with an oval face and a nose that would shame the beak of a water bird.

She wore dark blue trousers and a black vest, a daring choice for a woman. Her rolled-up shirtsleeves exposed strong sinewy forearms that were still red, evidence she had scrubbed them with the harsh bar soap used in the morgue, but her apron was still white, proving she hadn't started the autopsy yet.

The doctor was a very skilled butcher of men, but not so excellent as a bedside healer; she was a blunt speaker and without a grain of sentimentality. I found her a good friend.

The only other occupant of the room was a woman I knew little about but recognized: Madame Nyght. She was a flashy bird among us plain crows, dressed in a bold black-and-white striped satin, with the smallest waist the best corset could make, and a stylish hat that dripped with jet fringe.

You might mistake Nyght for a rich man's mistress. In truth, she was a huckster, a fraud who amused the rich. I wish I had her clientèle.

"I don't care who told you to be here. This is my surgery and I am in charge here," snapped Dr. LaRue.

"Do you think I wish to be here looking at your dead meat? Taken from my home and escorted here by a guardia?" Seeing her wild gestures puncturing the air made me believe the rumor that she had once worked on the stage before becoming a Ghost Talker.

Madame Nyght pointed at me. "First you ask for my help, then you insult me by bringing this donkey here?"

"As I've been saying, I don't want you here," replied Dr. LaRue tersely.

"Is she calling me a donkey?" I asked, turning to Inspector Barbier.

"Don't feel insulted. She called me a mule, and Dr. LaRue, a goat."

"A fixation on barnyard animals, perhaps?"

"You'd have to take that up with a mind-doctor. I only catch them, not explain them."

Madame Nyght made a dismissive hiss and waved her hand at us all. "Do I crawl into the gutters and look for dead bodies? No. I am Madame Nyght. I am genteel and talk with spirits in the drawing rooms of the best society."

Behind me, a voice with the harshness of a northern accent said, "And tonight we will be grateful for whatever your talents can reveal to us about this mystery."

The Duke de Archambeau had arrived.

CHAPTER TWO

Mysir de duke commanded the room. Men cast their gazes down, and women patted their hair into place. Even Doctor LaRue tucked a stray wisp behind an ear.

He was taller than average, with a square jaw, a faint scar across his chin, and wide, sharply defined cheekbones. Wearing immaculate evening clothes of black velvet trousers and matching coat, and a waistcoat that shimmered with its white brightness, it seemed he had just left a social engagement. Opera or theater? I put him down as a music aficionado.

The duke's entrance lit the room like a spark to gas. The first to recover was Dr. LaRue. She jerked her head toward Madame Nyght. "Remove this person from my morgue."

"In due course," the duke replied coolly. His northland burr placed his origin as close to the border of Zulskaya, our country's closest neighbor. A barely civilized wilderness of snowcapped mountains and thick forests, though I have been told the skiing is enjoyable.

"The Crown appreciates your time and sacrifice, Madame Nyght," he told her.

I spoke up. "Naturally, I wouldn't want to disturb Madame Nyght's session. I can wait my turn."

The duke's measuring gaze, if I were a horse, would have sent me to the knackers. "Who are you and why are you here?"

How embarrassing. Apparently, the donkey in the room had gone unnoticed, but before I could introduce myself, Madame Nyght flung an accusing finger at me. "She is a little guttersnipe Ghost Talker who slanders others!"

"Madame Guttersnipe, at your service," I said, giving a slight bow of my head.

Inspector Barbier explained. "Madame Chalamet helps us with our cases, Mysir de Archambeau. I requested her to come here before I realized you had commandeered Madame Nyght to our service."

Dr. LaRue fumed. "This is my morgue and my body. You sent this Nyght woman here without my permission, and when you show up, start deciding what to do with a body I haven't examined."

We all looked towards the body lying on a metal table in the center of the surgery. A damp sheet clung to it, shielding our delicate sensibilities. Though it was doubtful we needed protection, as we all appeared to be as stout as cart horses. Well, maybe the duke was a nicely bred racehorse, but I could see a bit of mule there. He'd go the distance out of sheer stubbornness.

"I completely understand, Dr. LaRue, and I sincerely apologize for any inconvenience. However, Madame Nyght is here at the request of the government to tell us all she can about this poor misfortunate fished out of the river."

Madame Nyght showed some fight in her. "Your man sent to fetch me did not give me a choice."

Perhaps we needed flattery to get things moving along?

"Madame Nyght is much admired by the elite in Alenbonné. It would be an honor to see her work." I spoke only the truth. She specialized in fleecing Le beau idéal, the aristo set, and fake Ghost Talking always interested me.

Before Nyght could protest again, the duke said, "Than shall we all watch as Madame Nyght raises the dead?"

The surgery was a working space: walls were of smooth brick, and the floor sloped to a drain that ran along one edge, making it easy to clean up after a session of examining bodies. Metal cabinets with a steel counter running along one wall. To increase illumination, gas sconces had mirrors behind them, but at Madame Nyght's request, these were dimmed.

Using a traditional arrangement of alternating males with females, Nyght placed each of us around the body. It was rather an old-fashioned idea about sexual spiritual energy; that a woman's undisciplined heat needed the cooling of a man's or the female flow would grow destructive. It was a foolish notion, but it produced drama when a woman gave her hand to a man.

The duke stepped forward immediately to Nyght's right-hand side. I ended up between the inspector and the sergeant. Dupont's hand was icy, almost freezing, while Barbier was warm; I was holding a candle with one hand and a snowball with the other.

Barbier leaned closer to me and whispered, "You don't do it like this."

I almost replied, but the duke's expression at the inspector's words made me press my lips together. There would be plenty of time to talk afterward. By pivoting my heel, I pressed the heel of my boot onto the inspector's troll-sized shoe to stop any further commentary. He gave me an offended puppy-dog look.

"Do not break the circle or one of us will die."

Madame Nyght's words produced silence; even Dr. LaRue stopped her muttered cursing. Nyght definitely had a flair; I tucked that melodramatic statement under my hat for the next time I had an unruly audience.

"Spirit, hear me! Make yourself known. We desire to speak with you."

The room was silent now except for our breathing. I didn't know if mysir de duke was a disbeliever, but even for those who might scoff at Ghost Talking, there was always that small doubt that the three planes existed: Earthly, Beyond, and Afterlife. And for those who did not doubt, there was the hesitation of wondering if you wanted to know what spirits could tell us.

Slowly, Nyght began a low chanting that grew in volume. The tone was guttural and the words nonsense, punctuated with her raspy, deep breathing. The air was heavy with a sense of taut expectation and for a moment I wondered if Nyght was indeed the fraud I thought she was, for the hairs on the back of my neck rose and a shiver went down my spine.

Something was happening. A high-pitched, unnatural squeal echoed around the room. The dimness of the room forced me to squint in order to make out her features. She tilted her head back, exposing a pale neck above her lace collar and around her lips, a wispy whiteness appeared.

Really? Ectoplasm?

It took shape, expanding, growing into a gray-white cloud stream.

If the two officers of the law weren't holding my hands, I might have clapped in admiration at Nyght doing a trick as old as the Zulskaya mountains.

However, one amongst us had had enough of the show and took drastic action. Mysir de duke dropped Nyght's hand and lunged towards the misty white trail. Grabbing it fiercely, he jerked his fist back, while Madame Nyght clamped down on the wispy fabric she was producing from her mouth.

She tried without success to shove him away, but his was the superior strength, and their tug of war made her stagger sideways.

Off balance, her out-flung hand contacted the corpse on the table. Nyght shrieked, and out came the wad of gauze from her mouth. As Dr. LaRue turned up the gas jets, the duke held the incriminating evidence high in the air, triumphant.

Madame Nyght, hand at her throat, cried, "How dare you treat a lady in this manner, sir!"

The duke ignored her outburst and addressed the rest of the room. "I requested Madame Nyght's help tonight because I wanted to expose her as a charlatan before impeccable witnesses."

"I am not—" But madame's protest died off when Mysir de Archambeau shook the length of gauze, the "ectoplasm," in her face.

To hide my smile, I looked down and saw on the floor a piece of tubing about the diameter of my pinky finger. I picked it up, and squeezing one end of the tin attachment, found it produced a shrill whistle. It was the unnatural sound made during the séance. Releasing the pressure caused the rubber attached at one end to re-inflate.

"Madame Nyght has played on the sorrows of grieving mothers and distraught fathers long enough with her Ghost Talking tricks."

I was barely listening to the duke as I was busy examining Madame Nyght's toy whistle. Before I could help myself, I squeezed it again, causing it to emit another eerie shriek. The duke stopped talking, narrowing his eyes to stare at me. I blushed, putting my hands behind my back.

"You are taking revenge against me for what I said about your wife," Madame Nyght accused him.

Before Mysir de Archambeau could address the medium's accusation, the inspector gave a phlegmy cough into his hand. Barbier said, with a note of apology in his voice, "The longer we go without Madame Chalamet Ghost Talking this fellow, the less information we will get from the corpse, mysir de duke. Or that has been my experience."

The duke's gaze went from the inspector to me. He handed the "ectoplasm" gauze to Sergeant Dupont and told him, "Good. Arrest Madame Nyght and take her down to the station. I shall stay here and see what farce Madame Chalamet can produce."

This was a night full of entertaining insults!

As bidden, Dupont handcuffed the medium with a pair of come-alongs, and pushed her out the door. Inspector Barbier stayed behind.

Well, time to begin my work.

I asked Dr. LaRue, "Could you move the table over there?"

Uncrossing her arms, she and Inspector Barbier rolled the table with the corpse against the wall. From my satchel, I took out a leather pouch filled with my custom mixture of resins that summoned and protected. Too many forgot the second, but not I.

"Before we begin, since we have a newcomer in our midst, I shall share some information."

"Someone dies if we break the circle?" asked the duke sarcastically.

"Not at all. However, Ghost Talking produces only limited results, as the inspector and the doctor know. A body quickly deteriorates after death, thinning the tie of the soul to the Earthly plan, and thus it affects the quality of the answers I can gain."

"Naturally. The perfect excuse."

If mysir de duke was going to interrupt me at every point, this would be a long night. However, I had faced skepticism before and would again, so I shrugged away his ridicule.

Pulling back the sheet from the face of the dead man, I examined it with a clinical eye. I'd guess about three days or fewer, but Dr. LaRue would know better after her postmortem.

"From my experience, I think we may have time for three questions before the man's spirit becomes confused. Do you have specific ones you would like to ask?"

"Who murdered him would be a good one," said the duke,

folding his arms. Yes, that mulish side of him was pinning its ears and giving me a kick or two.

"No, that would not be a good one," I corrected him. "He may not have seen his killer or recognize him. What he doesn't know, we won't know. Do we know his identity?"

"No."

"First, we ask who he is. Obviously he would know this unless he is a mental deficient. Second, a recounting of his last hour alive would provide clues for you to work with. The third question I suggest leaving open-ended until we learn more."

Because I couldn't resist, I asked our noble guest, "Do you wish to look down my throat, your Grace, and make sure I haven't stuffed it full of cotton?"

He folded his arms and glared.

"No? Alright, let the performance begin."

Chapter Three

In the past, Ghost Talkers ate the eyes of the dead to receive visions. Thankfully, in these enlightened times, there are better methods to know what the dead last saw.

Setting a coal in a brazier, I waited until the edges became white with heat before sprinkling tree resin on top. As it smoked, I used my left hand to wave the cloud into my nostrils before doing the same to the corpse.

Like alternating women and men in a séance circle, this was a traditional ritual, but it was one that worked. Air is the medium of communication, and this plant resin was effective in calling back the soul to its physical body.

Finished, I placed the bowl safely out of the way. From my bag, I took a vial of Eyesbright and placed several drops in my eyes. The room blurred, and I blinked rapidly, letting the liquid settle. My vision became tinted with a hazy purple-silver, letting me know I would now see the unseen.

Between the drops and the smoke, I was feeling light-headed, ready to step into the spiritual plane.

"Let's see what we have here."

Being in the water hadn't helped his appearance. I placed three drops of Eyesbright into each of his eye sockets and carefully stoppered the bottle before slipping it into the dress pocket that didn't hold my man-stopper.

After my father's death, I spent five years training with the Morpheus Society. While my younger self had struggled to learn the proper trance state, now I slipped into it easily. Holding the palms of my hand over his face, I centered my spirit before sending out a silent call. It took only moments before I found the spirit belonging to the flesh lying on the table.

"Come to me," I demanded.

The air grew heavy and thick, like the atmosphere before a rainstorm; it was a signal of the corpse's spirit drawing closer. Around me, I heard indrawn breaths from the others; he must have materialized. It surprises many to discover that ghosts appear as firm and real as the living. But they cannot hold that form for long and the man's mental acuity was already slipping away without a living body to anchor it.

"Give us your name and the title you held in life," I asked, pulling gently on that spiritual string that anchored us temporarily together.

"Giles Monet."

Behind me, the duke shifted, letting out an involuntary curse under his breath. So someone knew the name but not the face. How interesting.

"Tell us about the last hours of your life, Giles Monet."

From Monet's mind, I projected his knowledge into a physical existence. The images solidified as if it was a play on stage, and he carried out his last movements for us all to see.

The duke asked, "Is she using a magic lantern?"

"It's more like those new moving pictures," said the inspector.

Monet eats alone in a shabby room that combines bed, sofa, and a washstand in a cramped space. Then he leaves, going down two flights of stairs, and out a door into the street. Turning right, he walks two blocks and enters a corner store—a place selling news sheets and necessary household goods. I made note of the name, though I did not recognize it.

After making a small purchase, he takes a quick-cab to a night-club (not in the best side of town, my guess it was in the Hells). There, he walks through a group of toughs at the entrance who recognize him. Inside, he finds a seat close to the stage. A three-man band plays while a woman with blond hair sings a catchy musical number; it was the same tune as the rooster song the students had sung.

Suddenly, images started breaking apart as Monet's spirit frayed. That surprised me; though recently dead, Monet should have given us more, but his essence was weaker than it should have been. Why?

With no time for discussion, I asked quickly, "What person did you see last?"

A woman's face, a round face with enormous eyes and blond hair, formed before the image blew away, snuffed out like a candle's flame.

I opened my eyes, working hard to smother a yawn as my stomach growled. After rubbing my hands together briskly to bring life to them, I started cleaning up and packing my bag.

Across the surgery, the duke de Archambeau was at the doorway talking with Barbier. The last thing he said before leaving was, "Bring that woman to the station."

That is why I was sitting on a hard wooden chair in an office at the gendarmes, waiting for the dawn to break, instead of in my soft bed at the Crown hotel. Inspector Barbier apologized again, but his words were as weak as the tea he had given me.

"What does His Grace want with me?" I asked, irritated, my head and neck aching.

"When he finishes questioning Madame Nyght, he will come and release you." Barbier promised me.

"I don't understand why you aren't in charge of this case." My comment only gained a shrug from Barbier. "The gendarmes are fine for the everyday people but when a crime happens among le beau idéal, well, they want one of their own in charge."

"Maybe those are the very people who shouldn't be in charge," I said tartly.

Barbier gave a cough to hide his grin. "I don't know that I want the job investigating who murdered the king's cousin. Better let the blame fall on this duke's head when he can't solve the mystery. With royalty involved, this is a high profile case that could result in someone finding themselves fired, or worse, disappeared."

"Do you think he won't be able to find the murderer?" I asked, curious. Some crimes, like my father's, did go unsolved, but a surprising amount of murders were simply about finding who was in the right place with the right motive.

He gave another shrug. "Look, I need to be going. Are you sure you can wait on your own?"

I nodded. He stood up, making his way to the door, but he had one last bit of advice for me. "These nobles can be touchy. Don't rile him up, Elinor, I know how you can get on your high horse when you feel offended or when someone isn't listening to your advice, but this case could become a firecracker."

"I'll stay on a low, to the ground, horse. I promise you."

"Sure you will." He grinned, shaking his head, as he walked out the door.

Alone, I brought out the bottle of Eyesbright from my pocket and fitted it into my satchel. I removed the bullets from my small pistol and placed both into a false bottom of my bag.

Standing, I put my hands over my head and gave a deep stretch. I took a tour around the office, examining what hung on the walls and what items were on the desk in plain view. It only took moments to scan the room, and bored, I returned to my chair.

My corset was the only thing keeping me upright; my chin nodded down, touching my chest. Asleep, I started a dream of my father. He was polishing a deep red stone the size of his thumb. He held it under the bright lamp he used when working on jewelry, his fingers moving it so it glowed, refracting the light.

"Rubies are the heart-blood of dragons, Elinor."

A door slammed, jerking me awake. Mysir de Duke de Archambeau demanded, "What are you doing here?"

Exhausted, I did not answer in the kindest manner. "You told me to wait here. Remember?"

"Yes, yes I did. I forgot about you. The inspector told me about you— the daughter of a master jeweler." He wiped a hand across his forehead, disarranging his black, wavy hair. It seemed I wasn't the only one not fully awake in the early hours of the morning, but while his gesture might make him appear human, I would not let my guard down.

He gave me a long puzzled look, asking abruptly, "Why do you wear black? It doesn't suit your pale coloring. When I first saw you, I took you for much older."

"Too kind, sir! And what color do you recommend for a trip to the morgue?" I asked sarcastically.

"A dark satin blue, with perhaps a black velvet jacket. That would go well with your sandy blond hair and blue eyes." Ignoring my outraged look, he called out loudly, "Guardia!" In a moment, an officer I did not know entered the room, saluting Archambeau. From his coat pocket, the duke pulled out a leather wallet and handed several folded notes to her.

"A pot of coffee from across the street, strong and black, with a pot of cream. And pastries. Fruit, if they have any this late in the year."

After a salute, the officer left, closing the door behind her.

"You left me here to starve for hours, so I hope you plan on sharing that."

"Of course." He waved me to the chair sitting in front of his desk. "This one is more comfortable."

"Perhaps you can explain why you have an office here? You are not a member of the gendarmes." I spoke with confidence, having worked with the inspector since my graduation from the Morpheus Society.

"You are correct. I work for the Crown. But sometimes it is good to have a place to interview subjects in a more, shall we say, neutral place?"

"And that it happens to be close to the jail, I'm sure is a benefit?"

He didn't respond, and since we both looked foolish standing, I took the seat he offered while he chose the chair behind the desk. He was still wearing evening wear, so had not returned home either, which only reminded me of my grievance.

"Will you tell me why I'm here and when I can go home?"

"It's complicated."

"Not really," I countered. "Giles Monet gave you what information he could, but there's nothing more I can do. He's gone."

He looked down at his hands, the long fingers splayed out across the desktop.

"You heard things you should not have."

"I can forget whatever it was just as fast."

The corners of his mouth gave a closed-mouth twitch.

"Like I said, things are not simple. Exposing Madame Nyght ended a yearlong investigation. She is part of a confidence scheme that traces all the way to the capital."

"How did you know she was a fraud?"

"That would require divulging private information."

"Well, I already know too much, according to you, so knowing more won't hurt me."

"I didn't say it would hurt you," he said, giving a slight emphasis to the last word.

Others often describe my face as a friendly one that encourages confidences. I get told about illicit affairs while on the train and at the market hear the latest gossip about wayward sons who marry the wrong types. My face did not fail me now, for after a sigh, mysir de duke began his tale.

"Against my wishes, my in-laws had Nyght conduct a séance, trying to reach my wife. During it, Nyght revealed details of an intimate nature, known only between Minette and myself. I could see no way she would know such information, and it made me curious about her."

Because I was tired, I was more blunt than diplomatic.

"These con artists worm out information. A man thinks his wife keeps their secrets, but there is always a confidant, a close friend or relation, that she discusses heart matters with. Or letters exist. A journal. Servants."

"I found no such leak," he stated firmly. His eyes gained a bit of fire at my suggestion.

"If Madam Nyght had access to any of your friends or family, she would have learned even more than I have in the few hours I have known you. It is doubtful that your household servants would keep the knowledge of a quarrel between their master and mistress private. Servants are a notorious fountain of information about their employers."

"No one talked," he insisted.

"Conjecture can reveal more than you think. I imagine Madame Nyght had a dossier filled with facts about your family before that séance took place. The rest she fished out of you."

"I told her nothing—" he began, but I cut him off with a wave of my hand.

"Logic, mysir de duke! Logic! I have never met you, but I know you and your wife to be estranged. That you hold ill feelings about her. Perhaps even hate her?"

"How dare you!" He rose from his seat, slamming his fist on the desk. I also stood, just as furious.

"Your Grace, you have run through my patience. You state Madame Nyght is a fraud. I agree! Now, I show you how she does it and you dare to snap and bite at me?"

A ligament in his jaw jerked as he regained control of himself. He sat down again, gesturing for me to do the same. "You have not explained how you know this."

Refusing to sit, I walked a tight circle around the room, gesturing as I schooled him. "You admit this is your office for interrogation, so one would not expect personal items. However, still the room reveals you. It is sterile. Not even awards or boring art graces the walls. The drawers only hold a lone pencil rolling about. You do not see this as a personal office, but somewhere you pass through. This implies your actual office is elsewhere."

As I continued, his expression changed to one more thoughtful than angry.

"But your appearance is where I find the real clues. Your emerald cuff links are in excellent condition, your shoes and clothes perfection— the sign of an excellent tailor and valet, but there is no presence of a wife. For a wife of your station would have made sure you had a boutonnière before leaving the house for an evening's entertainment.

"Yet you wear a gold wedding band. So there is a wife, somewhere. Your lack of a flower shows she is missing. Called away this evening? Dead or estranged? The pupils of your eye just constricted— so she is dead. Not recently because you attended a social function tonight. Not dead long ago, because you still wear the wedding band.

"Unlike the cuff links, your watch, your starched collar, which are all pristine and correct, your gold band is scratched and dull. Uncared for. What could this mean but that you attach no importance to it? Yet, still feel some obligation to wear it. Why? We have choices: because society demands it? You are not the type. Out of respect? Ah, I see by your smirk that is not the reason. Perhaps guilt, Your Grace?"

He cut me short. "So my ring gave me away?"

"That and how your mood changed when I mentioned my findings. A fraud like Nyght deciphers every expression, every word said, as well as what is not. It is how the confidence medium works, Your Grace."

He gave a slow, strange smile. "But not you."

"No, not me."

He returned to the arrest of Madame Nyght.

"I do not believe my ghostly wife gave any information to Nyght, but I couldn't decipher how she knew what she did. My curiosity focused my attention on her activities and associates. Our investigation revealed Nyght headed a ring of spiritualists who defrauded their victims of thousands, but worse, they cruelly used people's hopes to steal the dignity of their loved ones. In the last four hours, my team has apprehended over eleven members of her gang in Alenbonné alone."

"I am surprised to learn she had such a large organization. You should inform the Morpheus Society, Your Grace. They will want to let our members know. While the Society isn't affiliated with the government or gendarmes, they do investigate fraudulent mediums to expose them. I have brought Madame Nyght to their attention several times."

"I informed them but received no answer, Madame Chalamet."

At this moment, the coffee and breakfast tray arrived. The guardia placed the tray on the desk before leaving. The duke poured out, letting me decide on how much cream I wanted. Over strong coffee and a glazed bun, he said, "While you may not be part of their enterprise, Madame Chalamet, you are still alarming. Quite alarming."

"How so?"

"Inspector Barbier tells me you do not request or receive any financial compensation for the work you do for the gendarmes."

"That is true. I do it out of civic duty, as I am financially independent. Though I have private clients from time to time."

"Yes, I've confirmed that with your bank manager."

Taken aback, my second bun paused on the way to my mouth. I asked, "In the middle of the night? Do take pity on my bank balance and remember, I am only a single woman who is making her way in the world, not a titled lady with a large inheritance."

"Duly noted. Also, that you are the daughter of a jeweler who did work for King Guénard, according to Barbier. How much do you remember of your father's commissions?"

"I have kept his papers and his memories."

"Can you authenticate gems?"

"Yes. I don't use those skills any more, but yes, my father trained me when I was young.

There was a speculative gleam in his eyes that did not bode well for me. He switched tactics. "What is most pressing is you are not a fake, which presents me with a dilemma."

"How so?"

"Remember Giles Monet? Our dead body?"

"Of course."

"He's a bastard relation of the royal house. Until we sign the peace treaty next week, I shall keep all the information about Giles Monet and his doings locked down."

"Fine, I'll keep quiet about it," I assured him.

He shook his head sadly.

"No, Madame Chalamet, you misunderstand me. This is a Crown matter now. The guardia and the coroner I can rely upon, but you? You, I do not know."

"I promise not to utter a word about it!" I crossed my heart twice, making an X.

"No, madame, there is only one answer."

"You can't lock me up!" I rose to my full height of five feet, two inches.

"To protect the king, we all must make sacrifices."

CHAPTER FOUR

Instead of a jail cell with iron bars, I was given a golden cage.

In his carriage, the duke agreed I could send a message to my servant for anything I would need during my confinement. A note he fully intended on reading, he informed me.

Anne-Marie would have loved this trip in His Grace's private carriage. A very glamorous equipage in polished black with doors displaying his crest in colors of gold, green, and red, pulled by two flashy matching bay horses. But I could not find the enthusiasm and rested my tired head on the back of the leather upholstery.

Like many city houses, a decorative black iron fence made the boundary of a napkin-sized front yard. Built of white stone, the windows had black shutters to batten down during the storm season. Ivy climbed up the front facade, softening the hard edges of the building, and each window had a copper roof over the top that matched in style the one at the top of the building.

A maid was sweeping the front doorstep when the coach stopped and in a moment the duke was out in a flash. His hand helped me down and then he was gone, marching up to the double-set black doors with their polished brass door knockers. The duke's long, purposeful stride had him entering his home while I clambered out from the coach. The maid gave me a sideways, curious look as I passed by her.

Like the outside, everything inside spoke of understated taste on an expensive scale. The grand height of the foyer, the staircase with its carved walnut balusters, the leaf and rope details in the white plaster moldings on the ceiling, and a floor of imported white and pink marble, were all evidence of no money spared.

My tiredness caused me to lose track of what my jailer was saying. I caught him in mid-sentence, addressing another maid. "—to a guest room. Whichever one she fancies. Her belongings will come at a later date. You will join me for dinner?"

It's not exactly a question when the person walks off in the middle of asking it. Fuming, I said to the servant, "Well, go ahead. Show me to a room. I'd like to know what my cell looks like."

She appeared confused by my comment, and after a moment, asked me to follow her up the stairs. On the third floor, after being shown two rooms, I selected the one facing the back gardens. If I was to suffer being here, I would not listen to the street noise of hawkers and carriages. I unpinned my hat, setting it on a hexagon table placed under the window.

"Could you please fetch me pen and paper?"

She gave a bob and headed away. I looked around to find that the room was not as big as my suite at the Crown, but far more luxurious.

The wallpaper was pale pink with a thin gold stripe, and the heavy, thick drapes were a deep rose velvet. The furnishings included a bed big enough for two, a desk with a chair, a sitting area that included two upholstered chairs, and a small settee that faced a fireplace mantle made from a dark red stone with black veining. Like the marble floor below, it was another luxury imported from the Zulskaya mountains.

As a jeweler's daughter, I appreciated the expense of the room's decor. It was a testament to wealth and good taste: a gilt bronze clock on the mantle, silver candlesticks, and a music box that I wound up and set aside before examining the framed watercolors. These were of the countryside, showing gently rolling hills and lakes.

However, it was the painting of a woman wearing garments of a hundred years ago that dominated the room. She held a shepherd's crook while lambs frolicked in the background. From her insipid dress, I was pretty sure she hadn't smelled a sheep in her entire life.

Next to the main apartment was a dressing room with a daybed. I would invite Anne-Marie to come, for I am sure she would hate me forever if she lost a chance to see how the aristocracy lived. It would serve the duke right to have two of us to watch.

Another door revealed a bathroom, and I wet a small towel to clean my face. The dirty air of the city got onto everything, no matter how thick your hat's veil. I started removing the barrettes, unwinding my hair from its sagging bun.

"Madame? Your paper."

The maid had reappeared with the materials I would need to send a note to Anne-Marie. I couldn't imagine my assistant being panicked, but surely she was wondering where I was. Well, I would ask her to bring me every black dress she could stuff into a large trunk.

"What is your name?"

"Georgette."

As I wrote, I asked, "Georgette, I am to dine with mysir de duke this evening. What does that entail, exactly?"

"Tonight he is hosting a party of twenty. A few diplomats and department heads. His sister, Lady Fontaine, will be hostess."

"And the evening dress protocol? Shoulders exposed, plunging neckline, all my wealth in my hair, around my neck, on fingers and wrists? I expect that's how they dress in high society?"

Being an excellent servant, Georgette did not startle easily, though her eyelashes couldn't suppress a flutter at my plain speaking. She said meekly, "Off-shoulder is the current style, madame."

Tempted as I was, I did not press her for details about Minette, the duke's dead wife. That would come later; the duke said his household did not talk, and I would discover who did.

After a long nap, I took a bath. On a bathroom shelf, I found little stoppered glass bottles packed with flowers and scented oils. I couldn't resist mixing and matching and by the time I ended experimenting with them, the entire suite was as steamy and fragrant as a florist shop.

The water at the Crown was notorious for never being truly hot. Henri Colbert, the manager, told me it was because too many people taxed the boiler. Here, steam was still rising from the water's surface. While the hot warmth caressed my skin, I considered my position.

A logical mind, such as mine, should be open to the right persuasion; I would not want to be accused of being narrow-minded. If mysir de duke wished to keep me in a golden cage, I might want to enjoy it for a while before making my escape.

I heard the door open and voices. Ah. Georgette and Anne-Marie. By the time I toweled off and entered the bedroom area in a guest robe, I found my servant was alone, surrounded by a couple of steamer trunks, hatboxes, and three carpetbags. Anne-Marie had packed for an extended engagement.

Anne-Marie had dressed the part, wearing a neatly pressed gray gown, with her braids pinned up. The only wrong note in her appearance of respectability rested on her head: a jaunty cap she had swiped from a news boy just last week.

"Goodness, madame, you've landed us in swansdown this time!"

I gave her a small smile. "Well, I'm not sure I would call our situation that. We must stay here, our every move watched, for a week. Once the new trade treaty is signed, we can leave."

My words didn't seem to bother her, for she asked eagerly, "How many footmen do you think His Grace has? It took four to help get your things upstairs."

"I have no idea!" I glanced at the clock. "Come along, Anne-Marie. I need to get my hair brushed and styled. I have an hour before dinner."

Anne-Marie turned quickly, opening up trunk latches and throwing dresses onto the bed. "Which dress for tonight, madame?"

"Whichever one you think is the blackest black. With shoulders showing."

Anne-Marie didn't ask silly questions. She held up a dress for approval. "What about this one?"

This evening dress had two rows of flounces at the bottom, which visually made me look shorter than I already was. It had the required deep neckline, along with off-the-shoulder puff sleeves of silk organza. In style, it was about three years out-of-date, but it was the nicest I owned and would do for tonight.

"Yes, that one. And my choker of gray-mist pearls with the diamond spacers."

While Anne-Marie tossed clothes, stockings, and shoes onto the bed, I went through the bags that she had brought at my request. The books I wanted to read, I placed at my bedside table. I thumbed through the stack of my correspondence and calling cards and pulled those that would require attention.

Some clients would need hand holding in person; that was something I would need to discuss soon with the duke.

~

Anne-Marie was finishing my hair when there was a discreet knock on the door. It was the maid, Georgette, and another woman dressed in an expensive and fashionable evening gown that was not three years old.

"Lady Valentina Fontaine, madame," Georgette introduced the newcomer and then stepped back to fade away down the passage.

Lady Valentina looked to be about five or more years older than her brother, perhaps in her late thirties or early forties. She seemed nervous, for her eyes flitted like startled birds around the room, avoiding my gaze. They took in my opened trunks, garments still lying on the bed, and my stacks of books. The frozen room was now cluttered with life.

"You are my brother's guest."

"I must be if His Grace says I am."

"My brother did not say you were a widow."

Ah, the black again.

"I am not," I said. My statement and my refusal to expand upon it seemed to flummox her.

"I was told to bring you down."

"How kind of you."

Lady Valentina's gown was a pale gold-cream color and from the drape of the fabric and how it moved like a waterfall, it was worth far more than my poor satin. Decorating the skirt were pearls, which I am sure made it a nightmare to clean the fabric. Scallops of gold lace edged the neckline and gave her flat chest some dimension, even if it was an illusion.

I was a black crow beside her as we left, our skirts swishing down the hall, our only audience the paintings of various frowning people in outfits of long ago. It was quiet, and I assumed this floor of the house was not in use at the moment except by myself.

"I do not know if my brother said—" Lady Valentina began again, flustered. "This is a very important dinner for him. He is working with men and women at the highest level to arrange for the safety of King Guénard when he arrives."

I started down the stairs, forcing Lady Valentina to hurry her step if she didn't want to shout her advice.

"There is a certain decorum to be observed at this, the highest level."

"Certainly," I said automatically, already bored to death with decorum.

"A person from your walk of life may not have the skill to navigate such—"

We had made the second turn on the staircase and could see the front hall, where guests wearing evening dress mingled, handing their wraps, coats and hats to staff. One bright red-gold head of hair caught my eye. Holding up my dress skirt to prevent tripping, I galloped down the last steps with as much grace as a farmer's cart horse.

"Elinor!"

"Jacques! I did not know you were back! Why didn't you send me a message?"

Both of his hands were on my waist and he twirled me around, my feet leaving the marble floor for an instant. We burst into laughter at the same time.

"I sent a message to the Crown, but got no reply. Whatever are you doing here?" he asked. We had drawn attention from the other guests, two women and an older man wearing a military uniform who walked stiffly as if his back hurt.

Jacques explained our behavior to them. "An old family friend."

Faces turned politely away. When Lady Fontaine joined the group, the others trailed after her into an adjoining room. We two were last, and entered hand in hand, like children.

In a deep whisper, bringing his head down close to mine, Jacques asked, "Are you here to lay Archambeau's ghost?"

Chapter Five

The dining hall of the duke's residence was as beautiful and expensive as the rest of it. It was as large as my entire suite of rooms at the Crown, and to my ears my heels seemed to echo rather loudly as they clicked across the marble floor. Several heads turned to notice my entrance on Jacques arm, and a fan or two fluttered up to hide a comment to their partner.

One question of "who is she?" I heard, and I hoped the warmth of my cheeks might be marked down to the heat from the immense number of beeswax tapers in silver candelabras that were placed down the long table. The candlelight gave off enough glow that it removed any dark corners of the room. Snow white plates rimmed in gold, and glass goblets each etched with a stylized flower from the Chambaux crest, decorated the table.

As Jacques pulled out my chair, I noticed the wallpaper: a dark blue field with a winding vine of green holding bunches of yellow grapes. It was only then that I connected the crest on the carriage door that had looked faintly familiar, with the grapes, and the Archambeau name to the province of Chambaux. *Wine!*

Stupid of me not to have made the link before, but it was difficult to visualize one of the most established and celebrated wines of Sarnesse with that of the face of Mysir de Archambeau himself. He did not look like the one who toiled the earth.

The room filled with guests and Jacques took his place further down the table, so we could not continue our interesting discussion. Instead, on my left was an elderly deaf man who was interested in only food, and on my right was a determined flirt who was busy pursuing the lady across the table. Jacques was enjoying company far more engaging than my own, so cheerful smiles sent my way were few.

I sighed. Mysir de Archambeau had silenced me by removing anyone who could have been a sympathetic confidant. Looking to where he sat at the head of the table, I tilted my glass of white wine to him as a salute. The corner of his mouth twitched, and he returned a subtle toast of his own glass towards me.

Thus, thwarted from conversing, I devoted myself to the delicious food and observed the guests.

My host's sister, Lady Valentina, sat at the opposite end of the table from her brother. Since she was closer, I could hear her talk about Sarnesse's complicated history with our across-the-ocean neighbor, Perino. She appeared to be in her element, the early nervousness gone.

It was during the fourth course when the woman who was the object of my flirting neighbor said, "Now I remember who you are. You're Madame Chalamet, the Ghost Talker. I'm surprised Tristan would have your sort at his table."

"Pardon me, but I don't believe we've met?"

"No, we haven't. Perhaps because I have no dead relations that I would like to speak to!" She gave one of those light laughs that are as frothy as whipped cream and about as fulfilling to the soul. "I am Lady Josephine Baudelaire, a dear friend of Tristan and Valentina. We've known each other for years; I'm practically family."

The look she gave under her eyelashes to Lady Valentina was indeed familial. In my line of work, I'd seen it before; it usually ends with someone dying under mysterious circumstances, along with a lost will, and the gendarmes involved.

A woman somewhat younger than Archambeau and his sister, Lady Josephine, with her blond hair, plucked eyebrows, and subtly tinted cheeks, was every drop a sophisticated lady of society seen in a fashion plate. She wore a gown of deep purple, and with no shoulders to hold it up, it relied on her bosom to keep everything in place. It had ample support.

"That is a beautiful necklace. An heirloom, by chance?" I asked her.

Her hand went up to touch the piece.

"Yes, it is a piece from my husband's family, handed down for over six generations to the heir's wife. A gift from Queen Marcelina."

There was no way not to notice it. The old-fashioned diamonds were cut in a style done over 400 years ago and which had recently become popular again. The elaboration on a table cut was easy to identify due to the criss-cross cuts over the diamond's surface. The silver links that held the square stones together were of heavy links to support the weight of the diamonds, and gave off the unpleasant notice of a dog's collar.

The showstopper though was the middle diamond, even larger than the others and faceted with the old-mine cut. Not matching the others, it might have come from another piece or had been added later. It attracted my attention.

Lady Josephine happily entertained me with her family's illustrious history: a long list of famous battles where Baudelaires saved princes and high lords aplenty, and were gifted castles and land by various nobles. This recitation of every exploit of her husband's bloodline while dropping names occupied her from the fourth course to the seventh.

"The earl was most be appreciative of how Avellino risked his life to save his daughter."

"I can only imagine," I commented.

Having scraped his plate clean, my elderly seat mate announced in a booming voice, "Vineyards."

"Yes, Sir Vincent, we have vineyards." Lady Josephine nodded at each word like a marionette, giving him a fixed smile, as if talking to a child or an imbecile.

"Next to Archambeau's estate."

Lady Josephine said quickly to me, "Madame Chalamet, tell me, as I have been dying to ask. Are you here to speak with the spirit of Tristan's dead wife and lay to rest the rumors of how she died?"

Mysir de duke must have hearing like a cat, for I felt his gaze upon me from the head of the table, six seats down. If he wanted to test me, I would tease him with his distrust.

"Can you keep a secret?"

The corner of her sharply defined, painted lips quirked up to form a sharp V she couldn't quite suppress. "Oh, indeed."

"I think he brought me here to evaluate his jewelry. After all, I am the daughter of Augustus Chalamet, the jeweler who selected the pieces gifted to King Guénard's bride."

She shrank back and her hand flew again to her necklace, but now in a protective posture. So Lady Josephine knew it was fake. *Interesting.* However, she quickly regained her composure and fired back with a carelessness that did not fool me.

"Oh yes, now I remember your father. Wasn't he murdered?"

"Yes, he was. They cut his throat from ear to ear," I confirmed calmly. Lady Josephine wasn't the first to bring up the subject and nor would she be the last. I had met many more insulting questions about my father's death than this one.

A servant removed my plate, and set the mignardise, the last course, in front of me. Attentive staff laid new silverware, removed glasses, and placed a cup of steaming coffee next to the bite-sized dessert. Each guest had the initial of their first name drawn in dark chocolate icing across the smooth white cream surface of the mignardise.

A dessert though did not distract my opponent, for Lady Josephine had the tenacity of a terrier. "Do you use your talent to speak with him? Your father, I mean. Beyond the grave?"

Her surname Baudelaire was an old word meaning dagger, but those who play with knives sometimes cut themselves.

"Oh yes, we chat all the time," I said. "But he doesn't speak of his death; he only talks of his trade. The jewels he's handled and set. And how no matter how well cut, glass never outshines the brilliance of diamonds."

Lady Josephine quickly returned to flirting, ignoring me for the time being. From the corner of my eye, I saw Archambeau raise his coffee cup towards me in his second salute of the evening. My, my, what mighty fine hearing the gentleman had.

Dinner over, our Lady Valentina stood up, and the party followed her into the adjoining receiving rooms, where guests mingled with the people they truly wanted to speak with. Now I suspected the real art of negotiation and deal-making would begin. I wondered how many had trade concerns the treaty and its increased taxes would impact?

Jacques sought me out, and I found I could breathe again. I gave my first honest smile since dinner. Our mothers were childhood friends, and we had carried on the tradition.

"Whatever are you doing here, Jacques? Your sister told me you were in Zulskaya, wooing three women at the same time."

"The number of my conquests is greatly exaggerated. There were only two, and it turned out they had huge brothers and fathers with no sense of humor. But to answer your question, I'm here in Alenbonné as an attaché to General Reynard Somerville. Writing his correspondence, managing his calendar, getting ready for the big parade."

"The general is that gentleman in the army uniform talking to Mysir de Archambeau?"

"Yes, but I don't want to talk about him." Jacques took my arm and guided me behind a plant, some tall monstrosity with leaves larger than my head in a brass pot. In a low voice, he said, "I want to know why you are here, as the guest of a man who hates Ghost Talkers?"

"I can't really discuss that. I'm under orders."

"Do you know about his marriage?"

"Yes, and that a Ghost Talker was called in after she died."

"But did you know it was his wife's family who dragged in a Ghost Talker, because they wanted to prove it wasn't a proper marriage in order to get her family property returned?"

Not a genuine marriage was an insinuation that it was unconsummated. Not insulting at all. I'm sure someone as prideful as mysir de duke took all of that placidly.

Before I could reply, I heard my name spoken across the room.

"Do you think spirits are really just sewage gas, Madame Chalamet?" Lady Josephine's voice carried across the room and it made the other conversations sputter to a stop. She was standing next to Lady Valentina, who did not look pleased at all with her dear family friend.

Their group included two men: a young man in his twenties with light blond hair and an overeager face, and an older, sandy-haired man who had flirted with Lady Josephine at dinner. Both wore expensive clothes and haircuts, and carried themselves with a certain weary, bored expression on their faces that seemed to be part of the required costume of their social class.

Jacques extended his arm, and I took it. As we walked over to the group, I felt we were leading a charge into enemy territory. When we were close enough to discuss things in a normal tone of voice, I answered the question.

"The fumes from sewage, especially in a confined area, can

cause health concerns. Mind-doctors say the air can produce hallucinations, illusions that seem real."

"I told you, Stephan," said the younger man, giving an elbow jab into the other man's ribs. The recipient of this hilarity said with a laugh, "Madame Ghost Talker, so you're confirming that spirits are nothing but vapors from a leaky toilet?"

Lady Josephine tittered at his witticism.

"No, but every vapor, every will-o-wisp seen, any shadow on the wall without something to cast it, is not always a ghost."

"I doubt Lance can tell the difference between swamp gas and ghosts," said Stephan.

The two shot acrimonious looks at each other, and I suspected gaining the attention of winsome Lady Josephine might be at the heart of their competition. It would be better to calm them down before I caught the blame for any unpleasantness.

"When faced with the unexpected, my advice is first always to check for a scientific explanation. Do the walls, windows, and floors produce a draft? Next, record your findings. Is this vapor seen only once, by only one person, and in what places? Science can explain many things that, upon first glance, appear to an uneducated eye as supernatural."

"There must be a way to identify ghosts. To know where to find them and when?" said Stephan.

"I'm sorry, but unlike a reliable clock, which produces always the same results if wound correctly, ghosts are less predictable. They randomly move between the two planes."

"What do you mean?" Lance's question was one I had answered many times.

"The Morpheus Society believes there are three planes of existence: the Earthly, the Beyond, and the Afterlife. The Earthly is the physical plane we inhabit. Once we die, there is a transition period where the spirit or soul travels to the Beyond, where they may become ghosts, although most souls travel on to the Afterlife, and are never heard from again."

"But what makes a ghost?" Stephan asked.

"All we have been able to determine at this point is powerful emotions, traumatic death, perhaps an important point in history, can weigh a soul down and prevent its transition. From our study of the paranormal, it seems spirits use the energy of the living to cross back to the Earthly plane."

"Why doesn't some of your lot go to this Beyond and find out more?" Stephan's comment was more sneer than question.

"So far, we've only been able to reach into the Beyond through astral projection, in dreams, or in meditation. But it can be very dangerous to linger too long. Remember, living energy gets drained where ghosts reside. My advice is to leave the Ghost Talking to the professionals."

"Not fair, madame!" said Stephan. Even Lance agreed. "That's an evasion! What of those who want to hunt ghosts themselves?"

"I wouldn't want to lose my income, mysir. This is best left to those trained by the Morpheus Society to do it."

During our conversation, Lady Valentina continued to cast glances to where her brother was standing with the general and two ladies. From their countenances, it was a serious discourse. Probably something about taxes. Taxes always gave me that slight bilious look.

Lady Josephine interrupted our discourse.

"If you wanted to ghost hunt, Stephan, why not start tonight? After all, we have access to a professional." Lady Josephine gave the duke's sister a snake smile. "What an amusing evening it would make for you guests, Valentina."

Lady Valentina was not looking happy, and neither was I. This was deep water, and would no doubt anger the duke. Before I could think of a graceful way to decline, Lady Josephine clapped her hands to gain the attention of the entire room.

"Madame Chalamet, a Ghost Talker, wants to conduct a ghost hunt. Who would like to come with us?"

Chapter Six

Stopping Lady Josephine with words was a useless effort as the duke's sister discovered.

"It will be entertaining, Valentina! Not everyone wants to stand around listening to Sharlyn play the piano yet again. This will make your party the hit of the season."

Suddenly, the duke joined our party and placed his hand on his sister's arm. "Forget trying to convince Josephine to see sense, Val. If she wants to get her expensive dress dusty climbing in through our garret, I will not stop her."

The siblings exchanged a look, but I didn't have the codebook to decipher what it meant.

"That's settled," said Lady Josephine rather smugly. "Who's joining us?"

Not everyone wanted to stumble around in the dark, which suited me just fine. A few begged off due to work commitments for tomorrow. Others simply wanted to discuss the politics of the day over some of the best wine the province of Chambaux could produce. Jacques would have stayed with me, but General Reynard Somerville beckoned him to his side.

Lady Josephine wanted the ghost hunt to take place in the dark to increase the thrill, but the duke ordered his staff to bring lanterns and candles for the guests. As these were being handed out, the duke told his sister, "You stay here with our guests. I shall accompany the ghost hunt."

"Are you sure, Tristan?" Her white teeth worried at her lip.

"Certainly. Besides, Madame Chalamet is my personal guest, and I have been lax in my duty of giving her a tour of our home."

The duke held out his arm, and taking it, I felt a moment of pleasure when I saw how it angered Lady Josephine.

"Wouldn't you like to be at the front with me to guide us, Tristan?" She asked in a tone that dropped sweet acid.

"Oh, I think you should be the hostess for this evening's entertainment. After all, you know the house so well," he replied smoothly.

"But what if a ghost frightens me?" she asked, giving him a coy smile. Her posture shifted subtly, displaying a well-developed cleavage. However, mysir de duke proved immune to both pleas and bosom.

"Isn't that the purpose of this little jaunt? To enjoy being frightened? I would never stand in the way of your pleasure, Josephine, no matter the consequences."

In the end, there was a mixed group of ladies and gentlemen that numbered nine. Lady Josephine, Mysir de Archambeau, Lance, Stephan, and junior members of the dining party who seemed more interested in being with each other in the dark, rather than finding spirits.

Speaking without moving my lips, I muttered, "This wasn't my idea."

"Come along," he said, leading me after the others who were already leaving.

From the ground floor, Lady Josephine showed her familiarity with the house's floor plan as she took a winding path of corridors that led us eventually to the kitchen. Cleaning up after a state dinner, the busy kitchen staff didn't seem impressed by the invasion of party guests. Lady Josephine ignored their irritated looks, ushering her group further into the bowels of the house. But Mysir de Archambeau stopped and addressed the woman who seemed in charge.

"Madame Darly, the meal was superb. Madame Chalamet here told me your dishes outshone even those served at the Crown hotel by the famous chef, Gerhard Perdersen."

He squeezed my hand, and I took my cue. "A superb meal that I will always remember," I told her.

Frustrated looks melted away, replaced with beaming smiles directed at the duke.

"That's good news, Your Grace," said the woman, wiping her hands on her apron. He gave her a nod, and than we moved past the staff to catch up with Lady Josephine.

I told him, "Accomplished liar."

Mysir de duke responded, "Did you want burned toast at breakfast tomorrow? The last time someone came into the kitchen unannounced, Darly gave us cold coffee and eggs for a week."

We were late and made it to the cellar door after the group had entered. Lady Josephine had stopped midway down the stairs to face an audience arranged below her. Coming down behind her, I vigorously fanned my hand back and forth to make the lady's lantern flicker wildly. As the flame guttered, she exclaimed, "Look at this wild flame! A spirit is nigh!"

I almost burst out laughing. Mysir de Archambeau whispered in my ear, "Behave, Ghost Talker, or I may have you arrested."

Hearing us, Lady Baudelaire spun around.

"You two are late! Come down and stand with the others."

Meekly, I stepped past her and joined her audience. Staying on the stairs, she held the lantern under her chin so it cast distorted shadows over her face, and began her tale.

"When Alenbonné still had dirt for streets, in this spot sat not a noble house, but a bawdy tavern named the Bell and Drum. A favorite with soldiers, the place was known for two things: the quality of its ale, and the beauty of its mistress. But beauty often spawns hate and jealousy. And none were more jealous than the beauty's husband, who saw her flirtatious way with the customers as a slight upon his honor."

Even under the sleeve of his coat, I could feel Archambeau's forearm stiffen as his hand balled into a fist.

"The couple ran the Bell and Tavern together— she, with her bright smile, drew the men who would spend their earnings, and the miser would count the coin every night. Wait!" Lady Josephine's hand went to her ear. "Do you hear the coins being counted?"

Of course we didn't. There was no male ghost down here, but Lady Josephine's dramatic presentation had gotten a few to shivering.

"Every day he became meaner, about his money and with his wife. He grew bitter, wanting what he couldn't have: his wife's affection. His jealousy drove her away from him. All she wanted was to make the world a happier place. There is more to life than mopping floors and washing dishes. Or being one man's companion."

A light sigh caressed my ear.

"Her husband tried to control her smiles, laughs, and joy. When nothing worked, he beat her, hoping that a spoiled face would stop her suitors. Little wonder that she sought to run away with her lover, but her husband caught her before she could escape. Down here, in this cellar. He shot her lover and beat her to death. Then he walked up the stairs, these very stairs, and drowned himself in the sea."

There was a grave moment of silence before Lady Josephine said in a stage whisper, "Some can still hear her laugh. Do you?"

She had primed her audience, and they were feeling a suspended dread. From the corner of my eye, I saw Stephan lightly touch a woman on the back of her neck. She screamed in surprise. Seeing him laughing, she slapped him across the face.

"Don't touch me again!"

"Stella!"

"Leave me alone!"

Grabbing her skirts, the young lady stormed up the stairs in righteous indignation. Stephan followed in hot pursuit, apologizing the entire way. Once the door at the top of the stairs banged shut, Lady Josephine told those who remained, "Let's see if we can catch a ghost in the green room."

She stepped upwards, with the others following. I placed my hand on Archambeau's sleeve to stop him from taking the stairs. In a low voice, I asked, "Do you have a handkerchief?"

Irritated, he asked with a sneer, "To wipe away a tear? Don't tell me that sentimental claptrap touched your heart?"

"Do you have one or not?" From an inside pocket he withdrew a white square, and I suggested, "Kiss it for me?"

He rolled his eyes, gave it a kiss, and handed it to me with a flourish. I laid it out on one of the storage barrels and told the ghost, "A gift from one of your admirers."

A breezy, light laugh tickled my ear and a sudden steep drop in temperature made goosebumps start up my bare back and neck. We must have stood there at least five minutes in silence before the temperature returned to normal.

"We can leave now. She's gone."

Now it was Mysir de Archambeau's hand on my elbow, which stopped us from leaving. "No manifestation this time?"

"Old haunts are more like memories, often confused. They have little power except for what they gain from the living to manifest."

"You mean she's draining our life force to be here?"

I chuckled. "Don't be so melodramatic. Of course not. The amount of power she would use from us would be negligible, but yes, it is our emotions that power her shifting from the Beyond to the Earthly. But if it bothers you, I could probably dismiss her to the Afterlife, if you want her dispelled permanently."

"You could do that? Banish any spirit I wanted?"

"This one, most likely. She's weak. But really, that seems mean-spirited, don't you think?" I started up, but his hand on my arm stopped me, putting us at eye level since he was lower on the stairs. Both of our lanterns had guttered, the fire quenched by the ghost's need for energy so the only light was traveling down from the open doorway.

"Why the handkerchief?"

"I thought she'd appreciate a gift from a man as handsome as yourself."

"Oh, you think me handsome, do you? I don't like flattery." I couldn't imagine why he sounded angry, or why he gave my arm a little shake when he spoke.

"You have two eyes that work, a nose in the right place, vast wealth, and a title. I'm sure that is handsome enough to please a hundred-year ghost."

Mysir de duke laughed, and the odd tension between us melted away.

"Thank you, madame," he said, giving me a dramatic bow worthy of the theater.

"Now, can we go upstairs and find out what other mischief Lady Josephine is up to?"

Up we went, and down the long corridor, past the kitchen staff, up four steps and down a hall that took us back to living areas of the house.

"Everyone thinks I'm here because you want to Ghost Talk with your wife."

"I don't," said Archambeau grimly.

"How did she die?"

"You do like getting to the point, don't you, Madame Nosy? Doesn't your power of deductions explain how it happened?" We had stopped and were now standing together in a hallway on the first floor. His arm went across my path, blocking me. "Have you ever wondered, madame, if your curiosity will get you into trouble one day?"

"Oh, it's gotten me into lots of trouble. But I like trouble."

"It isn't a secret. She died from River Fever five years ago. With the drought, and the water in the canals at a low point, there was an outbreak of the disease throughout Alenbonné that year."

His stare was intense, a mix of anger and something else.

"You're lying."

Someone shouted, "Here they are!"

Archambeau drew back and the person who had spotted us ducked back into a room only for Lady Josephine to exit into the hall. "Finally, our Ghost Talker has arrived. Did you get lost?"

Thankfully, Lady Josephine didn't wait for an answer. We entered the green room, and she followed us, closing the door behind her. With great fanfare, she announced to everyone, "Let's see if the famous Madame Chalamet can guess what happened in this room."

Surveying the green room, it seemed to be a public area done in a utilitarian masculine style. There were a couple of desks with comfortable chairs, but also a two-chair nook nestled against a draped window, bookshelves, and maps on the walls. As a government office, I dismissed the furnishings as anything that could provide clues.

Ignoring the energy of the living, I felt for the aura of a spirit. Those who have died but who remain on the physical plan have a different spectrum. A few untrained people feel them— eliciting comments of someone walking over your grave, or that sensation of being watched. With training, you can feel more: the air was vibrating. There was a damp furriness to the atmosphere, signaling a presence.

I did not like clients who wanted me to display my skills like a circus pony. Besides, Lady Josephine Baudelaire was not my client.

She wasn't even my host. And even if she were all of these things, I still wouldn't like her.

It helped that the haunt in this room was of the malicious type.

I fed it energy.

All the candles blew out, a girl screamed, and the room descended into chaos.

Chapter Seven

Books flew off the shelves. Not one volume, but a battery of missiles hit the back of people's heads. A thick religious book hit the face of Lady Josephine squarely on her nose. Before I could gloat, a hand grabbed mine to pull me to the floor.

Archambeau shoved me under the knee opening of a massive wood desk. Gallantly, he positioned himself to the outside so the inkwell flying off the desk only hit him. It splattered his luminous white waistcoat with black drops.

"Was that really necessary!?"

"I can't hear you over the screaming," I shouted back.

He brought his face closer to mine, and I could smell his cologne, a scent of basil, tangerine, and star anise.

"You caused this to happen. On purpose," he accused me.

"Technically, this is the work of a Noise Ghost who doesn't like women. I can't help it that Lady Baudelaire was in the wrong place at the wrong time."

It had grown quieter. Most of the living had run sobbing or screaming from the room. However, the air was still heavy and chilly, and sitting on the ground, I felt the coldness of vapor signaling we still had a Presence. Best stay where I was for now.

"What did you and Josephine discuss over dinner?"

"Oh. Well, she seemed surprised that you had invited me to dinner. Apparently I'm not fit company, being an ordinary person of the trade class."

"Hm."

"I really did not suggest a ghost hunt. That was her idea, though I think she did it to humiliate me or you. I hate to speak ill of a dear family friend, but she really doesn't like you."

Now that the inkwells had stopped flying, he sat back on his heels and looked over the top of the desk to survey the room. "Do you think it's safe to emerge now?"

I closed my eyes and scanned the unseen. "Yes, it's gone."

Giving me a hand, Archambeau helped me stand up. The room was a mess with broken windows, and scattered books. The heavy drapes were being whipped about by the wind and chairs were on their sides or upside down. Well, we could be thankful that it hadn't started a fire. Tricky temperamental things, Noise Ghosts.

"Do you realize this is my office?"

"No? Really? Sorry." I returned to the subject of Lady Baudelaire which interested me far more. "What do you think her purpose was for doing the ghost hunt? I had the feeling she had an ulterior motive."

"Curiosity killed the cat, Chalamet."

"And satisfaction brought it back."

In the still darkness of the room, his shadowed eyes were in black sockets, featureless and blank. He said, "Families marry families, the goal is to amass more wealth. Her estates adjoin our own and I am sure to her mind it was a logical idea that a union should have happened after Minette died. But after being sold once into marriage like a prized pig, I wasn't keen on doing it again. She did not take my rejection well. I imagine this stunt of Josephine's was for revenge. You were to contact Minette and publicly humiliate me."

"You mean reveal your marriage was a sham?"

"You love grabbing the tiger by the tail, don't you? Well, Madame Nosy, I assure you that despite my in-laws' belief, Minette did not die a virgin."

"So, what could she say?"

He gave a bitter chuckle.

"How she died, of course. I have the feeling that Josephine suspects that Minette did not die of fever."

"And she didn't?"

"Of course not. I murdered her."

Walking off without explaining himself was the method the duke de Archambeau used to end uncomfortable conversations. After the dramatic confession last night, and his refusal to expound upon it he had turned his back and simply walked away.

Breakfast the next morning was strangely uneventful. The duke was behind the newspaper, while his sister, Lady Valentina, busily thumbed through a society magazine, careful to pay me no attention.

Also seated around the table were three young men and a woman. One was Stephan, who seemed to be some sort of government clerk in the daylight. They were a subdued lot, mostly talking quietly among each other. From their conversation, it seemed they assisted Archambeau in his work for the king.

In the light of day, I couldn't believe what he told me last night was true. The duke did not behave like a murderer. Could a man enjoying his buttered toast and coffee while scanning the newspaper kill his wife? I had met many victims, but few murderers. How did he kill her? Why? And why tell me? Was it a test?

My head was spinning with speculation so at first I didn't hear my host address me.

"Pardon me?""

"I said, Inspector Barbier is here." Archambeau folded his newspaper and set it aside. "Stephan, you and the men clean up the office. No, not Deena. Until we take care of it, there is a haunt in the room that dislikes anyone female. She can work in my private office until we get things sorted out."

He rose, and I hastily wiped my mouth with a napkin before joining him. The clerks all cast me curious glances, while Stephan asked hesitantly, "But is it safe for us, Your Grace?"

"Certainly, for the men. And if it isn't, give us a scream or two and we will bring Madame Chalamet to vanquish the spirit." His promise did not seem to comfort them, so I added, "Don't worry. The ghost is most likely exhausted from last night, so I expect things will be quiet today. If not, just remove yourself from the room if it hasn't locked the door."

I followed the duke and, together in the hall, I asked him, "Is Barbier here to discuss the case of Giles Monet?"

"I expect so. That is what I've set him out to do, and I would be very disappointed if he didn't have some information for us."

The other office wasn't as grand or as large as Archambeau's original one, but it seemed more of a personal place with casual clutter and a fireplace with a cheerful blaze that removed some of the fall damp. With all the books lining the walls I guessed it had once been a library.

Inspector Barbier was alone, and as we entered, the inspector took off his hat, addressing me first.

"Madame Chalamet, I hope you are doing well."

"Oh, yes, except for being held prisoner and forced to dine with snobs."

Archambeau closed the double doors and invited Barbier to sit. We all arranged ourselves around the hearth. Carved from black stone with green veining, it was a lovely piece, and, of course, expensive. What was it like to grow up around such wealth? What ideas did it put into your head? How did it shape your character? I suspected it could make one arrogant enough to murder his wife.

"Do you have any news for us, inspector?"

From his coat pocket, Barbier pulled out a little leather-bound notebook. He released the tied ribbon and flipped it open. I didn't bother looking over his shoulder because I knew it would be unintelligible to me. From our long acquaintance, I knew he used a specialized shorthand known only to him; he was a careful bloodhound.

"With Madame Chalamet's Ghost Talk information, we found Monet's lodging. He was living rough, as a lodger at a house that took in transients at five royals a month."

"Does he not have funds? I would think the king would still support him, despite Monet being a bastard." Neither man seemed shocked by my use of the word. I am sure Lady Valentina would have gasped, but luckily, the duke's sister was not around.

Archambeau explained. "Giles visits court only occasionally and usually lives with his mother at her estate about an hour away from Alenbonné by train. Still, I agree. If he wanted to be in town, his allowance should have allowed him to afford something better. I would have expected him to be at a hotel, such as the Crown or the Royal."

"Maybe he didn't want to run into old acquaintances?" I suggested.

"You mean other aristos?" asked Archambeau. I nodded. "What of his friends, Barbier? What crowd did Monet run with?"

"The turf set, it seems. Sponsored a horse or two at the races. A punter. Loved to gamble but, talking with the bookmakers, they said he wasn't in deep and everyone thought him a pleasant chap. No particular enemies. Described as good-natured and was well-liked. When he lost, Monet would always front a round for everyone."

"Doesn't sound like a revenge killing to me," I said.

"The public face is not always the true nature of a man," said Archambeau.

Barbier flipped over some more pages of his notebook.

"The odd thing is, no one has seen him for weeks. His best horse had a race last weekend, and he was a no-show. The damn thing won at twenty to one."

Archambeau rubbed his square chin before tapping a forefinger on his lips. He confided in us. "I received a message from court late last night and Monet was at Winterbride with the king last month."

"Then royalty is involved!"

The duke shot me a sideways look. "Some of the king's jewelry might have disappeared when Monet left." At my gaping mouth, Archambeau said. "You don't think I locked up the daughter of Augustus Chalamet for my personal entertainment, did you? Having someone familiar with royal trinkets could come in handy."

While I was still re-grouping all my assumptions, he asked Barbier, "What else did you discover, inspector?"

"Here's a list of the contents of the room." From the back of the notebook, Inspector Barbier pulled out a folded looseleaf paper and handed it over to Archambeau. The duke read it over, while the inspector continued.

"Because of his accent and appearance, the landlady thought him an aristo down on his luck. Nothing remarkable in that. Gambling or drink too often overextends these types until they blow their brains out or their parents bail them out from debtor's prison. For women, it's the bills for millinery, jewelry, and cards."

My mind flitted to Josephine Baudelaire and her diamonds. Did the duke know they were fake? Was she in need of money?

"The landlady is a tough bird. She's strict and allows no visitors to the rooms. But his hallway neighbor knew Monet regularly lunched at a local café popular with the theater crowd. Saw him there with a baby-faced blond girl."

The inspector gave a nod in my direction. "That statement tallies with what madame showed us last night. We traced the girl to a cabaret called the Nightingale. It has nightly shows— dancers, magicians, jugglers, and even an animal act with trained dogs. Turns out we raided the district two nights back and had a few still in custody to interview."

"It will be interesting to see if the postmortem of Monet shows that he died about the same time as the raid."

"About that—" Barbier pulled out a packet of folded papers from inside of his coat pocket. "Dr. LaRue sent you a preliminary report, but she wants you to know this isn't her last word on the matter."

Archambeau took the report and started scanning Dr. LaRue's crabbed script.

"As I suspected. Monet's death could have happened the night of the raid. A blow to the back of the head, and probably unconscious when he drowned in the canal. What more from your interviews?"

"The gals we interviewed said the blond filly goes under the stage name Gabriella. Everyone had the same story: an aristo has been hanging around the Nightingale flashing money and Gabriella was wearing new jewelry. The aristo matches the description of Monet. Not many men have a mole to the right of their nose."

"Have you brought her in for questioning?" asked Archambeau.

"No one knows where she is. Scampered during the raid and, like a lot of these girls, no known address. We searched her trunk left behind at the Nightingale but didn't find any money or jewels. Not even a card from lover boy."

Archambeau fell into a brown study while the two of us waited in silence. Finally, he asked, "Will the Nightingale re-open?"

"The owner paid the fines, so I expect so."

"Find out and let me know. We need to visit incognito and discover what they didn't tell the gendarmes."

Before I could help myself, I gleefully clapped my hands, earning a suppressed, tight-lipped smile from Archambeau.

"Not done getting into trouble, Madame Nosy?"

"Not by a long shot."

Chapter Eight

The rest of the day was my own, and I had much to do. Anne-Marie brought me several messages, and I spent a few hours writing responses. My letters had to be reviewed by mysir de duke before posting. That was an irritation, but more for him than me since I composed the longest and silliest letters I could imagine.

After sending him the sixth one, he came to where I sat at a desk in the room, his hand overhead, waving my latest letter.

"I do not need my busy day being interrupted by—" He read from my letter in his hand, "—did Margarette really wear that dress sent to her by her lover, or—" The duke shuffled the paper to another letter. "Why ever did Poppy take her dog to the park?"

"You said you wanted to see everything I was writing," I said sweetly, trying to put on an air of innocence. It was hard to do so, but the duke was in one of his rushing-about moods where he walked away before a conversation was properly finished. "Fine, madame, I will let you write and send off your letters if you promise me, on your honor, not to discuss the king's business."

"Of course! Now, may I meet with a few of my clients here?"

"Madame Chalamet, what is the point of having you here,

under my eye, if you are going to write letters and meet who you please?"

"Exactly my thoughts and why you should let me go home."

"No. I need you at hand. Things are moving quickly and your expertise, and silence, could be helpful. Surely you can sit in this golden prison for ten days? I promise no more dinner parties. Occupy yourself in solitary activities. Read a book."

"You can't expect me to suspend my business because you think I'm a blabbermouth or because I could identify some random piece of jewelry. You haven't exactly hidden yourself away from your duties."

Stephan came into the room with a piece of paper in his hand and stood silently, waiting for the duke to address him. Archambeau shot him an irritated glance. "Madame, who do you want to meet today?"

"Just a handful of old clients. I promise I won't discuss anything related to you-know-who."

As a second clerk appeared behind Stephan with a bundle of papers clasped to their chest, he threw up his hands. "Fine. See your clients, but I want their names and if one whisper reaches the news dogs, I know who I will blame."

"Certainly. I'll even give you their addresses."

Before he left, he said, "Please adjourn from the music room and go to the conservatory to meet your clients. My mother and sister use this room during the day." He directed the footman to assist me in anything I might need, and after he left, I asked the servant his name.

"Ruben, madame."

"Good. Now Ruben, I will need these letters posted." I opened up my portfolio and brought out a stack of letters I had saved back, awaiting either a slackening of the rules, or when I could leave the house. "But this one, I need hand delivered to the café's owner."

"Yes, madame." Looking at the address, he said, "The letters I can post on my way to the café. I can return within the hour if I have your permission to take a quick-cab?"

"Of course." I fished into my leather wallet that had once been my father's. Decades of use had discolored the leather, but I would not replace it out of affection. Handing Ruben a handful of coins, including a mix of royals, castles, and knights, I told him, "If this is not enough to post the letters, and for the quick-cab, when you return I shall pay the cab myself."

"This should be more than enough, madame."

"Good. If there is any left over, treat yourself from a street vendor or save the coin. Your choice."

My first client arrived before Ruben returned and it was the servant girl, Georgette, who brought her to me. Madame Smit-Vossen was a widow who believed she was being haunted, but it was only her memory playing tricks. It was longing that made her smell her husband's cologne on the pillowcases, and her absent-mindedness that moved his favorite books and trinkets around their house.

After revealing the truth of her husband's 'haunting' two years ago, she still liked to meet with me to discuss what was happening in her life. With her children grown and with families of their own, she needed someone to listen. Though my expertise was in Ghost Talking, I learned after finishing my training by the Morpheus Society that most of my work was comforting the grieving hearts of the living.

Her round face filled with wonder as she gazed around the conservatory. It was a rich man's confection located on the roof. Over the housetops you could see the distant harbor, and the masts of ships. If you wanted to look closer, there was a brass telescope.

"Mysir de Duke de Chambaux's residence! You could have

knocked me over with a feather when your letter told me where to find you. I see you are finally getting the recognition you deserve."

She wore a white widow's cap edged in a modest lace over her tight brown curls and a wool day dress in brown with a pattern of tiny white daisies. She settled into one of the wicker chairs, causing it to give a small squeak of protest at her matronly bulk.

"Thank you, Madame Smit-Vossen, but this is merely a temporary situation. Soon I'll be back to my own humble abode at the Crown."

"Still, to rub elbows with the aristo set! And look at how they are treating you," she said, indicating the cart of treats that Georgette had brought us. Not only was there a silver teapot that looked to be an antique, but an assortment of desserts that was almost as good as the Crown's cream tea. I poured out while my guest wavered over a chocolate truffle or a slice of lemon cake.

"The duke has a talented staff, but I prefer Chef Perdersen at the Crown. I was just trying a new confection of his the other day. An incredible mix of flavors."

"There's nothing like home, is there? Every time my dear Leo came back from a business trip to Zulskaya. Lou-Lou, he'd say— he always called me that even though my real name is Louisa— there's nothing like being in front of your own fire and eating your good cooking."

I was glad to see the mention of her husband produced only a slight misting of her eyes. Helping her to remember him without experiencing crippling grief was my goal for the widow and it had taken us months to get to this stage.

"Tell me what your daughter is doing. Has her baby arrived yet?"

"Oh, yes!"

The next half hour was a pleasant chat about what clothes a baby might need and what would be a gift that Louisa could send that would outshine whatever the in-laws might choose. We talked over the best way to get baby milk out of clothes, the latest model of sewing machine she was considering, and her never-ending quest to find the best grocer in Alenbonné as defined by the lowest prices yet with the best quality.

For Madame Smit-Vossen was foremost a woman who enjoyed discussing the richness of her domestic life. She displayed no curiosity about why I was in the duke's house, and it was easy to keep my promise to Archambeau.

By the time we finished, Ruben had returned from his errands. He escorted Madame Smit-Vossen out, and as they left, I heard him answering her question of whether the rumors of the bathroom taps being gold were true.

My next client, Mysir Joris Jakobsen, was an Alenbonné merchant with a thriving spice trade. This was our third meeting, and he still hadn't gotten to the point of what he wanted from me. Instead, we had discussed the price of chocolate from Perino (lamentable!) and the time needed to repair a ship in dry dock.

The only thing I knew from gossip was mysir's business partner had died of a heart attack on the docks of Alenbonné when he was overseeing the unloading of one of their ships.

Jakobsen was a small man, in his fifties, partially bald, and wore wire-rim glasses with round lenses. He rearranged the teacups on the tray, holding up one close to his eyes to examine the fineness of the pattern on the thin porcelain.

He said, in an overly precise voice, chopping his syllables very fine, "You have never asked me, Madame Chalamet, why I have come to you."

"I have wondered, mysir, but I believed you would approach it in your own time."

"It's a troublesome matter. Very difficult."

"Sometimes an unexpected death leaves behind untidiness."

"Exactly. I am so relieved you understand. It's a messy matter." He shuddered. "It's the paperwork, you see."

"Business papers? Contracts? Or a will?"

"Embarrassing. So embarrassing." His precise voice shook a bit, and whether this was from disgust at things being left messy or anger, I wasn't sure. Probably a bit of both. "Conrad promised to leave paperwork that would insure I could buy his side of the business if anything happened. As did I. But I cannot find it. I have searched our offices three times and gone through each file folder. There is nothing!"

"And his heirs aren't being helpful? Are they causing problems?"

"No. I mean, yes, my goodness. They will hound me into my grave with their nonsense!"

"What nonsense?"

He went back to rearranging all the items on the tea cart, sorting them into a row of largest to smallest.

"His wife and son accuse me of being a liar. That I told them Conrad was on a business trip when instead he was in town. Insisting that he worked late in the office when I say he did not. They are driving me mad with their accusations! Worse, my suppliers are taking notice of their slander."

"What was your relationship in the past with them? Cordial?"

"Certainly. We saw each other in passing. I knew of no problem."

"Yet, now they proclaim you a liar and want a portion of the business?"

He frowned at the sugar tongs and started polishing them with one of the cloth napkins.

"No. Oddly enough, they have not. They have no interest in the business, for Conrad's son is well established in other work. I have offered to buy out their portion, but before she signs the paper, she wants me to admit that I knew what Conrad was doing—"

"Doing?"

From his inner waistcoat, he pulled out a crisp white handkerchief and, unfolding it, he revealed an oval locket. Jakobsen dangled it by its chain before dropping it into my outstretched hand. "I discovered this in his desk drawer."

The front of the locket was very ornamental, with an elaborately etched flower. I opened it to find a daguerreotype of a woman in her thirties. She stared back at me with solemn eyes. Framing her portrait were four small, round gems.

From around my neck, I pulled out a chain holding my father's jewelry loup which I had been wearing since the duke expressed an interest in my ability to appraise jewelry. Anne-Marie had brought it with my things.

Standing up, I took the locket and loup to the windows, using the natural light to examine it better under the magnifying glass. Afterward, I closed my eyes, thinking back over what my father had taught me.

Mysir Jakobsen asked eagerly, "What is it? Is Conrad's ghost talking to you?"

I went back to my seat and, cocking my head, said, "Do you know the language of love, mysir?" My question baffled him. Before he could guess, I continued. "About two decades ago, there was a trend where gems were used to spell out a loved one's name or a phrase such as 'adore.' It is more common with women's jewelry than with men's."

I twisted my hand so he could see inside the locket.

"From the newness of the prongs that hold the four gemstones: emerald, malachite, malachite, and amethyst; is the woman in this locket named Emma?"

He didn't reply.

"Not Conrad's wife, I presume? She isn't your wife, by chance?"

"Indeed, not, madame! I am not married! Of course, I recognized her face. She is the wife of one of our sea captains. He died a natural death, fever, and was buried at sea over a year ago."

The weight of the locket in my hand grew warm; it responded to the name. I gained the feeling of a secret relationship deep with confidences.

"This is my suggestion, mysir: have a private chat with Emma. I feel strongly that she can tell you where this missing paperwork is. Convince her to write a letter to your partner's wife, giving credence to the fact you knew nothing about the affair. If this suffices to convince the widow to sign the papers, I advise you to give this captain's wife a finder's fee; perhaps a two percent interest in your company?"

He bristled. "Are you mad? To a captain's wife? A woman?"

"Without her help, you may find yourself in court, and your business reputation in shambles. Treating fairly with her could be for your benefit."

"But I want nothing to do with this affair!"

If he was going to be like that—! I closed my eyes and held the locket to my forehead, and deepened my breath, summoning what spiritual residue remained attached to the locket in order to capture the resonance of Conrad's speech pattern.

"Joris, you must take care of her. My spirit will not be at peace until I know my beloved Emma is safe and my sad wife Sophia has her answers." Ending with my false voice, I opened my eyes, pretending innocence. "Did I say something? I feel as though I went into a trance."

Mysir Jakobsen's hand shook as he took back the locket and wrapped it carefully, tying the handkerchief in a knot, before returning it to his pocket. When he cleared his throat, the apple in his throat bobbed up and down with a heavy gulp.

"Most helpful, Madame Chalamet. I do not think I need to see you again."

"Always glad to be of service, Mysir Jakobsen."

Chapter Nine

I looked at my watch pinned on my jacket and wondered if the client I next expected would arrive. As if he was a mentalist, professing to read my thoughts, Ruben opened the door, admitting a lady. Her hat's veil was thick and obscured her face, making her a thin black silhouette.

"She did not give her name, madame. His Grace insisted I get names," the footman told me, clearly disapproving of this break in etiquette. I waved him away. "Don't worry, Reuben, I will explain to mysir de duke."

He cast my guest a disapproving glance before slowly closing the door.

"Thank you for answering my summons."

"I am here," she said flatly.

She said nothing; her figure swayed slightly, and I took a few deep breaths, quieting my breathing. While my other two clients of the day had not taxed my abilities, this lady would certainly test me.

One drizzling night walking along the boulevard, I saw her standing on a bridge. The stillness of her form intrigued me and because, like myself, she was alone. No passersby noticed her as she mounted the parapet. Shouting, I ran towards her, but she jumped before I could reach her. Looking over the side of the railing to the canal, I saw no splash, no sound, no body, and it was only then that I realized she was a ghost.

Madame Ghost was a repeater, an image that returns to the Earthly to reenact a tragic event: her death by suicide. She was a puzzle that I had been trying to solve for over a year. But it was a grief, so deep, so vast, it was hard to quench it.

I knew from experience she would stay only for a moment. Before she could fade, I sent forth a summoning into the Beyond, calling her lost child to me. The room grew colder and darker, as if clouds had covered the sun. The towering palms in the room loomed over me, their greens darkening into shadows.

Overwhelming grief, loss and yearning filled my heart as a little boy of exactly seven years and three months, a blend of the heart's yearning and the mind's hope, ran from the shadows to greet his mother.

"Mama!"

"Jantje!" She held him tightly, this child more precious to her than life.

The mother who had killed herself in despair after losing her child; the son who died from a fire when the candle in his nursery caught the drapes— their forms merged, becoming one shadow before winking away like a falling star.

Some time later, there was a discreet tap at the door before Ruben entered.

"Yes?"

"There's another to see you, madame, but I told him you were with someone. He is very persistent." His curious eyes shifted, taking in the room, now empty of everyone but me.

"She's gone, Ruben," I said tiredly, still feeling the backwash of melancholy that came from such an intense encounter. At the alarm on his face, I reassured him. "Don't worry, your employer will not have cause to reprimand you for not seeing her out. Now, who is this person who insists on seeing me?"

"A young person, madame," he said. From the tone of his voice, what he really meant was someone not acceptable to be a guest at the duke's residence.

I rose and went to the door. Sitting in the hall on a bench was a boy of about twelve, wearing the clothes of a day laborer. They were man sized, making him appear even younger than his years. He had a spotted bandanna tied around his neck, and shoes that probably had holes in the soles. When he saw me, he sprung to his feet.

"Marcus! How did you know I was here?"

"Anne-Marie told her da where she was going. He told me."

Turning to Ruben, I asked, "Can you bring us something for lunch? Something fattening or sweet?"

At my words, the boy's eyes gleamed. I waved for him to enter, and Marcus followed me up the steps into the conservatory. I shut the door after the duke's servant, to prevent our conversation from being overheard.

Marcus immediately went to the brass telescope and started fiddling with it, pressing his eye to the eyepiece. From there he examined the harbor, where ships moved in and out, the pulsing life of Alenbonné's economy.

"Tell me how you've been. I haven't seen you for weeks. How's your sister?"

"She's well enough, madame. Still be moaning about Dorrie not being home enough. Same old story. I blew out of there. Can't stand the howling."

Maybe his sister had the right to complain about an absent husband, but trying to convince a boy of a woman's needs was a lost cause. Any attempt at that would earn quick scorn, as I already knew.

The boy had dark curls and gray eyes that held the hard-earned wisdom of a street urchin. His father left before he was born and his mother died two years back from the dreaded city cough which collapses the lungs. Though he claimed to live with his older sister and her husband, more often than not, he was playing pranks or stealing hats on the streets.

That is how I met him. Two summers ago, he hitched a ride inside my quick-cab to evade the gendarmes who were hunting for him after some such prank. The boy used a pleading face and wide eyes to melt soft hearts, and I was no exception. That day he jumped into my cab had made me laugh on a day I felt like crying, so I quickly forgave him for his scam.

Ruben returned and perhaps he knew something about hungry boys, for there was bread, cake, biscuits, thick-cut pieces of farm ham and sausage, with cheese and olives. The tea was fresh, and I poured out before handing him a cup. "Enjoy."

Juggling it, he reached into his pocket and pulled out something in a crumpled brown box. He handed it to me, saying triumphantly, "Found it."

"Really?" I said, unable to conceal my excitement.

"Matches the description you gave me."

With my heart beating fast, I opened the square box to reveal my father's pocket watch. I had not seen it since his murder. My hands trembled as I picked it up, the box falling from my lap to the floor.

"Where did you find it?" My voice shook.

"Some Uncle in the Hells had it."

Marcus wasn't referring to a relative but to a pawn broker. Someone who re-sold goods that others had sold onward. I felt a moment of guilt knowing where Marcus had found this treasure so dear to my heart. The Hells was not a place I would knowingly send a child to, but it would not do to chastise him. Marcus was like a cat and if you stroked his fur the wrong way, he would bite and scratch, or worse, leave.

"How much did it cost? Let me pay you."

"Nothing, madame." He said proudly, "I stole it."

"Marcus!"

"Well, if it is your papa's, it was already stolen, right? Taking it was only fair."

"I'm more concerned about the danger you put yourself into stealing it! Someone might notice it missing and deduce it was you who took it."

"Whatever." He sounded peeved.

"I appreciate your help," I said sincerely, attempting a balance between praise and worry. "There is no way I would have found this, but remember, whoever killed my father will not stop at killing a street-rat."

He shrugged. "It was in a pile of old junk. No one will miss it."

Marcus showed he was done with discussing it by stuffing his mouth with food.

As a jeweler, my father had kept his pocket watch in perfect condition, but wherever it had been the last twelve years had taken its toll. The dented case, the latch release missing, and the golden bronze metal scratched, would have made him furious if he could see it now.

How it brought back so memories! Seeing it spinning from its chain (now missing) over my head as Papa teased me with it; him opening it to check the time, commenting that I was late back from school; and me, as a child, naming the precious stones that spelled my mother's name: a beryl, emerald, lapis lazuli twice, and last, another emerald.

I pried open the case to see inside and felt a rush of anger as I saw the gems were gone. Not only had they murdered my father, but they had tried to destroy his Belle, my mother with their vandalism. My fingers grew white as they convulsed over the watch. Too many emotions swamped me and I struggled to control them.

"You did well, Marcus. Thank you." I turned and made my

way to the door, my heart and head too full. "Eat all you want, take the leftovers, and let the footman know when you are ready to leave."

Outside, still finding it hard to breathe, I told Ruben to look after Marcus before going down the stairs to my room. Thankfully, Anne-Marie wasn't there. I locked my door and sat on the edge of the bed. The watch metal was wet from my tears. I used my sleeve to polish it, but my tears were coming faster, and I did the motion blindly.

Twelve years ago I had come home to find my father on the floor of his workshop, his throat slit, his body cold, and pools of blood. At seventeen, I knew nothing about talking with ghosts, and ran looking for help.

During my apprenticeship I tried many times to contact him but met with no success. Leona explained that his soul had not lingered but had moved to the Afterlife. There he was lost to me. We could not speak to anyone who was in heaven. Let it go, she said. Let the gendarmes see if they could find justice.

But that had never satisfied me and when I started my own practice seven years ago, I immediately sought out the gendarmes to offer my services. But while solving other murders, I still met dead ends to find resolution for my father's. Now, I finally had a lead that I might use.

Rising from the bed, I went to the bathroom. My fingers shaking, I washed my face, cooling my hot cheeks. I was not without skill, but fully trained in psychometry.

Life was vibrations and the items we keep close can absorb and hold those impressions. Accessing those memories from Jakobsen's locket had allowed me to imitate his partner's voice.

How many times had my mentor, Leona Granger, told me that receiving such information took a calm mind? Emotions had no place in our work. A grieving heart wanting answers might invent what it wanted, and not the facts of a matter.

I lay on the bed and cleared my thoughts as I stared at the ceiling. I placed the watch over my heart, the chill of the metal almost pleasant against my skin. Mouthing a silent chant quieted my jangled nerves with its rhythm and my emotions became a still pool.

A tentative impression grew stronger: a mean face full of low brutal emotion, who was the last to touch the watch. Twelve years of faces rushed by me but I was looking for a certain something—what the Morpheus Society called a frequency.

More than any vibration, violence makes the hardest stamp. The metal casing warmed as I shuffled backward through time, memorizing personalities of those who had carried my father's dearest possession. Until I hit a long period of silence when the watch had no human contact.

Like a boat trapped in rapids, suddenly images flooded me. There was no turning back. It grabbed me and spun me around and down, overwhelming me like a riptide. Psychically, I fell back from the emotional impressions, and in shock, I sat up; the watch dropping away, leaving a crescent burn on my breast.

What I had seen: my father sitting in his chair, bending over to examine something he held when his killer standing in the shadows behind him slit his throat.

My father was notorious for keeping his workshop closed to visitors and would only have allowed someone he trusted inside. This had been no stranger, but someone my father knew! Someone who he felt comfortable enough to turn his back to in a workshop filled with precious metals and valuable gems.

The gendarmes were wrong! The break-in was staged, and the murder made to look like a burglary. These weren't opportunist robbers.

I wasn't looking for an unknown villain, but possibly a favored client, a friend of his, who wanted him dead.

Chapter Ten

At breakfast, the duke ordered his sister to escort me to her modiste for new clothes.

"If I need something new, I'll buy it myself," I said.

"Do you want to come with me to the Nightingale or not?" was his reply.

Archambeau did a wonderful impression of a wall which you could throw yourself at with no result. I took my irritation out by cutting up a piece of sausage on my plate in very tiny bites.

His sister also tried protesting, to no avail.

"Dear Tristan, I have a very busy schedule today. I am sure Madame Chalamet can take a quick-cab herself to Rue de l'aiguille without my assistance."

"You have a sense of style, Valentina, which could benefit Madame Chalamet. I shall foot the bill for anything you buy in the Needle District. Pick out a pretty hat for yourself. Or even a new dress."

She was still speaking when he walked from the dining room. He had a terrible habit of doing that. If he was my brother, I would blockade all the exits before discussing anything with him.

Lady Valentina looked across the table at me. I shrugged.

Which all made for a very uncomfortable ride to the dress-maker, especially as we had, during our brief acquaintance, discovered a mutual loathing of each other. We knew each other to be the obverse, and it repulsed us. She, born to nobility, which had gold-plated bath faucets and me, the daughter of a tradesman, whose soap was three for a penny. Even more so than her brother, everything about her spoke of privilege, the benefit of her station's breeding, and the contempt she had for those not born within her sphere.

I felt no jealousy, though perhaps I did envy that bathroom. For with her life came the rules, the restrictions, the must-not-do's which would have never suited my nature.

Lady Valentina's face had her brother's wide, thin mouth, but her jaw was a softer, feminine version of her brother's. However, unlike the duke, her features lacked any humor to lighten their severity; I could forgive much from those who laughed with their eyes.

Lady Valentina started by complaining about the debacle at the house party. It seems Lady Josephine Baudelaire had suffered a contusion to her face, requiring a week's rest at home.

"When she left last night, her face was swelling. Her maid informs me it is quickly becoming a black eye! If you hadn't insisted on this foolish ghost hunt—"

"I'm afraid you are under a misapprehension, Lady Fontaine. It was Lady Baudelaire who wanted to search for ghosts."

The corner of her mouth tightened. It would have been easy to miss, but I was a noticing sort of person, so didn't.

"My dear friend would not have taken the notion into her head except for your presence last night. And why you should be there, I still do not know. It disarranged my entire seating arrangement and cook was much put out."

"I was a guest of your brother," I reminded her.

"Do you have some hold over him? Is it about Minette?" At

the mention of the duke's dead wife, I gained the impression that she was afraid.

"No, it has nothing to do with your brother's wife. I've never met her alive or as a ghost." Ah! Her gaze shifted away from my own. She definitely knew something about the Duchesse de Archambeau's demise. I tucked that tidbit away for later. "Your brother and I are working on a criminal matter. You will need to ask him about it, as he has sworn me to silence."

Her irritation shifted to something else to complain about.

"My brother is a man of position, a confidante to the king, and bears a noble name. Buying clothes for a woman who isn't family? It borders on scandalous."

"I didn't ask for the duke to buy me clothes. Your brother seems to have a fixation on what I wear."

"He doesn't like black. It reminds him of when our father died. We were both children, and though I barely recall it, I know Tristan suffered greatly with my father's funeral and the aftermath. And then Minette—"

She looked out the window, either to hide her expression or to think about the past. I wasn't sure which. The rest of the ride was conducted in silence.

Despite her brother's request to be my guide, Lady Valentina quickly divorced herself from the proceedings once we reached the dress shop in Threadneedle. After introducing me to the madame who managed the establishment, she strode away, fingering merchandise on the displays. A salesgirl jumped to attention.

"I wish to try on hats," she said, her back to me in a clear snub.

That suited me fine. I figured if I didn't order something, Archambeau would subject me to another annoying lecture about wearing dowdy clothes, so I would get my revenge another way.

To the manageress, I said, "Mysir de Duke de Chambaux sent me here to select a few outfits. To be charged to his account."

"Indeed?" she said, evincing surprise. The woman wore a deep rose-colored dress tailored to perfection. Her dark brown hair lay smooth against her skull and the bun at the back of her head had not one hair daring to escape.

Lady Valentina waved a hand vaguely in my direction, her attention staying firmly on hats. "My brother desires her to be made fit to be seen in society. I am sure I can count on you to make that happen."

The manageress made a slight bow in Lady Valentina's direction before asking me to follow her to a consultation room. She pulled aside a drape revealing a hallway and, stepping through the passage, I smelled a faint whiff of perfume accompanied by a ghostly touch on my shoulder. There wasn't enough energy for the spirit to materialize; it was an old memory replaying, with no consciousness, something that happened to ghosts that fragmented.

The private consultant room was a place of enchantment. Fabric of all colors hung on rods fixed on the walls, and drawers were bursting with gloves and stocking, feathers and buttons. There were two upholstered chairs with a table between them, overflowing with stacks of fashion plates.

To take measurements, the sales madame helped me undress to my undergarments. In the mirror I could see the crescent burn mark my father's watch had caused right above my heart; thankfully, no one commented upon it. Seeing my discarded dress laying limply over a chair, I asked her rather timidly, "Do you think black makes me look old?"

As she whipped her tape around my waist, she answered diplomatically. "Black is a diverse color appropriate to many walks of life. A servant and a judge both wear black. A widow uses it to show the world her grief. And in the right evening gown, a woman can become a beauty."

That really didn't answer my question.

"Black is helpful in my line of work. As a Ghost Talker, my clients are usually grieving over a loved one and black is a sympathetic color."

"If you wish to wear black, may I suggest combining it with a color? Let me show you." She steered me to stand in front of a mirror. From a drawer behind her, the dressmaker pulled out a yard of black satin and a colorful silk scarf of blue and yellow, draping them both over my shoulders. "See how the right color near the face enhances the glow of your skin? Shows off the fire in your eyes? But using the wrong color?" She changed the layering, putting the black closer to my face. "Your features risk becoming dull."

She was right. Which meant Archambeau was right. How annoying!

"What colors do you think would be best?"

She smiled. "What type of outfits would you require?"

Oh, mysir de duke, I hope your pocketbook is deep!

"A few day dresses for when I meet clients. And something for the evening."

"Certainly, madame."

Deciding on a wardrobe turned out to be complicated and time-consuming.

"We must build you from the inside out, or the clothes will not drape well," she explained. Operating on trust alone, I nodded, knowing I was in over my head.

First, there were the undergarments: a silk chemise and the options of what lace to have around the neck. Over that went the latest design in corsets. Thankfully, fashion had changed, and these gave a long, smooth, elegant silhouette, not the artificial shape of a strutting pigeon. You could actually breathe in it!

Next, we chose fabric for walking dresses, tea dresses, and finally, an evening gown for my upcoming adventure to the Nightingale.

"This dress I need within a day. Is that possible?"

"For the Chambaux family, of course. We could deliver it to you this evening. To what address shall we send it?"

"To the Duke's residence. I am staying there for now."

At that moment, her assistant reappeared, holding a shoulder wrap of white fur with black tips. Before I could protest, they draped it over my shoulders; despite myself, I started stroking it.

"It is lovely but—"

"Mysir de Archambeau always insists on the best. His wife was one of our finest patrons," said the modiste. As I continued stroking the soft fur, she added, "If it displeases you or the duke, send it back to us with no charge."

Even if the duke didn't agree to pay for it, I knew I wouldn't be able to part with it. Well, if I bought it, I'd consider it an early midwinter gift to myself.

With a glint in her eye, the modiste said, "I think we have something new that will appeal to your practical nature, Madame Chalamet."

From a wardrobe closet, she brought out three garments: a long skirt in a light brown wool with a green stripe, a matching coat, and a white cotton shirt.

"It's called a walking skirt. The hem ends at the ankle, preventing the skirt from being dragged in the mud or getting caught in the gears of a cycling machine. You can pair it with a coat of the same color as the skirt, or in a complementary color."

The jacket closed with buttons, and had a soft belt in matching fabric which fastened over the front, accenting the waist. The coat's skirt ended right below my knee, making it easy to move when wearing it!

Where had this been all my life?

"I want several of these," I blurted out.

Madame modiste bent to mark the hem and around the pins in her mouth said, "They will be quite suitable playing tennis or cycling at Chambaux."

"Oh, I doubt I'll ever see the Duke's estate," I said absentmindedly, still distracted by the view in the mirror. The pockets were just the right size to hold my man-stopper.

"How soon would my lady need these?"

"Oh, I'm not a lady. You can address me as madame. I'm a working woman like yourselves." Twisting in the mirror to see the back of the coat, I asked, "Could I wear this one when I leave?"

"Yes, if you can wait a few more minutes? That is why I love these new separate pieces; they are so easy to work with and are simple to adjust."

I disrobed and handed it to the assistant, who whisked the garments away to the mysterious workshop in the back. The door opened and I could hear the whirring sound of a sewing machine.

"I imagine Lady Fontaine has exhausted her interest in hats by now."

"Lady Fontaine left over two hours ago. Shall I have a quick-cab hailed for you?"

"Yes, that would be helpful."

In less than half an hour, I was back in my favorite new ensemble. Madame dressmaker twisted a scarf in soft sky blue around my neck in a stylish manner that I could never replicate. I would have to have Anne-Marie examine it. As the daughter of a sailor she was clever with knots.

"Remember, a lady should wear something that makes her feel special every day." I smiled at our faces in the mirror. She took my hat and positioned it on my head, gently fixing my hair. "It's been a pleasure to serve you, Madame Chalamet. I speak for all of us here — we are happy to see Mysir de Archambeau taking an interest in life again, since his dear duchesse's passing."

My mind thinking about murder, I asked, "How long ago was it when she died?"

"Four years ago. No. It must be five. I remember it was in the late spring when she last visited us. She bought a heavy winter coat in deep red. That was a hard color to match and had not sold.

When I heard she died of fever, I thought she must have been feeling the onset of the disease even then. No one would buy such a thing heading into summer."

A girl came to tell us the cab was ready. They stacked my parcels on the seats and floor of the carriage. Freed from Lady Valentina I made a break for freedom and gave the cab driver the directions to the morgue.

We had traveled some blocks when I suddenly realized the staff had mistaken me for the duke's mistress. I burst out laughing.

CHAPTER ELEVEN

Before I could reach the Alenbonné morgue, I was lucky enough to spot my target: Dr. Charlotte LaRue. I rapped the roof and asked the cab driver to stop.

"Charlotte! I was just heading your way for a visit."

Dr. LaRue greeted my hail and stepped over to the curb. She wore a dark blue check pattern in trousers, vest, and coat, with a carelessly tied stock around her neck, and a derby hat. In her hand, she held her cane. Not that she needed it for support or style, but because it held a sword stick she wasn't reluctant to use.

Dr. LaRue's outfit might have stood out as bizarre on Glamour Row, but in the student section of town, she blended into the strange artistic rabble found in the district.

"To meet me? Then it must be about Giles Monet. You only visit me because of my bodies."

"Not true!" I said, stepping out of the cab. "I saw you on your birthday."

"You do realize, Elinor, that was two months ago?"

To the quick-cab driver, I handed up a five-royal bill. "Would you take my things to Mysir de Archambeau's town home on Lunea Street? Do you know where that is?"

"I do indeed, madame." He touched the crown of his hat before turning his horse in the middle of the street. The u-turn earned him a shouted string of curses from a young student wearing a black scholastic robe whose cycle almost collided with him. The driver only gave him a backward wave over his head, his horse trotting quickly away.

Ready for a chat, I wrapped my arm around Dr. LaRue's.

"Well, I want to know more about our dead body. Can we do it over lunch? I haven't eaten since breakfast."

Dr. LaRue's eye gained a speculative glint.

"I know the perfect place. My treat. Come, it's further down the street."

The wan blue sky had that texture when winter replaces the halcyon fall. The breeze was brisk, and my new attire made me feel quite cozy and stylish even among the avant-garde residents of the student quarter.

"Nice outfit, by the way. You look younger."

"I've been shopping."

"Looks good on you. Better than all that black."

"Why does everyone feel a need to comment on my clothes?"

"Who's been commenting?"

I didn't answer her as Dr. LaRue had stopped to survey the front of a café. It didn't look out of the ordinary, with its two bay windows facing the boulevard and a black door between them. Inside, the crowd seemed thin, but I assumed that was due to it being past the prime lunch hour.

Dr. LaRue patted my arm. "Come along, I'm friends with the owner. They have a haunt they need your help with. The situation is ruining my best lunch spot, and that can't continue. Think of my stomach!"

When the staff saw Dr. LaRue enter, the man behind the bar greeted her and a server stopped washing glasses to rush over. Wiping his wet hands on the towel at his belt, he showed us to a clean table. A short man with a round, firm drum of a belly and white curly hair that was thin on top, showing shiny pink skin, came from the back room to our table. His round eyes were dark as polished nuts.

"Is this her?" he asked my companion.

"It is indeed," said Dr. LaRue.

"Good, good," he said, smiling wider. "Whatever the two of you want is on the house."

The older man bowed to us and left, chiding the staff, who had stopped their work to gaze at us. After we gave our food order to the server, I asked my companion, "Are you going to fill me in, or is keeping me in the dark part of the fun?"

Dr. LaRue broke apart the rustic loaf in the basket at our table and started heavily buttering a piece. "About a year ago, there was an argument out on the boulevard, right in front, and a man died. Two students fighting over the same woman is not anything extraordinary on the surface of it, but a few months ago, this place started experiencing activity."

"Sudden death can cause unrest. If the spirit died with a grudge, that could cause problems for the living."

"Exactly." Dr. LaRue pointed at me with her buttered bread before taking a bite from it. "Unfortunately, the disturbances are getting worse."

"Is the owner doing any renovation?"

"Not that I know of."

Our soup arrived and Dr. LaRue dived in. She had a system of scooping and holding her spoon to blow on it while she talked, before hastily swallowing and dipping for another spoonful. It was fast and efficient and held a rough beauty to its rhythm.

"They want the ghost gone."

I grimaced. That was always the first thought from the living.

"I can't guarantee that. If the haunt has intensified, it is being triggered by something. Remove that and things may calm down, but getting rid of a ghost completely? That rarely can be done, no matter what a gutter-medium will tell you. Besides I prefer not to vanquish ghosts; that is the last of their soul. I feel it's a better idea that they decide to leave on their own."

"What would trigger a ghost?"

"Oh, there are a dozen of things it could be. Construction and remodeling. Maybe they've hired a new person who disturbs the haunt. Someone here could be a sensitive, unknowingly feeding it energy."

"Like another Ghost Talker?"

"More like someone who has the potential, but no training. It might surprise you, but there are people sensitive to spirits who never develop it into anything more than an odd feeling or an awareness when something unnatural is nearby."

Our main meal arrived, and I quickly forgave the doctor's deception in bringing me here. The braised chicken thighs in a cream sauce flavored with mushrooms and onions were delicious. I almost asked the server if they had a bottle of Chambaux, but figured it would be too expensive for a place of this type to carry.

"What happened to the other man in the duel?"

"Arrested and hung. Dueling's been illegal for over two decades; Alenbonné doesn't want that pastime coming back into style. It's exactly something these idealistic fools would take into their head to make popular given a chance. Noble love and broken hearts. Stuff and nonsense that appeals to the young."

"The woman?"

"She was in court, but I couldn't understand one word of her testimony through the blubbering. Pretty thing, but clueless. What did she think would happen when her husband found out she was going to elope with her lover?"

"When does the activity usually start, and where?"

She checked the watch pinned to her coat lapel.

"In about an hour."

"Fine. Time enough to discuss Giles Monet over a coffee and dessert."

Dr. LaRue chuckled and waved for a server. They had several

interesting choices for dessert, and I selected the one I knew the least about to broaden my horizons. When we were alone again, Dr. LaRue gave me the details of the autopsy.

"Overall, a pretty straightforward business. Got conked on the back of the head with something hard and smooth. I'm thinking it was a rock. Like a cobblestone. He hit the water still breathing, so the official cause of death is drowning."

"Boring for you, I imagine."

"It would have been, except I also ran some blood tests, which made it more interesting."

She took her time, wiping her mouth first, and then making a performance of lighting one of her pencil-thin cigarettos. I think she enjoyed increasing my anticipation by waiting.

"Monet was a zhimo addict. Zhimo addiction changes the skin, making the dermis thinner. Plenty of bruising and marks not caused by being dumped in the canal. Long-term addicts lose their hair and the nails get a yellow color before they peel away."

"He was living in a boarding house. How could he afford zhimo!?"

Dr. LaRue gave another throaty chuckle, blowing smoke off to the side. "Once it gets a hold of you, you find a way to pay for it, trust me. From looking at his big toe, and calculating the slow growth rate of the nail, I'd say he's had a full-on habit for at least three months."

"You know how long it takes to grow a toenail?" I asked.

"Of course I do. We scientists measure everything. It gives us something to argue about at our clubs."

"Scientists have social clubs?"

"You do! Why shouldn't I have a place to retreat to? Where else can I talk shop? You don't think I have intellectual discussions with my students, do you? Ha! All students want to do is lecture their professors!"

Our attentive waiter took our plates and replaced them with a brass pot filled with black coffee. That was another benefit from our trade agreement with Perino; Sarnesse would riot if they lost this magical brew.

We were the last diners in the café when the owner reappeared. His smile was uncertain. "Has madame agreed to help us?"

I fingered my earring, thinking. There was no reason not to help, but some things needed to be understood first. "I will investigate the matter and then we shall talk over my findings. I make no guarantees about what I can do."

He was quick to agree; a tendency I've seen plenty of times in the desperate.

"Tell me what this haunt does? Does it manifest? Become embodied, or is it just a mist?"

He came closer and spoke in a low voice, as if he feared being overheard. "It is a man. A young man with dark hair tied in a bun at the nape of his neck. He does not speak but sits at that table."

Ah, that was why no one had sat there, even though it had a lovely view of the boulevard. A haunted space. I went over and took a seat at the table and, closing my eyes, spread out my inner senses.

At our table, I heard Dr. LaRue say, "Don't worry, Madame Chalamet is a professional. I let her talk with my dead bodies all the time."

Yes, the temperature here was colder. There was also that special wet feeling in the air that a sensitive person would detect. I regretted not having my bag with me. Well, I would have to improvise. Slipping into a light trance, I opened the door to my mind. Connecting, I fed power to the spirit to help it materialize.

"That's him," I heard fear coarsen the café owner's voice.

A handsome young man sat across from me. He wore a long linen frock coat over a festive plaid vest with matching pants. Rather a dandy.

The haunt had a well-groomed mustache with long hair pulled back into a tidy bun at the nape of his neck. His mouth was full, what a woman might call sensual, and his eyes were large and prominent. A woman married to a tyrant and looking for love might describe them as soulful.

Overall, I had the impression of an artistic, mercurial personality that would feel things intensely, and who might take affront easily. Provoking a haunt was not a good idea, so I proceeded cautiously. I asked gently, "Who are you waiting for?"

"She will be here. She promised to come. To leave him."

"She didn't?"

"She will be here. She promised to come. To leave him."

It seemed my ghostly companion was a bit stuck. I noticed what was under his hand, resting on the table, its petals limp.

"Is that her favorite flower?"

"It is our signal. For a meeting. When I saw her in class, if I carried a red rose, she knew to meet me later. She will be here. She promised to come. To leave him."

The problem with the dead is they are not very intelligent and are powered by emotions rather than logic. Unfortunately, mostly those feelings were of a darker nature: greed, anger, jealousy, and loss. I haven't met a ghost yet bursting with joy and happiness.

In the background, I heard a few arguing voices which I ignored. It was not a good thing to break your focus when speaking with spirits.

"What are you doing here? With this man?" Archambeau's demands surprised me as I hadn't been paying attention to my surroundings, only to the haunt sitting across from me, who appeared as solid as a living being. It slowly turned his head towards the duke.

"How dare you speak to her like that?" The ghost stood, but Archambeau gave it one of his dismissive looks. "Sit down, sprout. I was talking to Madame Chalamet."

"You will not speak to her like that. She has had enough of your cruelty."

"What in the devil are you talking about?"

"Your Grace—"

Archambeau cut me off. "When I was told your packages had arrived without you, I knew you'd escaped. Ran off. Just like a woman, not listening or caring if you put yourself in danger. If anyone knew you were in that morgue Ghost Talking they might think you knew who had killed—" He stopped revealing Monet's name just in time, but he wasn't finished being angry. "I'm trying to protect you, you fool."

"Protect her? You keep her in a cage and won't let her be free. You are not worthy to kiss the train of her dress, monster!"

If he was a living man, I'm sure the haunt would have slapped the duke and challenged him to a duel. Instead, it did something worse: it stepped into Archambeau's body and possessed him.

Chapter Twelve

The haunt embraced me tightly, and I found my nose being tickled by the duke's cravat and its cologne of tangerine, basil, and star anise.

"Now we can be together forever, my love."

"Let's approach this calmly—"

Before I could speak further, it pressed the duke's lips against my own. It wasn't a pleasant kiss since it was from two men: an ardent boy still in love with someone else, and the other a confused aristo held against his will. I couldn't help myself; I gave them both a resounding slap.

"Nicole, Nicole, have I angered you?"

"Unhand her!" Charlotte pressed the point of her cane sword into the back of the duke de Archambeau. On the floor was the discarded casing. The manager wrung his hands, repeating, "Oh my, oh my, oh my."

A lot more suddenly happened.

The rack of glasses shattered, and dishware fell off the wall behind the serving bar. It was a hallmark move of a Noise Ghost— a poltergeist— which uses the kinetic energy of the living to cause havoc. And like the one in Archambeau's office, they could be terribly temperamental and violent.

It shoved me backward as the haunt spun about, using Archambeau's forearm to bat away the rapier. The blade went spinning out of the doctor's hand, clattering on the tile floor.

There were several screams and a stampede to the back door.

Charlotte grabbed the coffeepot as the haunt lunged for her. Using it, she hit him hard on the temple and they both came crashing to the floor, where the duke's head made a resounding whack onto the tile.

It was deathly quiet now, and the shop owner peered over the bar where he had retreated to hide. I commanded the shop's owner as I came down to kneel beside Archambeau. "Wet a clean towel."

Mysir de duke was trying to sit up, and his hand reached up to where blood was running down a cut at his temple.

The ghost had made quite a scene, but they can't sustain the amount of energy needed to move physical objects, even when draining it from their hosts. From experience, I knew an episode like this would leave the duke exhausted and disoriented. Only time would tell if the entity had completely left him or not.

"How do you feel?"

He removed his hand and, squinting at me, said in his natural voice, "You slapped me."

"Yes, I'm sorry about that, Your Grace." Over the duke's head, the manager handed me the wet towel, but at the words "Your Grace" he bolted like a frightened rabbit for a doorway that removed him from sight.

"Here, let me see the damage." I gently cleaned his face. "You interfered with my reading and the ghost took advantage of you. I'm very sorry, Your Grace, but don't blame Charlotte. Dr. LaRue was trying to get the ghost to unhand me. She wasn't attacking you."

"Madame Chalamet, you are a lunatic." He tried to get his feet under him, but they weren't under his full control just yet.

They splayed out like a newborn colt, causing him to fall on all fours.

"Charlotte, maybe you should take a look at him?"

"I can see him from here," she said. "I'd guess a concussion, but his head doesn't seem cracked."

"Please, Charlotte."

The doctor came over and gingerly searched his head and looked at his eyes. "Hm. He's got a lump and a cut. The face bleeds easily, so that needs a plaster. Now let me see his arm."

The blade had sliced through the duke's coat, and blood was seeping through. "Help him out of this jacket, Elinor."

"I'm fine."

"No, you are not. Be a good boy and let her look."

Archambeau complied sullenly, but weak as he was, he really had little choice. We helped him sit in a chair and wrestled off his coat.

"Elinor, get me some alcohol from behind the bar and a clean towel or napkin."

I did as she asked. The duke sucked in hard when she sluiced the wound with liquor, but otherwise said nothing. Charlotte bandaged it with what I could find.

"I'd suggest getting him home and replacing that dressing. Some pain-killer would be good. Probably a mild concussion, so monitor him."

Because I doubted he would thank her, I did. I asked, "Can you hail a quick-cab for us, Charlotte?" After snapping her blade back into its case, she exited out the front door, and I heard her shout for a cab. "I thought you would want to be home, but do you need more time before we go?"

"We must go. I've already wasted enough time on finding you, and I have a meeting with General Somerville in the next half hour. This is enough public humiliation for me today."

"Come along," I encouraged him. "Lean on me, but take it slow. Use the chair to get up."

Gripping the chair's back, and with my help under his arm, Archambeau regained his feet. Without his coat, he looked very vulnerable, especially with the white shirt sleeve stained with blood. The bell on the door jingled, and Charlotte poked her head inside.

"I have a cab. I've asked the driver to help us with him."

With the doctor holding the door, and me at Archambeau's side, we carefully maneuvered him onto the sidewalk. The confusion of being possessed made him weave about like a baby first walking.

"What is this neighborhood coming to? A sad thing to see men fighting drunk before nightfall," said the driver, shaking his head.

"I am not drunk!" Unfortunately, the duke's slurred speech did nothing to convince the driver, who gave me a wide wink behind the duke's back.

"Of course not, mysir, my mistake. Now take it easy up this step. Here you go. Lean back like a good boy." With the duke seated inside, the driver became very solicitous towards me. Dr. LaRue must have given him a good tip. "You sure you don't want to catch a different cab, madame? Get a rest from the husband before going home?"

"Oh, he isn't my husband. Just a friend. A business acquaintance."

His eyes quickly traveled to my hands, both free of any rings. His solicitous manner cooled. "All right, madame, as you see fit."

Ignoring him, I scrambled into the cab beside the duke, firmly closing the door behind me. I stuck my head out the window and told Charlotte, "You need to send the name of this ghost, or anything else you know about him, to me at the duke's residence. The quicker, the better."

"Will you be fine—?" She gave a pointed look to the limp figure beside me that could barely keep himself upright.

"I can handle him. But I need that information as soon as possible. Please."

On the carriage ride back, I took the duke's pulse and tried to examine the pupils of his eyes. He weakly slapped my hands away.

"Stop fussing." His voice sounded more like his own, without the high youthful tone the ghost had spoken with. He was also sitting more upright. All were good signs that he was mastering his body despite the possession.

"Your Grace, I must explain to you that walking into a Manifestation, and addressing it, acknowledging its existence, opened a conduit between the two of you. It allowed the entity to possess you—"

"I wasn't possessed," he stubbornly insisted.

"Being a male ghost, your energy probably enticed it."

"That boy? You call that a man? He was nothing but a puppy. *I am a man!*"

Archambeau gaped like a fish at the last words rushing out of his mouth. As I feared, the ghost was hitching a ride.

"Please, Your Grace, understand me. This young man died during a duel over a woman. It is best that you humor him until I can get him to leave. No insults about masculinity or any disdain towards women, if you please. He seems sensitive about those areas."

He leaned his head back against the cushions, closing his eyes. I asked anxiously, "You don't feel nauseous, do you?"

"I didn't until you said something."

"Do we need to stop so you can be sick?"

"Stop-talking-about-that."

I folded my hands in my lap, wondering what I could say to buck him up.

"Possessions aren't forever. We need to find out what the ghost wants in order for him to feel at peace and ready to move on to the Afterlife."

"Jolly," muttered Archambeau.

"Dr. LaRue will send us what she can discover, but for now all

I know is his unfinished business concerns a married woman named Nicole."

The metaphysical glow that I had been observing emanating from the duke's form intensified. "*Nicole. I waited. Why did she not come?*" cried the ghost, using the duke's mouth.

I promised him. "We will find out, but you must give me time."

Archambeau shook his head, opening his eyes. "Did you say something?"

"Not a peep," I assured him.

When we arrived at the duke's residence, Archambeau stepped out of the cab into the street under his own power and thus earned a low, admiring whistle from the cab driver. I paid him out of my purse because the duke ignored us. He exited slowly and walked carefully to the front door by slowly placing one foot in front of the other.

The cab driver touched the brim of his hat.

Shaking his head, he said, "Le beau idéal, indeed! Who would want to emulate that! Fighting and drinking in the middle of the day? It might not be worth it." He gave me a meaningful glance before advising me, "Look after yourself, madame." With a cluck to his horse, they headed off at a brisk pace down the pristine and wealthy boulevard.

I caught up to Archambeau when the front door opened, revealing his sister, Lady Valentina Fontaine, and next to her, an older woman. From their walking dresses, they looked about ready to leave the house, but the duke was leaning against the door frame to remain standing and was blocking their exit.

"Are you drunk?" demanded the older woman.

"I'm told by a premier authority that I am merely possessed," said the duke calmly.

"Tristan, how could you? It's that woman leading you to this madness, isn't it?" asked Valentina. She pointed her parasol savagely in my direction.

"Madame Chalamet, may I introduce you to my mother, the Duchesse of Chambaux. Mother, this is Elinor Chalamet, who is helping me with a case of importance to the king."

That was quite a long speech, and by the end, he looked even paler.

"I believe His Grace needs to be seen to," I said, concerned.

Ignoring my words, the Duchesse de Chambaux asked her daughter, "Who is this Chalamet person?"

"That's the woman I was telling you about earlier, mother," said Lady Valentina.

I was growing more concerned about Archambeau. Through the hallway, I saw General Reynard Somerville, with Jacques Moreau.

"Jacques, please." At my plea, he looked first to the general and, receiving his permission with a nod, came to where we were standing.

"What can I do?"

"Can you help the duke upstairs? He banged his head and has wounds that need attending."

Archambeau straightened, pushing away from the wall. "I can make it upstairs alone."

"No, you can't. Stop being stubborn," I chided him. At my words, his sister gasped and his mother frowned. I ignored their outrage and told the duke, "Being possessed isn't easy. It's worse than recovering from the city cough."

"I bow to your superior knowledge, madame," he said sarcastically. "If I have your permission, can we go inside and stop making a farce for my neighbors?"

It was then I noticed the small group of people who had paused in their stroll along the boulevard who were gaping at our tableau.

"Mother, Valentina, Madame Chalamet," Archambeau said politely before walking stiffly towards the bottom of the staircase. I waved Jacques to follow, and he stepped up beside the duke. But the stubborn man refused his offer of a supporting arm. Well, if Archambeau fell down the stairs, it wasn't my fault.

The duchesse de Chambaux demanded, "Follow me, Madame Chalamet. I have things to discuss with you."

Chapter Thirteen

I followed the two ladies into a receiving room where everything was even more opulent than the rest of the house. The walls were cream, the carved plaster moldings were white, and the grass-green drapes were trimmed with gold-thread tassels. The furniture was in a pink-rose velvet, and the wood was gilt while exotic rugs from Perino weavers covered the floor.

It all gave me the feeling of walking into a very high-end box of sweets.

The art was less sugary. Landscape paintings showed castles and manor houses with expansive views. Painted lords and ladies aplenty frowned down at me with suitable severity. Hopefully, there was a secret room where the more humorous family members resided.

In a bay window, instead of a seating arrangement, there was a five-foot bronze statue of a man trying to bridle a willful stallion. The man and the horse looked equally determined to get their own way, and their facial expressions immediately made me think of the duke.

The Duchesse silently pointed at a seat across from her own

chair. As I took it, she arranged the handle of her parasol to lie across the crook of her elbow; the pose was one of a queen on her throne holding a scepter.

"Madeline, bring us tea, and close the door."

She addressed a servant who had followed us. She now left, and the footman standing in the hall closed the doors. Instinctively, I looked to the window, calculating distance. We were on the ground floor, so escape was possible.

"It is my understanding you are a guest of my son," said the Duchesse de Chambaux. I made my features blank as she continued. "Chalamet. I have heard that name. Ah. Yes. A jeweler. I haven't heard of him lately. He must have gone out of fashion."

Archambeau's sister, Lady Valentina Fontaine, didn't meet my eyes, but toyed with a small book she picked up from a side table. Considering the title was about planetary movements and she was holding it upside down, I think it was safe to judge she had no interest in astronomy.

"Stop fiddling, Valentina. A lady's mind should be in charge of her body at all times. It is what sets us apart from the lower order of grocer, dressmaker, and merchant."

I think my pleasant face froze around the edges, but I survived; a frost only kills tender plants.

A door opened on the wall, revealing a disguised second entrance behind a painting of some military dignitary of the last century. The painting's frame cleverly hid the seam. After Madeline rolled the tea cart to the side of Lady Fontaine, the duke's sister dismissed her. She left by the same entrance, pulling the painting back into place.

Lady Fontaine poured out a cup for her mother and set it within easy reach of the duchesse on a small black table, lines of gold paint bringing out the details of the fluted legs. She ignored it.

"Are you married?" the duchesse asked me.

"No, Your Grace," I replied, and she grimaced.

"I cannot believe—" she began, but with that control that

only ladies of quality have over their bodies, the duchesse stopped herself. "You must be here because of my son's work. There is no other reason Tristan would involve himself with a Ghost Talker. We do not concern ourselves with such ghoulish people."

I said, keeping my voice level with effort, "Yes, I am here because of a matter Mysir de Archambeau is investigating. I have been told not to discuss it, so if you wish to know more, you shall need to ask him to explain."

After a silent stare and a small sip of her tea, she said, "Today, I was told you conducted a Ghost Hunt last night in this very house. Only the lower classes resort to such vulgar entertainments. I do not hold with the Morpheus Society or their blasphemous doings."

I couldn't stop myself. After all, I hailed from the lower orders and thus lacked regulation. "Lady Baudelaire requested it."

If you really watch the face, it reveals much. The fine line of her nostrils flared as she took a deep breath and under her rouge, her skin grew white with fury.

"Lady Baudelaire is under the mistaken impression that her acquaintance with my son's late wife has given her some right to command at Hartwood House. The next time she pays a call here, Valentina, send her to me. I will correct this misapprehension of hers."

"I'm sure she didn't mean to overstep, Mother. She's known us since we were children—"

The duchesse halted her daughter with a glance that cut. "You are naïve, Valentina. She is using you."

"But I thought— I only invited her because I thought you favored her?"

"Once, perhaps, but Tristan will have none of it, so her schemes will never bear fruit." Realizing she was discussing family matters in front of a stranger, she returned to her original grievance. "Having a Ghost Hunt in this home is a dangerous activity.

There are ancient, restless spirits here that are not to be trifled with."

"Like the cellar girl, murdered by her lover? Or the Noise Ghost in the study who hates women?"

"Not to be trifled with." The duchesse repeated firmly. "Such things are best left alone, undisturbed." She clicked her cup into its saucer and set it aside. "We've had enough interference from your kind. Another Ghost Talker tried her tricks here, but I saw through her. I sent her packing and now the newspapers finally proclaim that Madame Nyght woman to be exactly what I knew she was all along— a liar."

"The Morpheus Society does not endorse her."

"Endorsed by them? A group that plays upon the grief of families in order to earn their coin?" The duchesse's words dripped with acid. "Frauds and tricksters, the lot of you. Well, Madame Chalamet, you will gain no money from me for your trouble."

This was probably my cue to storm out of the room. I stubbornly stayed where I was, for no one had offered me tea. The silence stretched on and Lady Valentina's fingers fiddled again with the cover of the book resting in her lap.

The Duchesse de Chambaux broke it first. She stood and taking her parasol handle in her right hand, tapped its tip against the rich carpet.

"It is time for my walk," she announced before leaving, with Lady Valentina hurrying afterward.

Alone in the room, I poured a cup for myself. Finding it cold, I set it aside and walked over to examine the false wall.

Once you knew what to look for, it was easy. There was an indent for your fingers, and a button under the edge of the picture frame to push, to release the locking mechanism. Opening it, I peered into a corridor, but hearing someone coming, quickly closed it.

It was Jacques. How well he looked in his military dress uniform of scarlet and black.

"Elinor! How did you fare with the old dragon?"

"Only slightly scorched. But tell me of the duke. Is he well?"

"Nicked some flesh, but from the healthy quantity of complaining about my help, I think he will recover just fine. He's with Axe now. That's the nickname for the commander, for he can quickly chop you down to size."

He tucked my hand under his arm and returned me to the seat I had abandoned. Pulling up a chair close to me, he laid his arm along the back of my chair. "We didn't have time to talk last night, but now we can have a cozy chat. What a strange place to find you! Hobnobbing with Le beau idéal."

Perhaps it was the recent interview with Duchesse de Chambaux but I found myself feeling offended by his words. "Do you think I do not belong here? That I am not as good as these people?"

He chuckled which perhaps offended me more.

"Of course not. It's just not your usual place, is it, Elinor? I mean you're more to be found with the salt of the earth types. Merchants, bankers, sailors, tradespeople." He drawled out the last word, accenting it.

"My clients come from all levels of society," I said frostily, for after all wasn't Archambeau one of my clients now? "And if you think I do not belong here, why do you think you do!? Our families came from the same neighborhood!"

"I'm a soldier," he said smugly. "Our uniforms not only blur the line of class, but we are invited to all the dances and fêtes to fill out the numbers. Now, don't get your hackles up, little cat, and tell me the real reason why you are here."

"I am working with His Grace on a case," I said stiffly. "But discussing a client's business would be a breach of confidentiality. You don't tell me military secrets."

"Is it about his wife, the fair Minette?" he pressed, his eyes watching me intently.

"No."

Since I was curious and he seemed to know something he wasn't telling, I asked, "People keep mentioning his dead wife to me. Did you know her?"

His hand came up my back and played with the feather on my hat. "I met her the year she came out. You were training with Madame Granger then. Anyway," he sighed, leaning further into the sofa's back. "She was a gorgeous thing. Heads above the other girls who were being presented at the time. No one coming after her, has surpassed her in beauty or wit."

"Did you court her?" His animosity towards the duke might be rooted in something more simple.

His smile grew a little sly. "Now, that would be tales out of school." Jacques became lost in the past as he reminisced. "That was a special year for me— the year I earned my bars. Minette was dazzling, both men and quite a few ladies. Clothes, jewelry, horses, parties— anything she put her hand to sparkled brighter and better than anyone else. She was in demand everywhere. At the end of the season, though, she gave us the biggest surprise of all."

"How so?"

"She became engaged and later married Mysir de Duke de Chambaux. We were baffled! She could have had anyone, far wealthier, but she picks a man whose estate is in the farthest corner of Sarnesse, far away from the glitter of the city? Nor had she paid him any special attention before the announcement. No one could figure out the attraction— they were as different as chalk and cheese. Their union made little sense."

"Perhaps it was an arranged marriage?" I said quietly, trying to put the puzzle together.

"That could explain things I never understood. Soon after the grand wedding, I was sent off to Zulskaya and didn't see her until about five years ago. The marriage changed her." His mouth became grim as he paused.

"In what way?" I prompted.

"She was so unhappy. Miserably really though she pretended

otherwise. Some of their arguments were very public and nasty. There was abuse."

"You know this?"

Instead of answering me, he shifted and said as his gaze went to the statue of the man trying to tame the horse. "His wife's now a haunt. And she's dangerous. She's still jealous— women get pinched, slapped, jewelry mislaid, and she pushed one poor soul down the stairs. The woman survived, only breaking her arm, but no one stays overnight at this house except his mother and sister."

"Thanks for the warning, but I've seen nothing so far to indicate she is here, and if she does, I know what to do."

"I'm serious, Elinor. You need to get out of here. I don't want to see you hurt."

I shook my head. "Forget it. This is exactly the type of ghost I would love to meet. Now, changing subjects, tell me why are you and your general here?"

"Organizing the royal procession and the public treaty signing between the king and the Perino delegation. After they sign, there will be a huge banquet, a ball, and handing out some medals. It's simple work and I'm glad. Last time, we met Perino on some hill surrounded by a swamp where it rained the entire week."

"Sounds very unpleasant."

"Swamps usually are. Lots of biting insects the size of your hand. And mud. Talk about the mud! The damp gets into your kit, making everything mildew, while your horse's hooves rot away."

"It sounds far more fun to host them in our lovely city."

"It would be, but there's always a fly in the ointment, and this time it is those damn student protesters. Blocking entrances, shouting non-stop outside of hotels where you just want to sleep. Don't they have classes to attend?"

"Maybe if the university had proper funding, they wouldn't protest."

"Oh, you little rebel. Ready to wave a sign and stop one of our patrols, huh? Well, the royal family is an easy target. King Guénard is such a fat fool."

"Who is a fat fool?" asked the round man who had just entered the room.

Jacques jumped to his feet and bowed to the king of Sarnesse while I sunk into a curtsy.

Chapter Fourteen

My knowledge of King Guénard was from afar and secondhand. At the moment, I wished myself very far away indeed.

Behind the rotund figure of the ruler of Sarnesse was the tall, trim one of the Duke de Archambeau. He was wearing a clean coat and a pristine white shirt with an elegant necktie, his left arm held stiffly against his side. Beside him stood General 'Axe' Somerville, who barked at us.

"You two, step aside."

We rapidly complied, moving over to stand in front of the long green drapes, hoping to be forgotten. The king sat down heavily in the chair the duchesse had used earlier and it may have creaked a little under his weight. The king's face held a florid color that made me wonder what Dr. LaRue would think of him.

"Is that her?" he pointed one short, pudgy finger my way.

"Yes, Your Majesty," replied Archambeau.

"She talked with Giles?"

Archambeau quickly looked behind him, giving a nod to the footman to close the door. It was the same young man from earlier. Did he never leave?

"Yes, your majesty. She provided information that helped us to locate where Monet was lodging at the time of his death."

"She can speak for herself, I imagine."

Yes, the woman could speak. Given permission.

King Guénard waved me forward with a limp, tired gesture. "Tell me."

"Yes, your majesty, I did Ghost Talk with a man that identified himself as Giles Monet. Mysir de Archambeau was present, and the gendarmes representatives Inspector Marcellus Barbier and Sergeant Quincy Dupont. Dr. Charlotte LaRue was the attending physician."

When I paused, weighing what details to relay, the king demanded. "Go on. Don't mind the sensibilities of this fat fool. Giles was my cousin, a son of my mother's half-sister. He was a hanger-on, a sponger, with too many friends from low places. Nothing much would surprise me."

"The images I translated gave Inspector Barbier enough to find out Mysir Monet was seeing a dancer at a nightclub called the Nightingale. Other than that, I learned little. I regret to inform your majesty, while the Ghost Talk session revealed his last few hours, it did not show us his killer."

"Ha. Ghost Talking is a neat parlor trick, but does it do anything but make ladies scream, claiming a ghostly hand was up their skirt?"

With surprise, I heard Archambeau defend me.

"The session gave us his lodgings, a hole in the Hells, where he lived under an assumed name. From there, we have tracked his lover, who might possess what we seek. Without Madame Chalamet, none of this would have been possible."

"Fine, fine," grumbled the king. "But what I want to know is, what are you going to do about my dead relative, Giles Monet?"

"I have made plans for us to visit the Nightingale."

"Haven't heard of the place."

Eager to redeem himself, Jacques interjected, "It's a skirt-and-tails show, your majesty. Dance hall girls, magicians, jugglers, and clowns. Very popular with nobles who want to slum it in the Hells."

The king gave a grunt, clearly not interested in a place he wouldn't be seen dead or alive in. Archambeau asked, "You've been there?"

Jacques gave a deprecating chuckle. "Well, that was some time ago." Seeing the general's face grow grimmer, he quickly added, "When I was much younger and far more foolish. Pretty rough customers and the management serves drinks that could strip paint. But the girls are all right."

Archambeau turned to the general. "Can I have the use of this man for the next day or so?"

"Gladly," growled the general. "Find something unpleasant for him to do. Like digging a trench for a latrine."

"What I want to know," demanded the king, pounding his fist into his meaty thigh encased in white dress breeches that were skin tight. "Is what did Giles do with my tiara?"

At the mention of jewelry, my ears perked up. "Which, of the twenty-four tiaras Your Majesty owns, do you mean?"

He groaned, his hands coming up to pull on the hair on either side of his ears.

"The most inconvenient one in my collection! That damn thing I need in five days time or the Perino dignitaries will walk away without signing. They insist on its return, claiming it as a treasured relic we stole from them over a century ago. No tiara, no trade agreement." The king smashed his fist against the chair arm. "Giles would pick that one to steal! Why couldn't he take some other bauble to pay off racing debts or his skirts?"

My father had worked on several pieces for King Guénard, right up to his murder. It meant I had memorized the list of the king's treasures long ago.

"Do you mean the one with the three rubies? That is the only one with Perino heritage that I know of."

"Yes, the one with the three rubies," the king repeated, mimicking my voice. "We had the damn thing out to be cleaned about four months ago, and Giles expressed an interest in seeing it. When he left abruptly, so did the tiara. I should have known it would cause trouble again."

"What do you mean?" Archambeau asked sharply.

"Two women who have worn it have died," I said.

"Three," corrected the king. "The third death was hushed up. First, was the death of a princess, murdered by her husband. Second, was a lady-in-waiting who drowned herself. In my childhood, a servant put it on as a joke and that evening she jumped from the west tower. I was looking forward to dumping the cursed thing on the Perino's."

"But how do you know Mysir Monet took it?" I asked.

The king wiped his mouth with the palm of his hand, rubbing his lips hard.

"Giles' mother showed up about six weeks later, demanding to know where her boy was. I told her he was probably drunk in a gutter somewhere and now it seems my guess was pretty accurate. That's when we discovered the tiara was missing as well."

"You didn't suspect the staff?" asked the duke.

"The staff wouldn't touch that thing with a ten-foot pole; they know its reputation. Besides, if they wanted to steal something valuable, the palace has enough trinkets. They could pocket plenty of them without me ever knowing."

"How long ago was this, your majesty?" I asked.

"About four months ago."

Archambeau asked me, "What are you thinking, madame? I see the wheels spinning in that nefarious brain of yours."

"When I met with Dr. LaRue this afternoon, she said Giles Monet had become a recent zhimo addict. Did you suspect that, your majesty?"

"No. Giles was a waster, but drink was his weapon of destruction. Last year, he stayed a month and drained an entire rack of my best wine. Some of it was vintage Chambaux, which I wouldn't mind you replacing, Archambeau."

Thinking out loud, I said, "Perhaps the drug made him desperate enough to steal the tiara?"

"To pay his debts, you mean?" asked Jacques.

"Or his dealer got him hooked and then influenced him to steal it. When he passed it off, they killed him," I said thoughtfully. "But why did they want the tiara? Being rubies, it isn't especially valuable without its history. Was it stolen to sell to a private collector?"

"Or stolen to cause unrest," said Archambeau. "We need it or the entire trade treaty falls apart. The Perino delegates will be angry when they discover their national treasure is missing."

Reminded of his troubles, King Guénard groaned, putting the heel of his hands over his eyes, and said, "Leave me. I have a headache."

We shuffled together in a line to the exit. Before the door fully closed, I heard him give one last order to Archambeau.

"Bring me a bottle of Chambaux. And cake. A lot of cake."

In the hallway, General Somerville was talking with the duke.

"I'm proceeding ahead with our plans on the security. I'll leave recovering the tiara to you, Archambeau. That," he pointed at Jacques, who was standing at attention, "you can have. He's my representative in this. Moreau, consider the duke to be my voice."

After the general left, the duke gave directions to Jacques to return with his gear. "You seem to be familiar with this Nightingale place, and I would like to know more of what you can tell us."

Behind Archambeau's back, Jacques gave me a wink as he left. Alone in the hall for the first time, I asked mysir de duke how he was doing.

"Fine, madame," he said rigidly.

"Can we talk about what happened?"

"No."

"I really think it's best. Being possessed is uncomfortable at best, and at worse, dangerous. We need to encourage your ghost to leave as soon as possible."

"I will deal with it in my own way."

This must be how parents feel about children who refuse to eat their vegetables.

"Can I go with you to the Nightingale?"

"The Nightingale is not a place I would take my sister or any lady of my acquaintance," he qualified.

"Yes, but I'm not a lady, as your mother has pointed out to me, and so should be able to manage well at the low type of establishment the Nightingale seems to be." A bit of that mulish look was returning, so I hastily added, "This girl of Monet's? If we find her, she is more likely to talk to another woman than a man. I can also go where men cannot, such as the dancer's dressing room."

"I am sure plenty of men gain the back rooms if they pay for the privilege," he said cynically. "However, I will concede your point. Having a woman with us could be useful, not only in disguising our real purpose, but perhaps as an appeal to the suspect if we find her. And if the tiara is found, your expertise may be needed."

"If we find the tiara, I think it is best that I'm the one who handles it. This curse is of the Uncanny, and it would be best to treat it cautiously."

"You think there is some substance to this curse?"

I frowned.

"My father thought the rubies were more likely to be drops of dragon blood, than true rubies."

"Dragons?" Archambeau laughed. "I'll give you credit for ghosts, Chalamet, but now dragons? Do you take me for a gullible fool?"

"Don't scoff. Our naturalists have fossils and accounts that dragons existed hundreds of years ago. Historical documents fearing their Uncanny powers before they died out."

"But how do you jump from the idea that these rubies are drops of dragon blood?"

"While I have never seen dragon stones, I have read about them." I didn't want to tell him about that snatch of a dream I had experienced in the gendarmes office. "My point is the tiara has a curse on it, something ordinary jewelry does not have. It comes from Perino (a place that once was a breeding ground for dragons), and I know what it looks like. All good reasons for me to come to the Nightingale."

The mule became thoughtful. I pushed my point. "Don't you think Monet's behavior is puzzling? He has access to wealth, doesn't run up large amounts of debt, and is well-liked. But out of the blue, he steals a tiara that has a curse upon it. One that is needed for an important trade agreement between Sarnesse and Perino. What a timely theft."

He grimaced at my words.

"I agree. It's all a little too convenient. What I fear is at the root isn't some imaginary dragon, but anarchy. Giving this thing back to Perino was a gesture of goodwill and to go back on his word would be a public humiliation that would be hard for the monarchy to recover from. It would give fuel to the anti-monarchists who want more power given to parliament."

He gave me a searching look before agreeing.

"Fine, Madame Chalamet, you may come, but you will do exactly as I tell you and if there is any danger at all—"

"I'll dive under the table at the first sign of trouble. I promise."

Chapter Fifteen

In my room, I found Anne-Marie unpacking boxes newly arrived from the modiste.

"Look at this!" she cried, holding up a silk lace chemise. "So much nicer than that old cotton stuff you wear. It feels so nice!"

"I'm glad my undergarments meet with your approval."

"And the dresses!" From the bed, she grabbed a garment and placed it over her chest. I bowed to her, and taking her hand, we twirled around the furniture in a popular three-quarter time dance. When we finally stopped, laughing and out of breath, she said, "This latest job must pay well for you to splurge like this, madame."

"All of this is courtesy of Mysir de duke."

Her eyes grew round. "Are we living here for good? I could get used to it."

"Certainly not. We should be back to the Crown by next week."

Anne-Marie tried to hide her disappointment as she put away my new outfits. "So this high life isn't for keeps?"

"Well, the clothes are mine, but staying here? I might have to eat breakfast with his sister every day. And have you met his mother? Now, Anne-Marie, the dressmaker was supposed to send me a gown— oh, there it is. I'll be using that one tonight."

Anne-Marie tried her best to conceal her disappointment. "I guess it's for the best. It's only been a bit frosty downstairs."

"Have you been mistreated? Tell me!" I asked, alarmed. Shot through with energy I was about to march down and give mysir de duke a piece of my mind.

The girl shook her head, smiling. "Oh, don't get worked up, madame. It's nothing I can't handle. It's only the duchesse's personal servant, that Madeline. Thinks she knows what's best for the family as she's been here for donkey years."

I sat down on the corner of the bed, watching her. "What's been happening?"

"She doesn't like you or me staying here and has made sure the rest of the servants know she disapproves. And that her employer would like us dumped in a back alley of the Hells rather than look at us!"

Thinking of my interview with the duchesse I could only imagine the unpleasantness that my servant in this household had been given.

"I'm so sorry that you've been subjected to that. We will be home soon, so don't worry."

"I'm not worried. Some of them have been very nice to me, showing me around the house when you all were down to dinner. Letting me peek into the rooms. But I'm certainly going to enjoy telling them about your new clothes!"

That made me laugh. "Get a bath running so I can get ready for tonight."

After a quick soak, and change, she was putting my hair up when there was a low knock on the door. It was the maid Georgette.

"Madame, His Grace says he wants you downstairs for a meeting in the library in about an hour."

Downstairs, in the duke's study, I found a war council already in session.

Archambeau, Jacques, Inspector Barbier, and Sergeant Dupont were in the middle of a discussion when I entered. Dupont, as rumpled as ever, fading into the background, was the only one who didn't greet me.

The men stood around a table where lay a large piece of white butcher's paper. Coming closer, I could see it was a roughly sketched map of the city area known as the Hells. Unlike the planned areas of the city, where the streets made decorative crescents along the canals, these were crooked narrow lanes. A black square was marked with the letter N, for what I assumed was the location of Nightingale.

"It looks like a rabbit warren," I commented.

"The oldest part of the city," said Archambeau. "Probably the only area to survive the blaze of '02, though I think a fire could improve it."

"A thousand places for thieves and felons to hide," said the inspector. "If you get into trouble there, getting you out might be difficult."

"I understand," said the duke. "But the Nightingale is our best clue and we must try. Now, Inspector Barbier will have plainclothes guardia here, here, and here." Archambeau pointed with a pencil at places on the map that he marked with penciled small X's. "They won't come in unless we need them. Do we know anything more about the woman Giles Monet was visiting?"

"We found her lodgings finally, but not Gabrielle. According to her landlady, no one has seen her since Monet cashed his chips in," said the inspector. "Her act is on tonight, but I doubt she'll be there."

Archambeau said confidently, "If she does not, we can use our time to discover more about her. Her clients, the manager, and the other girls. Someone will know something."

"My people had no luck," said the inspector sourly. Barbier wasn't enjoying the duke's highhandedness, and I felt a wincing sympathy for his difficult position. He had worked hard to become inspector, even breaking his leg while chasing a thief over the rooftops which later resulted in a limp and shortened leg.

Yes, he had paid his dues on rough streets, and I am sure he was wondering what mysir de duke had done to earn anything, let alone the right to tell the gendarmes what to do.

"I'm not saying your people haven't done good work, inspector, but the Nightingale's patrons will be naturally suspicious of the gendarmes. But a man of means interested in her favors, and who is happy to flash the paper, will be tempting bait."

To this, the inspector said nothing, but his back remained stiff and his manner disapproving. Turning to Jacques, the duke said, "Moreau, you come in uniform and act like an officer on leave, ready for a good time. But wait about thirty minutes after we arrive before you make your debut, and do not acknowledge us."

"Fine, but I still don't think Elinor should join us."

"She wants to come. And we may need her expertise."

"About ghosts?" asked Jacques with surprise.

"I'm coming for the tiara. I have some acquaintance with my father's notes that he took about the royal collection when he surveyed it, and I can also tell real goods from false. Besides, have you all forgotten about the curse? In this room, who has experience with the Uncanny?"

The room grew quiet and the only noise for a moment or two was Archambeau tapping his pencil against the map.

"Fine. Warning taken. We need to be careful. No one touch the thing except Madame Chalamet or myself. If we find Monet's girlfriend, I suspect we will learn the fate of our missing tiara."

He nodded to Inspector Barbier to begin.

"Gabrielle Meijer. She's in her early twenties, but looks

younger, with a round baby-face, brown eyes, and blond hair. A dancer well-known to the Nightingale and its patrons. Not seen for a week, but since we don't have her body in the morgue, at this point we are assuming she's gone to ground somewhere."

Looking around the group, Archambeau said, "If she's at the Nightingale, we take her with us. If she isn't, who are her friends? Her confidants? Does anyone know her favorite haunts?"

Jacques shook his head. "There's some big bull, a thug who controls the backstage. He won't let anyone through unless you pay for a girl's time."

"I'll leave that mission to you, then. Madame Chalamet and I will canvas the front of the house," said Archambeau. "Now, Madame Chalamet found out some interesting information about Monet this afternoon."

I told them about Dr. LaRue's discovery of Monet's drug habit.

"She thinks it started about three or four months ago, which would work with the timeline of him visiting the king and taking the tiara. Did he get his drugs at the Nightingale or from Gabrielle? Is his supplier involved in the tiara theft?"

Jacques said, "He could have stolen the thing to sell it to pay for his drugs; zhimo is not a cheap high."

"Or extremists used his addiction to force him to prevent the treaty," said Archambeau. "The trade treaty between Sarnesse and Perino is to be signed in four days. As a gesture of goodwill, King Guénard will return the tiara stolen from them during our last war. Without this former national treasure, that treaty is as good as dead in the water. So, gentlemen and madame, can we try really hard not to risk an international incident?"

After Barbier left, I was alone with Archambeau and Jacques. If I expected mysir de duke to say anything about my new outfit, I was in for a disappointment. At least Jacques knew how to hand out a compliment.

"Elinor, you look lovely!" He took my hand and gave it a kiss.

"I could say the same for you. So handsome in your scarlet and black."

Archambeau wore a black tailcoat in wool with silk lapels; his white waistcoat gleamed and his cufflinks were onyx. He shrugged into a thick gray wool overcoat that Ruben the footman held for him.

"Wait a moment, madame!" called Anne-Marie as she trotted down the stairs holding my new fur wrap. Jacques placed it around my bare shoulders and, without further ado, our party went out the front door.

At the curb, Jacques opened the door to his own quick-cab and jumped in. "Good hunting!" He waved out the window as his vehicle rolled away.

Archambeau handed me into another carriage. Unlike his personal coach, this one had no coat of arms on the polished black door. As the two horses started forth, their hooves clip-clopped loudly against the cobblestones. I settled back, my heart racing with anticipation.

"I am guessing your fur is a recent acquisition."

My hand automatically went up and stroked it. "Indeed, your Grace. One of several treats I rewarded myself for putting up with you and your family."

My comment didn't seem to offend him because he chuckled. "I better check my bank balance."

"Does a duke need to check? I would think the Chambaux family would have enough credit to buy a country, let alone a few dresses."

"From the amount of boxes I saw going up the stairs this afternoon, I did buy a small country. *Well, I think you look lovely.*"

The last startled me until I realized the duke's ghost had said it.

Worryingly, Archambeau hadn't seemed to notice the slip. The two needed to be separated, and soon.

"I know you may not have much trust in Ghost Talking, Your Grace, but it is important that we evict your ghost as soon as possible. Meanwhile, please try to keep better control of it."

"I am in control."

Nothing like a man in denial. Time for a lecture.

"There are several common types of ghosts. The recently dead, like Giles Monet, can produce a spiritual vision of his last moments through a Ghost Talk. A true ghost is an entity that shifts between the realms of the Earthly and Beyond; they return because of a powerful emotion or a horrific death."

There was a moment of silence before the duke said diffidently, "Have you heard what they say about my dead wife? That she walks my house and attacks women?"

I would not lie to him. "Jacques told me something about that. Even your mother warned me from contacting her."

From his corner seat, the duke's face flickered in and out of shadow as we passed gas street lamps glowing in the dark. I could not read his expression as he asked, "Have you seen her?"

"No. But I haven't looked either. I won't, unless you ask me to do so, for it would be a breach of your privacy."

"I have not seen her, but sometimes I think I smell her perfume."

We had entered the Hells, and without street gas-lamps Archambeau's corner was now very dark. I could only make out the gleaming white of his waistcoat and gloves.

"You think loudly, madame, did you know that? Even in this dim light I see the shine of your eyes wondering, hear the gears of your mind ticking away like a hall clock. Wondering if I indeed killed her like I said. Trying to figure out why or how, or if I could be mistaken. No. It was no accident, no death by unintentional means. It was a gunshot wound to the heart which killed Minette instantly. I am an excellent marksman, even at twenty paces."

I wet my lips about to speak, but Archambeau changed the subject.

"Enough of the past. Let us speak of tonight. We are to play-act as jaded nobles, seeking amusement."

"I do not think anyone of quality would be foolish enough to visit such a place, Your Grace."

"I have visited far worse for my king," he muttered under his breath before saying in a normal tone, "Our cover story is that I'm showing you the seedier side of Alenbonné for a cheap thrill. Some foolish people deliberately court danger in order to feel more alive. This is the reason for our presence, so be sure to look pleasurably shocked, yet thrilled, when we get inside."

"I shall try my best."

The carriage slowed to a stop. I looked out the window and cried out so loudly that heads turned our way, "Oh, look at the funny people! Why is that man sleeping in the gutter? He'd better get up before he catches cold."

When mysir de duke handed me down, I stumbled against him, giggling. Pressed against him, he whispered in my ear, "Is that a weapon I feel in your pocket, madame?"

I gave him a playful shove away from me. "Don't ask a girl to reveal her secrets! Not until I see a show and dinner. Remember, you promised me both!"

He held his arm out for me, and I tucked mine under his. Together we weaved past the drunks, the whores, and the gamesters to enter the Nightingale.

Chapter Sixteen

A boisterous crowd packed the Nightingale. Inside, Archambeau used his bulk to push through the crowd, ignoring the disgruntled looks and curses his actions received.

A haze of smoke from cigars and cigarettos made my eyes water, and underneath it all was a smell of beer and unwashed bodies. It made a woman question the sanity of why bother to perfume her bath and wear an elegant dress that cost as much as a year's earnings to slum in such a place.

I bumped into the duke's back when he stopped to hand a server a wad of bills. After taking his time to examine each bill as if we were trying to cheat him, the server cocked his finger for us to follow him. He made his way to a table near the stage where a man and two women were sitting. The women wore heavy stage makeup with red lips and eyes like black holes; their skimpy dress showed leg all the way to the knee.

"Scram," said the Nightingale man. The women hopped up immediately and left, but the man rolled back in his wooden chair, putting hands in his pockets, striking a tense, defiant pose. "What if I don't want to?"

The waiter gave a swift kick to the front of the chair, tipping it over and sending the man sprawling. His victim tried to gain his feet, receiving a kick to his head that sent him splattering back to the floor face down. Someone from the crowd emerged, a giant among the other men, with a boulder head sitting on a mountain body. Without further ado, he dragged the injured man away. Throughout the incident, the raucous din in the Nightingale never stopped.

Archambeau bent over and righted the discarded chair. "Have a seat, madame."

I took it, but was careful not to let my fur slip to touch a floor sticky with blood and beer. Archambeau took a chair next to mine, and the waiter left with our order, along with more money.

Less than ten feet from our table was the stage where an act of three little dogs were jumping through hoops. They were being ignored by almost everyone in the room, but when it ended, I applauded vigorously. The trainer gave me an elaborate bow. Archambeau tossed some coins up on the stage, which made the three dogs stop what they were doing and give our table a series of adorable tricks.

The waiter returned to set down two mugs of beer. After he left, I told Archambeau, "How do we begin?"

"Relax, Chalamet, and have some patience. When you fish, you don't scream at them to jump on your hook."

"I've never fished, so wouldn't know."

"Don't worry— the money I'm spending has already attracted their interest. No. Don't look around. Watch the stage."

The next act was two clowns, both dressed in floppy men's clothes with a bright plaid pattern. They tipped their top hats to the crowd while taking a wide bow, earning them a few drunken cheers. Someone from the back yelled an obscenity.

The pantomime act was one of crude humor: pelvic thrusting, pratfalls and splits, interspersed with punches and slaps. The female clown was the butt of all the jokes, which seemed to please the crowd but I only wished a dog from the previous act would rush in and bite the man kicking her.

Archambeau must have noticed my mood. "Not amused?"

"No."

Disgusted, I moved my attention to the audience, examining them with an interest I made casual. Most of them looked to be locals, men wearing baggy working-class coats, with colorful cotton handkerchiefs tied around their throats instead of the white muslin cravat that Archambeau wore. Not as many women, but those that I did see wore gaudy dresses that didn't match their dour expressions. I found the place depressing in its crudeness and poverty.

Seeing both of our mugs empty, I asked Archambeau, "You didn't drink that?"

"That swill? Not likely. Ditched it under the table."

As the server hurried by, Archambeau flashed a folded bill between his fingers and the man stopped. "Do you have any wine? I'm celebrating tonight."

The waiter vanished almost as quickly as the money. After he left, I muttered, "This is a waste of time. We won't find her sitting at this table."

"Maybe not her, but I've already found someone here who I didn't expect."

"Who?"

"One of the Perino ambassadors, and it looks like he's waiting for someone. He's sitting almost directly across from us at the other end of the room."

I swept my eyes past the area Archambeau indicated, and saw a much older man with white hair who wore the standard business garb of a merchant. That was all I could gain before the crowd shifted, blocking my view.

"Do you think he's here about the tiara? But why? The king will give it to them soon enough."

"If they can bypass royal authority and grab it, it would probably soothe their feelings of having lost it in the first place. It seems too coincidental he would be here at the same time as us. Perhaps he also waits for the appearance of Gabrielle Meijer."

The clowns ran off the stage and suddenly the men started clapping and hooting as a trio of dancing girls pranced on stage, swinging their short skirts. Two of the three were the girls who had been at our table.

Their dancing wasn't elegant, but they did it enthusiastically. The crowd roared and everyone started pounding on the tables to the time of the piano music being hammered out by a man who had no respect for a tune.

The waiter reappeared to set down two glasses and a bottle. From the corner of my eye, I saw a tall blond man in a black and scarlet uniform shoving himself through the crowd. Jacques had arrived.

"Girls!" he shouted happily. "I'm back!"

He threw a scattering of coins on stage before grabbing an empty stool and joining a table of others wearing military coats. With the coins, the kicks on stage grew higher and everyone greeted the show of more leg with wild applause.

"*She shouldn't be up there*," said Archambeau, confusing me.

"Who?"

"*Nicole.*"

Oh, no. This was not a good time for the duke's ghostly companion to come awake. As he stared at the third girl, I suggested in a mild tone of voice, "I don't think that's Nicole."

"*Why is she here? She promised to leave him.*"

The dancers finished their performance and immediately stepped down into the audience to be greeted with suggestive shouts, and grabs at their waists or arms. But the women were savvy to their games and moved like slippery eels through the crowd.

Archambeau's ghost waved to the one that had grabbed his

attention, and after she spoke with our server, she made her way to us.

"Hello, gorgeous," she said to the duke as she sat down. She showed no interest in me; her big brown eyes, outlined in black with bright blue eyeshadow, were only for the man at the table.

"*Waiter!*" called Archambeau's ghost. When the server appeared, he said, "*Whatever this lady wants, please bring.*"

"Oh, I want so many things," said the dancer, batting her eyes at him. This close, she wasn't as young as she had appeared from on stage, and her face showed a rapacious cunning learned from hard years.

"*Nicole, how I've missed you!*"

"You can call me whatever you want, handsome," was her answer.

"Please come back, Your Grace. Shove him away," I begged Archambeau, but he was too far gone. This was exactly what I had feared: the duke had lost control of his possession; it was pulling vigorously from the crowd's raw power and it would take time for the ghost to wear itself out and leave.

Through the parting of the crowd, I saw a stranger, a thin man with a skimpy mustache, approach the Perino delegate. I dug my elbow into the duke's ribs, and hissed at him, "Someone has joined our ambassador."

Lost in love memories, he was holding the dancer's hands as the ghost poured all of its attention upon the woman he had mistaken for his old lover. There was no shaking the spirit out of the duke; not when it had a powerful fixation to keep it motivated.

The Perino man rose from his seat and left with Mysir Mustache. Jacques didn't notice my intent stare or the quick jerk of my head towards the two leaving. He was at the bar, his back to me, buying a round of drinks for his new brothers-in-arms.

"I think I shall go to the ladies' powder room. Where is that?" I asked the show girl.

The dancer thrust her chin, pointing off in a direction behind us. I doubt she heard my thanks, for Archambeau was now stroking her cheek. Restraining a desire to slap his hand down, I left. I was not as successful in negotiating my passage as the dancers, for someone tried to grab me as they offered to take me home.

"Another time, mysir," I said, pushing him away.

My quarry had exited to another room and, entering it, I saw a gambling den. Men and women were playing at cards, piles of coins and bills on the tables. No one spared a glance at me. The two men passed through another door, and quickening my step, I followed.

But I was too slow, for when I entered a corridor with many other doors, I didn't know which they had taken. Suddenly, one of them flew open, almost hitting my face, forcing me to take a step back. It was the animal trainer, with two of his dogs yapping at his heels, and the third in his arms.

"Excuse me," I said. "I was to meet a friend back here. A man with white hair?"

"Just went in— third door down on the right."

"Thank you," I said.

"Come along, girls, time to take a break outside." They left using the door at the end of the hall, which must have been an exit, as I felt a draft of cool air.

At the door the trainer had shown me, I stopped. The question really was how to proceed without Jacques or Archambeau. Before I could decide, a high-pitched scream sounded from within and, without thinking further, I pulled out my gun and rushed inside.

It was a storeroom, full of extra furniture and stage props. Huddled in one corner was the screaming woman, her hands on top of her head, as Mysir Mustache was shaking and shouting at her. "Stop being crazy and give it to me, Gabby!"

To my right, the ambassador stood against the wall, pretending as if nothing was happening.

"Unhand her!" I demanded.

What I hadn't accounted for was someone being behind the door. A man sprung forward and hit my outstretched arm, and the gun went flying from my hand. He grabbed me from behind, pinning my arms and though I struggled, kicking as hard as I could, he held me easily. He was the big man who had dragged the man away from our table and my slight build was no match.

"Who's this pigeon?"

"I dunno," said Mysir Mustache, letting go of the girl in surprise.

From him calling her Gabby, and her doll-like face, I guessed she was Giles Monet's missing girlfriend. Her round childish face was weeping and on her head, almost obscured by her hair, was a gold tiara with three egg-sized rubies. It looked far too heavy for her small head.

The tiara grabbed my attention. It was a spectacular piece of ancient primitive make, not at all like the delicate pieces popular today. But what was the most fascinating thing about it was the tiara started singing to me, throwing images in rapid succession into my mind. It wasn't human speech, but more like ghostly impressions I would receive when in a trance state.

I felt my body relax, growing languid under its spell, even as I resisted.

Take me, release me, take me, free me...

"Do any of you realize that a ghost dragon possesses that tiara?"

Chapter Seventeen

The three men all reacted differently to my revelation.

Mysir Mustache scratched his head. "That could explain why sis is acting loony."

"Enzo, shut up! Who is this wench?" growled the man, shaking me.

"I don't know, Jean." Mysir Mustache, now identified as Enzo, said.

"Gentlemen, I am here only for the tiara. You promised me the tiara. I wish to take it away now." This was from the Perino delegate, who we all ignored.

I identified myself. "As an official representative of King Guénard, it would be best for everyone concerned if you turn it over to me."

"Certainly, madame," said Enzo, giving me a wide, sweeping bow full of theatric mockery. "We'll just hand it over."

He gave a loud laugh, slapping his thigh, as if he had made a tremendous joke. The rest of us did not join in with his laughter.

Jean snarled. "We aren't letting it go without being paid. I don't care if it is the king or Perino who hands us the cash, but we went through too much trouble for it not to get the money Monet promised us."

"You promised me first chance at purchasing the tiara. We are the rightful owners of it," said the Perino ambassador in a prim, yet strident voice.

"Ownership? We own it," snapped Jean.

I said soothingly, "I'm sure I could persuade King Guénard to give all of you a finder's reward, no questions asked."

At the mention of a reward, he dropped his hold on me. Before anyone could stop me, I quickly picked up my gun and put it back in my pocket, immediately feeling better. While I hoped to win this battle with words, not a firearm, doubtless having one would put me in a better negotiating position.

"I know that Giles Monet stole the tiara from the king's palace and that Gabrielle is his lover. But this plot to sell it to the Perino delegation and bypass the king is not a good idea. That is a treasonous act against the Crown, the penalty being to be drawn and quartered."

At my statement Jean and Enzos' faces showed dismay while the diplomat from Perino edged towards the door, silently slipping away. Wise man.

"That was Giles' plan, but we had nothing to do with it," whined Enzo.

He was a thin man, like one of those stick insects, but with poor posture and a face as pale as a ground worm. Enzo bore little resemblance to the girl he called sister, making me wonder if they had different parents, or if the word was slang for some sort of other relationship.

Out loud, I outlined my theory.

"The dragon ghost in the tiara beguiled Giles Monet to take it, but the voices in his head frightened him and he used zhimo to stop hearing them. Somewhere along the line, you two discovered what he had stolen. Or were you in it from the beginning? Regardless, what none of you had planned was Gabby putting the thing on her head."

"How did you—?" asked Enzo in astonishment.

"Who cares? She knows too much and could get us all killed!" snapped Jean, lunging towards me. I stopped him by pulling out my gun, but before we could discover the winner, the dance girl stood up from her crouch and said in a creepy, Uncanny voice, *"Don't you dare harm her! She's mine."*

The hair on the back of my neck stood up as the room temperature dropped by a good twenty degrees. Unfortunately, my fur stole lay on the ground where it had fallen when I had been so rudely grabbed.

"Gabby!" cried Enzo.

I shook my head as he stepped towards her. "Don't touch her. That would be dangerous."

The tiara on Gabrielle's head started glowing and emitting an eerie whine.

Enzo asked in a frightened voice, "What's happening?"

Take me, release me, take me, free me...

The chant was rolling around in my head, trying to find a hold on me. I cleared my throat, trying to focus my thoughts, using words. "Those aren't rubies in the tiara, but three drops of dragon blood. It's a common mistake because dried dragon's blood is as hard as rubies, but what gives it away is the unusual size. And rubies don't have that gold striation nor do they pulse like a beating heart."

Gabrielle's eyes were shining red as the creature in the tiara whispered into my brain: *"You are intelligent. Help me."*

"Save my sister from that thing!" Enzo begged me. "She's not talked sense since she put it on her head, and I can't get it off of her."

The dragon in the tiara must have taken that as a threat, for Enzo suddenly crumpled to the ground. Seeing his partner go down, Jean showed some intelligence. He bolted, slamming the door and locking it behind him. Unfortunately, that meant I was alone with Enzo, a mad girl, and a ghost dragon.

"Help me. Free me."

The creature came closer, and I moved away, training my little gun on him. I wasn't prepared to shoot him as I was sure the creature would just jump to another person. I only had two bullets.

In trying to keep something between us, I bumped into stacks of costumes and props that fell, scattering across the floor. When I stepped over Enzo, he suddenly became animated and grabbed my ankle.

The same voice that Gabrielle used now issued from her brother. *"Why do you flee from me? I can give you everything you want. Wealth. Love. Vengeance."*

I'd never seen a spirit control more than one person at the same time. This couldn't be good. A kick of my heel into Enzo's face got him to release me, and I scrambled to my feet.

"Where did you come from?" I asked. I had never communicated with a ghost animal, let alone one that was a dragon, but surely it would want to talk? Explaining their point of view seemed to be a universal thing amongst the dead.

"From the tiara, of course," said Gabby.

"By way of Perino," said Enzo.

"Don't you want to go back to Perino? Your home? I can get you there."

"I want to be free of this prison. That is all I want."

They cornered me: Enzo took one hand, Gabby the other. The grip was so tight that my hand became numb and dropped my gun. Their hands were hot, like someone with a high fever; the ghost dragon was drawing off their life force at a rapid rate: Gabrielle's skin looked almost translucent and Enzo's eyes now held nothing but madness.

"I want my freedom," repeated Enzo.

"Explain the problem to me," I said, keeping hysteria out of my voice with effort. "Maybe I can figure out a solution."

There was a pounding at the door, and I heard Jacques and Archambeau shouting my name. It would be best if they didn't come in here and give the thing more food, more power to feed off of.

"It's easier if you join us," said the creature, controlling Enzo.

"Take me. Put me on your head." Gabrielle dropped my hand and started dancing in a circle, her hands going to her head to touch the tiara. *"Free, free, free me!"*

"I promise to help you, but first you must release these two, and agree to stop possessing people. How can I trust you if you keep grabbing people?"

"I agree to nothing until you put me on your head!" shouted Enzo. He was so close to my face that spittle hit my cheek, and his grip on my wrist was bruising.

The door was starting to splinter in its frame as it was being battered from outside. There was only one way to protect Jacques and Archambeau.

"Fine. Give it to me," I told Gabby.

She gave a wild laugh and took it off her head and handed it to me. The tiara felt warm, like a living creature, and it squirmed in my hand like a snake. I brought it over my head as the door jamb broke, revealing Jacques and Archambeau.

"Don't, Elinor!" yelled the duke.

"Throw it away!" shouted Jacques.

I did neither. I took the creature and settled it down on my head.

The thing laughed in my mind.

"Now we can have a good long chat."

Chapter Eighteen

I was sitting in a chair holding a teacup in the conservatory at the duke's residence. For a moment, I thought I had dreamed everything at the Nightingale until the thing that wore Gabrielle's body addressed me.

"I am so glad we could meet in a more pleasant location."

Beyond the glass panes was a fog of white. Nothing outside of the conservatory existed except the void. I wasn't at the duke's home; the ghost-dragon had brought me to the Beyond and created a reality from an image it took from my mind.

Shocked, I barely took in what the creature had said. My frantic mind raced hither and thither, closing access, as I tried to remain calm.

"It's always best to have serious conversations in a neutral place. Much like negotiating a peace treaty or a ceasefire." At least my voice was steady. The teacup in my hand felt real under my fingers, but it was empty of anything to drink. It seemed the creature had a limited imagination.

How the creature brought me here I did not know. But any member of the Morpheus Society knew staying in the Beyond tempted madness. The Beyond rejected the living, and it dealt with us unkindly if we lingered too long.

Gabrielle looked ghastly. Her red eyes, pale death-like complexion, and the thinness of her body made her seem a walking ghoul. If my guess was correct, the creature was using Gabrielle's life to power this elaborate illusion and keep me imprisoned here, something unnatural since the Beyond rejects life. I couldn't imagine the energy that would take; she'd be dead soon.

Her body prowled around the octagonal room like a wild thing in a cage. She stopped behind my chair and, leaning over the back, said, "You aren't like the others. You're special."

I forced a smile. "You probably say that to everyone you terrorize."

It laughed, throwing itself away from me, and went back to pacing. "I like you. Smart and funny. A delicious treat."

As it circled, coming back into view, it now wore the face and body of Enzo. Only the bulging, glass-red, insect-like eyes remained the same.

"You must be ancient. King Guénard said the tiara has been in his family for some time."

"King Guénard!" The thing snarled, displaying unnaturally pointed teeth inside Enzo's mouth, showing some hybrid mix of its selves. It took all my will not to shrink back into my chair.

"You dislike the king?"

Enzo flung himself into the only other chair in the place with such violence that it rocked back temporarily on its back two feet. "Guénard's ancestors took me from the Perino people. Stole me from a shrine where they venerated me as a god!"

"Worshiped as a dragon? Or as a tiara?" I asked, my curiosity aroused.

"In Perino, they imprisoned me in this bauble." It pointed a finger at its head, but there was no physical tiara there. I imagine it was still sitting on my head back in the Earthly plane. "Still, in

Perino, they at least gave me my due. I was worshiped as national treasure and given sacrifices to survive."

"Then why not let the king return you to Perino? That was his intent. Don't you long to go back to being worshiped?"

Enzo hissed. "That is not the freedom I crave, Elinor. I hope you will let me call you Elinor. I feel we will be great friends."

"Of course. After all, you are in my head now, aren't you? Trying to find a way in to control me?"

It leaned forward, a nictitating membrane flashing over its human eyes, wetting them with moisture. Another sign that the thing blended itself with its human host.

"You keep so much locked away from me. Give me the key to your mind and I can make your dreams come true. How can you resist me?"

For a moment, *wanting the answer to my father's murder* flashed into my head. I locked that errant thought down; no way was this thing going to give me what my heart desired. I shrugged and said, "I'm sorry, but my training sealed off parts of my mind. My mentor, Leona Granger, gave me protections I cannot remove."

It leaned back in the chair, and Gabrielle's figure and face replaced Enzo's. They were both looking worse for the wearing, like a shabby winter coat you kept despite lost buttons. It had to draw on them both to keep itself and this illusion intact. It would soon run out of power. *What then, Elinor?*

"I think the last dragon sighting was at least five hundred years. I wonder how old you are?"

"Six hundred fifty-eight years ago is when the last dragon flew."

"Oh, were you the last one?"

It made a disgusted sneer with Gabrielle's borrowed mouth. "No. I died seven hundred eighty-six years ago."

"By humans?"

"No. Natural causes. From wounds I gained in a mating fight."

"That's too bad—" It cut me off with a roar of rage, leaping from the chair to return to its maniac pacing. "My body could not lie in peace. No! Humans came and harvested my hide, my bones, and even, yes, my blood to make these so-called rubies."

The glass in the window frames shook and, and the entire image of the conservatory faded. I felt the chair drop from under me as the ghost-dragon struggled to maintain its illusion as reality. While it was distracted, I tried to make the teacup in my hand disappear. *Yes!* It faded away until finally vanishing. A minor victory for me proving I could influence this environment.

After the storm quieted and the image of the conservatory was once more around me, the thing begged. "Free me, Elinor. Let me have access to your mind."

"Perhaps if you tell me more, I could help?"

"I want out of this ruby prison! Out of the tiara, and be returned to the skies in my dragon form."

The dead wanting life again wasn't a new idea. It's part of why they possess the living.

"I'd recommend possessing a bird with wings since dragons are no longer around."

"Birds are too primitive a mind to serve my needs. Humans are better hosts, for they help me keep my mind, my thoughts intact, even though you are lesser beings than dragons."

Absentmindedly, it started picking at the flesh on Gabrielle's hand, peeling the skin back to expose bone, throwing the discards on the floor. Strangely enough, Gabrielle's hand didn't bleed even though the exposed flesh was raw, exposing sinew and muscle.

As its gaze grew abstract, I feared for Jacques and Archambeau. Enzo and Gabrielle were dying or already dead; this mind-place in the Beyond was already fading and would need more fuel to keep it in place. Fuel from the living.

"I think I know a way you can gain your happiness."

Its head swiveled on its neck with a distinct reptilian movement. "Tell me!"

"Locked away from the world, perhaps you don't know that medical science has made strides in helping people solve these types of problems."

When I paused, it demanded again. "Tell me! *Now*. I want my freedom."

"Alienists use something they call a talking cure."

"Talking? Haven't we been talking already?"

"This is a specialized talking. You must peel back all the layers, be totally honest, bare yourself, and bring down all the barriers if you wish to obtain true happiness." I gave a heavy sigh, shaking my head. "But I don't think you're ready, for only the strongest and bravest can make such strong magic work."

"A dragon is the strongest and bravest thing on earth."

"But you're not a dragon anymore. Not really. For hundreds of years, you've let yourself become polluted by us lower human vessels."

"What do you mean?" In its irritation, the thing scraped a deep gouge down Gabrielle's cheek, exposing the bone of her jaw.

"You've polluted your dragon-ness with human thoughts and desires. No wonder you haven't become free in six hundred years. You don't really want that; you enjoy being human." I tried using a pitying voice.

"Liar! I am nothing but a dragon!"

"Really? How many humans have you possessed and devoured? Gabrielle, a poor dancing girl; Enzo, some gutter thief? Giles Monet, some princesses and servant girls. What are you now but a messy mixing pot of their desires? You wear their faces and identities."

In a split second, its face was nose to nose with mine. The shock of it made my heart bolt, but I kept my face calm.

"I am a dragon, no matter what form I wear!"

"Prove it. Let go of your human memories and show me your true self. Release Gabrielle and Enzo."

"Why should I?"

"Possession mixes the spirit with the living. No matter what you think, the living will dominate the twinning: our life-force makes it so. Our desires and needs will always rule over the dead. When I last saw Gabrielle, she couldn't stop herself from dancing, although you controlled her. How many times has she expressed desires you thought were your own?"

"Fine. I shall release her. She is dying anyway."

Quickly, Gabrielle's face disappeared, and the creature was now Enzo. At least he didn't have hands showing bone and raw muscle.

"You must release Enzo as well. He is hiding your dragon-ness."

The creature gave me a mock bow before Enzo vanished to be replaced with the face and form of Giles Monet. It was strange seeing him animated. "Part of the talking cure includes telling the alienist the 'why'? Why make Mysir Monet take you? Or did he steal you?"

Monet's face held a cast of cruelty to it, that I hoped wasn't his real expression because it was vastly unpleasant. "Giles was easy to corrupt. Do not think he went to me unwillingly. He was unhappy, begging for scraps, and I offered him much more than your weak king ever did."

"Maybe not as willing as you believe. Didn't he try to use drugs to stop from hearing you in his mind? The same reason a girl threw herself from a tower."

Mad with rage, the creature seized a chair and threw it against the walls. Shattering the glass panes, the chair spun away into the void. Then the creature turned to me, its stolen face inflamed with violence.

"Yes! He refused my command to hand the crown to the dancer. Said he would destroy me instead! But I had my revenge. I made his lover kill him. A rock to the back of the head during a romantic stroll along the canal."

He started laughing hysterically.

Remain calm, Elinor.

"But your satisfaction at being revenged didn't last long, did it? You were soon hungry again. Giles, Gabrielle, Enzo. None really gave you what you craved, did they? Your freedom."

"No," it agreed in a sulky tone that I might have expected to come from Marcus. Thinking of my interactions with the boy, I tried to strike an encouraging tone instead of one of authority.

"You must release your hold on Giles and go back even further. Only by casting away the human souls contaminating your thoughts can you return to your pure dragon state. And therein find true freedom."

It paced, hands behind its back, talking to itself in a rapid-fire and disturbing litany. "She cannot be right. I need them all. I've kept their memories. Lived their thoughts. They are me. Me. I am them? Aren't I? I could eat this one, gain the knowledge I need. No. She might die, her mind-doors closed to me. I need to be me. A dragon. Pure dragon. I cannot dilute my essence with the foulness of my prey."

While it fretted, distracted, I drew on my memories, imagining the smooth pearl handle of my man-stopper, the coolness of the barrel resting in the palm of my hand. If I could unmake in this strange place, I could make.

"I do not want these humans contaminating me! I shall eliminate them!"

Monet's face vanished, replaced by a disturbing sequence of bodies that he wore like an overcoat— men, women, and even children. It was like a spinning carousel of images that, in their quantity, became vastly disturbing as you wished that the next would be the last, only to see another. Each face shrieked in pain which became a high pitched whistling of screams that stabbed at my ear drums.

I watched fascinated and horrified until finally the creature's frantic pacing took it in front of the broken glass where it had thrown the chair.

Formed by my will and imagination, I felt the hardness of the mans-stopper in my hand. I brought it up, and taking aim, fired the pistol.

The creature staggered, screaming as it tried to grab my mind. Springing from my chair, I closed the distance between us and fired again in rapid succession. It fell backward, falling into the white void of the Beyond.

Chapter Nineteen

“She's still talking about the proper way to cut a diamond,” said Mysir de Archambeau.

I blinked, trying to focus my eyes, and in a very quavering voice said, “That's because if you cut a diamond wrong, you ruin its brilliance.”

“Elinor!” That was Jacques. *Dear Jacques.* With my vision restored, I saw the two men were sitting opposite of each other on either side of my bed. A hospital bed, it appeared to be. Jacques was sporting a black eye but was wearing ordinary clothes; Archambeau was still wearing the evening clothes from the Nightingale. They were very wrinkled, and the starch had long gone out of his cravat; now the ends lay untied, showing off his suntanned throat.

“Where is the tiara?” My hands flew up and located it still on my head. *How funny.* I removed it from the tangles of my hair and handed it to the duke. “The king can have it now. It's curse-free.”

Archambeau took it gingerly. It did not seem that he wanted it, with or without a curse.

“The doctors wanted to remove it, but mysir de duke insisted they keep it on your head until you awoke," said Jacques in a disapproving tone.

"That was probably wise." I pulled myself up in my bed. Jacques quickly stepped behind me to reposition my pillows like a good boy. I folded my hands in my lap. "Where is my fur? You didn't leave it behind, did you?"

Jacques gave a huge laugh of relief. "The duke said you'd worry about it. I handed it off to Anne-Marie for cleaning."

Archambeau informed me. "You've been here for two days, Madame Chalamet. Perhaps you can fill us in on what happened?"

"Gabrielle and Enzo?"

"Dead."

"A dragon ghost spirit inhabited the tiara. It's been using people like puppets, possessing them, and draining their energy to keep its sense of self, of memory, alive inside the tiara."

"I don't get it—" said Jacques.

Feeling stronger, I was enjoying the chance to explain.

"A ghost that ancient would have long ago fragmented. Because after death, memories decay over time. You see this phenomenon in old ghosts that appear but can't communicate with us on the Earthly plane; all they can do is repeat actions, like walk a corridor or go down a staircase. But the tiara's dragon used humans to feed it energy over hundreds of years, allowing it to keep most of its original identity and personality intact. Although its soul-sucking ways didn't keep it sane."

"How did you defeat it? I assume you did so?" asked Archambeau, nonchalantly studying his fingernails. What was that shadow on his jaw? Hadn't he shaved this morning?

"The creature brought me mentally into the Beyond, creating a space from my memories of your house, Your Grace. Whatever was imagined into that space acted as if it was real— the chairs, the glass— my gun. I've never heard of that being done! I can't wait to write a paper and present it to the Morpheus Society— won't

Parnell Lafayette, he's their current darling, have to eat crow? He said it couldn't be done."

"Chalamet, what happened?"

"Sorry, but you don't realize how incredible this was. The Earthly plane repels ghosts as they don't belong here, just as we don't belong in the Beyond. While some close to death have described the sensation of being there, the Beyond rejects the living. Like how the wrong end of magnets won't connect. That ill-begotten thing was trying to keep me where I did not belong against the very forces of nature."

I grimaced, thinking of Gabrielle and Enzo and not being able to save them.

"It drained the life force from Gabrielle and Enzo to hold me there. And it still remembered all the souls of the people it possessed and murdered across the centuries."

"But how did you get away? Is it gone?" asked Jacques.

"I made it toss aside the human personalities that were keeping it sane. Being so old, I gambled it wouldn't remember what it actually was anymore. While it was trying to remember, I shot it. Since everything in its created illusion in the Beyond acted as real, so did my gun."

That was a lot to say, and it wore me out. I sunk back into the pillows.

"I doubt it was as easy as you make it out to be, Chalamet."

I gave the duke a tired smile. "Now, tell me what happened at the Nightingale?"

"When I discovered you weren't sitting at the table, I came to ask the duke where you had gone." When Jacques stopped, Archambeau continued the story. "What your friend isn't telling you, to spare my dignity, is that his solicitude earned him a punch to the face. Bastiaan Hagen didn't like being interrupted."

"Who's Bastiaan Hagen?"

"My ghost," said the duke, stone-faced. "He managed a few poorly thrown punches, tarnishing my reputation forever, before fading away. When I regained my senses, the girl at the table told us where you went. When we got backstage, we saw that Perino fellow running from a room and I guessed correctly he must have been fleeing some chaos you wrought."

That seemed to explain everything. My stomach rumbled.

"Isn't there anything in this place to eat?"

~

Not for the first time, Dr. LaRue apologized again to the mysir de duke for her attempt to stab him.

"Think nothing of it, doctor. You thought your friend was in danger and acted accordingly."

"Enough, Charlotte!" I said. "Can't you see you are embarrassing the man?"

It was two weeks since I awoke from the hospital bed and the three of us were in the duke's carriage. The tiara had made it to King Guénard one day late, but the Perino government wouldn't admit to trying to grab it from behind his back, so in the end, we diplomatically blamed the delay on the king's indigestion, a stratagem well-known to his subjects to avoid work. The Perino delegation agreed to the tariffs Sarnesse wanted, signed the treaty and sailed away with the tiara, to the relief of many.

Life had almost returned to normal, but there were a few loose ends, and one of them was the reason the three of us were sitting in a chilly coach, waiting for a stranger to enter the park. From Dr. LaRue's information, Nicole Bakhuizen should arrive at any moment, as it was her habit to walk the park in the morning regardless of the weather.

"How do you feel?" I asked the duke.

"More embarrassed each time you ask me," he replied coldly, causing Dr. LaRue to utter a snorting laugh that she quickly smothered. Before any of us could say anything more that would embarrass a titled gentleman, Dr. LaRue exclaimed excitedly, "There she is! She's the woman in the dark blue dress."

"You didn't tell me she'd have a baby carriage with her!" I replied to the doctor sitting beside me, but the duke paid us no attention. He was already stepping out of his coach and striding down the sidewalk towards the lady in question.

"You stay here!" I commanded the doctor and hastily climbed out. I was forced to trot after Archambeau in order to reach his side. "Remember, she doesn't know the duke, or that Hagen is here."

"*I know her*," said the ghost possessing Archambeau.

"Let me make the introductions," I begged. "We don't want to frighten her."

We were closing the distance quickly and now I could see that Nicole Bakhuizen had blond hair and brown eyes, was about the same height, with a figure very much like the Nightingale's dance hall girl. There the resemblance ended, which really showed how little cognitive thought continued after death.

This woman had a faded elegance of an educated, well-bred woman. This close, I could see that the tragedy of her husband being hanged and her lover dying by his sword had marked her with grief. Her face was pale and strained, with shadows under her eyes and a dullness to her hair.

"Hello, Madame Bakhuizen," I said before the duke's ghost could speak. She startled and perhaps it was the intensity of our interest that made her say nervously, "I don't know you. Are you reporters? If you follow me, I swear I'll scream!"

She wheeled the baby carriage around and started walking rapidly in the opposite direction. Risking the scream, we followed. I said to her straight back, "We are representing Mysir Hagen."

That made her stop and whip around. "What do you mean?"

I wasn't sure what to say, but Hagen did. "*May I see the child?*"

Madame Bakhuizen took a moment in weighing the risk of us being baby snatchers against having an honest reason for seeing her babe. I like to think it was my presence and my nice, comfortable face that convinced her.

She bent over and took out a child wrapped in a fuzzy yellow blanket. A fur-lined baby's bonnet revealed an edge of dark, fluffy hair that framed a rosy complexion. It looked to be less than six months old.

"What is the child's name?" asked the duke.

"Bastiaan."

Named after her lover. Well, that explained the unfinished business.

"May I hold him?"

"Do you truly represent Mysir Hagen?"

"We mean you no harm," I reassured her. "Truly, we are here to help."

She reluctantly gave the duke her baby, but her eyes were watchful, ready to grab him back if Archambeau showed any sign of being a lunatic or a reporter, which was pretty much the same thing.

"He's precious," I said, knowing that all babies were to their mothers.

"He's already pulling himself up," she said proudly.

Archambeau or his ghost must have known something about babies, for the infant broke out in a gumless smile, a starfish hand reaching out for the duke's nose. He bounced the baby gently against his shoulder.

We hadn't discussed what we were going to do other than allow Hagen a chance to see his true love and, in return, he would move on to the Afterlife.

"We heard things got a little rough for you since— everything happened."

"I don't complain."

The very public trial exposing her infidelity had ruined her reputation. In Alenbonné, we accept love outside marriage as long as the affair is discreet, but a duel in the streets and a murder trial didn't have that distinction. Yes, her family had taken her back, but they used her as an unpaid servant, according to Dr. LaRue.

The baby gurgled, and the duke shielded his face behind the child's bonnet, as he asked, "*Nikki, why didn't you come that day to the café?*"

"Laurence found out I was running away, and locked me in my room," she said, responding without thought.

After a sigh that warmed the foggy air, the ghost of Bastiaan Hagen faded away from the Earthly plane and crossed to the After-life. The duke's body position changed: his posture became straighter, his shoulders widened. The baby started fussing and Archambeau handed him back to his mother, whose arms were eager for his return.

"As Madame Chalamet said, we are here as representatives of Mysir Hagen. He reached out to us before meeting your husband that fateful day. It is unfortunate that it has taken us almost a year to find you, but we have good news for you."

She was patting the baby's back, and Bastiaan gave a loud burp at the end of the duke's statement. Madame Bakhuizen asked warily, "What news would that be?"

"He put money back for your future, thinking the two of you would be together. Those funds are now yours to do with what you wish." From his pocket, Archambeau handed her an envelope of folded papers. "Here is all the information you need to claim it at the Royal Bank of Alenbonné."

Madame Bakhuizen slowly put the baby back into his carriage and hesitantly took the documents. She opened the bank book and as she read the numbers, tears started sliding down her cheek.

"Madame," said mysir de duke and, after a curt bow, he took my arm and we turned away to make our way back to his carriage. When we were out of earshot, I asked Archambeau, "Hagen was a student and poor as a church mouse. You set this up, didn't you?"

"Having someone live in my body is an unsettling experience. This seemed the best way to insure he would not come back."

I smiled. "Are you saying you paid off the ghost? Not because of any sentimental feeling about his lost love, but only so he would leave you alone?"

He asked me curiously, "Has a ghost ever possessed you, Chalamet? In your line of work?"

"For short periods of time, to deliver a message, but nothing like you experienced. I think my nature is anathema to being possessed. I wasn't exactly a natural and the Morpheus Society almost gave up on me ever becoming a Ghost Talker, but I was determined."

"Do you always get what you want?"

"Most times. If I really want it."

EPILOGUE

I sat on the edge of the bed watching Anne-Marie finish packing my boxes and trunks. "Were you able to find out any information from the staff about that woman who fell down the stairs?"

"Yes, madame. She was an overnight guest invited by the duchesse. It was a small group of select lady friends."

"Do we have a list?"

Anne-Marie fished in the pocket of her dress and handed a folded piece of paper to me. I scanned it, immediately noticing Lady Josephine Baudelaire's name along with three others. "Was the duke here at the time?"

"No. He was traveling in Zulskaya. The lady fell down in the middle of the night when everyone was still asleep. They found her in the morning on the landing, knocked out from the pain."

"What was she doing going downstairs? All these suites have bathrooms, do they not?"

"Yes, madame. I asked Ruben about it and he said the lady always makes a big to-do about refusing food at dinner in order to keep her figure, but late at night she sneaks downstairs to the kitchen hunting for something sweet to eat. Makes Cook quite angry about it since a whole cake went missing on one of her other visits. Mighty particular about her kitchen is Madame Darly."

"Interesting," I said, lost in thought.

"I think these are ready to go now, madame. Should I get Ruben to take them down to the coach?"

I nodded. Soon young men filled the room, and all the way down the hall, Anne-Marie instructed them on how to carry the boxes. Their voices grew fainter as they drew further away from my room. It became quiet, and the air stilled, heavy with expectation. My nostrils flared, senses on high alert, but I felt, heard, and smelled nothing.

I rose. Only one last thing to check before leaving the duke's residence for good. Finding the hall empty, I went to the top of the stairs. Sitting on the top step, I checked the lay of the carpet. Nothing that would trip anyone, but my glove's tip snagged, and I bent to examine the cause.

There was a nail with a head projecting from the baseboard. The painted head blended in color with the wood trim. Opposite from the nail, I examined the top balustrade on the staircase and found a thin line scoring the paint as if something had cut across it. None of the other balustrades showed any such mark. String would be too soft. Wire?

"May I ask what you are doing, madame, examining my carpet?"

Mysir de Archambeau was on the landing, gazing up at me with a touch of irritation in his face. I stood up.

"I thought I dropped an earring here on the night we went to the Nightingale." Before he could ask any further questions, I got up, brushed off my skirt, and stepped down to meet him. We walked down the stairs, side by side. "Where is Jacques? Not here to send me off?"

"Returned to General Somerville."

We were now in the foyer, and the open front door gave a view of my baggage being packed on the roof of the duke's carriage. As a sailor's daughter, Anne-Marie was very explicit on how she wanted the ropes tied and was correcting each footman on how to stack everything.

"I think this is goodbye." I held out my hand. Two heartbeats later, he shook it.

"Good day, Madame Chalamet."

"Good day, Mysir de Archambeau."

I went out to the carriage and stepped up into the cab. Anne-Marie climbed in after me, snapping the door shut. Yes, it was back to the Crown, to clients, and continuing my private investigation into my father's murder. But as the carriage pulled away, I cast one look back, my busy mind wondering who had strung a wire across the top of the duke's staircase and why.

Find more great reads
by Byrd Nash
at her website
ByrdNash.com

Author Notes

I've always been fascinated by ghosts and have wanted to write a story about them for some time. Pair that with a longstanding love of Sherlock Holmes, that started when I was about nine, and you have the Madame Chalamet series.

A big thank you to my team of beta readers: Ami A., Charlotte Z, Davida, Diana P., Elizabeth C., Inas M., Jennifer H., Jessica F., Laurie H., Merricat A., and Stephanie A.

Beta readers get the first look at the story and provide helpful and valuable feedback on pacing, characters, and plot. Your thoughts helped me develop the story and make it better.

A shout-out to my editor, Emma, who did a very thorough developmental edit on this book. Her suggestions made me reach deeper to polish up Elinor's adventures.

As always, to my readers who keep me going through their follows and reviews, I greatly appreciate you!

BYRD NASH

NOTE: This fantasy world is inspired by 1910 France, but is not a part of it.

For convenience sake, American spellings have been chosen for this fantasy series. For example, instead of grey, gray is used.

For use in this fantasy world, Guardia refers to an individual police officer. Gendarmes to the police force, or a group of police officers.

Cast of Characters

- **Elinor Chalamet** (Shall-ah-may)— A Ghost Talker residing in the city of Alenbonné (Alan-bon-ay) in the country of Sarnesse (Sar-nessie).
- **Tristan Fontaine** Duke of Archambeau (Are-shem-bow)— is a member of Alenbonné nobility, **Le beau idéal**. For simplicity, duke is only capitalized when it is used with his title, either Duke de Archambeau or Duke de Chambaux (province title).

Family and Friends:

- **Minette Fontaine**, the previous Duchesse de Chambaux (deceased)— wife of Tristan.
- **The Duchesse de Chambaux** (Sham-beau)— Tristan's mother.
- **Lady Valentina Fontaine**— Tristan's sister.
- **Lady Josephine Baudelaire** (Bowed-lair)— a society lady who was a friend of Minette's and the Chambaux family.
- **Augustus Chalamet** (deceased) Elinor's father— was murdered about 12 years ago at the start of Ghost Talker. He was a well-known jeweler to the king and nobility.
- **Jacques Moreau** (More-row)— a childhood friend of Elinor's who is now a soldier.
- **Dr. Charlotte LaRue** (Lah-roo)— the city's coroner and university instructor. A friend of Elinor's.

- **Inspector Marcellus Barbier** (Bahr-bee-er)— a guardia inspector who Elinor met when her father was murdered. She works with him now to solve crimes.
- **Sergeant Quincy Dupont** (Dew-pon)— Barbier's subordinate.

Servants and Helpers:

- **Anne-Marie**— Elinor's servant, a daughter of a sailor.
- **Marcus**— an orphaned street urchin who occasionally helps Elinor.
- **Ruben**— a footman in the de Chambaux household.
- **Georgette**— a house maid in the de Chambaux household.
- **Madeline**— the duchesse's personal servant.
- **Madame Darly**— the duke's cook in the de Chambaux household.

Clients and Ghosts:

- **Giles Monet** (Mo-nay)— a victim of a crime, and relative to the king.
- **Bastiaan Hagen**— a student killed in a duel.
- **Natalie Bakhuize** (Ba-kozie)— Bastiaan's lover.
- **Louisa** (Lou-Lou) **Smit-Vossen**— a widow (husband Leo, deceased)
- **Joris Jakobsen**— a merchant.

Ghost Theory & the Morpheus Society:

- **The Morpheus Society**— an intellectual group of amateurs who study the paranormal using scientific methods. Founded by Lady Alouette Sarte.

- **The 3 planes**— Physical where living humans reside; the Beyond, a transitional place where ghosts reside when not in the physical plane; and the Afterlife.
- **Ghost Talking** (not to be confused with a séance)— raises the dead to see their last memories through a ritual used by those trained by the Morpheus Society.
- **Spirit Projection**— this is a moving mind-image (Ghost Talking) that can be created from the recently dead through a Ghost Talk.
- **Noise Ghost**— a Poltergeist that uses energy from the living to cause trouble.
- **Possession**— an uncommon occurrence and usually short term in duration due to the amount of energy a ghost needs to maintain a connection with a human.
- **Binding**— when a living person holds a soul captive because of powerful emotions. This prevents the dead one from transitioning to the Afterlife.
- **Attachment**— when a ghost won't let go of a living person or an obsession and exists in the Beyond, refusing to transition to the Afterlife.
- **Death Remembered**— sentimental jewelry for mourning, often holding a photo or lock of hair of the deceased.

Countries:

- **Sarnesse** (Sar-nessie)— a land of rolling hills, with an extensive coastline. Vineyards. Provinces. **King Guénard** (Gie-nar) is the ruler with an elected parliament.
- **Zulskaya** (Zul-sky-a)— the closest neighbor with a large land border. Mountainous.
- **Perino** (Pa-rin-o)— a country of tropical rain forest, separated from Sarnesse by an ocean.

Addresses:

- **Madame** (Ma-dahm)— address for any financially independent and professional woman or those who are married. Any woman managing her own household. Also, A spinster would be addressed as madame. Elinor is 29 and independent, hence the address used for her.
- **Mys** (Miss)— address for financially dependent young ladies, and unmarried débutantes. Typically denotes an immaturity in the title of address, and someone well under the age of 25.
- **Mysir** (my-sur)— address to any man, suitable for all social levels.
- **Lady**— address denotes a woman of upper class, nobility.
- **Lord**— address to any man of clear nobility, or title.